TRUTH

Truth

Peter Temple

Quercus

First published by The Text Publishing Company Pty Ld, Australia in 2009
First published in Great Britain in 2010 by

Quercus
21 Bloomsbury Square
London
WC1A 2NS

A CIP catalogue record for this book is available
from the British Library

ISBN (HB) 978 1 84916 153 4
ISBN (TPB) 978 1 84916 154 1

10 9 8 7 6 5 4 3 2 1

Printed and bound in Great Britain by Clays Ltd, St Ives plc

For Anita and for Nick: the lights on the hill.

And for MH, whose faith has transcended reason.

'But because truly, being here is so much; because everything here apparently needs us, this fleeting world, which in some strange way keeps calling to us. Us, the most fleeting of all.'

Rainer Maria Rilke

ON THE Westgate Bridge, behind them a flat in Altona, a dead woman, a girl really, dirty hair, dyed red, pale roots, she was stabbed too many times to count, stomach, chest, back, face. The child, male, two or three years old, his head was kicked. Blood everywhere. On the nylon carpet, it lay in pools, a chain of tacky black ponds.

Villani looked at the city towers, wobbling, unstable in the sulphurous haze. He shouldn't have come. There was no need. 'This air-conditioner's fucked,' he said. 'Second one this week.'

'Never go over here without thinking,' said Birkerts.

'What?'

'My grandad. On it.'

One spring morning in 1970, the bridge's half-built steel frame stood in the air, it crawled with men, unmarried men, men with wives, men with wives and children, men with children they did not know, men with nothing but the job and the hard, hard hangover and then Span 10–11 failed.

One hundred and twelve metres of newly raised steel and concrete, two thousand tonnes.

Men and machines, tools, lunchboxes, toilets, whole sheds – even, someone said, a small black dog, barking – all fell down the sky. In moments, thirty-five men were dead or dying, bodies broken, sunk in the foul grey crusted sludge of the Yarra's bank. Diesel fuel lay everywhere. A fire broke out and, slowly, a filthy plume rose to mark the scene.

'Dead?' said Villani.

'No, taking a shit, rode the dunny all the way down.'

'Certainly passed on that shit-riding talent,' said Villani, thinking about Singleton, who couldn't keep his hands off the job either, couldn't stay in the office. It was not something to admire in the head of Homicide.

On the down ramp, Birkerts' phone rang, it was on speaker. Finucane's deep voice:

'Boss. Boss, Altona, we're at the husband's brother's place in Maidstone. He's here, the hubby, in the garage. Hosepipe. Well, not a hosepipe, black plastic thing, y'know, like a pool hose?'

'Excellent work,' said Birkerts. 'Could've been in Alice Springs by now. Tennant Creek.'

Finucane coughed. 'So, yeah, maybe the scientists can come on here, boss. Plus the truck.'

'Sort that out, Fin. Might be pizza though.'

'I'll tell the wife hold the T-bones.'

Birkerts ended the call.

'Closed this Altona thing in an hour,' he said. 'That's pretty neat for the clearance.'

Villani heard Singo:

Fuck the clearance rate. Worry about doing the job properly.

Joe Cashin had thought he was doing the job properly and it took the jaws to open the car embedded in the fallen house. Diab was dead, Cashin was breathing but no hope, too much blood lost, too much broken and ruptured.

Singleton only left the hospital to sit in his car, the old Falcon. He aged, grey stubble sprouted, his silken hair went greasy. After the surgery, when they told him Joe had some small chance and allowed him into the room, he took Joe's slack hand, held it, kissed its knuckles. Then he stood, smoothed Joe's hair, bent to kiss Joe's forehead.

Finucane was there, he was the witness, and he told Villani. They did not know that Singleton was capable of such emotions.

The next time Cashin came out of hospital, the second time in three years, he was pale as a barked tree. Singo was dead by then, a second stroke, and Villani was acting boss of Homicide.

'The clearance rate,' Villani said. 'A disappointment to me to hear you use the term.'

His phone.

Gavan Kiely, deputy head of Homicide, two months in the job.

'We have a dead woman in the Prosilio building, that's in Docklands,' he said. 'Paul Dove's asked for assistance.'

'Why?'

'Out of his depth. I'm off to Auckland later but I can go.'

'No,' said Villani. 'I bear this cross.'

HE WENT down the passage into the bedroom, a bed big enough for four sleepers, mattress naked, pillows bare. Forensic had finished there. He picked up a pillow with his fingertips, sniffed it.

Faintest smell of perfume. Deeper sniff. The other pillow. Different perfume, slightly stronger smell.

He walked through the empty dressing-room into the bathroom, saw the glass bath and beside it a bronze arm rising from the floor, its hand offering a cake of soap.

She was on the plastic bag in a yoga posture of rest – legs parted, palms up, scarlet toenails, long legs, sparse pubic hair, small breasts. His view was blocked by the shoulder of a kneeling forensic tech. Villani stepped sideways and saw her face, recoiled. For a terrible heart-jumping instant, he thought it was Lizzie, the resemblance was strong.

He turned to the wall of glass, breathed out, his heart settled. The drab grey bay lay before him and, between the heads, a pinhead, a container ship. Gradually it would show its ponderous shape, a huge lolling flat-topped steel slug bleeding rust and oil and putrid waste.

'Panic button,' said Dove. He was wearing a navy suit, a white shirt and a dark tie, a neurosurgeon on his hospital rounds.

Villani looked: rubber, dimpled like a golf ball, set in the wall between the shower and the head of the bath.

'Nice shower,' said Dove.

A stainless-steel disc hung above a perforated square of metal. On a glass shelf, a dozen or more soap bars were displayed as if for sale.

The forensic woman said, 'Broken neck. Bath empty but she's damp.'

She was new on the job, Canadian, a mannish young woman, no make-up, tanned, crew cut.

'How do you break your neck in the bath?' said Villani.

'It's hard to do it yourself. Takes a lot to break a neck.'

'Really?'

She didn't get his tone. 'Absolutely. Takes force.'

'What else?' said Villani.

'Nothing I can see now.'

'The time? Inspired guess.'

'Less than twenty-four or I have to go back to school.'

'I'm sure they'll be pleased to see you. Taken the water temperature into account?'

'What?'

Villani pointed. The small digital touchscreen at the door was set at 48 degrees.

'Didn't see that,' she said. 'I would have. In due course.'

'No doubt.'

Little smile. 'Okay, Lance,' she said. 'Zip it.'

Lance was a gaunt man, spade beard. He tried to zip the bag, it stuck below the woman's breasts. He moved the slider back and forth, got it free, encased her in the plastic.

Not ungently, they lifted the bag onto the trolley.

When they were gone, Dove and Weber came to him.

'Who owns this?' said Villani.

'They're finding out,' said Dove. 'Apparently it's complicated.'

'They?'

'The management. Waiting for us downstairs.'

'You want me to do it?' said Villani.

Dove touched a cheekbone, unhappy. 'That would be helpful, boss.'

'You want to do it, Web?' said Villani, rubbing it in to Dove.

Weber was mid-thirties, looked twenty, an unmarried evangelical Christian. He came with plenty of country experience: mothers who drowned babies, sons who axed their mothers, access fathers who wasted the kids. But Old Testament murders in the rural welfare sumps didn't prepare you for women dead in apartments with private lifts, glass baths, French soaps and three bottles of Moët in the fridge.

'No, boss,' he said.

They walked on the plastic strip, passed through the apartment's small pale marble hall, through the front door into a corridor. They waited for the lift.

'What's her name?' Villani said.

'They don't know,' said Dove. 'Know nothing about her. There's no ID.'

'Neighbours?'

'Aren't any. Six apartments on this floor, all empty.'

The lift came, they fell thirty floors. On the sixth, at a desk, three dark suits, two men and a woman, waited. The plump fiftyish man came forward, pushing back limp hair.

'Alex Manton, building manager,' he said.

Dove said, 'This is Inspector Villani, head of Homicide.'

Manton offered his hand. It felt dry, chalky.

'Let's talk in the meeting space, inspector,' Manton said.

The room had a painting on the inner wall, vaguely marine, five metres by three at least, blue-grey smears, possibly applied with a mop. They sat at a long table with legs of chromed pipe.

'Who owns the apartment?' said Villani.

'A company called Shollonel Pty Ltd, registered in Lebanon,' said Manton. 'As far as we know, it's not occupied.'

'You don't know?'

'Well, it's not a given to know. People buy apartments to live in, investment, future use. They might not live in them at all, live in them for short or long periods. We ask people to register when they're in residence. But you can't force them.'

'How was she found?' said Villani.

'Sylvia?' said Manton. 'Our head concierge, Sylvia Allegro.'

The woman, dolly face. 'The apartment's front door wasn't fully closed,' she said. 'The lock didn't engage. That triggers a buzzer in the apartment. If it isn't closed in two minutes, there's a security alert and they ring the apartment. If that doesn't work, they go up.'

'So there in four, five minutes?' said Villani.

Sylvia looked at Manton, who was looking at the other man, fortyish, head like a glans.

'Obviously not quite,' said the man.

'You are?' said Villani.

'David Condy, head of security for the apartments and the hotel.' He was English.

'What's not quite mean?'

'I'm told the whole electronic system failed its first big test last night. The casino opening. Orion. Four hundred guests.'

'The open door. The system tells you when?'

'It should do. But what with . . .'

'That's no?'

'Yes. No.'

'Panic buttons up there.'

'In all the apartments.'

'Not pressed?

Condy ran a finger in his collar. 'No evidence of that.'

'You don't know?'

'It's difficult to say. With the failure, we have no record.'

'That's not difficult,' said Villani. 'It's impossible.'

Manton held up a pudgy hand. 'To cut to the whatever, inspector, a major IT malfunction. Coinciding with this matter, so we look a little silly.'

Villani looked at the woman. 'The bed's stripped. How would you get rid of sheets and stuff?'

'Get rid of?'

'Dispose of.'

The woman flicked at Manton. 'Well, the garbage chute, I suppose,' she said.

'Can you tell where garbage has come from?'

'No.'

'Explain this building to me, Mr Manton. Just an outline.'

Manton's right hand consulted his hair. 'From the top, four floors of penthouses. Then six floors, four apartments each. Beneath them, it's fourteen floors of apartments, six to a floor. Then it's the three recreation floors, pools, gyms, spas, and so on. Then twelve more floors of apartments, eight to a floor. Then the casino's four floors, the hotel's ten floors, two floors of catering, housekeeping. And these reception floors, that's concierge, admin and security. The casino has its own security but its systems mesh with the building's.'

'Or don't.' Villani pointed down.

'Under us, the business floors, retail, and hospitality, ground floor plaza. Five basement levels for parking and utilities.'

In Villani's line of sight, the door opened. A man came in, a woman followed, even height, suits, white shirts.

'Crashing in,' said the man, loud. 'Introductions, please, Alex.'

Manton stood. 'Inspector Villani, this is Guy Ulyatt of Marscay Corporation.'

Ulyatt was fat and pink, cornsilk hair, tuber nose. 'Pleasure, inspector,' he said. He didn't offer a hand, sat down. The woman sat beside him.

Villani said to Manton, 'This person's got something to tell us?'

'Sorry, sorry,' said Ulyatt. 'I'm head of corporate affairs for Marscay.'

'You have something to tell us?' said Villani.

'Making sure you're getting maximum co-operation. No reflection on Alex, of course.'

'Mr Manton is helping us,' said Villani. 'If you don't have a contribution, thank you and goodbye.'

'I beg your pardon?' said Ulyatt. 'I represent the building's owners.'

Silence in the big room. Villani looked at Dove. He wanted him to learn something from this. Dove held his eyes but there was no telling what he was learning.

'We Own The Building,' said Ulyatt, four distinct words.

'What's that got to do with me?' said Villani.

'We'd like to work with you. Minimise the impact on Prosilio and its people.'

'Homicide, Mr Elliot,' said Villani. 'We're from Homicide.'

'It's Ulyatt.' He spelled it.

'Yes,' said Villani. 'You might try talking to some other branch of the force. Impact minimisation division. I'm sure there's one, I'd be the last to know.'

Ulyatt smiled, a genial fish, a grouper. 'Why don't we settle down and sort this out? Julie?'

The woman smiled. She had shoe-black hair, she'd been under

the knife, knew the needle, the dermabrasion, detailed down to her tyres like a saleyard Mercedes.

'Julie Sorenson, our key media person,' said Ulyatt.

'Hi,' she said, vanilla teeth, eyes like a dead deer, 'It's Stephen, isn't it?'

'Hi and goodbye,' said Villani. 'Same to you, Mr Elliot. Lovely to meet you but we're pushed here. A deceased person.'

Ulyatt lost the fish look. 'It's Ulyatt. I'm trying to be helpful, inspector, and I'm being met by hostility. Why is that?'

'This is what we need, Mr Manton,' said Villani. 'Ready?'

'Sylvia?' said Manton.

She had her pen ready.

'All CCTV tapes from 3pm yesterday, all lifts, parking,' said Villani. 'Also duty rosters, plus every single recorded coming and going, cars, people, deliveries, tradies, whatever.'

Ulyatt whistled. 'Tall order,' he said. 'We'll need a lot more time.'

'Got that down?' said Villani to Sylvia Allegro.

'Yes.'

'Also the CVs and rosters of all staff with access to the thirty-sixth floor or who could allow anyone access. And the owners of apartments on the floor and other floors with access to the floor. Plus the guest list for the casino function.'

'We don't have that,' said Ulyatt. 'That's Orion's business.'

'The casino function was in your building,' said Villani. 'I suggest you ask them. If they won't co-operate, let Detective Dove here know.'

Ulyatt was shaking his head.

'We'll show the victim on television tonight, ask for information,' said Villani.

'I can't see the necessity at this stage,' said Ulyatt.

Villani delayed looking at him, met the eyes of Dove, Weber,

Manton, Allegro, not Condy, he was looking away. Then he fixed Ulyatt. 'All these rich people paying for full-on security, the panic buttons, the cameras,' he said. 'A woman murdered in your building, that's a negative?'

'It's a woman found dead,' said Ulyatt. 'It's not clear to me that she was murdered. And I can't see why you would go on television until you've examined the information you want. Which we will provide as speedily as we can, I can assure you.'

'I don't need to be told how to conduct an investigation,' said Villani. 'And I don't want to be told.'

'I'm trying to help. I can go further up the food chain,' said Ulyatt.

'What?'

'Talk to people in government.'

Awake at 4.30am, Villani was feeling the length of the day now, his best behind him. 'You'll talk to people in government,' he said.

Ulyatt's lips drew back. 'As a last resort, of course.'

'So resort to it, mate,' said Villani, pilot flame of resentment igniting the burner. 'You're dealing with the bottom feeders, there's nowhere to go but up.'

'I certainly will be putting our view,' said Ulyatt, a long sour look, he rose, the woman rose too. He turned on his black shoes, the woman turned, they both wore thin black shoes, they both had slack arses, one fat, one thin, the surgery hadn't extended to lifting her arse. They left, Ulyatt taking out his mobile.

'No garbage to leave the premises, Mr Manton,' said Villani. 'I've always wanted to give someone that instruction.'

'It's gone,' said Manton. 'It goes before 7am, every day except Sunday.'

'Right. So. How do you get up there?'

'Private lifts,' said Manton. 'From the basements and the ground floor. Card-activated, access only to your floor.'

'And who's got cards?'

Manton turned to Condy. 'David?'

'I'd have to check,' said Condy.

Villani said, 'You don't know?'

'There's a procedure for issuing cards. I'll check.'

Villani moved his shoulders. 'Getting into the apartment?' he said. 'How's that work?'

'Same card, plus a PIN and optional fingerprint and iris scanning,' said Condy. 'The print and iris are in temporary abeyance.'

'Temporary what?'

'Ah, being finetuned.'

'Not working?'

'For the moment, no.'

'So it's just the card?'

'Yes.'

'Same card you don't know how many people have.'

Villani turned to Dove.

'I'm off,' he said. 'If we don't get the fullest co-operation here, I'll be on television saying that this building is a management disaster and a dangerous place to live and residents should be alarmed.'

'Inspector, we're trying to be . . .'

'Just do it, please,' said Villani, rising.

In the ground-floor foyer, he said to Dove and Weber, 'One, get Tracy onto the company that owns the apartment. Two, ID's the priority here. Run her prints. See what vision they've got, get someone to take down every rego in the parking garage. And get that casino guest list.'

Dove nodded.

Weber said, scratching his scalp, 'Fancy set-up, this. Like a palace.'

'So what?' said Villani.

Weber shrugged, awkward.

'Just another dead person,' said Villani. 'Flat in a Housing Commission, this palace, all the same. Just procedure. Bomb it to Snake.'

'Excuse, boss?'

'Know the term, Mr Dove? Honours degree of any use here?'

'I'd say it's a technical Homicide term,' said Dove. He was cleaning his rimless glasses, brown face vulnerable.

Villani looked at him for a while. 'Follow the drill. The procedure. Do what you've been taught. Tick stuff off. That way you don't have to ask for help.'

'I didn't ask for help,' said Dove. 'I asked Inspector Kiely a few questions.'

'Not the way he saw it,' said Villani. His phone tapped his chest.

'Please hold for Mr Colby,' said Angela Lowell, the secretary.

The assistant commissioner said, 'Steve, this Prosilio woman, I've had Mr Barry on the line. Broken neck, right?'

'They say that.'

'So he understands it could be an accident. A fall.'

'Bullshit, boss,' said Villani.

'Yeah, well, he wants nothing said about murder.'

'What's this?'

'Mr Barry's request to you. I'm the fucking conduit. With me, inspector?'

'Yes, boss.'

'Talk later, okay?'

'Yes, boss.'

Ulyatt hadn't been bluffing. He'd gone close to the top of the food chain. Perhaps he'd gone to the top, to Chief Commissioner Gillam, perhaps he could go to the premier.

Dove and Weber were looking at him.

'Media out there?' said Villani.

'No,' said Dove.

'No? What happened to media leaks? Anyway, if they show up, say a woman found dead, cause not established, can't rule out anything. Don't say murder, don't say suspicious, don't say anything about where in the building. Just a dead woman and we are waiting for forensic.'

Dove blinked, made tiny head movements, Villani saw his anxiety. His impulse was to make him suffer but judgment overrode it.

'On second thoughts, you do it, Web,' he said. 'See how you go in the big smoke.'

Wide eyes, Weber said, 'Sure, boss, sure. Done a bit of media.'

Villani passed through the sliding doors, the hot late afternoon seized his breath, his passage was brief, no media, down the stairs, across the forecourt, a cool car waiting.

On the radio, Alan Machin, 3AR's drive man, said:

. . . 35-plus tomorrow, two more days and we break the record. Why did I say that? People talk as if we want to break records like this. Lowest rainfall for a century. Hottest day. Can we stop talking about records? Gerry from Greenvale's on the line, what's on your mind, Gerry?

'Radio okay, boss?'

'Fine.'

. . . years ago, you ring the cops, the ambos, they come. Five minutes. Saturday there's shit across the road here, I ring the cops, twenty minutes, I ring again, it's a bloody riot out there, mate, girls screamin, animals trashin cars, they throw a letterbox through my front window, there's more arrivin all the time, no cops. I ring again, then there's two kids stabbed, another one's head's smashed in, somebody calls the medics.

So how far's the nearest police station, Gerry?

Craigieburn Road, isn't it? Too far's all I can say. Twenty-five minutes for the ambos to get here, they say the one kid's dead already. And the ambos load them up and they're gone before the bloody cops get here.

So it's what, more than an hour all-up before the police respond, is that . . .

Definitely. You notice they find hundreds when some dork gets lost bloody bushwalkin? That sorta thing?

Thanks for that, Gerry. Alice's been waiting, go ahead, Alice.

It's Alysha, actually, with a y. I wanted to talk about the trains but your caller's bloody spot on. We get riots around here, I'm not joking, riot's the only . . .

Where's that, Alisha, where's around . . .

Braybrook. Yeah. Police don't give a stuff, let them kill each other, gangs, it's like you don't see an Aussie face, all foreigners, blacks, Asians. Yeah . . .

'They don't like cops much, do they, boss?' said the driver.

'They can't like cops,' said Villani. 'Cops are their better side.'

IN HIS office, Gavan Kiely gone to Auckland, Villani switched on the big monitor, muted, waited for the 6.30pm news, unmuted.

A burning world − scarlet hills, grey-white funeral plumes, trees exploding, blackened vehicle carapaces, paddocks of charcoal, flames sluicing down a gentle slope of brown grass, the helicopters' water trunks hanging in the air.

. . . weary firefighters are bracing themselves for a last-ditch stand against a racing fire front that threatens the high country village of Morpeth, where most residents have chosen to stay and defend their homes despite warnings to heed the terrible lessons of 2009 . . .

When it was full dark, his father and Gordie would see the ochre glow in the sky, Morpeth was thirty kilometres by road from Selborne but only four valleys away.

A plane crash in Indonesia, a factory explosion in Geelong, a six-car freeway pile-up, the shut-down of an electronics company.

The wide-eyed newsreader said:

. . . four hundred A-listers, many of them high-rolling gamblers from Asia, the United States and Europe, last night had a preview of the Orion, Australia's newest casino and its most exclusive . . .

Men in evening dress, women in little black dresses getting out of cars, walking up a red carpet. Villani recognised a millionaire property developer, an actor whose career was dead, a famous footballer you could rent by the hour, two cocaine-addicted television personalities, a sallow man who owned racehorses and many jockeys.

A helicopter shot of the Prosilio building, then a spiky-haired young man on the forecourt said:

The boutique gambling venue is housed in this building, the newly commissioned Prosilio Tower, one of Australia's most expensive residential addresses. It's a world of total luxury for the millionaire residents, who live high above the city behind layers of the most advanced electronic and other security . . .

His phone.

'Pope Barry is pleased,' said Colby.

Villani said, 'About what?'

'Prosilio. The girl.'

'Nothing to do with me. The absent media, who arranged that?'

'I'd only be guessing.'

'Yeah, right. This Prosilio prick, Elliot, Ulyatt, his company owns the building. Came on like we're from the council about overhanging branches.'

'And you said?'

'Well I said fuck off.'

'Well I can say he went somewhere. I can say that.'

'I don't like this stuff, boss.'

'They don't want bad news.'

'The casino?' said Villani.

'The casino's not it, son,' said Colby. 'Up there in the air there's like a whole suburb of unsold million-buck apartments. All spruiked to be as safe as living next door to the Benalla copshop in 1952. You make all this money and you can buy anything and then some deranged psycho shithead invades your space and kills you. Fucks you and tortures you and kills you.'

'I see the unappealing part of that.'

'So you'll also try to grasp the charm of a murder in the building.'

Anna Markham on the screen, cold, pinstriped jacket. He had looked at the dimple in her chin from close range, thought about inserting his tongue into the tiny cleft.

'I'll work on that, boss,' he said.

'Front and fucking centre. In the big game now. Not in Armed Robbery anymore. Not you, not me.'

. . . today's poll shock, the threat of a nurses' strike, the questions over the Calder Village project and next week's demonstrations in the Goulburn Valley. With the election weeks away, Premier Yeats has a few things to be worried about . . .

She had the private-school voice, the expensive tones.

The anchorman said:

. . . political editor Anna Markham. Now to finance news. In a surprise development in the media world today, a new . . .

The phone. Mute.

'Media on the line, boss. Mr Searle.'

'Stevo, how you going?' Hoarse cigarette voice.

'Good. What?'

'To business. Like that in a man. Listen, this Prosilio woman, got anything?'

'No.'

'Okay, so we keep it off the agenda till you have, no point in . . .'

'If we don't ID her before,' said Villani, 'I want her on all news tomorrow.'

'My word,' said Searle. 'And obviously it's not stressing the Prosilio angle, it's a woman we want identified, that's basically . . .'

'Talk tomorrow,' said Villani. 'Calls waiting.'

'Inspector.'

Villani sat for a long time, head back, eyes closed, thinking about the girl-woman who looked like Lizzie lying in a glass bath in a glass room high above the stained world.

Three levels of security, panic buttons, so many barriers, so insulated. And still the fear. He saw the girl's skin, grey of the earliest dawn, he saw the shallow bowl between her hipbones and her pubic hair holding droplets like a desert plant.

The water would have been bobbed, flecked and scummed with substances released by her body. He was glad he hadn't seen that.

Time to go, put an end to the day.

No one to have a drink with. He could not do that anymore, he was the boss.

Go home. No one there.

He rang Bob Villani's number, saw the passage in his father's house, the phone on the rickety table, heard the telephone's urgent sound, saw the dog listening, head on one side. He did not wait for it to ring out.

Inspector. Head of Homicide.

He knew he was going to do it but he waited, drew it out, went to the cupboard and found the card in her spiky hand. He sat, pressed the numbers, a mobile.

'Hello.'

'Stephen Villani. If I've got the right number, I'm exploring the possibility of seeing someone again.'

'Right number, explorer. When did you have in mind?'

'Well, whenever.'

'Like tonight?'

He could not believe his luck. 'Like tonight, I would have that in mind, yes.'

'I can change my plans,' she said, the arrogant voice. 'I can be where I live in ... oh, about an hour.'

'You want to change your plans?'

'Let me think. Yes, I want to change my plans.'

'Well, I can be there.'

'Don't eat. Be hungry.'

'So that's how hunger works,' said Villani. 'Give me the address.'

'South Melbourne. Eighteen Minter Street. Exeter Place. Apartment twelve.'

He felt the blood in his veins, the little tightness in his chest, the way he felt in the ring before the bell, before the fight began.

'SATISFACTORY,' said Anna Markham.

'Can I get a more precise mark?' said Villani.

He was on his side, he kissed her cheekbone. Anna turned her head, found his mouth. It was a good kiss.

'It's binary at this stage,' she said. 'Satisfactory, unsatisfactory.'

'Before I rang,' he said. 'Where were you going?'

'To see a play.'

'With?'

'A friend.'

'Male friend?'

'Possibly.'

'There are ways to tell.'

'I like uncertainty,' Anna said. 'Don't you want to know what play?'

A test. Villani felt the great space between them. She had been to university, the apartment was full of books, paintings, classical music CDs fanned on a sideboard. He had no learning beyond school, he learned little there that he could remember, in high school he had been in a play, shotgunned by a spunky teacher, he saw her face. Ms Davis, she insisted on the Ms. All he knew about art and music came from Laurie dragging him out until she grew weary of it. He read the newspapers, Bob had instilled the habit in him, he watched movies late at night when he couldn't sleep.

And trees, he knew a fair bit about trees. For a start, he knew the botanical names of about fifty oaks.

'What play?' he said.

'*The Tempest*. Shakespeare.'

'Never heard of it.'

He put his head back and after a while he said, 'The cloud-capp'd towers, the gorgeous palaces, the solemn temples, the great globe itself, yea, all which it inherit, shall dissolve...'

Fingertips dug into his upper arm.

'And, like this insubstantial pageant faded, leave not a rack behind,' Villani said.

'Who are you?'

'It's the new force,' he said. 'We find Shakespeare relevant. Plus inspirational.'

She moved onto him, silk, her hair fell on him. 'I had a feeling you might be the thinking woman's investigator. Great screw too. If a little hasty.'

'I'll give you hasty.'

She was thin but muscled, she pretended to surrender, then she resisted him, he tried to pin her down, aroused.

He saw the girl in the back seat of the car, blurred lipstick. Fear flooded him.

'What?' she said, 'what?'

'I thought you were . . . fighting me.'

'I like fighting you. What's wrong?'

'Nothing.'

'Turned you off?'

He rolled over, saw the matted hair on his belly, there was flab.

'Just tired,' he said. 'Up early.'

She said nothing for a while, reached for her gown, rose like a mantis, no effort. 'Take a shower, we'll eat.'

Villani was towelling his hair when his phone rang.

'Dad.'

Corin.

'Yes, love. What?'

'I'm a bit spooked. There's a car hanging around.'

The fear. In his stomach, in his throat, instant bile in his mouth. 'Hanging around how?' he said, casual.

'Drove past as I got home, two guys. Then I took the bin out and it's parked down the street. I went out just now and it was gone and then they came around the block and parked further up.'

'What kind of car?'

'They all look alike. New. Light colour.'

'Won't be anything, but lock up, be on the safe side. I'll get someone to come around, I'm on my way. Twenty minutes max. Ring me if anything happens. That clear?'

'Sir. Right, yeah. Thanks, Dad.'

His precious girl. Thanking him as if he were doing her a favour. He speed-dialled, spoke to the duty person, waited, heard the talk on the radio.

'Car four minutes away, boss,' said the woman.

'Tell them I'll be there in twenty, hang on for me.'

Anna was at the kitchen end of the big room, hair up, barefoot, thin gown. She turned her head.

Villani walked across the space, stood behind her.

'Prime rump strips,' Anna said. 'To build strength.'

There was an awkwardness. Villani wanted to pull her against him. 'Prime rump's cost me my strength,' he said. 'I've got to go. Urgent stuff.'

She stirred the wok. 'Slam bam.'

He tried to kiss an ear, she moved, he kissed hair. 'I'm sorry,' he said. 'This is probably all a mistake.'

'Let's not do this as tragedy,' she said. 'Just a screw.'

'You should have gone to the play.'

'It's on for a month. You, on the other hand, could close at any time.'

'You should probably consider me closed,' he said, a wash of relief, walked, gathered his coat from the sofa without breaking stride. At the front door, he could not stop himself looking back, down the gunbarrel. He saw the length of her neck.

All across the hot shrieking city, he thought about Corin, the joy of her, the lovely breathing weight of the tiny child asleep on him on a baking afternoon at the holiday house, he rehearsed the selfish pain he would feel if anything happened to her, the responsibility he would bear for having a job where animals hated you, dreamed of revenge, would kill your family.

In Carlton, at the Elgin intersection, he spoke to her.

'There's something happening out there,' she said. 'Cars.'

'The force is with you. Stay inside, I'm a couple of minutes away.'

Turning into the street, he saw the cars, pulled up behind them. A uniform came to his window.

'Couple of dickheads, boss,' she said. 'The one's separated from his missus, she's renting number 176 down there, he reckons she's rooting his brother. So him and his mate, they sit in the Holden sipping Beam, now both pissed, they're waiting for the poor bloke to arrive.'

'Wasted your time then,' said Villani.

'Definitely not, boss,' said the woman. 'So many loonies around. These idiots, we give them a scare. The car'll be here till tomorrow. Going home in a cab.'

Villani parked in the driveway, went in the back door. Corin was waiting, anxious face. He told her.

'Sorry, Dad.'

He kissed her forehead, she put up a hand, rubbed the back of his head.

'Sorry is the day you don't call me,' he said. 'Jesus, it's hot.'

Corin said, 'You think kind of, your dad's a cop, you're bulletproof.'

'You are. Just a car in the street.'

'Yeah. Dumb. Eaten?'

'Not recently, no.'

'TCT suit?'

'TCT and O. Shavings of O.'

'If there's an O. You grate the cheese.'

Like old times, girl and dad, in the kitchen, side by side, Villani buttering bread, grating cheddar, Corin slicing a tomato, an onion. Not looking, she said, 'Damp hair.'

Villani felt his hair. 'Showered,' he said. 'Long day. A sweaty day.'

'You shower at work?'

'Often. Head of Homicide has to be seen to be clean.'

Corin said, quickly, 'Sam in my tute, he works a shift at this place, he says you were there with a woman.'

'He knows me?'

'Saw you on TV.'

'Canadian criminologist,' Villani said. 'She's got a grant to study Commonwealth police forces. Beats being interviewed in the office.'

An elaborated lie. Too much detail. These porkies usually fell over when you stared at the teller for ten seconds.

Corin went to the sink.

'Sam says it was Anna Markham, the television woman. It was after midnight.'

'There is a resemblance,' he said. 'Now that you mention it.'

'Dad. Don't.'

'Don't what?'

'Lie to me. I'm not a kid.'

'Listen, kid,' said Villani. 'It was nothing.'

'What about you and Mum?'

'Well, it's difficult, a difficult time.'

'Don't you love her anymore?'

Corin was twenty-one, you could still ask a question like that.

'Love's not just the one thing,' he said. 'There's love and there's love. It changes.'

In her eyes he saw that she had no idea what he was saying. 'Anyway,' he said. 'Where's Lizzie?'

'Supposed to be staying with a friend for the weekend.'

'See her today?'

'Heard her. She was in the bathroom when I left. When did you last see her?'

Villani couldn't remember exactly. Guilt, there was always guilt. 'Few days ago. Where's your mum this time? I forget.'

'Cairns. A movie.'

'Never worked out why these people have to take their own caterer. Don't they cook in Cairns? Just raw fruit?'

'You should spend more time together,' said Corin.

Villani pretended to punch her arm. 'Finish law first,' he said. 'Then the grad-dip marriage counselling.'

He ate his toasted sandwiches in front of the television, reading the *Age*. Corin lay on the sofa, files on the floor, taking notes. With the plate on his lap, he fell asleep, waking startled when she took it from his hands.

'Bed, Dad,' she said. 'You've got to get more sleep. Sleep and proper food and exercise.'

'The holy trinity,' said Villani. 'Goodnight, my darling.'

IN THE lift, Birkerts joined him. 'I saw the lay pastor of the Church of Jesus the High Achiever sharing a moment with Mr Kiely the other day,' he said. 'Possibly planning a lunchtime bible-study group.'

'At least Weber shows me some respect,' said Villani.

'He probably prays for you,' said Birkerts. 'Could lay hands on you, whatever that means.'

'I want to encourage prayer,' said Villani. 'I want people to pray not to be transferred to Neighbourhood Watch Co-ordination.'

'There's a few here who don't mind kneeling before the right man.'

'Got nothing against Catholics,' said Villani.

In his office, Villani checked the messages, summoned Dove.

'How you going?' said Villani. 'Your health.' He didn't much care but you were supposed to be concerned. Dove was the force's first indigenous officer shot on duty.

Dove rolled his shaven head, hand on neck. 'Fine,' he said. 'Boss.'

'Headaches?'

'Headaches?'

'Get headaches?'

'Sometimes. I had headaches before. Sometimes.'

'It says,' said Villani, 'it says headaches are a common post-traumatic stress symptom.'

'I don't have post-traumatic stress, boss.'

'Flashbacks?'

'No. I don't have flashbacks, I don't relive the prick shooting me. I remember it, I've got a perfect memory of being shot, everything till I passed out.'

'Good. And stress? Feel stressed?'

Dove looked down. 'Can I ask you a question, boss?'

'Sure.'

'Ever been shot?'

'No. Shot at, yeah. Few times.'

'Get flashbacks?'

'No. Dreams. I've had dreams.'

Dove held Villani's eyes, he wasn't going to look away. 'Can I see your medical records, boss?' he said. 'Discuss them with you?'

Villani thought about Dove's attitude, always bad, not improved by being shot. He was a mistake. The best thing would be to issue formal cautions, starting today with insubordination. Then he could be posted elsewhere. In due course, someone else could fire him.

'Right,' said Villani. 'You seem normal to me. It's a low base-line but there you go.'

'This's because of yesterday. Boss? My questions to Kiely? Simple questions about procedure.'

Villani saw a chance. 'Inspector Kiely to you. I get the feeling you're unhappy here. No names, no pack-drill transfer might be the go.'

Dove held his gaze. 'No, boss,' he said. 'I'm happy. To do whatever you want me to do.'

'That's normally the way it works in the force.'

'Yes, boss.'

Tracy from the door. 'Boss, bloke won't give a name. Old mate, he says.'

'His number, I'll call him back.'

To Dove, he said, 'Get Weber.'

They were back in seconds.

'So tell me,' said Villani.

'It's not good,' said Dove. 'They haven't provided the video for the parking and the lifts. They claim technical difficulties. The publicity says state-of-the-art but nothing worked. Could be a building in the 1950s.'

'New world of total security,' said Villani. 'New world of total bullshit. What about cards, the PINs?'

'They actually have no idea who could get into the apartment. Just about anyone in security can make a card, program the PIN. Then later they could change back to the old ones.'

'Shit. Okay, moving on. Scientists.'

Dove inclined his head at Weber.

'No prints, they say DNA's unlikely, it's cleaner than a hospital,' said Weber, the bright look.

'No longer a benchmark, hospitals,' said Villani. 'What's the butchery say?'

Weber had a printout. 'Time of death around midnight on Thursday. C5 snapped, very likely head jerked back, no bruising or abrasions. Recent intercourse. Tearing to vaginal and anal passages. No semen. Used cocaine. She's sixteen to twenty. Scar on left tricep, more than a year old. Bruising on her ribs left side, probably punched, that's recent. Slightly displaced septum, probably in the last six months.'

Silence.

'So what do they offer?' said Villani.

Weber coughed, he looked at Dove.

Dove said, 'She's possibly had her hands tied, she's gagged, something soft, there's vaginal and anal intercourse, he's behind her, he's very big, as in huge or he's wearing something or it's an object, that kind of thing. He at some point jerks her head back violently, breaks her neck. He would have her head in his hands. He places her in the bath and washes her, pulls plug.'

'Then,' said Weber, 'then he disposes of her clothes, shoes, everything and wipes all surfaces touched.'

'Just another homey night in the Prosilio building,' Villani said. 'Before the sex, they probably ate pizza, watched a DVD. Checked for that, did you, Mr Dove?'

Dove blinked. 'Ah, no. No.'

'Possibly *Pretty Woman*,' said Villani. 'Religious text for hookers. Hooker's New Testament. Message of salvation. Familiar with it, Mr Weber?'

Weber made a smile, perhaps he forgave the levity, they would never know. 'You're saying that, boss? A hooker?'

'No,' said Villani. 'I'm just leaning that way. I'm close to falling over. Checked the laundry chute, the garbage?'

'Nothing in the laundry chute,' said Dove. 'Garbage taken on Friday morning. It's in the landfill.'

'That's really promising,' said Villani. 'The manager produce the other stuff?'

'I don't think Manton's flat out on this,' said Dove, stroking his head. 'He referred us to Ulyatt, to Marscay. The owners.'

Ulyatt. The man who could speak to someone who could tell the chief commissioner what to do.

'What about the casino guests?'

Dove looked at Weber. Weber said, 'Uh, I left that with Tracy, boss. Casino security is run by a company called Stilicho. Sounds like it's part of Blackwatch Associates.'

'Well, retrieve it,' said Villani. 'That's not her job. Since when do Blackwatch do this kind of thing?'

'Don't know much about Blackwatch, boss,' said Weber.

'The name Matt Cameron mean anything?'

'The cop?'

Villani had served under the legendary Matt Cameron, gone to the scene of the killings of his son and his girlfriend, taken part in the massive, fruitless man-hunt.

'Once the cop. He runs Blackwatch. Part owns.'

'This lot is a new company,' said Dove. 'I think it's Blackwatch in partnership with someone else.'

'Okay,' Villani said. 'Dead woman, no clothes, no ID, no idea how she got there, no vision, so we have dogshit.'

'Encapsulated it, boss,' said Dove, the little smile-smirk.

Villani rose, stretched his arms up, sideways, rolled his head, some bones clicked, he went to the window, he could not see the eastern hills, lost in smoke. He thought about his trees. If they went, he would never go back there, he would not be able to bear that sight. Smoke, he needed a smoke, he would always need a smoke. Weber would always be a pain, his purity a living reprimand, but he would worry and lose sleep, do a good job. Dove was another matter. Too clever, too cocky, not enough dead seen.

Villani thought about the dead he had seen. He remembered them all. Bodies in Housing Commission flats, in low brown brick-veneer units, in puked alleys, stained driveways, car boots, the dead stuffed into culverts, drains, sunk in dams, rivers, creeks, canals, buried under houses, thrown down mineshafts, entombed in walls, embalmed in concrete, people shot, stabbed, strangled, brained, crushed, poisoned, drowned, electrocuted, asphyxiated, starved, skewered, hacked, pushed from buildings, tossed from bridges. There could be no unstaining, no uninstalling, he was marked by seeing these dead as his father was marked by the killing he had done, the killing he had seen.

Villani said, 'Tell Mr Searle we want her on all channels tonight, hair up, hair down, a women found dead in an apartment in the Prosilio building in Docklands.'

'Is that like being murdered?' said Dove. 'Is murdered a word
that can be used?'

'That's it, Detective Weber. Detective Dove, a minute.'

Weber left. Villani gazed at Dove, blinked, gazed, didn't move
his head, his hands were in his lap. Dove blinked, moved his head
back and forth, wouldn't look away, blinked, touched an ear.

'Understand that I don't like a smartarse,' said Villani. 'You're
only here because when they offered you around trying to get
rid of you, I took you on. Now all you've got going for you is
you got shot. The sympathy vote.'

'Haven't exactly had much of a chance,' said Dove.

'This is your chance,' said Villani. 'Don't stuff it up. Tell Manton
we don't get everything today, staff names, CVs, who came and
went, we will say some very nasty things about the Prosilio building. And we want that Orion guest list too.'

He did paperwork, read the case notes, wrote instructions,
gave instructions, spoke to squad leaders. Things were in hand,
the day ticked by. At 5.40pm, he left, bought Chinese on the way,
reached the empty house in time for the television news. They
showed her face. The resemblance to Lizzie was strong, he hadn't
imagined it. Even in death, she was lovely, serious, but she looked
no more dead than if it were her passport photograph.

No mention that she was found broken-necked. No mention
of the Prosilio building. Just an unidentified young woman. He
changed channels, caught the item on Ten. The same.

He rang four numbers, he could not find Searle or anyone
else to rage at, left a short message for Dove.

He was watching the 7pm ABC news when Dove rang.

'Before you say anything,' said Villani, 'who decided no broken
neck, not found at any particular place?'

'Not us, boss. I used your words. A young woman found dead
in an apartment in the Prosilio building.'

The woman on screen. Hair down.

. . . police are appealing for information about the identity of this young woman. She is Caucasian, brown hair, in her late teens and would not have been seen for several days . . .

New image. Her hair was up.

. . . please contact Crime Stoppers on . . .

'Searle will turn in the wind for this,' said Villani. 'Anything comes in, let me know.'

'Is that any time, night and day?' said Dove.

'When you make a bad call, I'll tell you. It's a sudden-death thing.'

Saturday night. Once high point of the week. He showered, found crumpled shorts, opened a beer, went shirtless into the hot night. He took a piss on the former vegetable strip along the fence, dead hard-baked soil, heard voices, laughter from two sides. A splash, splashes. How had he missed a pool going in next door?

He sat in a deckchair on the back terrace, drank another beer, ate cold Chinese. It wasn't bad, possibly better cold than hot, hot was less than wonderful. He registered the rough brick paving underfoot, laid by another him and another Joe Cashin in another age. It took a weekend.

Sudden craving for red wine. He found a bottle, the second last one in the case.

In the kitchen, the corkscrew in hand, his mobile on the benchtop sang.

'Is this a good time?' said Dove.

'Speak,' said Villani.

'Crime Stoppers call from a woman in Box Hill. I just talked to her.'

'So?'

'She's pretty sure she saw our girl at a truck stop on the Hume about two months ago, sixteenth of December, about 9pm. This side of Wangaratta.'

'Saw her how?'

'In the toilets. There was a man waiting outside for her and they spoke in a foreign language. Not Italian, French or Spanish, she reckons, she's been there. Went to a new Holden SV, black or dark green. Another man was driving. She says there might have been someone else in the back seat.'

'Rego?'

'No.'

'So what are you going to do?'

'Well, HSV, that's a muscle car, only driven by men with big balls,' said Dove. 'Web's asking our traffic and New South if they had an offender on the day.'

'That's not stupid. I'm off to sleep soon, looking forward to it like a first root. Tomorrow I'm going up country. You don't get me the first time, keep trying. Reception's rough up there.'

'I'll just keep bombing it to Snake,' said Dove.

'Quick learner,' said Villani. 'You're a bright young man.'

He sat outside, drank wine, it seemed to be getting hotter. He showered again, went outside and rang Bob Villani. It rang out.

VILLANI ROSE in the dark and stifling house, stood in the shower, dressed, took his canvas bag and left. The world was spent, only the desperate were on the streets. On the ramp before the exit, a tall black man, head shaven, was walking, behind him a shorter person, hidden in grey garments.

In the mirror, Villani saw she had only a slit through which to see the world.

It took three hours, the country drying out, the last stretch up the long yellow hills, paddocks skun, the livestock skinny, handfed.

. . . today is a day of total fire ban. Four fires are still burning out of control in the high country around Paxton and the town of Morpeth has been evacuated. Firefighters fear the blazes will join into a sixty-kilometre fire front . . .

From a cafe called Terroir in the last town before Selborne, Villani bought poached chicken breasts, a loaf of sourdough, a lettuce and a container of mayonnaise. He asked for the bread to be sliced.

'If you wish,' said the man, too old for his tipped, gelled hair, silver nostril stud. 'You realise it won't keep as well.'

'I have no long-term plans for it,' said Villani. 'I propose to eat it within weeks.'

The man tilted his head, interested. 'You local?'

Passing through Selborne, he looked for changes, it was his town, any alteration or addition caught his eye. And then the last winding stretch, the gate. Villani got out, did the lift and drag, twice, he drove down the driveway and parked beneath the elm. He had climbed this tree a hundred times, it was not looking good.

Out of the vehicle, he stretched, tested his knees, looked at the house. His father came around the corner, something different about his walk, the way he held himself.

Nodding, nothing said, they shook, soft hands, they were beyond gripping. Having touched like boxers, they could get on with it.

'Grass's a bit fucking much,' said Villani. 'Serious fire hazard.'

'Gets this far, you're buggered anyway,' said Bob.

'That's not what the CFA manual says.'

'They know fuckall, they start the fires. Lukie's coming, staying tonight.'

'Thrilling news. When d'you last see him?'

'He's busy.'

'When?'

'Haven't seen your lot for a while. Bloody years.'

'Kids,' said Villani. 'You know.'

'No, never worked out kids.'

'Well, lack of effort could be involved.'

His father never asked about Laurie and she never asked about him. From the start, she and Bob behaved like dogs who'd had a bad fight, shifty eyes, didn't kiss, had nothing to say to each other.

'Eaten?'

'Yeah. Brought us lunch.'

'Cup of tea?'

'Might do some mowing first. Get this stuff down.'

'Can't mow. Total fire ban day.'

'Leaving it's a bigger risk than the mower.'

'Gordie'll do it.'

'Not sure I want to trust my inheritance to Gordie coming around one day.'

'Who made you the prince? I'll leave the place to Luke.'

You did not want to take Bob seriously, he could take and give, he could dissolve everything you thought solid.

Villani got the Victa out of the garage, fuelled it, pushed it around to the front. He opened the throttle and tried to pull the cord. It wouldn't move. He upended the machine, tried to move the blade, brushed his knuckles, quick blood. He went to the woodpile, chose a length, came back and hit the blade, the third blow shifted it.

'First resort,' said his father. 'Brute force.'

'Yes,' said Villani. 'Learned from you.'

He righted the mower, pressed the nipple a few times, it was covered in grease and dirt. He pulled the cord. The motor plopped. He tried again. Again. Again, a wire of pain up his arm, into his shoulder.

'Not getting juice,' said his father. 'More tit.'

'Filthy, this machine. What happened to never put a tool away dirty, that's what you always said.'

'Dust,' said his father. 'Whole fucking Mallee's blowing over here.'

Villani thumbed the plunger until he smelled fuel, stood up and pulled the cord: a piston puff, he tried again, the engine puffed twice, he gave another rip. A roar, dust, lapwings rose from the grass. He trimmed the throttle, pushed the mower down to the northern corner of the house block and began.

On the second tank, he saw Bob Villani wave. They sat on the gap-planked verandah and drank tea. The dog, yellow of hair and eye, lay with his long snout on his master's boot.

For another half-hour, he pushed the machine. The dust he raised mingled with petrol fumes and stuck to his skin, a headache began. It was over thirty, wind gone, nothing stirring, a hot, dead world smelling of smoke. On the long east-west run, itching, dust in his eyes, sticking to his face, he could look at the blue-grey mountain, the treeless dark of the upper slope. It appeared close but it was an hour away, the country was deeply folded.

At noon, he throttled back, the motor stuttered, didn't want to die. It was minutes before he could hear the silence. He walked to the tank, disturbing a pair of crested pigeons. They strutted off, offended. He washed his hands, splashed his face. When he opened his eyes, the world dimmed. You didn't notice this in the city, you needed to be away from the smog for clouds to change the colour of the land, of your flesh.

'Missed a bit down there,' said Bob, pointing.

'I didn't actually drive up here to cut your grass,' he said. 'The phone rings out. What happened to the answering machine?'

'Buggered,' said Bob.

'Well, get another one.' He drank from the tap. The rainwater tasted ancient, of zinc nails held in the mouth.

Villani cleaned the mower, sprayed it with WD-40, pushed it into the garage. He went inside, washed his face and hands in the kitchen sink, made chicken sandwiches with mayonnaise and iceberg lettuce.

They ate in the kitchen, the dog under the table.

'Bread's tough,' said Bob.

'It's expensive bread, handmade.'

'They done you, mate.'

'Mark been here?'

'The doctor doesn't need his old man.'

'Maybe he phones and no one answers.'

'He doesn't phone.'

'Yeah? The phone doesn't work. I'll talk to him. The compost heap's dead. No tomatoes in either.'

His father chewing, eyes on the ceiling. 'Not growing anything, you don't need compost.'

'Not over yet, Dad. You're still eating, I presume?'

Bob Villani said, 'Gordie's growing vegies for a fucking army, what's the point me growing tomatoes?'

'Fair enough. How's he going?'

'Gordie's Gordie. Be here five minutes after Luke shows up.'

'Doesn't do that for me.'

'Scared of you.'

'Bullshit.'

Bob said nothing, took his plate to the sink.

'Anyway he's a boofhead,' said Villani. 'Always been one. Like his mother. Why you limping?'

'Fell.'

'How?'

'No particular way.'

'What, your hip?'

Bob turned. 'You're not the doctor, boy,' he said, 'you're the fucking copper.'

Bob wasn't going to look away. Villani put up his hands, they went outside.

'Ibises,' said Bob. 'Never seen so many ibises. That's a very bad sign.'

'What happens when the fire gets here?'

Bob turned his head, the long, appraising, pitying look. 'Fire's not coming,' he said. 'Fire's going where the wind says.'

'Just got lucky the last time.'

'That's what I am. Mr Lucky.'

'I hope so,' Villani said. 'I very much hope so. Let's have a look at the trees.'

'You go,' said Bob. 'I'll wait for Lukie. Take the dog.'

Villani looked at the dog. It was studying the ground like an anteater waiting for food to appear.

'Walk?' he said.

The dog looked at him, alert, cheered, a sentry relieved at last. They walked across the bottom paddock, it had provided no horse feed this season, went through the gate to the big crescent of dam, stood on the edge. The dog wandered down the dry fissured side to an unhealthy yellow-green puddle, stepped in and lapped. The hole was carved before they began planting, a man came with a bulldozer on a truck, shifted tonnes of earth, rerouted a winter creek. For years, it was never empty, often it overflowed, its lip had to be raised.

Below them a forest, wide and deep and dark, big trees, more than thirty years old. Planted by hand, every last one, thousands of trees – alpine ash, mountain swamp gum, red stringybark, peppermints, mountain gum, spotted gum, snow gum, southern mahogany, sugar gum, silvertop ash. And the oaks, about four thousand, grown from acorns collected in two autumns from every russet Avenue of Honour Bob Villani drove down, from every botanical garden he passed. He stored the shiny amber capsules in brown-paper bags in their own fridge, place of origin and date, sometimes a species, written in pencil in his squat soldier's report-writing hand.

In the spring, Villani helped him fence off a big rectangle behind the stables, rabbit-proof fence. They put the acorns in plastic pots, in a mixture of river sand and soil, a weekend just to do that. Villani was thirteen that year, already alone all week with Mark, making their breakfast and tea, sandwiches for school, washing clothes, ironing. He remembered the delight of the morning he saw tiny green oak tips had broken the soil, dozens and dozens, as if they had received some signal. He couldn't wait for Bob to get home to show him.

'What's wrong with the others?' said Bob. 'Water them?'

The others emerged in the next weeks. All that summer, he watered the seedlings by hand, half a mug each from a bucket filled from the tanks.

On a Saturday morning in late summer they walked down to the bottom gate and across the road that went nowhere, stood at the gate opposite. Bob waved a hand. 'Bought it,' he said. 'Hundred and ten acres.'

Villani looked at the overgrazed, barren, pitted sheep paddocks. 'Why?' he said.

'A forest,' Bob said. 'Going to have our own forest.'

'Right,' said Villani. 'A forest.'

That winter they dug the first holes, at least a thousand, left paths, clearings, Bob appeared to have a master plan in his head, never disclosed. They dug in icy winds and freezing rain, numb black hands, your cold skin tore, you only found out you had bled when you washed off the dirt. Towards spring that year and the next two, Saturdays and Sundays, eight hours a day, they created the forest. They planted the oak seedlings and the bought eucalypt seedlings through squares of old carpet underfelt, protected them with house-wrap cut from fifty-metre rolls, Bob got these things somewhere, perhaps fallen off the back of some other driver's truck, like the plastic pots.

In the cold spring when it was done, when Bob said it was done, Villani was heading for sixteen, marginally shorter than his father.

Now he looked at what had once been a burrowed, bumpy landscape covered with little silver tents, then with hair-transplant plugs, and said to himself, 'Looking good.' The sight filled him with pleasure, with joy even.

He went around the dam, the dog came up, muddy-pawed, and they entered the shade by the path once wide as a street, now narrowed to a track. From the time the trees were head-high, every time he walked the forest he heard new bird calls, saw new groundcovers spreading, new plants sprung up, new droppings of different sizes and shapes, new burrowings, scrapings, scratchings, new holes, fallen feathers, drab ones and feathers that flashed sapphire, scarlet, blue, emerald, and soon there were tiny bones and spike-toothed skulls, signs of life and death and struggle among the arboreal mammals.

'Lots of little buggers in there now,' said Bob one day. 'Echidnas, bandis, God knows where they come from.'

The walk took almost an hour. When they got back to the house, Villani said, 'We should've done something about the understorey a long time ago. Well, got to go. Long day tomorrow.'

Bob raised a hand. 'He'll be here in a minute, hang on.'

'See Luke some other time.'

'Give him a chance. Don't often get two of you here.' He rose. 'Come. Got two new horses.'

They walked along the horse paddock fence. The ten-year-old Cromwell had sensed they were coming, stood near the trough with his rough head over the wire.

'Having a little rest, Crommie,' said Bob. He fed the horse something, stroked his nose.

'What was the last payday?' said Villani.

'Third at Benalla, that'd be . . . a while. Still, got a run or two left in him.'

'Encourage them to have a race for ten-year-olds,' said Villani. 'No more than four non-metropolitan wins. A level playing field.'

They went into the stable, a long building, doors open at both ends, cracked and pitted concrete floor, twelve bays. It smelled of manure and urine and straw. Two heads looked at them from adjacent boxes on the left.

They stopped at the first one, a big animal, colour of rust. 'This's Sunny,' said Bob. 'Red Sundown, six-year-old. Bought him off Billy Clarke at Trenneries, three hundred bucks, he's got this leg. Only had the six runs but he's out of St Marcus.'

'If he can't actually run, he might as well be out of St Peter,' said Villani.

'I'll fix him,' said his father. 'The lawang.'

'The what?'

'Oil. From a tree in Indonesia. Costs a fucking bomb.' He fed the horse something out of his cupped hand.

'What happened to magnets? Last time it was miracles from magnets.'

'Lawang's better than magnets.' Bob moved to the next horse. 'My baby. Tripoli Girl.'

The coal-dark animal was skittish, jerked its head, white-eyed them, backed off, toed the floor. Bob showed his palm, closed his hand, opened it, took it away, turned his back on the horse.

'Cairo Night out of Hathaway,' he said. 'Cairo won two, maiden by ten lengths. He bled and then he came back and run terrible, they gave up on him after a year or so. Just produced the four fruits.'

'All duds?'

'Bad luck early, badly handled, that's the way I read it.'

'How much?'

'Cheap. Cheap. Dollar Dazzler.'

Tripoli Girl was nudging Bob with its silken head, moving it from side to side. He turned, kept back from the horse, extended an empty hand. The horse nosed it, looked at him. He offered the other hand, opened it slowly, Tripoli nuzzled into it, found something.

They went back to the house, shoes disturbing the dry mown grass. Bob fetched two beers, a VB and a Crown. He gave Villani the Crown. It cost more than the VB.

'Said he'd be here around three-thirty,' said Bob.

They sat on the shady side of the house. After a while, Villani said, 'Why's Gordon scared of me?'

Bob wiped a beer tidemark from his upper lip. 'Well, you know. People.'

'What?'

Bob frowned at the landscape. 'You've got a manner.'

'What's that?'

'Boss manner.'

'Since when?'

'Since a kid. Just got more so.'

Villani could not believe that he had always had a boss manner. 'No one's said that.'

'Be like telling a bloke he's got red hair.'

'Where would I get a boss manner from?' said Villani.

'Don't look at me.'

They sat drinking, Bob looking at his watch every few minutes. They heard the car, Bob was up, gone. Villani sipped beer and looked at the hills, row upon wavy row, greying now, darker in the foreground. He put the bottle on the table and got up.

Luke got out of a black Audi, embraced his father, kissed his cheek. A woman got out, tall, dark hair pulled back. Luke saw Villani.

'Steve. Been a while, mate.' He had a tan, he'd lost weight, white shirt worn outside his pants.

Villani stepped off the verandah. They shook hands.

'This's Charis, works with me,' Luke said. 'Charis, this's my dad, best bloke on the planet, my brother Steve, he's another matter entirely.'

'Hi.' Charis smiled, uneasy, offered a hand.

She was young, a teenager.

'You didn't say Steve was coming,' Luke said to his father.

'Didn't know. Beer time.'

They sat on the verandah. Bob brought beers, glasses. Luke and the woman drank Crown from the bottle. Luke was a race-caller, all he ever wanted to be. He did all the talking, asked questions, didn't hear the answers, gave answers himself. The woman giggled at everything he said.

'Charis does T–WIN weather,' he said. 'Just a start, she's going to be big-time.'

Charis smiled, showed all front teeth, a for-the-camera smile.

'Oh, Luke,' she said.

'How's Kathy?' said Villani. 'The kids.' There were two. He couldn't remember their names.

'Great, good.' Luke didn't meet Villani's eyes. 'Yours?'

'Same, yeah.'

A cough. Gordon McArthur, the neighbour's son, approaching thirty, a fat twelve-year-old face, checked shirt beneath clean overalls.

'Gordie, my man.' Luke went to him, tapped his cheeks, hard, both hands. 'How you doing, big fella?'

'Good, Lukie, good.' Gordie's eyes were lit.

'Charis, meet Gordie. Seen Charis do the weather, Gordie?'

'Seen her,' said Gordie. He didn't quite look at Charis and she didn't quite look at him.

Villani's mobile went. He stepped away, to the far end of the verandah.

'Tried you a few times, boss,' said Dove.

'Comes and goes,' said Villani. 'What?'

'Two things. One, got an HSV doing 130 on the Hume about 9.40 on the night of sixteen December. Driver is a Loran Alibani, address in Marrickville, Sydney, vehicle registered to him.'

'That's good. What shows?'

'We're waiting. Second thing, Prosilio now says it's got no vision at all from the lifts and the parking, the basement, from Thursday 4.23pm to 8.55am Friday. Recording malfunction.'

'This is shit. Happened before?'

'That's not clear,' said Dove. 'The company runs the electronic security for the building. Stilicho. They offer cutting edge, you expect bugs. It's the first time they ran the full casino system and it sort of blew other bits. The CEO is blaming the techs, they're not happy.'

'How do you know that?'

'Weber. He talked to people.'

Villani was looking at the mountain. 'Really?' he said. 'That's an old-fashioned thing to do.'

'He's from the country,' said Dove. 'Manton says Prosilio management's not responsible for Stilicho's technical failures. He says talk to Hugh Hendry, he's the Stilicho boss.'

'Is that Max Hendry's son?'

'Don't know, boss.'

'Find out. And the other stuff?'

'Running the names. Unless someone pops up for killing women, even one, it'll be a while.'

'Takes as long as it takes,' said Villani. 'Do it right and sleep tight.'

Oh God, another Singo saying. He killed the call before Dove could say something clever, walked back down the verandah.

'Got the meat, the Crownies,' Bob Villani said to Luke.

'Can't, Dad,' said Luke. 'The talent dropped out, some weak-dog excuse. I can't say no, it's in the contract. Really pisses me off, been looking forward to talking ponies.'

Luke rose and they all stood. Luke put an arm around his father's shoulders, walked him along. It struck Villani that he now looked completely unlike Bob. At the car, the girl inside, Luke took out a wallet, thumbed fifties.

'Thursday,' he said. 'Benalla. Stand in the Day in the third. The little thing's rough as a brush.'

He tucked the notes into Bob's shirt pocket.

'Four hundred,' he said. 'I'll give you a bell about ten if it's on, you and Gordie pop over to Stanny. Probably a hundred each way, the rest, we'll box a few. Thirty per cent commission, how's that?'

'Reasonable,' said Bob. 'Stand in the Day. Good name.'

'Just my dough, Dad, okay?' said Luke. 'No insurance here, could run stone motherless.'

He turned to Villani. 'Want to be in this?'

'No thanks.'

'Oh yeah, forgot you'd given it away.' He offered a high-five to Villani. Villani didn't take it, he was not a high-five man.

'Catch you, mate, right?' said Luke. 'Soon. Ring you.'

'Good.'

Luke put his arms around Bob. 'This fire gets serious, mate, I want you out of here, okay? I'll come up and drag you out myself.'

'Be fine,' said Bob. 'Got Gordie to look after me.'

'Do that, Gordie,' said Luke. 'I'm holding you responsible for this bastard.'

'Do that, Lukie,' said Gordie.

Luke hugged him.

They watched the car reverse, swing, fat tyres spat stones, Luke gunned it down the drive.

'My turn to go,' said Villani.

His father looked down, rubbed his stubble. 'You could stay, have the barbie,' he said. 'I'll get you up at sparrer.'

To say no was in Villani's mouth, he had the excuses. But his father turned the grey stone eyes and he could not utter them. 'Why not?' he said. 'The meat, the beer.'

'Fire up the bugger, Gordie.'

'Total fire ban,' said Villani.

'For dickheads,' said Bob.

The day ended slowly, a fever in the western sky. Villani ate too much steak, smoked Gordie's cigarettes, slept in his old bed. Some time after midnight he woke, felt the storm coming, the trembling stillness, then the first solid movement of air and the thunderclap, it shook heaven and earth, a wind struck the house, squeaked the timbers, squealed the roof iron, rain hit like buckshot, two or three minutes under heavy fire, gone, the dying sluice of water in the downpipes.

His father didn't have to wake him. When he came into the pewter day, Bob was there, shorts, bare-chested, all rib and bone, sinew and muscle.

'No need to get up,' said Villani.

'Hear the rain?'

'Woke me.'

'Yeah. Done buggerall, need a soaking.'

'The finances,' said Villani. 'Coping?'

Bob Villani flexed his arms. 'Why wouldn't I be?'

'Just asking.'

'That boss stuff,' said Bob.

'I'm not worrying about it,' said Villani.

'The way things were, you looking after the little buggers.'

'You can let this fucking house burn down,' said Villani, 'but if the forest goes I'm coming after you.'

They shook hands, just touched skin. He wanted to hug his father as Luke had done and give him something, some evidence that he too was a worthy son, but that was not possible.

Before first light, still cool, he drove down Selborne's curt main street. Beneath the pub's sole elm, a man slept on his ute tray, he was embalmed in a grey blanket, one naked marble-white foot showed. Around his head was a rough semi-circle of empty stubbies.

On the main road, Villani switched on the radio.

... firefighters arrive from West Australia today to support the weary teams battling to save three towns now under threat in the high country ...

When the mobile rang, the towers were in sight, he was in the early Monday commuter traffic, all slit-eyed men, close-shaven, dreaming of Friday afternoon so far.

'Villani,' he said.

Birkerts said, 'Three dead, it's a shed in Oakleigh.'

'Three?'

'Yeah. Pretty fucking rough.'

THE SMELL was of a slaughterhouse, of excrement and piss and blood and fear.

Breathing shallowly, Villani stepped over the black creek and stood just inside the tin cavern. Light from the doorway lay across a man near them, on his front, his fluids had formed a clover shape before they ran out under the door.

Ten metres away, against a side wall, two men sagged from steel roof pillars, hands tied above their heads with gaffer tape. They were naked, covered in caked blood, feet in black ponds.

'Jesus Christ,' said Villani. 'Jesus H. Christ.'

He took the long route to the first upright man, kept close to the wall, stopped well short.

The man was tanned, muscular, big-calved legs, small paunch, tracks on his arms. His hair appeared to have been burnt off, his genitals cut off, a thing of flesh lay on the concrete, head like a kicked cabbage dipped in blood, glint of teeth. Skeins of viscous material, gobbets of flesh, stuck to the tin wall behind him.

Villani went to the second man. He was paler, bigger beer gut, semi-circle of scar tissue under his left nipple. The same damage had been inflicted upon his face and genitals.

He looked around. The shed was a vehicle tip – carcasses of cars, doors, bonnets, windscreens, wheel rims, pistons, seats, dashboards, steering wheels, engine parts, they lay as if dropped from the sky.

Behind him, Birkerts cleared his throat. 'Forensics two minutes away. Ditto coroner.'

'We're out of here, then.'

At the door, it was dead quiet, Villani heard something, looked up and saw a starling in ragged flight beneath the silver ceiling it had bounced off.

They passed through the door, the uniforms parted for them, and they went outside and stood on the concrete apron and sucked the dirty city air, so clean now. Birkerts offered, they lit.

Gawkers lined the side fence, workers from the car repair shop next door.

'Shit,' said Birkerts. 'This is a step up.'

'Who found them?'

'Security bloke. Walking along that fence, he saw the blood, went around to the front of the house, door open, no one home, he came through and had a look. He's in shock.'

A warm wind from the north-east now. Villani looked at the sky, thin streaks of high cloud the colour of tongue fur, heard the sound of a train, the rip and flap of a loose truck tarp in the nearest yard.

'Well, three,' he said. 'Three is just one times three.'

'Simple as that,' said Birkerts, he was looking over Villani's shoulder. 'The scientists.'

People in blue overalls were coming down the side of the house, the crime-scene team, blood, ballistics, fingerprints, photography, they carried bags, not in a hurry. They walked across the concrete yard, chatting side-on, could be tradies coming on site.

Two of Birkerts' crew came around the corner, in black, scratching, yawning, Finucane in front, work needed on his shave, as much hair on face as scalp, the pitbull Tomasic behind him.

Next was the forensic pathologist, Moxley, a balding ginger Scot. Villani raised a hand.

'Doctor Death,' he said.

Moxley grounded his bag. 'The head of Homicide. Isn't this early for someone so important?'

'Never sleep. Three deceased here, two with no clothes on. May I request an extreme hurry-on?'

'ASAP is always the aim,' said Moxley.

'Of course,' said Villani. 'Must be painful always to fall short.'

'Well, it takes more than your nine or ten years of third-rate schooling to understand professional procedures.'

'Yeah, but in Australia,' said Villani. 'Outranks a Glasgow PhD.'

'Probably couldn't find Glasgow on a map,' said Moxley and left.

Villani watched him go. 'When I kill him, I want three days' start,' he said. 'Like Tony Mokbel. Sum up the position for these two, Birk.'

Birkerts said, 'Three dead. One shot, the others, the Christ knows, could be tortured to death, make you puke, I can tell you. Found by security. That's it. Boss?'

'It would be at night,' said Villani. 'Can't be long ago.'

The day was warming quickly, cracks and pings from the tin building, the structure around them. 'Not exactly in the bush,' said Villani. 'Someone around here must have seen something.'

'Kill three people,' said Birkerts. 'Tie two up. How many does that take? You'd want to come in force, wouldn't you? Say two cars, at least.'

'Unless they came in a little bus,' said Villani. 'Like an outing.'

'Non-linear thinking, boss.' Birkerts gestured at Finucane, Tomasic. 'Let's get out there and ask about the place, start with those dorks at the fence.'

'Media,' said Finucane.

Villani looked. Television crews were arriving at the side fence, jostling.

A faint chop in the west, a television helicopter, a second one, bugs on the surface of the huge pale pond of sky. He said to Birkerts, 'Since you look so sharp, when the time comes, you talk to them.'

'People love to see me on television,' said Birkerts.

'So do we all. Say nothing. Check the whole street for security vision, that's the priority. Along with all mobiles in the vicinity, starting, oh, 6pm Saturday.'

'My exact thoughts,' said Birkerts.

'What took you so long then?' said Villani. 'Are we assuming the killers took these boys from the house to the shed to work on them?'

'I am,' said Birkerts. 'The back door's been smashed in.'

Villani crossed the concrete apron, inspected the back door. The latch was lying on the floor, all four screws forced out, that was one heavy, practised blow. He smelled disinfectant before he entered the kitchen, clinically clean.

The smelling he learned not on the detective course but from Singleton, who walked around murder scenes sniffing like someone with a lingering cold.

'Stay with you, smells,' Singo said. 'All your life.'

Villani did not know of any occasion when sniffing had detected something that would not have been found by other means. But the more he sniffed, the more doglike he became, the more aware of the smells of the world.

The day would come, sniffing would pay off.

Empty pizza boxes stacked beside a bin, plastic plates in a drying rack, empty sink, two scourers. He crossed the room. A dim passage with a bare parquet floor led to the front door, two doors to the left, three to the right.

He looked into the first left-hand room. A bedroom, single bed. Prim like the kitchen, bed unmade, two pairs of runners lined up under it, clothes folded on a chair, a comb stuck in a clean hairbrush, like a porcupine with a fin.

The room opposite, a bathroom, towels hanging from rails. Clean as the kitchen, it smelled of chlorine bleach.

Next, another bedroom, king-sized bed, not made, cheap Chinese cotton clothes peeled from a body, dropped to the floor, layers of clothes. He sniffed cigarettes, dope, alcohol breath, sweaty runners.

Something else. Perfume, cheap. He sniffed above the bed. A woman had slept in it recently. Or a perfumed man.

The next room on the right. Duplicate of the previous one but dirtier and with two drug pipes. Different perfume here, also cheap.

The room on the left, a sitting room. Oversized chairs of cheap leather, foam escaping through splits, glass coffee table three metres square, cracked from corner to corner, a landing strip for burger wrappers, empty beer cans, cans of Cougar, HotRod, Stiff, HighLand. A chrome hubcap served as an ashtray, it held perhaps forty or fifty stubs, others missed the ashtray, burned out on the table, left cylinders of ash, dark nicotine stains. A fifty-inch flatscreen stood on a stand, the sound muted, a man and a woman with thick make-up, sprayed hair were talking to the camera: a breakfast show. The male frowned at the end of sentences, his eyebrows sloped, a dog face, sometimes happy, sometimes puzzled, sometimes sad. The pretty woman was excited in an awkward way, she knew she was meat, they had told her to be herself, she had no idea of what she was herself except pretty, so that did not help.

Someone had slept on a sofa against the wall, an unzipped

sleeping bag on it, a grimy pillow, on the floor a full ashtray, a half-empty cigarette pack, a plastic lighter.

Beside the fireplace, newspapers were neatly stacked on a small table beside an obese and lumpy chair. Villani looked.

The *Age*.

Saturday's paper. In this house, who read the broadsheet of record, the druggies or the tidy man, the cleaner and disinfector?

They had always kept the *Age* for Bob Villani at the milkbar in Selborne. When he was driving all week, they accumulated. On Sunday mornings, Bob arranged them in order and father and son read them at a sitting, Bob passing each paper on as he finished it.

Villani went back down the passage, through the antiseptic kitchen, into the day. Moxley was coming from the shed wearing a green surgical mask, pushing it onto his forehead.

'Three Caucasian males, bullet wounds only on the one nearest the entrance, shot in the head, the two hanging have multiple wounds, including bullet wounds,' he said. 'No identification. Except.'

He handed Villani a card.

VOLIM TE IVAN, written in slanting capitals.

'What's this,' said Villani.

'Engraved on an earring on the nearest hanging male,' said Moxley. 'The two are both late thirties, I'd say. Give or take a few years.'

They watched him go back into the building.

'I like him more with the mask on,' said Villani. 'More kissable.'

He showed the card. The crew stepped close.

'I love you Ivan,' said Tomasic. He was an only child, his parents dumped him when he was seven, he was fostered, shopped around, spoke four languages. 'That's what it says.'

'In what?'

'Croatian. Slovak.'

Villani felt the little tingle, looked at Birkerts. 'Get in there and tell Moxley I'd like details of tatts.'

'That's going to be helpful?'

Birkerts had been Singo's star pupil, picked in spite of having a degree, in spite of getting up the nose of every superior he'd ever had.

Villani had an acid surge, beer, nicotine, vinegary tomato sauce. 'You reckon not, detective?' he said. 'Should I have asked you first?'

'Sorry, boss.' A small head bow, Birkerts went.

Villani and the crew stood in the warming day, the air alive with electronic squawk and grate and twitter, waited for his return, watched him step around the blood, come back.

'Both got a little shield with a sword across it,' said Birkerts. 'Like a chessboard.'

He patted his left upper arm. 'Here.'

'Matko Ribaric's boys,' said Villani. 'Who says there's no God?'

He walked to the building. They would have turned the third man onto his back by now, he could take pictures.

IN THE CAR, at the lights at Belgrave Road, the phone rang.

Kiely's fat vowels. 'Gather I'm the last to hear about Oakleigh,' he said. 'Makes me unhappy.'

'What's your unhappiness got to do with me?' said Villani.

'Just a comment. So I'm playing catch-up, what's the prelim scenario?'

Villani wanted to close his eyes for a long time, but the lights changed.

'Could be drugs,' Villani said. 'That's a possibility.'

'Really?' said Kiely, smart little inflection. 'I thought it might be something like, ah, farm produce.'

Kiely had a degree in criminology and an MBA, done part-time. He was head of Homicide in Auckland when he got the nod, they thought New Zealand was clean and green. Kiely was certainly green.

'We've had farm produce, mate,' said Villani. 'Many dead. The Mafia war. But you wouldn't know.'

The silence sang.

'Anyway,' said Villani, 'Tomasic's sent through three names, we'll get the paper on these boys soonest. The house is going to take all morning. That's the priority.'

'Shouldn't this be a Crucible matter?'

'Unnatural deaths. Homicide. Not the case in Auckland?'

'Just contributing to our ongoing professional conversation.'

'Whatever the fuck that is. Forget Crucible.'

Hunger.

Villani detoured to South Melbourne, parked in a disabled space, he felt disabled. They knew him at the greasy, run by Greek outlaws, he customised the hamburger with the lot, subtracted the cheese, he couldn't hack plastic cheese, the bacon with the pink stains of meat in the white fat. Four orders ahead of him, he went down the street, bought a paper, came back and watched the two-station assembly line at work.

Jim, the fat cook, changed the station on the radio and Paul Keogh came on in full voice:

. . . these killings, nothing official yet. We throw millions of dollars, that's millions, throw them at a so-called high-tech, super-sophisticated taskforce, dedicated to stamping out organised crime and what's to show for the Crucible spending? A few idiots jailed. That's it. And now this thing's happened in Oakleigh, which is . . .

'Know about this?' said Dimi, the thinner cook, big hairy hands cupping a mince patty, no gloves.

'What happened to the gloves?' said Villani. 'The food hygiene?'

'Fuck that shit,' said Dimi. 'Start with fucken clean hands, that's like fucken gloves, no? Anyway, fucken heat kills fucken germs.'

'I sincerely hope,' said Villani.

He ate in the car, reading the newspaper, listening to Keogh:

. . . the latest hideous symptom, it's a disease, drugs and the toler-ance and the rubbish that's grown up around drugs, the methadone programs, I ask you, we supply these spineless, gutless individuals with a free drug supposed to lessen their dependence, they now clamour for it, demand it as a right, it's like a superannuation scheme for junkies . . .

Phone. The secretary, Angela.

'Boss, first is Mr Colby, he requests a 9.30 meeting. And

Deputy Commissioner Barry, he'd like to see you as soon after.'

'Under starter's orders,' said Villani.

. . . Chief Commissioner David Gillam, the so-called new broom, done nothing except sweep the dirt around and under the carpet. Achieved sweet fanny. All the evidence is that right up to senior levels some of the cavalry have joined the Indians. I'm talking about corruption in my usual roundabout way. And then there is the massive problem of public order. Public safety. The right of law-abiding citizens to go about their business without fear. This city has a very, very serious public order problem, the government, that's our wonder boy Police Minister Martin Orong, they have done nothing to solve it and so that's quite rightly a massive issue in this election. Add it to the chaos that is public transport, the gridlock that stops this city twice a day . . .

Villani studied the hamburger, the cold grey meat, the globs of congealed fat, seam of egg, charred onion strands. He bit into it.

THEY WERE waiting for him in the meeting room, Colby, Dance, Ordonez.

'Like a Robbers reunion this,' said Colby. 'Should be in a pub. So let's be clear. It's the fucking Ribarics?'

'The Ribarics, boss,' said Villani. 'Confirmed Ivan wears that earring and Andy's got the knife scar Ivan gave him when they were kids. Also Andy's got a hole in his arse the Robbers know about.'

He gestured to Ordonez, head of Armed Crimes.

'Dates from a payroll job in Somerton in 1997,' said Ordonez. 'Security bloke shot him through the right cheek. Six years for that, Andrew, came out in 2002.'

'The third one,' said Villani. He took out the camera, found the image, offered the camera to Colby. 'You might remember this bloke.'

Villani had served in the Armed Robbery Squad under Colby, they went to an in-progress at a bank in Glen Iris, he and Colby and Dance, arrived on the scene late, it ended with Colby jumping onto the bonnet of a moving yellow Commodore, the front-seat passenger stuck his gun out, a Magnum, wrong-handed, fired four shots, took away a big piece of Colby's right pec, a bit of an ear. Colby crawled onto the roof rack, reached down, got his fingers into the driver's hair, pulled his head half out the window and banged it against the frame, repeatedly.

Doing around eighty, the Commodore crossed tramlines,

clipped an oncoming tradesman's van, hit a concrete bus shelter, broadsided into a tree, spun into a small park, rolled twice, came to rest beside a sandpit. Children were playing in it, chirping.

When Villani and Dance got there, the driver was dead, the shooter was dying, the third man, Vernon Donald Hudson, was unharmed, whimpering. Colby – skull fracture, broken arm, rib piercing a lung – was on his feet, face a blood mask, right arm hanging like a dead fish. He spat, blood and a tooth, looked down at himself and said, 'Jesus, a brand-new fucking suit.'

'Vern,' said Colby, eyes on the camera screen. 'Less hair but it's Huddo. He's a survivor. Was. Where's the cunt been?'

'We haven't heard of him for a long time,' said Ordonez. 'He's supposed to be in Queensland. Retired.'

'Retired now,' said Colby. 'So what's this shit about?'

'Ivan's an animal,' said Ordonez. 'Smack addict and animal. High on our list. We reckon he killed the SecureGuard bloke in Dandenong last October, executed him. Also shot the customer at Westpac at Garden City in March, no reason at all. There's other bashings, one woman's got brain damage, can't speak. We reckon these boys have done seven, eight jobs in the last two years. Maybe eight hundred grand. Dandenong was two hundred but that was lucky.'

'What a pity we couldn't cull the boys when we took out the old man,' said Colby.

The coroner determined that Dance and Vickery fired twelve shots at Matko Ribaric before Vickery hit him in the left eye, no skill, just luck, the slug came off the roof. It was not textbook stuff but then Matko was shooting at them in a shopping mall carpark with a Benelli M4 Super 90 semi-automatic shotgun, the pellets hitting the cars like steel hail.

'Anyway, this is all helpful and also not helpful,' said Colby. 'Who would kill the pricks?'

'No idea,' said Ordonez. 'These boys are just robbers.'

'I should say here,' said Villani, 'that the brothers have been worked over like I haven't seen since Rai Sarris. Noses, tackle cut off, hair burnt. There is pleasure involved.'

'Our belief,' said Ordonez, 'is that the Ribs have done jobs with one Russell Jansen and one Christopher Wales, both serious hardcases. Jansen is a near-fuckwit but he's good with cars. Stealing, driving. Wales is another druggy. Everything we know is here.'

Ordonez passed a folder to Villani.

'The Oakleigh address is in there?' said Colby.

Ordonez pulled a tight-lipped face. 'No, boss. We did not have addresses for any of them.'

'They lived there?' Colby said to Villani.

'At least four people lived in the house,' said Villani. 'That's at a glance. Vehicles parked all over the place, that'll take a bit of working through.'

'Mr Dance,' said Colby. 'Since you command the most expensive operation in the history of the force, you will have much to tell us about these cunts.'

Mr Xavier Benedict Dance smiled, long medieval face, ice-blue cattledog eyes. He had his chair well back from the table, ankle on a knee, buffed Italian shoe, cotton sock. Villani knew Colby had always thought Dance was gun-shy. Once, after a chaotic in-progress cock-up and a chase on foot, Colby stared at Dance and said, 'You practise running on the spot?'

'Our intelligence focus is on big players,' said Dance.

'Like calling the fucking phone book intelligence,' said Colby.

'Crucible's brief is crime networks,' said Dance.

'Yeah, mate, yeah. Read drugs. What's this look like?'

'Well, Ivan Ribaric only comes on our radar because he did

some muscle for Gabby Simon, that's a few years ago. But he nearly killed a bloke in the Lord Carnarvon in South Melbourne and that was too extreme for Gabby. In public, that is.'

'So what's your non-intelligence-based view?'

Dance held up his hands. 'Could be alternative dispute resolution involving ten million bucks. Could be argument over parking spot. The fuckers kill each other for anything. Nothing.'

'And the torture?'

'Torture is like a Playstation game for arseholes awake for three days on ice. I would say payback. By pricks who hate Vern Hudson a bit less than the Ribbos.'

'At least you didn't say gang war,' said Colby. 'Okay, gentlemen, let's get back to what I hear are called our silos. Inspector Villani, a word.'

'I EXPECT to hear first, son,' said Colby. 'From you or whoever. Not from God. Gillam rang me, girl's fucking hysterical. Then it's Mr Garry O'Barry, the Irish deviant.'

'Sorry, boss.'

'Yeah, well, listen, all the makings of a shit sandwich this. I see no joy, suffering all round.'

'Very early days.'

'I'm thinking get rid of it, handball it to Dancer. Crucible.'

'It's Homicide business.'

'Sometimes you worry me,' said Colby. 'You don't see the whole picture.'

'No?'

'No. All that Singleton justice-for-the-dead shit. Homicide, little island of fucking Boy Scouts. Get over it. Singo's gone, he's microscopic dust floating up there, he's air pollution. Stuff like this, the media blowies on you, bloody pollies pestering, the ordinary work goes to hell. And then you don't get a result in an hour and you're a turd.'

'We could get lucky.'

Colby sneezed, a detonation, another, another. 'Fucking smoke's killing me,' he said. 'Anyway, I'll say this. Get lucky or have plans B to D ready.'

'Do that then, boss.'

'Stay in touch. Close touch. I want to know.'

'Boss.'

When Villani was at the door, Colby said, 'Career-defining moment this could be. They come, you know.'

'Bear that in mind, boss.'

VILLANI SAT in the outer office, mobile off, eyes closed. Barry was on an important call, said the secretary. Villani didn't mind, enjoyed the peace.

'Commissioner Barry's free, inspector,' said the secretary, some signal given.

Barry's desk was side-on to the window, the venetian blinds half closed, the vertical lines of the buildings thinly sliced.

'Stephen,' he said. 'Sit. Just got the chief off the line.' He paused. 'Tell me.'

Villani became aware of the aches in his forearms, across his shoulders. The mowing, the whole body tensed, the gripping of the throttle bar. 'Ivan Ribaric and his half-brother,' he said. 'Croatians.'

Barry found a tissue, napkin-sized. He blew his nose, eyes bulged. 'Never had a cold in freezing bloody Ireland,' he said. He inspected the tissue, crushed it. 'Now is that Australian of Croatian descent or citizen of Croatia?'

'The first.'

'I've found there's a bit of sensitivity around this kind of thing.'

'It's a family with a wog name. Like me.'

'What about me?' Barry said. 'Is an Irishman a wog?'

'Mick is a kind of early wog as I understand it.'

Barry laughed, rolling pub laugh, he had hard bird eyes.

'Moving on. Knowing the dead's a step, catching the deaders, that's the trick.'

'Steep curve I'm on.'

Mouth too quick, always his failing. Villani looked at the view. He thought he liked Barry more than his predecessor, a useless Pom from Liverpool who left suddenly for a job in Canada.

'A joke, Stephen,' said Barry.

Villani nodded, humbly he hoped. He noticed a white substance on the side of his left shoe. Birdshit? Please, God, not something from Oakleigh.

'This election. Now I'm no expert on local politics but I'm told there could be changes coming, people moving around. That's likely.' He stared at Villani. 'We could work well together, you and me. A team. What's your feeling?'

'I think we could, boss.' Villani had no idea what he meant.

'Can I advise a bit of an investment in presentation? It's important. Couple of new suits. Dark grey. Shirts. Light blue, cotton, buy half a dozen. And ties. Red, silk, Jacquard silk. Black shoes, toecaps. Good for morale, shoes, the women know that.'

Villani thought it best to say nothing.

'Now I haven't offended?' said Barry.

'No, boss.'

'I'm looking out for you, Stephen.'

'I appreciate that.'

'Good. So Oakleigh, we need a result, that's the ticket. Your clearance rate overall needs a boost.'

'Boss.'

The clearance rate was all luck. A decent run of domestics gone sad, pissed fights, gatecrash stabbings, gang bashings, fatal clashes among the homeless and hopeless – easy, you could clear the lot inside a week or two, it looked pretty good, efficient.

'And the Prosilio woman? What's happening there?'

'Making progress in identifying her. A lot of work done. Yes.'

'Good, good. Keep me posted on anything I should know, won't you?' said Barry, raised his hands, made pistols, brought the muzzles together. 'Directly.'

'I will, boss.'

'And I don't think we need to refer to Prosilio. There's a degree of sensitivity about that too. With me?'

'Boss.'

Rising in the building's intestine, air like dry-cleaning fluid, Villani thought of lying down on a hard bed in a cool, dim room, pulling up his knees and going to sleep. His mobile rang.

'Tentative conclusions,' said Moxley. 'Man near entrance is shot in the head at close range from behind. The other two, multiple stab wounds, genitals severed, other injuries. Also head and pubic hair ignited, shot, muzzle in mouth. Three bullets recovered, 45 calibre.'

'So you can't rule out an accident?' said Villani.

'Any other questions?'

'Time. Not a problem on television, the cops get answers,' said Villani. 'Up to speed on modern forensics, professor?'

'No more than twelve hours.'

'That's something, I suppose.'

'May I say how much I miss the professionalism of Inspector Singleton?' said Moxley. 'Goodbye.'

VILLANI SAT at his desk and the phone rang.

'Mr Searle, boss.'

'Okay.'

'Steve, mate,' Searle said. 'Mate, I'd love to be first call on stuff like Oakleigh. Just someone give me a buzz. You know we never sleep.'

'There's a long queue for first call,' said Villani. 'Why don't you take it up with my superiors? As I plan to take up the issue of the strange treatment of the Prosilio murder on fucking Crime Stoppers.'

Searle whistled. 'Steady on, that's a bit hostile.'

'As intended,' said Villani.

'Right. I'll move on.'

'Giving me an explanation or what?'

'Some misunderstanding, that's all I can say,' said Searle. 'I take it Oakleigh will go to Crucible?'

'Don't you know a homicide when you see one?'

'Okay, okay. Huge story like this, I suggest I embed Cathy Wynn with you. Everything run by you, of course, you're in total control.'

Singo had hated Searle. 'Mongrels, every last fucking Searle,' he said when he heard of Geoff Searle's appointment. 'This prick's the runt of the litter.'

'Embed?' said Villani. 'Emfuckingbed?'

'I can promise you will be happy with the result. And the process. Absolutely no downside. At all.'

'Over my dead body.'

'Right. That's fine. Respect your view. Who should we liaise with?'

'Inspector Kiely.'

Searle coughed.

'Steve, mate,' he said, 'Singleton had it in for me, buggered why. But can we move on? I mean, we've both got jobs to do, right?'

'I've got a police job, yes,' said Villani.

'Well, managing your profile can't hurt, can it?'

'I have no idea what that means,' said Villani. 'Nor do I wish to. Call-waiting. Homicide business, murders, that kind of thing. I'll get back to you.'

'Appreciate that,' said Searle. 'Cathy Wynn is your point of contact.'

Villani thought about his profile being managed. The phone rang.

'Mr Dance, boss,' said the switch.

'Okay. Dancer?'

'Comrade,' said Dance. 'Bloody Colby's arsier every time I see him. You'd think I dreamt up bloody Crucible myself. Anyway, just had a word from Simon Chong, our boy genius, he's run some program the nerds invented.'

'Yes?'

'It picks names out of the stuff we pull in. The soup. Our friend Ivan is mentioned. That's last week, six days ago.'

'Mentioned how?'

'One budgie says Ivan's got something to sell. He coughs. That means precursor. He says he'll get back but we don't have that. He didn't talk on the same line again.'

The other phone rang. Tracy Holmes, the senior analyst.

'Oakleigh,' she said. 'The name is Metallic.'

'Another stroke of genius. Thank you.'

'How many people you talking to there?' said Dance.

'No more than I have to,' said Villani. 'As the bullfighter said, these boys are robbers. What's with selling cough medicine?'

'The bullfighter is such a turkey, mate. It's not like it was. When we were young. Younger. No division of labour any more. Drugs, whores, robbers, it's all one fucking moshpit.'

Villani thought, a few seconds, he said, 'So this is likely some drug shit gone bad?'

'I would say so.'

'Do anything?'

'Mate, this shit we hear all the time. It's like air-traffic control for the whole world here. We passed it on to our drug comrades, whatever they're called now. Could be Illegal Substances Enjoyment Group.'

'Who's talking?'

'The first one we don't know,' said Dance. 'The second one is Mick Archer, he's a former Hellhound, been tight with Gabby Simon, club scumbag, that may be why he knows who Ivan is. I mentioned him and the Lord Carnarvon business. But Mick's also close to many other dangerous arseholes. Only mildly of interest to us.'

'Didn't know there was such a thing as a former Hellhound. Thought it was Hellhound or dead.'

'Mick walked and lived. There may be an explanation.'

'He'd do this if the Ribbos fucked him over?'

'Capable of anything. But Mick wasn't there. Nor his offsider. In Malaysia for sure.'

'How'd you get this?'

'The ether.'

'Well thanks, ether. What the fuck do I do with it?'

'We pass on intelligence.'

'The phone book.'

'Hurtful,' said Dance. 'You don't want to join the Colby gang. Like joining the Kellys. They are few. We are many.'

'Meaning?'

Silence.

'Steve, wake up. Collo's the last of the big land animals.'

'Brood on that. So much to brood on. You can buy me a drink when you've got a moment off television.'

'And fuck you too,' said Dancer. 'Our genius has sent you the audio.'

GAVAN KIELY in the door, putty slab of face.

'Welcome,' said Villani. 'Chance to do a haka over there?'

'Two things,' said Kiely, rat teeth showing. 'I've had Cathy Wynn from media. They're keen for forward planning on Metallic.'

Villani said, 'Tell her we're still planning backwards. We'll let them know how it works out.'

Kiely found a focus above Villani's head. 'Also, I think I should be playing a more upfront role,' he said. 'As the number two.'

'Never a good number, two. Upfront how?'

'Well, representing the squad.'

'You want to be the spokesman?'

'Rather than lower ranks, yes.'

'It's horses for courses,' said Villani.

'Excuse me?'

'The practice has been to let squad leaders speak. Birk'll keep you briefed.'

'Actually, I don't expect to be briefed by juniors,' said Kiely.

Villani gave him the stare, let the time pass. Kiely couldn't bear it.

'Here's an offer,' said Villani. 'You don't get hissy and I promise to be more inclusive. Is that the word?'

Kiely went from pink to something deeper.

The clock above the door: 11.40. 'That said, let's see if we can find the Ribs' mates Wales and Jansen.'

A HELICOPTER, glass buildings, silent explosions, people fleeing some unseen terror, a black-haired woman with a feline air said:

. . . homicide police were today called to the scene of a triple murder, three men found dead in a shed behind a house in Oakleigh in the city's south-east . . .

Helicopter vision, the red-tiled roof, at odds with the huge tin factories, workshops and warehouses surrounding it, the street full of vehicles, the workers and media along the side fence. Villani saw the clump of Homicide cops, thought he saw himself. Then ground-level footage of the yard and the shed. He was walking towards the door.

. . . a security patrol discovered the grisly scene just before 6am today. Homicide detectives and forensic experts are still at the premises. The people who live in the house have only been glimpsed say workers at the electrical equipment factory next door . . .

Then it was Birkerts, the long, pale Scandinavian face.

. . . we don't have any identification at this time but we hope to establish all identities shortly.

Can you tell us how they died?

All shot.

Can you confirm they were tortured?

The experts will tell us about injuries and cause of deaths. In due course.

Is this drug-related?

We can't rule out anything at this stage . . .

Next: wind-shift reprieve for Morpeth and Stanton, protests over train delays, a new political poll had Labor in trouble, four hurt in a crane accident in the city, a dog saved from a drain, a Jack Russell. It appeared to want to go back.

Villani pressed mute, dropped his chin. Why would anyone want the job? Trapped in a dream that shifted from one ugly scene to another, all seen through a veil of tiredness. The full stupidity of his life overwhelmed him and he closed his eyes.

When he opened them, he was looking at the cardboard box in the corner, Singleton's trophies and photographs, waiting to go somewhere. The silver boxer stuck out, crouching, throwing a left.

He saw it on his first day in the Homicide office, fresh from Armed Robbery, carrying a gruesome farewell-party hangover, keen to start anew, save his marriage.

'Should've got that Dance decision,' said Singleton.

'He caught me a few good ones,' said Villani. 'Boss.'

'Caught him a few more. Anyway, new life's begun. No more bash and crash. What's your wife say about this?'

'She'll cope, boss.'

Laurie was just about done with coping by then. Laurie had her own life, share of a business.

'My condolences to her,' said Singleton. 'Kiddies, I see.'

'Yes, boss.'

'They just lost their dad.'

Homicide ate you, your family got the tooth-scarred bone. Singo told them not to obsess but he judged them by how much they obsessed, how little time they spent at home. No one survived who didn't pass the HCF test: Homicide Comes First.

Villani thought, I'm another Singleton, have to know everything, don't trust anyone to do the job properly, interfere, try to manage everything.

Unlearn Singo. The man should have died in a jail and not a nursing home.

But the truth was that, once you got used to it, working for Singo was comforting. He was hard on people, handed out cold, vicious reprimands, blood on the floor. But he looked out for you, never stole your credit, covered for you, even covered terrible shit like Shane Diab, dead because he thought Joe Cashin was the second coming, would have followed him down a snake hole.

Villani looked at nothing. Singo and his father. The same hardness, the air of bad things seen, of the right to sit in judgment on lesser, weaker people.

Phone. Birkerts. Villani said, 'Had no time to miss you.'

'On our way back,' said Birkerts. 'Been to three old addresses for Jansen, two for Wales, one is so old, the house's history, four units on the site. Tomasic tells me they've done the first sweep at Oakleigh. He's sent for an MD and the X-ray.'

Villani could see Dove at his desk, stretching. He took off his glasses and rubbed his eyes, looked around, blinking. Tired, thought Villani, he's tired. What right does he have to be tired?

'Coffee,' Villani said to Birkerts. 'Pick me up. I'm not functioning.'

He put the plug in his ear, found the place on the player.

. . . listen, I've had a bloke, he's offering . . .

Coughing.

Y'know?

Yeah? Source?

My understanding is accidental discovery, like.

Quantity?

Back up the truck, he says.

Oh yeah? What kind of bloke is this?

You know him. Ivan Ribaric. Bad. Very bad.

No, mate, the word's not bad, the word is fucking lunatic, don't want to go there. No.

No argument, the cunt's mad but this is, this looks okay, it's just something, y'know, get rid of quick, make a buck. Yeah.

He's up for something? Jack trading?

No, no, no. What Jack's going to trade with the Ribarics, mate? Jesus.

Yeah, well I'm not ruling it out, basically, we'd be . . . you've got to be fucking sure. I'd say you be sure of, ah, quality, then we talk. There's cunts, I mean you do business, you have to kill them.

Okay. Get back to you.

Make it soon. Got a, ah, trip coming up. Holiday.

That's nice. Soon, mate, soon . . .

THEY PARKED as close as they could and walked under an open sky, hot smoky afternoon wind, sweating, seeing the sweat on the faces coming at them, moving to the pavement's edge to skirt a loose pack of tourists, bright garments, bodies all going south, Americans. A fat man fanning himself with a straw hat said, 'Dart painting? How in hell they do that?'

They ordered, sat at a table in the back corner. Villani said, 'Need some luck with this shit, fucking Orong'll be on us next.'

Birkerts said, 'Pretty basic brief from the Robbers. Not giving much away. How keen are they?'

'I would say not very.'

'And Crucible?'

Villani took the tiny player and the earphone out of his top pocket, gave it to Birkerts. 'Listen,' he said.

Birkerts plugged in, held the device below the table rim, eyes on it.

Villani flicked the room, stopped at a woman looking at him over a man's shoulder. Straight black hair, grey eyes, clever eyes. He liked clever, he liked grey, Laurie's eyes. The first time Laurie looked at him with her grey eyes, he knew she was clever. Clever had always been the sexiest thing. Looks he had never cared much about. Looks were a bonus.

Birkerts unplugged, handed back the player. 'Cut and dried then,' he said. 'Who are these people?'

Villani told him they had half the story. 'Archer's got a pretty good out. In Malaysia with his offsider.'

The coffee came. Villani put sugar on the crema, watched it sink, change colour. 'What shows out there?' he said.

'Three possible cameras in the vicinity. Tommo's looking now, don't hold your breath, nothing points the right way. Got the ID stash, there's licences, Medicare, credit cards, you name it. Plastic bag in the freezer, who'd think of looking there? No weapons so far. Half a million prints in the house. There's traces of a woman.'

'What traces?'

'Lipstick on cigarette butts in the sitting room.'

'Two women,' said Villani. 'Different scents in the bedrooms.'

Birkerts raised his eyebrows. 'Yeah?'

'Yeah. Phones?'

'Not a one, should have said that.'

Birkerts touched his chest, felt for his mobile, went outside.

Villani tasted the coffee, passable, some ashy sweetness. The place was unreliable, baristas came and went, sacked, poached, some did a geographical, moved to the country in the childish hope that a change of scene, the clean air, would help them kick their drug habits. He looked up and met the eyes of the woman, a second, he looked away. Once he had exchanged looks with a handsome, sharp-faced woman here, that was in the days of big shoulders. Her name proved to be Clem, an interior designer, the man on the till gave him her business card when he was paying.

'She said to give it to you,' he said.

Birkerts came back, spoke behind fingers. 'Three vehicles in the street registered to the Ribbos' dud names. Also two stolens, can't be stupid enough to park a stolen car in your own street.'

'You're not dealing with criminal masterminds here,' said Villani. 'You're dealing with fuckheads. We'll probably read the full story by Tony fucking Ruskin in the *Age* tomorrow, he'll give us all the details, we look like complete twats once again.'

His mobile pulsed. He wasn't going outside, it was too hot out there.

'Interrupting anything?' Cashin.

'Got a cold?' said Villani. 'Like a man with tampons up his nose.'

'Clearing my throat, first words of the day,' said Cashin.

'Of course. Mostly use sign language down there on the blue-balls coast. The two fingers, the kick, the fist. How's the weather?'

'We have wind today,' said Cashin. 'We have a great deal of wind.'

'And still the place sustains life. Forms of life. Amazing.'

'I saw Birk on television. What's this torture stuff?'

'Two blokes tied to pillars. Noses gone, teeth smashed, tackle cut off, hair burnt. Also stabbed and shot.'

Silence. 'Sarris,' said Cashin.

'In the style of Sarris, yeah.'

'It's him.'

'Plenty of torturers around, mate. But I'll send what we've got. Might spark something in a fucking obsessive like you. Semi-retired obsessive.'

'Fax it home if it's after six.'

'Be dark down there by then. Keeping warm? Is it true you should never wash your woollen longjohns? Loses the body oils?'

'It's summer here,' said Cashin. 'We are wearing shortjohns.'

'I thought you went spring-autumn direct? Well, give the dogs a few kicks for me. Little kicks. Affectionate kicks.'

'I was thinking about Bob just now. The heat's getting close.'

'He says he hasn't noticed anything unusual,' said Villani.

'That'd be right. How's Dove travelling?'

The grey-eyed woman was still looking at him. Villani gave her the measured blink, he could not stop himself, always the teenager panting for his first screw. Ashamed, he looked away.

'Made a full recovery,' he said. 'Gives cheek. Wants to see my medical records. Check if I'm fit to work. So you're now the only cripple on staff.'

'I'm not on staff, Steve.'

'Son,' said Villani, 'you're on staff till I say you're not. Currently on loan to police the sheepshaggers. Talk soon.'

Birkerts said, 'Cashin?'

Villani nodded.

'Tragic,' said Birkerts. 'Sarris is dead or he's on his arsebone in the Bekaa Valley, snorting Cloud Nine. Rai didn't invent torture. A bloke in Brissie, he's a nothing, subsistence dealer, they flog him with barbwire and then they put him on a massive gas barbie. The Supreme Ozzie Partymaster, six turbo wok burners.'

'Less Queensland information, please,' said Villani. 'Brief Kiely, will you? He's unhappy. Feels neglected.'

On the way out, he avoided looking at the woman. What was the point?

Near the car, his phone rang. Barry.

'Listen, boyo, I should have said when we were chatting earlier, there's a little function this evening. I want you to take a break, hour or so, show yourself in public. Good for you.'

'Not the best time, boss,' said Villani. 'Bit on, yeah.'

Silence. 'Well, you make your own luck in this life, don't you, inspector?' said Barry. 'And a good commander knows when to delegate. I'll say no more.'

Villani sidestepped two teenagers, a skinny ginger, a bow-legged fat wearing sunnies, neither walking straight, the skinny was moving his hands as if winding something, like wool.

'But I'll be there, boss,' he said. 'Thank you. Where is that?'

'Persius. The Hawksmoor Gallery. Six-thirtyish. They'll have your name.'

'Right.'

'Good. Buck's can probably fix you up with a suit that fits. Respectable tie, et cetera.'

'I'll try them,' said Villani.

DOVE AND Weber in the doorway. Villani nodded, they entered. Dove sat on a filing cabinet, Weber stood like a soldier.

'Go,' said Villani.

'First,' said Dove, 'this Alibani on the Hume, he flew to Greece two years ago, no re-entry. Dead end there.'

'Unsurprising,' said Villani. 'Pinched ID. Well, could be family, the thickheads stick close to home. Get the Alibanis unto the thirteenth cousins, the fucking lot, every name.'

Dove, looking at the back of his left hand, he tickled the skin, he said, 'Done that, asked for the names.'

'Don't make me wait to hear what you've done, detective,' said Villani. 'Whatever the practice was in the feds.'

A cough, Weber had his notebook open. 'Boss, the company that owns the Prosilio apartment? Shollonel, registered in Beirut?'

'Yeah.'

'Marscay says it's not obliged to disclose details.'

'I've had it with Marscay,' said Villani. 'Okay, let's be clear. A woman comes into this palace, we don't know how. Unless she's got a card, she can't get to the floor, she can't get into the apartment. She does, she dies there, maybe it's accidental, heavy sex. But the place is wiped, her clothes, everything she had, they're disposed of. Killer or killers leave. No CC vision, no one in the building sees a fucking thing. As for ID, three days, not a clue except a possible sighting on the Hume, probably crap.'

'That's about it,' said Dove. 'Boss.'

'Jesus, we are looking pathetic,' said Villani.

'Not a good look,' said Dove, the rictus smile.

Villani thought about how unsuited Dove was, he should be in some desk job, trading shares on a screen, that would suit him, you couldn't resent the screen, it didn't give a shit about your life, your history, your colour, your complexes, the size of your dick.

'Mr Dove,' he said, 'in shorthand, I'm saying I want some progress. Know shorthand?'

'Is that a disability?' said Dove. 'Boss.'

An officer shot in the line of duty. On the cold tiles, a small hole in his front, a fist-sized hole in his back, serious damage inside, the blood flowed, made a pool. And then, just before the curtain fell, it stopped flowing, it clotted.

In the main, cops hurt this badly you never saw again unless you went to visit them in retirement, bloated, semi-drunk, on anti-depressants, sleeping pills, wake-up pills, they often took to smoking dope, they had the stupefied look, the wife always angry, shouting at them, at someone on the phone, the fat little dog on the chair, farting.

Eleven weeks, Dove came back to work.

'I want you to shake Manton and Ulyatt, fucking Marscay,' said Villani. 'All details or we guarantee media about non-existent security in millionaires' building, residents gripped by fear. That kind of shit.'

'I'm authorised to make that threat?' Dove said.

'What threat?'

He remembered the call at Bob's. 'What's the security company called?'

'Stilicho.'

'Is that Max Hendry's son running it?'

'Yes, Hugh,' said Dove. 'I forgot to say. Blackwatch owns half.'

'What's Blackwatch want with another security company?'

'Stilicho's bought this Israeli technology, puts it all together – secure entry, the ID stuff, iris scanning, fingerprints, facial recognition, suspicious behaviour, body language, all the casino cameras. We're talking hundreds of inputs. Cameras, ID entries, door contacts, smartcard readers, all kinds of electronic stuff. They say it's a first. Stilicho's even trying to get access to the crimes database, photos and photofits, prints, records, the lot.'

'Why?'

'Well, preemptive strike. Your face's in the base, you show up somewhere Stilicho's doing the security, that's just come in the door, get into a lift, walk down a corridor, you're on camera. The technology recognises you, red light goes on somewhere, you are stopped, tracked, barred, whatever. Shot.'

'How do you know this?'

'Talked to people. Boss.'

Villani nodded, acknowledged the reference, did not show amusement. 'Interesting. Do away with cops. I can understand why the system doesn't work but this lost-all-vision shit, no, I'm unhappy. Make sure that message gets to Mr Hugh Bloody Hendry.'

'Tried that, boss. Repeatedly.'

Angela from the door. 'Your mate. The old days. Says it's urgent.'

Dove left, he took the call. Afterwards, he thought about Colby's advice. There was no upside to Oakleigh. It was just wading into a swamp. What did it matter if homicides went to some other outfit, they had enough dead people. He sent for Birkerts.

'I'm leaning to the view that Oakleigh should go to Crucible,' Villani said. 'Let's stick to women drown their babies, men knife their wives, that's our comfort level.'

'Well excuse me, we have . . .'

'Drugs,' Villani said. 'This is drugs, it's like spit, no natural end. You never nail anyone who matters, never have the final day in court.'

Birkerts' head inclined to the window. 'Well, just turn it over before we have a chance, I mean . . .'

'Not running a democracy,' said Villani.

'You can't run a democracy, that's the thing about democracies, they . . .'

'Tell Angela to ask Mr Kiely to step in, will you?'

Villani looked away until Birkerts had left, two fingertips in the hollow of his throat, feeling the pulse, before a fight it was a way to steady yourself, get your breathing right.

'Inspector,' said Kiely, face stiff.

'Take the media gig this afternoon?'

'Well, yes, certainly. Yes.'

'Give them the waffle. Can't name Ribarics. On the torture, it's out there, so the line is horrific and so on. We're shocked. Scumbags' inhumanity to other filth. With me?'

'Urge people to come forward?'

'Mate, absolutely. In large numbers.'

Kiely smiled, uneasy.

'Anyway, the communication expert will guide you,' said Villani. 'Ms Cathy Wynn. Just don't embed her.'

'What?'

'Nothing. Joke.'

'Your jokes,' said Kiely, 'are either very crude or very obscure.'

'Let me think about that, will you?'

'It'll probably take you a while.'

'That's cheeky for a subordinate,' said Villani.

'THE OLD DAYS,' said Vickery. 'My fuck, some good ones, right?'

They drank, set glasses on the counter cloth. The bar was in the basement of an office block, smell of pissed-on camphor balls, nylon carpet outgassing, the fears of failed salesmen.

'Think about them?' said Vickery.

'Oh, yeah. The good times.'

Villani often thought about the rushes, about being young, unbreakable, stupid. He never thought about them as the good times.

'We missed you,' said Vickery. 'Always miss a steady bloke. Reliable bloke. Bloke likes a joke.'

Vickery and a cop called Gary Plaice almost killed a half-arsed little robber called Ivanovich, they said he broke free, tripped and fell down a flight of stairs.

'The lesson the scum can draw from this,' said the boss, Matt Cameron, 'is that you don't get between Vick and a hard Plaice.'

Villani knew what Vickery was saying. 'Different jokes now,' he said.

'Oakleigh, got a joke there. Good fucking riddance. Listen, won't hold you. The reason is, we heard a story.'

'Yeah?'

'Um.' Vickery's tongue bulged his upper lip, did a few wipes over his gums. 'Lovett carked it, hear that? Lung cancer.'

'I heard that,' Villani said. He had felt no loss at the news, every day dawned brighter without Alan Arthur Lovett.

'Didn't break down myself neither,' said Vickery. 'But he's on a fucking video, coughing and spitting, the twat says we fitted the little Quirk bastard.'

'Why would he say that?' said Villani.

Vickery gave him the long look. 'Yeah, well, the drugs fuck with your brain, my brother-in-law, another prick, he came up with all kinds of shit, incest, you name it. It's the Super K.'

'When was it made?'

'What?'

'The tape?'

'Dunno. What's it matter?'

'Could matter a lot.'

Vickery turned his back to the bar, glass in hand, looked around the dungeon. 'Anyway, the problem here's the wife, bloody Grace's found God, fucking never-never-land shit and she's sent the DPP the tape.'

Down the bar a blade-faced man coughed and coughed, could not stop coughing, it was painful to hear, he bent his head, ejected something into an expectant palm.

'Fucked,' said Vickery. 'Another cunt going Lovett's way. My guy says they're talking second inquest. And there's people very keen to see us go down. So we need to consider taking steps.'

He looked into his glass. 'Coming man like you, you can raise this in the right places.'

'Don't know about that,' said Villani.

Vickery turned to be at a right angle to Villani, he was the same height, heavier, torso sausaged in cold blue polyester.

'Mate, mate,' he said. 'Clarity here. Courtesy this mad prick we can go down as killers, perjurers, eternal disgrace to the fucking force.'

In dreams, Villani always saw the fire escape, the kitchen's grey vinyl tiles, dirty, peeling, the blood, on the ceiling, on the walls, on the windowpanes, lying on the carpet like drops of scarlet syrup. He never saw Greg Quirk's face, never the blown-away throat, he never saw the face of the dying man.

'See what I can do,' he said, finished the beer.

Vickery made a nasal pipe-hammer sound. 'Stevo,' he said, 'we don't get smart here, we'll know what arsefucked by a whole footy team feels like. Those who don't already.'

'Well, you heard a story,' said Villani. 'Could be some mistake.'

'My whole life's a fucking mistake,' said Vickery. 'With one or two exceptions I can't remember. No mistake here.'

On the stairs, carrying his parcels, Villani passed two young women arguing, blotchy drug faces, hookers. The street door resisted him, then the outside hit, hot air of wood smoke and petrochemicals, fuels ancient and new.

'I'M NOT sayin Greg was a good boy,' she said that day.

'You wouldn't want to,' said Villani, 'because it would be a very big porky.'

He had been on his knees, pulling at the last clump of the couch grass, the roots yielded, no warning, his hands struck him in the mouth. He spat, an elastic string of sputum, no lift-off, the bloody line fell down his chin, lay on his T-shirt.

He put a finger into his mouth, felt his inner lip.

'Fingers in your mouth, son,' Rose said. 'That's a big no-no. Feedin yourself germs.'

She was on the verandah, a filter cigarette in a pink plastic holder.

'Pity I didn't meet you earlier,' Villani said. 'You could have spared me so much.'

'On the other hand, Mick,' she said. 'Always thought Mick would come good.'

'Just got in with bad boys, I know.'

Rose closed her eyes, tilted her head back, blew smoke. 'Too right. Rotten homes, every last one of that lot.'

Villani took the watering can to the rainwater tank behind the house. Tap watering was banned. It hadn't rained much for a long time but Rose's tank was always full. He didn't ask questions. It wasn't beyond her to pass through next door's rotten fence in the deep of night, connect her hose to their tap and fill the tank.

In the house, over time, he saw items well beyond the means

and needs of an aged pensioner, French cologne, a leather purse, handbags, chocolates, jewellery, CDs, DVDs.

Once he picked up a small camera. 'Where'd you get this?'

'Found it,' she said. 'At the bus stop.'

'Same stop as the Chanel No. 5?'

'Don't be cheeky, copper.'

'Hate to see you in court.'

'What, gonna dob me? Serve me bloodywell right lettin you into me house. And who the hell are you to talk? Bloody bent, every last prick of you. Believe me, sonny, I know.'

Villani came back, watering can brimming. 'Lucky with rain here,' he said. 'Microclimate. Tiny zone of high rainfall.'

After a while, Rose said, 'Kids. You don't want to blame yourself, do you? God knows, you done your best.'

'What if you haven't done your best?'

'Me?'

'No, me.'

'Well, you're not a mum.'

'No,' said Villani. 'That lets me off then.'

He sprinkled water, special attention for the carrots and potatoes in the drum. He liked underground vegetables. When he was seven, Bob Villani left him and Mark with their grandmother, Stella. Couple of weeks, son, he said. More than three years passed, he came back only twice that Villani could remember.

But he already knew by seven, knew from his mother, that what adults told you was only true while it suited them for it to be true. He had become expert at detecting grown-ups' moods, always alert for signs of anxiety, for false cheerfulness and unnecessary lies, for the appearance of sincerity. He knew all the danger signs – extra attention and being pushed away, hushed conversations, the unexpected and frightening outbursts that gave way to hugs and kisses.

The first spring, Stella showed him how to plant carrot seeds. She put them in a glass jar with sand, drew a furrow in the black soil of her back garden with a finger, trickled a line. When the tops came up, he went outside in the evenings, after tea, lay on the path next to his little carrot bed, warm bricks beneath his body, trying to hear the little carrots expanding, pushing downwards.

'Time to put the radishes in,' said Rose. 'Love a tiny little radish.'

'April,' said Villani, 'that's when the radishes go in.'

'April,' said Rose. 'Doubt I'll see April. Feelin a terrible tiredness. Body and soul.'

'Ten years you've been saying that,' said Villani. 'Still be saying it in ten years.'

Rose said, 'Ten years? Be bloody eighty. No desire to be eighty. I can see what bloody eighty looks like. Looks like bloody hell.'

Rose Quirk hadn't got much older since their first meeting. On his second visit, dusk on that long-ago October day, coming from a barren surveillance, he stood at her front door, regretting the impulse. 'Out this way, thought I'd see if you . . .'

'No,' she said.

'Nothing?'

'No.'

'Well, if something comes up, if I can do . . .'

'No,' she said.

Going down the cracked concrete path, Villani's eye fell on crusted earth, faded seed packets. At the gate, he said, 'Need to get the summer vegies in soon.'

'Greg did the vegies.'

They had shot Greg dead, he wasn't going to do the vegies. On the next Saturday, Villani woke early, heard Laurie's car grate the gravel in the driveway, it was her busiest day of the week. He lay in bed thinking about the old woman's vegetables, sighing. After making breakfast for the kids, he drove to a nursery and bought blood and bone, mulch, seeds, seedlings. Rose Quirk didn't answer his knocks. He went around the back, found a fork in the shed, dug up the beds, dug in blood and bone. He planted carrots, beans, two kinds of tomatoes, peas, cucumbers, beetroot, mulched the beds, watered thoroughly.

He was sweaty, looking at his work, the bright seed packets on sticks, when he heard the gate.

'What's this?' said Rose, hoarse cigarette voice.

'Put some vegies in.'

'What for?'

'I thought we could share them.'

'Why don't you grow your own?'

'No room.' A lie.

'Can't hardly walk, never mind lookin after vegies. Buy em at the super's easier.'

'They don't need much. I'll come around.'

Black eyes, Rose looked at him as if he were a Jehovah's Witness, wouldn't take no. He thought he had been stupid, he would take no. At the gate, he said, 'Got my number, Mrs Quirk,' he said. 'You can get me.'

'What kind of copper are you?'

'Not just a copper,' he said. 'I'm a human being too.'

'Yeah?'

'Yeah.'

'That'd be a first,' she said. 'Thirsty. Go a beer?'

'I could go a beer.'

They sat on the front verandah in fraying, swaying wicker chairs and drank Vic Bitter out of glasses with green and red bands around the tops.

'Smoke?' said Rose.

'Given up,' said Villani. He took one. Rose clicked a pink plastic lighter, he leaned across.

'Family man?' she said.

'Two girls and a boy.'

'Wife?'

'Wife. Their mother.'

'Where you from? You Melbourne?'

'No. A few places.'

'Why's that?'

'My dad was in the army.'

Loud clattering noise.

Villani jerked, alarmed, heads in the street, beanies.

Skateboarders.

The street sloped, full of holes, they would come from all around to run it. He put his head back, felt the tension in his neck.

'A wharfie, me dad,' Rose said. 'Bashed mum, bashed me, bashed us all. Me brother Danny run away, twelve years old, never ever saw him again. Biggest bastard ever lived, me dad.'

There was nothing to say about that.

'Broke me little doggy's head with a half-brick,' she said. 'No bigger swine ever lived.'

Villani was on the fire escape at the back door of the third floor unit when he heard the shots. He went in, weapon drawn, filthy kitchen, pizza boxes, beer cans, opened the door, a passage, went left down it, put an eye around the corner and saw Gregory Thomas Quirk, Rose Quirk's second-born.

So you say that from the fire escape you heard Detective Dance shout?

Yes, sir.

What did you hear?

He shouted, Put it down, Greg.

You heard that clearly?

Yes, sir.

It says here, you say here, he shouted it two or three times?

Yes, sir.

And then you heard the shots?

Yes, sir.

You were outside the back door?

Yes, sir.

How far away was the back door from the front door, sergeant?

I don't know exactly, sir.

I'll tell you, sergeant. More than ten metres.

That could be right, yes.

Certainly is. So you say that, across this distance, through double-brick walls, you heard Detective Dance shouting?

Yes, sir.

Put it down, Greg. He barked those words?

No, sir.

No?

He didn't bark them. He shouted them.

Of course. Sharp point, my apologies. Not a dog then. Nothing worse than a dog, is there, Mr Villani?

Detective. Sir.

Yes. Moving on, you say you heard Detective Dance shout and then you heard shots?

Yes, sir.

What was the interval between the shouts and the shots?

Quick. Short.

What, a second or two? More?

I can't estimate that, sir. He shouted, there were shots.

Four shots, you say here.

Yes, sir.

You could count them?

Yes, sir.

Widely spaced?

No, sir.

In the passage, he looked into Greg Quirk's black sleepy eyes. Greg's left hand was on his chest, blood running, over his fingers. He coughed, from his throat blood spurted, his chin dropped, long black strands of hair hid his face, he went to his knees.

Tell us what you saw when you first saw Greg Quirk.

There was blood coming from his throat. He dropped a firearm, a handgun, and he took a step and sort of knelt down.

And?

Detective Dance was in the door. Detective Vickery. Behind him.

And Detective Lovett?

I didn't see him. Not then.

Nothing prepared you for it: the volume of blood; the weak sounds of life leaking away.

COLBY SAID, 'So you put the sheepshagger on TV to say you have no idea who these dead pricks are.'

'No. Didn't do that.'

'That's the impression of the girl Gillam, who's been shat upon by the branchstacker Orong, who rang Mr Larry O'Barry to complain.'

'I told Kiely don't name anyone,' said Villani. 'I didn't say we don't know who they are. Anyway, he was in the hands of Searle's media expert. Cathy Wynn. Handpicked by Searle.'

'So she told Kiely what to say?'

'Well they tell you what not to say, don't they?'

'That's better. I don't know Cathy Wynn.'

On television, Anna Markham raised her chin and tilted her head a few degrees east. Good-looking women did that, it was in their genes, they had to do it.

'Just come on board,' said Villani, cold in his heart. 'From the *Herald Sun*, possibly the fashion pages. They say recently seen going into Lake Towers in Middle Park with someone. Two-thirty in the pm.'

'What kind of someone?'

'Resembling a communications expert.'

'That's from?'

It came from an off-duty uniform via one of Birkerts' squad.

'I forget,' said Villani. 'Reliable enough.'

'So the defence line is Homicide badly advised by said slut?'

'We are not the defendant, boss.'

'Moving on. Reconsidered passing this Oakleigh shit to Crucible?'

That impulse was gone. 'No, sir.'

Colby put the phone down. Villani unmuted. Anna Markham was speaking:

. . . in Wangaratta today new state Liberal leader Karen Mellish rated water, health, public transport, economic mismanagement, public safety and police corruption as key issues for voters in this election . . .

The Opposition leader standing on the back of a truck, hair pulled back, check shirt and denims, a sea of hats in front of her.

. . . Labor's brought this great state to its knees. They talk about being the party of working people. Rubbish. Party of the merchant bankers and the consultants and the investment advisors and the branchstackers, that's what they are. It's time to chuck them out . . .

Cut to the anchor, who said:

. . . Melbourne will tonight hear details of what its proposers call 'a public transport revolution' when a consortium headed by businessman Max Hendry outlines its plans at a function for city councils. Among the guests will be the premier, the leader of the Opposition and . . .

Villani muted, looked at what the computer offered on the current cases. It offered nothing except the blindingly obvious. He logged out, went back to the files, worked at the paper, the never-diminishing, self-replenishing paper, took calls, hoping for a call from Barry withdrawing the invitation. Maybe he should quit the job, take a package, he had the years. He could join Bob, use mysterious Indonesian oils to patch up horses, go to the races, look after the trees.

They had to think about thinning or it would be impossible to walk in some parts of the forest. Dig another dam too, it would rain again, sooner or later.

At 6pm, Stephen Villani took the pins out of the new blue shirt, changed into the new suit, dark grey, put on the tie, red, and the shoes, black with toecaps. He sat for a moment, head back, eyes closed, felt the weight of the day begun far away in the high country, before dawn.

VILLANI TOOK a glass of white wine from a penguin boy's tray, looked at the crowd, all suits, men and women, walked around the rim of the crowded room. It was in the sky, windows all around, it offered the city, the bay, the hinterland, the meek hills, all gauzed in smoke.

'Something of a view, is it not, Stephen,' said Commissioner Barry.

'Don't often get this high, sir,' Villani said.

Barry was drinking champagne. He looked different, shorter, his dark hair gleamed, his cheekbones glowed, there was mois-turiser involved. 'Nice suit,' he said. 'Also tie and shirt.'

His eyes went down. 'Ditto shoes. That's the way, Stephen.'

Villani felt a flush, he willed it away. He would not forget this moment, he felt like a girl.

'I've reassured my leaders on your handling of the media,' Barry said. 'A bit of paranoia at the political level. The problem is wanting always to be seen to be on top of the baddies. Now is that not a total misunderstanding of the world?'

'Yes,' said Villani. 'Thanks for the invitation. Happy crowd here.'

'Well, they would be, the oysters, the champers,' said Barry.

Probably Laurie's outfit, thought Villani, caterers to the big end of town, minimum hundred-and-fifty bucks a head, feeding the A-list on Cup Day was three hundred.

'Good to see you out of your silo,' said Barry. 'Can't have you buried like Singleton. Get some perspective. If you're going up, you need to have a wide view.'

He winked. 'Mind you, I say that to all the girls.'

Villani made a smile, looked away, into the eyes of a young woman.

'The minister and the chief commissioner are here, gentlemen,' she said. 'Would you care to follow me?'

'Of course,' said Barry. 'Lead on, darling.'

She took their glasses, gave them to a waiter. Then, like a safari guide, she led them through the throng.

As they skirted groups, Villani saw faces he knew from television, the newspapers. He saw the premier, Kelvin Yeats, slick brown hair, yellow eyes, he was laughing, bright teeth, looking at a man in his sixties, tanned, close-cropped grey hair: Max Hendry. The premier's plump, blinking wife was talking to Vicky Hendry, Max's second, third or fourth wife, a looker, shortish fair hair. As they passed, she met Villani's eyes, registered him.

Then came infrastructure minister Stuart Koenig talking to Tony Ruskin and Paul Keogh, radio bookends of the working day, some people's working day, two self-appointed opinion-makers. Sucking up to them before an election would be a priority for both parties.

They came close to a buffed couple, slash-mouthed Opposition leader Karen Mellish, kite-tight face, and her husband, Keith, usually called a farmer, he would have soft Collins Street hands.

From five metres, Villani saw the targets, two men drinking champagne: the police minister, Martin Orong, wolf-faced thirty-year-old, black hair, greasy skin, the latest model of outer-urban party branchstacker, and David Gillam, the chief commissioner.

As they approached, Gillam adjusted his uniform jacket. His features were a size or two too big for his face, as if they had grown ahead in the way of teenage boys' feet.

Barry got there first, shook hands. 'I'd like to introduce Inspector Stephen Villani, head of Homicide,' he said.

Orong tried some pathetic muscle, Villani didn't respond.

'How's this Oakleigh shit going?' said Orong, squeaky voice.

'We'll get there, minister,' said Villani.

'Drugs. Give it to Crucible.'

Villani looked at Barry, at the chief commissioner, read nothing in their faces.

'Homicide investigates suspicious deaths,' he said. 'I'm a traditionalist, minister.'

Gillam sucked his teeth. 'Tradition, absolutely. Steve, the minister's just been talking about balance. Informing the public, that's a given. While not creating undue alarm. Right, minister?'

Orong looked at Barry, at Villani. 'Absolutely,' he said. 'Had the premier on the subject this very day. Balance, that's the theme tune.'

Orong made a beckoning gesture. Gillam and Barry bent towards him.

'An example is Prosilio,' he said, eyes on Villani, 'where you don't want some hooker bitch thing to tarnish a multi-million-dollar project, flagship project, jewel in the crown for the precinct.'

Villani looked away, at the people intent on the expensive morsels, the French champagne. In the old days, Laurie brought experiments and leftovers home, they ate them at the kitchen table, drinking wine. It often led to sex.

'Find the sluts dead every day, right, inspector?' said Orong.

Villani paid attention.

'Dogshit on the shoes of society. In fucking alleys.'

The beautiful child in the bathroom in the sky, her palms open, her neck broken, pulled back and back and back until the man behind her gained the satisfaction he sought.

Lizzie. She looked like Lizzie.

Who was seeing to Lizzie? Not her mother, her mother was feeding a film crew somewhere. Where? What had Corin said? He didn't listen properly to family things.

'Certainly find women dead in alleys, minister,' said Villani.

'Oh yes,' said Barry.

'Druggy sluts,' said Orong. 'Good riddance.'

'Can I tempt you, gentlemen?' said a girl penguin. She offered a silver tray of tiny puffed pastry balls on toothpicks. 'Blue swimmer crab with *foie gras en croute*,' she said. 'But if you've got seafood issues, I'll . . .'

The minister took two. Gillam and Barry did the same. Villani took one. They would be four dollars a pop.

Orong added champagne to the puff in his mouth, chewed, looked around. The penguin was close.

'More, sir?' she said.

'Yeah,' said Orong.

He put his glass on her tray and popped puffs into his mouth – one, two, three, four, five, he collected toothpicks. Mouth full, he said, 'So anyway, you've acted responsibly over the Prosilio matter. The premier's pleased, I can tell you that.'

Without looking at the penguin, Orong held up his toothpicks, a delicate fence between thumb and forefinger. She took them impassively, surgically, put them on her salver.

'French,' he said, eyes on Villani. 'Not the local muck. In a clean glass. And bring the steak thingies, the Wagyu.'

'Sir,' she said.

'You following me, inspector?' said Orong.

Villani knew why he was there, what was at stake for him, how he should behave in the presence of this shoddy little arsehole, a nothing, no talents, just a political creature who knew how to slime around, how to get the numbers, how to suck up to those who could advance him, screw those who couldn't, how to claim credit, duck responsibility.

'Closely, minister,' he said. 'Balance.'

'Balance is the key,' said Gillam.

'Oh, definitely,' said Barry. 'Balance.'

'That's good,' said Orong, wiped his lips. 'The boss's got a saying. Can't lead unless you can follow. Can't give orders unless you can take them.'

Villani thought of the people he'd taken orders from. Bob Villani's army life, had he taken orders from dickheads and arselickers like this man? Did they have them? Was the army different? Was there another Bob Villani, a servile Bob?

'Being looked after, minister, gentlemen?' A big man with dense silver hair combed back, he tugged at his double cuffs, small ruby cufflinks.

Orong gleamed. 'Clinton, yeah, very nice, great. Listen, you know Dave Gillam, Mike Barry . . .'

'I certainly do,' said the man. 'But I don't think I . . .'

'Stephen Villani, head of Homicide,' said Barry. 'Meet Clinton Hulme.'

'Steve, good to meet you,' said Hulme, soft handshake. 'I feel very safe here. So many policemen.'

'Clinton's CEO of Concordat Holdings,' said Barry. 'Max Hendry's company. Our hosts.'

'Just one of them, please,' said Hulme. 'This consortium's so big only Max knows everyone.'

A soft drum roll, a plump man on the small stage, wired for sound, behind him his image on a huge screen. Villani knew he was once a television star, a game-show host perhaps. The amplified voice said, 'Ladies and gentleman, good evening and welcome. I'm Kim Hogarth representing the AirLine Consortium.'

Through the crowd, Villani could see television crews, still photographers.

'A great pleasure today to welcome so many people who serve our great city and our great state,' the man said. 'And at such a wonderful venue, the Hawksmoor Gallery at Persius.'

Applause, canned.

'I'd like to offer a special, special welcome to the premier and his ministers and their partners, the leader of the Opposition and her colleagues and their partners,' said Hogarth. 'We appreciate them joining us. The AirLine project isn't a secret. It's been speculated about in the media for months. Tonight we put an end to that. We'll spell out our dream.'

A long pause.

'Of course, we all know that dreams don't often come true. We give up because achieving them is just too hard, needs too much work, needs too much courage. And more boldness than we have.'

Triumphal symphonic music. On the giant screen, images of primitive machines and Saturn rockets lifting off, the Wright brothers and jet airliners taking off, three-masted sailing ships and supertankers, dusty paddocks and shimmering pictures of city skyscrapers, it went on.

Then the screen showed the city from a great height, zoomed in, cut to speeded-up helicopter-shot footage of gridlocked highways, bridges and city streets, of overcrowded railway platforms and rail carriages. Over the images, voices announced train delays and cancellations, warned of road blockages, diversions, malfunctioning traffic lights, sluggish flows, stoppages.

'AirLine has a bold dream, a bold vision,' said Hogarth. 'It comes from a great citizen of Melbourne, a great Victorian, a great Australian.'

Soaring music.

Still and moving pictures of a man, from slim youth onwards, hair short, long, short, running, playing football, laying bricks, beside a light plane, at a drawing board, in a hardhat on building sites, leading in a winning horse at Flemington, walking bunch-muscled through the shallows after a Pier-to-Pub swim, talking and laughing with politicians, Whitlam, Fraser, Hawke, Keating, Howard, Rudd, with artists, musicians, athletes, being hugged by Nelson Mandela.

It went on too long. It ended in silence with the man walking down a country road, fire-black tree skeletons and paddocks on both sides. An elderly couple came to meet him in front of a burnt-down house and outbuildings. He put his arms around them and they stood, heads together, a tableau of sorrow and sympathy.

Silence.

Hogarth said, 'Ladies and gentlemen, I give you AirLine's visionary, its founder and chairman, I give you Mr Max Hendry.'

Max Hendry was on the platform, moving easily.

'That bloke in the pictures,' he said. 'Looks a bit like Harrison Ford. Anyone remember Harrison? Only taller. And a damn side handsomer.'

Long, loud applause, the sombre mood dissolved. Max Hendry made a palms-out gesture.

'Guests, friends, it's good to have you here,' he said. 'And enemies too. You are all welcome. My father used to say it's hard to dislike a man who pours you a glass of the Grange.'

The crowd laughed, they liked him.

He waited, looked around the room. 'I want to ask you a question,' he said.

'Is there anyone here, and that includes you Mr Premier and your ministers, who can say with hand on heart that this city's public transport isn't woefully inadequate?'

Murmurings.

'No takers?' said Hendry. 'Of course not. Woefully inadequate is being polite. It's a disgrace. That's why our consortium wants to give this city at least one system that is super-fast, safe, and comfortable. A great system for a great city. It looks like this.'

The screen showed an elevated train bulleting along above a highway, passing another going the other way. Then a map of the city with bold lines along the arteries, all meeting in the heart of the city.

'It's not another toll road. It's not another train. It operates in the air, in useless space above the highways. In the airspace. We call it Project AirLine.'

More applause.

'We have no small ambition,' he said. 'We want to build the most advanced transport system in the world. Passive magnetic levitation, suspended pods, lightweight advanced metals, cutting-edge engineering. But we need the state government to help us. We need all the councils on all the routes to come to the party.'

Applause.

'We can have the Monash line operating in around twenty months from the go-ahead,' said Hendry. 'Imagine fifteen minutes from the outer suburbs to the heart of the city. Then we'll do the western feeder. Melton, Caroline Springs, ten minutes. And that's just the beginning.'

Longer applause, Max Hendry nodding, camera flashes winking.

'Two other things,' said Max Hendry. 'I like the idea of fear-free mass transport. Very much. Some people here know my wife's nephew was beaten to death near a station a few years ago. He was much loved.'

The respectful silence, the wait.

'Makes you think, that kind of violence, doesn't it?' he said. 'It plagues our city.'

On the big screen, a panning camera was on the premier, no expression, hands steepled under his bottom lip, bovine Robbie Cowper, the planning minister. It moved to Orong, to Gillam, to Barry. Villani saw himself. Then it came to a nodding Paul Keogh.

'So this will be the world's safest public transport,' said Hendry. 'I give my solemn word.'

He was on the screen now, five metres high, he pulled loose his tie, a man coming into the pub, friends waiting. He smiled. It was a good smile, all the better for being so long awaited.

'The second thing,' he said. 'I'll tell you a commercial-in-confidence secret.'

The wait.

'We're greedy bastards. We hope to make some money out of this. Of course, greedy bastards have built a lot of the world. Some things greed builds outlive the greedy bastards who built them.'

More applause.

'So our message for the state government and the councils is this. Forget about more freeways. They solve nothing and make many things worse. Forget about more tunnels. All they do is take the problems underground for a while.'

Pause.

'Ladies and gentlemen, this project is about actually doing something to stop this city choking to death. In the major corridors, we can take at least twenty per cent of passenger vehicles off the roads. We can cut greenhouse emissions dramatically. It's the greenest thing any level of government could do. It's a gift to the present and the future.'

Applause, flashbulbs popping. Hendry took breath.

'What will it cost? Frankly, we don't know precisely yet. Big bikkies. Our people are working flat out on costs. Do we seek a public-private partnership? Absolutely not. Do we have merchant-bank robbers involved? Bugger them. So do we want government contributions? Bloody right we do. Contributions from government at all levels, from the federal government down.'

Louder, longer clapping.

'So, you may ask, why make this announcement now? Because we've done our private talking. We've talked our heads off and we've had nothing more than polite expressions of interest. Now we want to go to the people.'

Thunderous applause.

'This huge project ramifies in all directions. It's political at every level. So, as we approach the state election and with a federal election less than a year away, we'd like this city's people to tell their representatives, local, state and federal, that they want the cleanest, greenest, fastest, safest transport option in the world.'

Someone handed Hendry a glass of water. He held it up.

'What's this liquid? Desalinated water? Never touch it.'

Laughter.

'Mr Premier, leader of the Opposition, members of parliament, mayors, councillors, I want to urge you to think about this chance to do something important for your city, your state, and, in a small way, for your country and the planet.'

A camera was on the impassive premier, they cut to Karen Mellish. She wasn't giving away anything either.

'I thank you,' said Hendry. 'This project's taken three years of my life, three years of spending my own money, which hurts, I can tell you. I've done it because I believe in it with passion. It will be the best thing I do in my life.'

Long and emotional applause. Hendry waited again.

'The challenge I'm issuing to all of you,' he said, 'and particularly those standing for election in a few weeks, is this. Declare yourself for or against this project. In principle. That's all we ask. Then we'll let the people of this city and this state speak with their votes.'

The applause lasted minutes. Gillam, Barry and Orong didn't join in. Clinton Hulme made a lot of noise.

'That's about as good as a speech gets,' he said to Villani. 'What do you reckon?'

'Has he done any public speaking before?' said Villani.

Hulme smiled, patted Villani's arm. 'I like dry in a man. Come and meet Max.'

'I don't think Max's hanging out to meet me,' Villani said.

'So wrong. He wants to meet you, Vicky wants to meet you.'

VILLANI WAS taken through the crowd, Hulme's hand in his back. A long-legged woman in black led them.

They followed Max Hendry on a tour, the spruiker Kim Hogarth and two women escorting him, they read name tags, did introductions, Hendry shook hands, he spoke, the guests laughed, he laughed, he went serious, they went serious, nodded, he left them with a few words, another clasp, a touch on the arm, a woman kissed him on his cheek.

The woman in black intervened. Hendry turned.

'Max, Vicky,' said Clinton Hulme. 'I'd like to introduce Stephen Villani, head of the Homicide Squad. He thinks you're too royal to meet him, Max.'

They shook hands. They were the same height. Hendry had light eyes, disconcerting, the colour of shallow water over clean sand.

'Meet Vicky,' said Hendry.

Vicky Hendry wasn't much older close up, fine lines, high-cheekboned, handsome.

'Stephen, I have to tell you my family thinks Homicide walks on water,' she said. 'After my nephew was murdered, someone rang every day, always saying you'd find them.'

Villani's scalp itched. Praise, flattery, to deal with them perhaps you had to be praised when you were young, he had very little experience of praise. For Bob, not getting things right was bludging, slackarse behaviour, not paying attention.

Stephen, don't take your kids' achievements for granted.

Laurie said that one day when he had found the time to read Tony's school report and just nodded.

'I suppose you know how much that means to people who've lost someone?' said Vicky Hendry.

'We try to understand,' said Villani.

The fourth of Singo's Five Commandments: *Thou shalt speak to the family as often as possible. As avenging angel, not fucking undertaker.*

'And you got them,' said Vicky Hendry. 'Because for them to be out there free, laughing, that was a knife in our hearts.'

Through a gap, he saw the shimmer of black hair, Anna, laughing, just metres away. Their eyes met, she looked away.

'We were watching television and you came on and my sister said, That's him, he caught them.'

'Well, it's always a team effort,' said Villani.

'Not always,' said someone behind him. 'Sometimes it's just one bloke with brains.'

Villani turned and saw Matt Cameron, the first time in years. Sixty-odd, he was still unlined, still whipstick thin, the big shoulders, the tight grey curls.

'If you say so, boss,' Villani said.

Max Hendry patted Cameron's shoulder, Vicky Hendry touched him too, affectionate, they knew one another well.

'This is about as secure as it gets,' said Hendry. 'Whole hierarchy of the police force and Mr Private Security himself. You know each other then?'

Cameron said, the soft voice, 'Taught the boy everything he knows. Things he shouldn't know too.'

When Villani joined the Robbers, Cameron was boss, in his early forties then, the hardest man, still boxing, just muscle and

sinew, a phenomenal reach. He sparred with him, it was like fighting Inspector Gadget. He left the force after his cop son and his
girlfriend were murdered on a farm near Colac, still unsolved. His
wife killed herself a month later. Now he was rich, co-founder
with Wayne Poland, another cop, of Blackwatch Associates, the
country's biggest security firm.

'Gentlemen, got to keep moving,' said Hendry. He put hands
on Villani and Cameron. 'Steve, Vicky'll arrange something. Do
us the honour?'

'Of course.'

Vicky Hendry offered a hand, she took his in both hands, silken,
the extra second of clasp, not flirting, the couple moved on.

'Interesting bloke, Max,' said Cameron. 'I see Colby's not choos-
ing your suits anymore. Nor ties.'

'Got a new advisor.'

'Smart people always take advice. But only from smarter people.
How's the Oakleigh thing going?'

'Not as fast as you'd like,' said Villani. 'Remember Matko
Ribaric?'

'Trying to forget Matko.'

'It's his boys. And Vern Hudson.'

Cameron smiled, the rare smile, Villani remembered it was
gold. 'Well, best fucking thing I've heard for a while,' he said.
'Vermin born of vermin. Be drugs. Everything's drugs.'

'Not unlikely.'

'Handballing to Dancer and the Crucible dancing girls?'

'No.'

'Brave. Still, boy's got worries enough. Machinery for deep-
level mining, can't crack a walnut.'

Cameron drank something pale from a whisky glass. 'I heard
about Lovett. Grace Lovett.'

'Before me,' said Villani. 'I heard ten minutes ago.'

'Out of the loop. Still, no leaks, media don't crack a fat, it'll go away. Working on that, are you? With Searle?'

'We're not that close.'

'Son, a Pom once said England had no permanent alliances, only permanent interests. Look after your permanent interests. With me?'

'Suck up to the prick?'

Cameron looked at him, Villani saw his father in Cameron's gaze, you never knew what it meant until it was too late, you had got it wrong.

'Well, world's imperfect,' Cameron said. 'Don't be the twat ends up on the cross. Need a hand, I still know a few people.'

Villani knew that he should bow his head and say something, with gratitude. He hadn't asked for a favour, he didn't want one.

'Thanks, boss,' he said.

A man came up, tall, handsome, floppy fair hair, fleshy mid-thirties. Villani knew who he was.

'The old man gives a nice party,' he said. He wore a grey suit, snowy shirt, no tie.

'Know Steve Villani?' said Cameron. 'Steve, Hugh Hendry.'

The handshake was perfect, firm, gentle.

'Your man Dove's a bloody Jack Russell,' said Hendry.

'Trained to be so,' said Villani. 'Paid to be so. Encouraged to be so.'

The perfect smile too, the big teeth, white and even. Rich teeth. 'Respect that. It's getting it over to him that we are pleading guilty to a software failure and not guilty to whatever else he has in his mind.'

'People feeding us bullshit,' said Villani. 'That's what we have in mind. Total loss of vision on this scale is new to us.'

The tiny narrowing of Hendry's eyes.

'We're a bit new on that too,' he said. 'Our techs are hot-bunking to solve the problem.'

'Doesn't the software write a log?'

'A log?'

'Have a code that writes a detailed log on glitches, break-downs?'

Hendry didn't get it.

'Certainly a technical challenge,' said Hendry. He was looking at Cameron in the way of someone who wanted to be rescued from a bore.

'Dead girl in the building,' said Villani. 'That's our technical challenge. Low-tech challenge. Girl screwed to death.'

Cameron ran a finger across his upper lip. It was a signal to Hendry. The feeling of being patronised triggered the icy rage in Villani.

'Maybe we should be talking to you, boss,' he said to Cameron. 'Maybe we're talking to the office boys. This's a Blackwatch cock-up, not so? Blackwatch high-tech challenge. No back-up, no log.'

Cameron smiled, not the golden smile now, no eye-crinkles, Villani knew this smile too and he wished he could take back all his words.

'Growing in the job, Stevo,' said Cameron. 'Crawling out from under Colby and Dance and Singleton. That's a good thing for a man your age. Mature man, family man.'

In the crowded room, in the hubbub, Cameron's words made their own silence.

'Got to move on,' said Cameron. He was looking over Villani's shoulder, raised a hand to someone. 'Keep sane.'

Cameron walked and Villani looked.

Anna. His hand was on her arm. She touched it.

He saw Cameron stoop, kiss her cheek, another cheek.

Jesus, when did he take up this shit? The last time he saw Cameron stoop to kiss it was to kiss Joey Colombaris with his forehead, the prick bled for so long they exhausted the shit paper, called the medics. Joey turned out to be a bleeder, needed a transfusion, almost died.

'Not the best few days,' said Hendry. 'Casino's screaming at me, the hotel, bloody Marscay. I'm supposed to be at the beach.'

'That's tough,' said Villani. 'A last point. This stuff doesn't go away. You and Marscay and Orion can fuck with us but we don't go away.'

Hendry put up his hands. 'No, no, we want to know what happened up there as much as anyone. We understand our obligations. But the technology failed us. The bloody Israelis gave us a demo in this hot lab in Herzliya. Worked like a charm. Infinitely scaleable, they said. You know what that . . .'

'I know what that means,' said Villani.

A couple were at Hendry's shoulder, the woman tall and thin, pale hair in a man's cut, her loose shirt showed hollows behind her collarbones deep enough to hold water. Small birds could sit on her shoulders and nod to drink. The man was shaven-headed, hooded eyes, an art dealer, Daniel Bricknell, often in the media.

She put a hand on Hendry's shoulder. 'Darling, that Orong creature made an advance,' she said.

She smiled at Villani. 'Oh shit, he's not your closest friend?'

'Like brothers,' said Villani.

'Caitlin Harris, Daniel Bricknell, Stephen Villani,' said Hendry. 'Stephen's the head of the Homicide Squad.'

'I know who Stephen is,' she said. 'I've seen Stephen on television. The serious face. It turns me on. Stephen, that old *City Homicide* show. Is it really like that?'

'Only the names were changed,' Villani said.

'You're not bad in the flesh,' she said. 'I mean without the make-up. That's unusual.'

'Nice to meet you,' said Villani. 'I have to go, attend to bodies.'

'Well, I'm a body,' said Caitlin. 'I need attending to.'

'Forgive her,' said Hendry. 'The beauty-brain imbalance. Scientists are working on it.'

'Nothing wrong with a beauty-brain imbalance,' said Bricknell. 'It's the ugly-brain balance I don't like.'

Villani passed close to Anna, Cameron gone, he met her grey eyes, he was a stranger, could read nothing.

Near the door, Barry came from nowhere. 'A rewarding outing, boyo. Talking to the right people. Doesn't hurt to get to know people, does it?'

'Thanks for the invitation,' said Villani.

'My pleasure. You went really well. Just a little tip?'

'Yes?'

'Smile more. You can be a bit forbidding, bit grim. Makes people uncomfortable, know what I mean? Like you're going to arrest them.'

Villani smiled, he felt the resistance in the muscles of his cheeks. 'Point taken, boss,' he said.

'Excellent,' said Barry. 'Now it's an early night. That's an order.'

ANNA WAS on his mind all the way home. So striking, so hand-some. And so clever, so confident. She could choose from all the smart people around her. Why had she slept with him? Perhaps she was like him, perhaps she felt the compulsion to possess.

The house dark, murmur of television from the back, the family room, no complete family ever gathered in it, one hundred and fifty thousand dollars worth of extension, half what the house cost, Laurie arranged the money.

Corin asleep on the sofa. He killed the television, said her name, twice, a third time, she was startled, grumpy, puffy-eyed, rose and went away without a kind word.

He went down the passage, sat on the bed, took off his shoes and his tie, unbuttoned his shirt, ready to shower, lay back, just for a little minute, closed his eyes.

It was not like television. His second or third month on the job, a late-night kicking in Flinders Street, the man unconscious, then induced coma, two days later they cut the power. The premier went on television, said symptom of all that was rotten in society, the whole force including traffic was on the case day and night, results expected hourly. The truth was they had nothing. They looked at security footage from every working camera in the area. All they got was a glimpse of four figures, grey shadows, a block away, the time right. Unless they got a dobber, they had nowhere to go and so the media unit fed a stream of rubbish about positive identifications in the hope that one of the pricks in the group who didn't actually kick the man more than five or six times would dob in those who did.

No one came forward. They took turns talking to the victim's family, rich people in Toorak, he didn't know anything about them, just rich people. He spoke to the mother and the father, they always thanked him warmly but he knew he was just a reminder of what they had lost.

On a night in August, freezing wind off the bay, it had rained at last light, Villani and Burgess went to Footscray, a sad domestic, woman stabbed, the blood-spattered husband was in the local cells, picked up at the milkbar while buying cigarettes. Villani tried to talk to the man, who was incoherent with drink, drugs, possibly this was his natural state. After a while, Villani went outside for a smoke, stood against the wall in the cold, stained concrete yard, the sky now blown clear, he could see the Southern Cross, the wind blew the cigarette coal white-hot.

A van came in, they unloaded two youths, black trackies, beanies, still full of fuck-you attitude, it showed they had been treated with the respect owed to citizens, even those who were lawless scum.

'What?' said Villani to the senior.

The man knew him from the Armed Robbers, most cops in those parts knew him, he had been seen in the company of legends, it attached to you.

'Bashing a black kid, kicking him, boss,' he said. 'We come around the corner, the hugely intelligent pricks run straight up a dead end.'

Villani flicked away his stub, watched the party go up the steps into the building and, through the legs of the cop behind, he registered the second youth was wearing Blunnies.

He followed. Inside, he said to the senior, 'Give us a minute with these dorks. One to start.'

The man looked at him, the moment of query, uncertainty.

'Sure, boss. Just do the paper, they come in unharmed, okay?'

They did the paper, put the boys away, it took time, it was late when Villani went into the smaller one's cell, his name was Jude Luck. Now the fuck-you boy was alone, had no beanie, no shoes, no trackie, he had some homey tatts, his eyes showed a lot of white, not good dairy white.

Villani started in the normal way, he smiled and said, 'Hello, Jude, I'm the chaplain from St Barnabas,' and he kicked Luck's feet out from under him, he fell sideways and Villani stopped him meeting the concrete, not with love, laid him to rest, put a shoe on his chest, tested his weight, moved it up to the windpipe and pressed, tapped, you did not want to mark the cunt.

'I've been looking for you, son,' he said. 'So long I've been looking for you. You and your fucking Blunnies.'

They recorded the interview with Jude Brendan Luck at 12.47am. A while later, they put Luck's story to the bigger one, Shayne Lethlean, he went to water. They picked up the other boys, the brothers, two years apart, ginger-freckled angels fast asleep on the floor in the garage of their sister's house in Braybrook, they did not wake when the door rolled up, they had to be shaken, slapped, there was some pleasure in the work.

Villani woke, fully dressed, unrefreshed, as if from a brief fainting spell, the new day was grey in the east window, the city was making its discordant birth cries.

CORIN WAS eating cereal. She was dressed to go, damp hair back, looking twelve or thirteen but for the nose, the neck, the strong shoulders.

'Early?' Villani said, whispery voice.

'Job interview,' she said. 'Six-thirty.'

Third year at university, so clever, she was always so sharp. He could not believe his sperm played a part in her creation.

'Where?'

'Slam Juice. Lygon Street.'

'Dawn interview?'

'They test you. When's Mum get back?'

He was looking into the fridge. 'I don't know. Jesus, this needs high-pressure steam. Don't you talk to her?'

'Don't you?'

'She doesn't phone you?'

'She's working, Dad. Do you ring me?'

Toast. Vegemite. Peanut butter. That would do.

'Heard from Tony?'

'He's in Scotland. Don't you know that?'

'Scotland? I thought he was in England.'

'He's on an island, working on a fishing boat.'

'Nobody told me that.'

'Maybe you weren't listening, Dad. Preoccupied.'

'Give me a break,' said Villani. 'I'm human. Lizzie talked to her mum?'

'I have no idea.'

Corin went to the sink, he saw the sad and lovely curve of her nose, it was his mother's profile in one of the two photographs he had, kept with her letter.

'Well, ask her,' Villani said. 'She may be in the loop.'

He sliced bread, it was good bread gone a little stale, he cut three slices, went to the toaster.

Silence.

He looked up, Corin was drying her hands.

'What?' he said.

'I can't talk to her,' said Corin.

'Your mum?'

'No. Lizzie.'

'Since when?'

'Since a long time. She's a stranger.'

'Say this to your mum?'

'Dad, you are so out of touch with this family.'

He depressed the toaster lever.

Corin said, 'Saw her yesterday near the market. Three-thirty, around then.'

'Yes?'

'With streeters. Shitfaced. She's crossed over, big time.'

There had been a previous episode of wagging school. How long ago was that? Months? A year?

'I thought this stuff was over?' said Villani. 'I thought she'd settled down.'

'No, Dad. The school wants to kick her out.'

'Well, Jesus,' said Villani, 'I don't know this.'

Corin was putting her plate and spoon away. Silence.

'Why?' said Villani. 'Why was I not told?'

'Dad, you only sleep here, you pass over this house like a cloud shadow.'

Corin left the room. He waited and he heard the front door close. She'd always kissed him goodbye. She'd never gone out without a kiss. Or had she? Perhaps she'd stopped long ago?

The toaster clicked, toast shot up. He removed the slices, burnt, wrong setting. He gave them to the bin.

He went down the passage and opened Lizzie's door, it was on the cool side of the house, the room dark, air dead, heavy with breathed air, sour, and faintly sweet. A small, curved, broken ridge rose from the landscape of the bed. He could see a thin arm, fallen to the floor, elbow joint white as an old bone, fingernails almost touching the carpet.

The room was a tip – clothes, bags, shoes, towels, no floor visible.

He went to wake her and then he could not bring himself to. Let her sleep, I'll talk to her later.

He closed the door and left the house. He knew he was being weak. He knew he should have woken her, talked to her, showed concern, put the hard word on her. What the hell was Laurie doing in Queensland while her daughter was running wild?

At the gate, he leaned out of the car window and cleared the mailbox: junk, bills.

IN THE ghostly city, he saw the newspaper bales being dumped, the lost people, the homeless, the unhinged, a man and a woman sitting on the kerb passing a bottle, a figure face down, crucified in a pool of piss, the unloaders of fruit and vegetables, men lumping pieces of animals sheathed in hard white fat and shiny membrane, a malbred dog in a gutter, eating something, shaking his grey eusuchian head. As he crossed the bridge, the mist opened and showed a skiff thin as a pencil, two men drawing a line on the cold river.

Parked, the world waiting for him, every minute would be taken, he sat head down. Laurie had begun to go on the two- or three-day advertising shoots around the time she fell pregnant with Lizzie, she didn't tell him until she was more than four months. It wasn't until Lizzie was about five that it occurred to Villani that she looked like neither of them.

He hadn't been much of a father to her.

He hadn't been much of a father to Corin and Tony either. He'd never given any thought to being a father. He wasn't ready for marriage, never mind children. He went to work, paid the bills. Laurie did the take and fetch, the school stuff, the worrying about temperatures, coughs, pains, sore throats, a broken wrist, tooth knocked out, parent-teacher meetings, reports, bullying. She told him, he half-listened, made sounds, went out the door or fell asleep.

He'd looked after kids. He'd had his turn. All the years seeing to Mark and Luke, *see to* was his father's term, you had to see to the horses, the dogs, the chooks – helpless creatures, they suffered, they died, if you didn't see to them.

Mark got his mother's genes, a teacher's genes, not the genes of Bob Villani, brumby-hunter's son left school at fourteen, found a home in army barracks, found his vocation in killing people in Vietnam. Luke was another matter. His mother was a bike called Ellen. Bob Villani bunned her in Darwin. Just before dark one July day, she arrived at the farm in a taxi, tight pants, red-dyed hair.

They were alone, the two of them, Bob was on the road, he was driving Melbourne–Brisbane then, gone the whole week, came home, five or six beers, four eggs scrambled, half a loaf of bread, he slept face down till around nine on Saturday. Mark went into his room every ten minutes from sunrise, looked for signs that he was breathing, studied him for signs of waking up.

Monday morning, Bob Villani left before dawn, blast on the airhorn at the gate, money on the kitchen table.

'He's not here,' said Villani.

'When's he comin back?' she said.

'Not sure,' said Villani.

She looked at Mark behind him, back at Villani. 'You his kids?' she said, she had a grating voice.

They nodded. She waved the taxi away.

'Brought your half-brother,' she said.

Luke came out from behind her, a fat little shit, long hair. For the first three days, he whined, she smacked him, he howled, she kissed and hugged him, he started whining again.

Bob Villani came back on Friday night just before nine. Mark and Ellen and Luke were watching the snowy television. Villani was making a model plane on the kitchen table. He caught the sound of the rig five kilometres away, the downshifts climbing

Camel Hill, the chatter of the jake brake as it slowed on the steep slope before the turn-off from the main road. And then the airhorn, long and lonely, hanging in the aching-cold black.

He went to open the gate, waited in the dark, shivering, the mover came around the bend like a building. It slowed, inched through the gate, towered above him, he closed the gate, walked down the drive.

Bob was out of the truck, stretching.

'Where's Mark?' he said.

'There's a woman here,' said Villani. 'Ellen. With a kid.'

Silence. Bob put a hand through his hair.

Deep in the night, the sounds from his father's room woke him. He thought his father was killing Ellen. It was the first time he ever heard fucking.

Mark woke. 'What's that?' he said. 'Stevie, what's that?' He was a boy who frightened easily.

'Nothing,' said Villani. 'She's having a bad dream. Put your head under the pillow.'

On Monday morning, Bob Villani took Villani and Mark to school in the truck, they rode like gods, they looked down on tiny cars, utes.

'They staying, Dad?' said Mark.

'We'll see,' said Bob. 'Keep an eye on Tomboy, Steve. Off his feed.'

When they got out, Bob gave Villani the thumbs up, said what he always said: 'Carry on, sergeant-major.'

On the Friday, when Luke was asleep, Ellen walked to the farm gate, a tradie gave her a lift to Paxton. She was never heard of again, not by the boys – not a letter, not a postcard. Villani and Mark came home from school, found the boy snailed on his bed, keening, snotted cheeks.

Looking at Luke, weeks after his mother had shot through,

Bob Villani said, 'And the bloody taxi driver reckons I owe him sixty bucks for taking her to Stanny.'

It came to Villani that, in never giving a thought to being a father, he was just being his father's son. All of Bob was in him: the big hands, the hair, the delegation of responsibility, the eyes that saw everything through crosshairs. Everything except the courage. He didn't have that. He had learned to behave as if he had it because Bob Villani expected it of him, took it for granted. He had joined the cops because he didn't have courage, started boxing because he didn't have courage.

Never take a backward step, son. Bad for the soul.

Bob Villani's terrible injunction had been at his throat all his life.

Villani raised his head. Winter, standing in front of his car, head forward, peering.

He got out.

'Worried me there, boss,' said Winter, a reed-thin man with a moustache grown to hide an unpredictable upper-lip twitch, some nerve short-circuit, two threads coming close, arcing.

'Meditating,' said Villani. 'Going inward. You should try it.'

In the lift, he said, 'Getting home before they're asleep?'

'Trying, boss, yeah.'

'Well, bear in mind the clients are the dead,' said Villani. 'We are the living. Although it may not always feel that way.'

'Staying level's my aim, boss.' Winter's gaze was down.

'And that's a receding target around here,' said Villani.

They arrived, Winter stood back. He was Singo's last recruit, a CIB junior. Singo had broken the rule that Homicide only took senior detectives. Senior detectives brought with them attitude. Singo wanted people in whom he could instil attitude. His.

At his desk, the trilling, the incoming paper. Soon, two calls on hold, two people outside. The morning went, he ate a salad roll at 11.30, standing at the window, phoning Laurie. Wherever she was, Darwin, Cairns, Port Douglas, she didn't answer her mobile. He sent an SMS: *Call me.*

What was Birkerts doing on Oakleigh? Why hadn't Dove reported?

Phone. Tomasic.

'Thought I should let you know, boss,' he said. 'Oakleigh, there's an electronics outfit around the corner. They just got back from a trade show thing, looked at their security set-up.'

'Yes?'

'Got a camera, triggered by sensors. Covers 90 degrees. They've got vision of the street. Vision Sunday night, early Monday morning.'

'Yes?'

'It's 2.23am, a vehicle. Then opposite direction, vehicle, 2.51am.'

'Get it in here,' said Villani. 'Maximum speed.'

THE VEHICLE in the frozen frame was a blur, red-tinged. In the top right-hand corner of the picture, a display said: 2.23.07.

'A Prado, I'd say,' said Tomasic. 'They all look a bit the same.'

2.51.17: vehicle, opposite direction.

'Prado again.' said Tomasic.

'Petrolhead?' said Birkerts.

'Just an interest, boss.'

'Let's see it coming and going,' said Villani.

They watched at different speeds.

'What's that in the background?' said Villani.

'Can't say, boss.'

'Street vision, please, Trace.'

On the big monitor, the overhead view of Oakleigh moved from the house across the tin roofs to the corner, changed to an eye-level view.

'Left,' said Villani. 'Stop.'

It was a long low building with showroom-sized windows.

'Run the tape,' he said.

The Prado, turning left . . .

'Stop,' said Villani. 'Back slowly . . . stop.'

Silence in the room.

'In the window,' said Villani. 'Numberplate light reflected.'

'Missed that,' said Birkerts. 'Fuck.'

'See what the techs can do,' said Villani. He looked at Birkerts appraisingly.

'Tommo, tell Fin we want all light-coloured Prados on the tollway from, oh, 2am to 3am, both directions,' said Birkerts.

'Yes, boss.'

'And the prints in the place,' said Villani. 'What the fuck's going on there?'

Birkerts put his head down. 'I'll check. Boss.'

Villani got back to the work. Life went on. Life and death.

Colby's words:

. . . stuff like this, the media blowies on you, bloody pollies pestering, the ordinary work goes to hell. And then you don't get a result quickly and you're a turd.

The post-mortem on the naked woman in her pool in Keilor said fluid in lungs greatly in excess of what drowning required. What did that mean?

A level-six resident of the Kensington Housing Commission flats found on the concrete five metres from the base of the building. Dead of injuries consistent with a fall from that height. Wearing panties, a bra and a plastic Pope John Paul mask. Male.

In Frankston, in a house, a girl, unidentified, around fifteen, strangled. Two unidentified males said to live there missing.

Somali youth stabbed in Reservoir. In the back with a screwdriver, into the heart. Phillips head. Dead on arrival. Sixty-odd people at a social gathering.

The radio:

. . . hoping for a wind shift as firefighters battle to keep the blaze from breaking containment lines above the towns of Morpeth and Paxton . . .

He found his mobile, went to the window, saw the liquid city, the uncertain horizon. It took three tries.

'It's me.'

'What?'

'You going now?' He knew the answer.

Throat clearing. 'Nah. Took the horses over to old Gill. Put them in with his. He's got a set-up sprays the stable. All day you have to.'

'You better get in there with them. You and Gordie.'

Bob's hard laugh. 'No, mate, no. Gordie's got an old firetruck. Full. Be our own CFA.'

'That's going to save my trees?'

'It comes, son, only the good Lord can save the trees.'

'First mention of him I've heard from you.'

'Figure of speech. Make it Father Christmas.'

'I'll ring,' said Villani. 'Answer the bloody phone, will you?'

'Yes, boss.'

His mobile rang.

'I came home,' said Corin, no breath. 'Lizzie comes out with this creature, he's old, filthy, dreadlocks, tatts on his face, between his eyes and she's got a bag, and . . . Dad, all my money's gone, four hundred and fifty bucks and my iPod and my pearl pendant and my silver bracelets, she's been through Mum's things, I don't know what she's taken and . . .'

'Stop,' said Villani. 'Stop.'

He heard her quick, ragged breathing.

'Now we will take a few deep breaths,' he said.

'Right . . . yes.'

'So. Slowly in, slowly out. Let's do that. In . . .'

They did four, he heard the calm come to her.

'Right,' she said. 'Over that now. I'll kill the little bitch.'

She was part her mother and she was part Villani. Bob would be proud, he would like the kill part, he knew when it was time to put something down, he took the old dog away and shot it, buried it, they never found out where.

'Darling, I want you to wait there,' he said. 'Someone'll ring soon. Give them descriptions of Lizzie, her clothes, the bloke, anything that'll help pick them in the street, in a crowd. The bag she's carrying, don't forget the bag.'

'Okay,' said Corin, brisk, composure regained. 'Fine. Should I ring Mum?'

'We'll reel Lizzie in first, no point making your mum sweat in Darwin. Wherever she is.'

'Cairns, Dad, Cairns.'

'I'll write that down. You shouldn't keep that much money in cash, that's not smart.'

'Gee, thanks, Dad. I'll write that down.'

'Tried ringing Lizzie?' He realised he didn't have her mobile number.

'It's never on,' said Corin. 'Anyway I don't want to talk to her. You ring her.'

'Give me the number.'

'Don't you have it?'

'Somewhere. Give it to me.'

Villani wrote it on a card, put it in his wallet. 'Wait for the call, love,' he said. He tapped Lizzie's number. Not switched on.

Sitting for a few moments. You could not do this like a civilian, you needed the brothers. He calculated the price, punched the numbers, identified himself.

Vickery came on, the harsh cigarette voice, 'Stevo. What can you do for me, son?'

Villani told the story.

'Touches everyone this shit,' said Vickery. 'I'll get the word out there. Someone will ring your girl shortly. Number?'

'In your debt,' said Villani when he had given Corin's mobile number.

'Mate, we're all in debt to each other,' said Vickery. 'Brothers, good times and bad. Know that, don't you?'

He was talking about their meeting, about Greg Quirk.

'Indeed I do. Call me direct?'

'Give me the number.'

Villani gave it.

'Get together for a gargle, you and me and other old comrades,' said Vickery.

'We will,' said Villani.

The phone, Tomasic, another hoarse voice.

'Boss, the window reflection, the techs got the first two numbers off the Prado.'

'I'm switching you,' said Villani. 'Don't go anywhere.'

He pressed buttons. 'Ange, take Tomasic off me for Tracy.'

Pause.

'Trace, Tommo's got two rego digits from the Oakleigh Prado. A little chance here.'

'On it, boss,' she said, a lilt of joy in her voice.

Sitting back, the adrenalin surge, he felt for a moment that he belonged in Singo's chair: Stephen Villani, the boss of Homicide. Someone who deserved to be the boss of Homicide.

A moment.

TRACY IN the door, alight.

'Boss, the numbers, a Prado on the tollway, the time's right. We match a James Heath Kidd, 197 Cloke Street, Essendon.'

Tracy was clever, overworked, not a sworn person. At any time, she could tell them she was going elsewhere. He feared that. She had been in love with Cashin, everyone knew it, Cashin knew it and it scared Cashin.

'A likely person,' said Villani. 'Let's look at his abode.'

'Ordinary house with garage, shed, that kind of thing.'

'Can I get a chance to initiate something?' said Villani. 'Feel like I'm the brains of the outfit?'

She smiled her downturned smile, left. Birkerts appeared.

'Cloke Street from on high, detective,' said Villani. 'High and well away, going somewhere else. Spook the cunt, they will patrol the Hume until they retire.'

Birkerts inclined his head.

'And have the Salvos take a walk around there,' said Villani. 'In minutes, no buggering around.'

He sat for a time, got to work reading the currents. It did no good to create more urgency than was useful. *Save a level of excitement for the Second Coming.* Singleton. The master's voice.

Then he went to Tracy's desk, stood behind her. She was looking at her monitor, wrists up, hands dangling over her keyboard. She had long fingers. He had never noticed her fingers. She looked at him, the light caught the down on her upper lip.

'What?' she said.

'Running him through the lot?'

'Of course. Inspector.'

Villani went back, eyed the big room – the hung-up jackets, desks lost beneath files, boxes, stacked in-trays, mugs standing on walls of folders, cropped domes facing monitors. As if from a grave, a hand came up and drew down a speckled mug.

Ten years, how many hours here, sixteen-hour days? Would your daughter be on the streets with scum if you'd lived some other life, ordinary civilian kind of life? Home around six, check the home-work, watch the news, join in the cooking, eat together, talk about things, what's happening at school. Next weekend, get your back-sides out of bed, I'll teach you to ride a board, taught by an expert, now an expert will pass it on to you.

He became aware of eyes on him, aware of the dead air, of the humming, of a running-water sound – perhaps a failed lavatory cistern seal, a ruptured air-conditioner, fire sprinklers soaking empty offices above them.

He went back and rang Kiely.

'Inspector,' he said, 'prepare to bring down the full weight of the surveillance state on this Kidd – family, friends, dogs, the lot.'

'Inspector.'

'But with delicacy. The prick gets a sniff . . .'

'I've run this sort of thing before.'

'In New Zealand,' said Villani. 'We're not talking mystery sheep killings here.' Too far – much too far, regret. 'A bad joke. No more sheep jokes. I promise.'

'Not a problem,' said Kiely. 'Runs off you. You know it's only shitheads keep making them.'

'Wow,' said Villani. 'That's a throat punch. Take out a big woolly ram with that punch.'

He called Barry.

'WE THINK we've got a vehicle at Oakleigh, boss.'

Barry said, 'Boyo, tell me it's much more than you think.'

'We got the last two digits of a white Prado's number off a security camera. We have a white Prado match on the tollway forty minutes on. The timing is right.'

'And you have the owner's name?'

'Yes, sir. Doesn't mean he's the driver.'

Barry spoke to someone in the room with him. Villani couldn't hear what he said.

'What's his name?' said Barry.

'Kidd. James Heath Kidd.'

'James Heath Kidd. Now that's promising,' said Barry. 'Told Mr Colby?'

'About to, boss.'

'Why don't you wait a few minutes, Stephen? Ten. That's a good wait.'

'We may need a Section 27 from him in minutes. Emergency authorisation.'

'Right. Do that then.' Barry made a gargling sound. 'You'll be taking proper care here, Stephen? To avoid stuffing this thing up.'

'My word, boss.'

'But you won't be taking too long?'

The call-waiting light.

'Not a second longer than it takes to avoid a stuff-up,' said Villani. 'Boss.'

'Good man.'

The waiting call.

Corin.

'Dad, this cop rang. I told her everything. I think I should call Mum. She's never going to forgive us . . .'

'Ring her,' said Villani. 'She doesn't return my calls. Tried Lizzie's mobile?'

'Yes. Every ten minutes. Off. What about you?'

'Same. You home tonight?'

'I'm having dinner with Gareth and his father. At Epigram.'

Gareth. Someone he should know. Someone who had a father, not a dad, a parent taken seriously, who took you to dinner at expensive restaurants.

'Gareth is?'

'I've told you. His father's Graham Campbell. Campbell Connaught Bryan?'

His daughter dining with a super-rich corporate lawyer and his son.

'Ah, that Gareth,' he said. 'Listen, you telling me Lizzie's on drugs?'

'Jesus, Dad, you a cop or what?'

'I'd be happier as a what. Just tell me.' He had set his mind against it.

'Well, on, what does on mean? She's hanging out with this shitface, don't be naïve.'

It came to that.

Villani said, 'Listen, when they find her, I might call you, spoil your evening, okay?'

Just one second too long. 'I don't actually want anything to do with her, Dad.'

'She's your sister, Corin.'

'First she's your kid.'

'Okay, forget it,' he said. 'Have a good time.'

'Dad,' said Corin. 'I'll come. Call me and I'll come.'

His girl. Someone who loved him. What the hell had Laurie been thinking? Lizzie was fifteen, no one at home most of the time, what did her mother think would become of her?

Then, as if looking into a mirror, he saw his stupidity and he looked away from himself, shamed.

Tracy.

'Boss, Kidd's ex-force. Special Operations Group for three years, five years' service in total. Resigned three years ago.'

'Oh Jesus, what's his record?'

'On the beat, second year, cleared of using excessive force on a mental who died. Since quitting, two speeding offences.'

'Get me the SOG boss, whatever musclebrain that now is.'

It took six minutes. Villani thought about Deke Murray, Matt Cameron's best mate, the Armed Robber who became SOG boss. He was called The Unforgiver, never forgot, never forgave.

The man's name was Martin Loneregan.

'Mate, a James Kidd,' said Villani. 'Left three years ago.'

'What's this?'

'Serious stuff.'

'Yeah?'

'Yeah.'

'Well, he quit.'

'Why?'

'People quit, they quit.'

Villani said, 'I'd appreciate your help here, Martin. Concerns dead people.'

'Kidd's involved?'

'The name's got our attention.'

'Well, there's procedure, privacy. All that.'

'Martin, Commissioner Barry will ask you the questions, that'll take a few minutes I'd like to save. This a mate thing?'

Spitting sound.

'Personality issues,' said Loneregan. 'A selection failure, basically.'

'Took three years to notice?'

'People comment on how you run Homicide?'

'Sorry, mate.'

'Yeah, well, I'll just say the arsehole pressed the down button three weeks after I took over. Had to send out for Kleenex for the whole squad.'

'Not lovable then. So some violent drug thing, you'd say that?'

'Any kind of shit you care to name. The boy's psycho.'

'Trouble you for an address?' said Villani.

'Hang on.'

He hung, closed his eyes, moved his head.

'You there?' said Loneregan.

'Here,' said Villani.

'It's a unit, 21, Montville, 212 Roma Street, South Melbourne.'

Villani tapped it in, the image of the area appeared, 212 arrowed. 'Much obliged.'

'Bob Villani. Relation?'

'My dad.'

'Vietnam?'

'Yeah, he was, yeah.'

'Still ticking?' said Loneregan.

'Last time I looked.'

'Mate, ask him about a Danny Loneregan. Daniel. My old man. Just got this one photo, it's three blokes, one's a Bob Villani.'

Another member of The Team. First in, last out. Ten years, four months, sixteen days, the longest serving unit in any war, just a thousand men in all and four Victoria Crosses, a hundred and ten other decorations.

My dad says your dad's got war medals.

That was how Villani found out about Bob's war. He would never have learned anything about Vietnam from Bob.

'Yes, certainly do that,' said Villani. 'Thanks for your help.'

'Given under duress. We'll be loaded with this cunt. Not the force, no. It only accepted him. It'll be member of elite Special Operations Group gone bad, all that shit.'

'Well, price you pay for fame.' Villani was looking at the close-up. There was a house over the wall from the parking area, a long narrow swimming pool. 'Kidd didn't leave any mates with you did he?'

'I can say not a single fucking soul.'

'Buy you a coldie, then.'

'Got my number,' said Loneregan. 'Listen, my old man. Ask, will you? When you see your dad. He might have a picture, y'know . . .'

In the kickarse voice Villani heard the boy who never had a father, only a photograph, a face, he would look for himself in that face.

'Didn't come back?' said Villani.

'No,' said Loneregan.

'Well. Honoured dead.'

'Shot outside a bar. Bar, whorehouse.'

'I'll ask Bob,' said Villani. 'Get back to you.'

He rang Colby.

'This is as of when?' said Colby.

'Just on the radar. We hope to need a Section 27. Mr Kiely will be on to you.'

'I'll pass the word. Run anything major by me. Think Cromarty, son. Think never again.'

Would they ever let him forget Cromarty? His crime was to trust senior officers to behave like trained policemen.

'Yes, boss,' Villani said.

'A fucking arrest, that's the ticket. Show we're getting somewhere. With me?'

'Boss.'

Villani looked at the tendon standing proud of his forearm. He relaxed his grip on the handset.

Birkerts outside. Villani waved.

'The Salvos have been there,' he said. 'Essendon is Kidd's aunt's house. Her name's Hocking. She says he stayed there long ago, still gets mail, still drops by. Gave her an early Christmas present this year – thousand bucks, cash. Wouldn't let her open the envelope while he was there.'

'You could love such a boy,' said Villani.

Kiely in the door.

'The chopper says no vehicle visible at Cloke Street. We've got a J. H. Kidd off the tenants' database. Roma Street, South Melbourne.'

'That's him,' said Villani.

'It's a block of flats, third-floor flat. The chopper's looking now.'

Villani waved, they left. He sat, hands in his lap, palms up, the scar ran from little finger to the right thumb pad, his first year in the job, sliced by a cook, the cut went to the bones.

Rose Quirk's garden.

Jesus. He hadn't been there since Cup Day, the day he put in the tomatoes.

He dialled. It rang, rang, he knew it was going to ring out, she answered.

'Ma, Stephen.'

'Where've you been?'

'Busy. Yeah. Really busy, tied up. You okay?'

'I'm fine. Just a bit weak.'

'Taking the tablets?'

She did a bit of her coughing, he knew her coughing, it was a tactical move. 'Make me feel sick,' she said.

'For God's sake, Ma, take them.'

'Weeds takin over here.'

'I'll fix the weeds. Take the tablets. Tomatoes coming on?'

'They like the hot. I give them a little drip every night.'

'Good. I'll be around soon as I can.'

'Screen door's buggered. Something wrong with the pump thing.'

'I can get someone to fix it.'

'Don't want a stranger here.'

'Okay, I'll do it. Listen, got to go. Be around soon.'

'PRADO'S AT Roma Street,' said Birkerts. 'At the back.'

'Nice work,' said Villani.

'There's a chance of vision from across the road. Building going up. Rear access.'

'Section 27 from Colby,' said Villani. 'A 26 and a 27, cover all bases. He's expecting you.'

'My view,' said Kiely, 'my view is if he's there we should take him out.'

'Talk to the dogs, Birk,' said Villani. 'Impress upon them the need to get the stuff in now, immediately, sooner, they have no higher priority. Or they will answer to the minister. Or God.'

'Sir.'

Birkerts left. Villani looked at Kiely. 'Arrest him, you think?'

'That's prudent, yes. I think so.'

'And then we've got him and he dobs the other pricks? Wow.'

'Wow?' said Kiely.

'Yes, wow. Wow, wow. He still gets twenty years, twenty-three hours a day looking at walls, your fellow crims wait, they want to kill you, fuck you, they do so love a doggy.'

Kiely scratched his collarbone. 'Well, not to move, I would say that should be cleared. Approved.'

'The New Zealand way,' said Villani. 'Interesting. Now here on the mainland we're different. What we don't do here is seek approval for what we do not want to do. And moving on, let me say that if we lose Kidd, even if the cunt takes off in a balloon, I will be holding . . .'

Kiely raised a hand. 'Yes,' he said. 'Made yourself perfectly clear.'

He left. Villani's mobile rang.

'What's going on?' Laurie said.

'Corin tell you?'

'Yes.'

'Well, that's what's going on.'

'Can't you find her?'

'Doing my best. People are looking for her.'

'People? What about you?'

'The whole fucking force is looking for her. Is that good enough? Is that doing enough?'

A sigh.

'I'll be there around midnight,' she said. 'Ring me if you find her.'

'I'll certainly do that. Keep trying her mobile.'

'I don't need to be told that, thank you.'

Line dead.

Villani tried Lizzie's number again. Off.

THE TARRED top of a building, a lift housing. The camera moved down, glass distortion, a room, a big television, squat furniture, coffee table holding bottles, cans, cups, junkfood containers.

Jerry the tech in headphones, fiddling, tapping, talking to his throat mike. 'Yeah, piss-poor, yeah, okay, here we go. On air, mate.'

Birkerts at the scene, scratchy, said, 'Across the road on the sixth floor, very trying conditions here, wet concrete, no windows, just holes.'

'Picture's very poor,' said Kiely, fiddling with his earpiece.

'Spot that?' said Villani.

Birkerts said, 'Prado's at the back, two ways in. Here we go, you can see a kitchen. So to speak.'

Slow zoom in to a littered countertop – boxes, bottles, a shiny object.

'Boy's got an industrial coffee machine,' said Birkerts. 'The red, that's from the back window, sunset in the west.'

'My, the west,' said Villani. 'Know your compass.'

'Pulling back, that's a door at left.'

A dark shape.

'Passage probably runs front door to balcony. The kitchen and lounge to left. Right, it's bathroom and bedroom.'

Villani said, 'We can get in the back?'

'Fire escape and there's a door to the lobby from the parking area.'

The camera roved left to a blank window, right to another, down to the floors below, to the forecourt, the street, parked cars, two men with briefcases, a car, another, a delivery van, a strung-out scuffle of teenagers, four, nothing.

They watched for a while. The camera went back to Kidd's windows, lingered, dropped. The street seemed to have darkened. Streetlights came on, small white flares.

Back. Kidd's windows dark now, the sun gone from the back of the building, fallen.

'Nice little street,' said Villani. 'You comfy there? Got the toothbrush?'

Angela motioned from the door. He went out.

'Mr Colby, boss.'

Villani took the call at his desk.

'Got him?' said Colby.

'Got his unit. Vehicle's out the back.'

'And the plan is?'

'A good look.'

'Steve, if the prick's there, take him. Get the SOGs.'

'And give away upstream?'

'Not listening, son. Still not fucking listening.'

'Can you say again, boss?'

He heard finger taps.

'The head of Homicide,' said Colby. 'You're in the tower, it's your call. We rely on your judgment.'

Villani went back to the operations room, put on the headset, looked at the dark building. The camera pulled back. Lights on in the units on both sides of Kidd's and the one below.

'Dunny,' said the tech. 'Someone's there.'

'How'd you hear?'

'The hard line. Phone must be close. Bedroom or the passage.'

Kiely coughed. 'Tell Mr Colby?'

'Nothing to tell,' said Villani. 'Could be anyone. Girlfriend. Flatmate. House-trained dog.'

They waited. Five minutes, ten, it was soothing, doing nothing, watching the camera wander around, the operator bored, up, down, sideways, along the street. Villani closed his eyes.

Lizzie. In the early days, he sometimes came home to find them asleep, in the big bedroom or on Lizzie's bed. Often they were in the armchair, mother and child as one, Laurie's hair fallen like dark thatch over the infant's face.

IN HIS ear, Birkerts said, 'He's gone back to sleep.'

Villani looked at his watch. Forty minutes since the lavatory was flushed. 'I'm coming to join you,' he said. 'On-site inspection.'

'We have nothing to hide. Please use the servants' entrance.'

Finucane drove, Winter came. A few blocks away from the street, Villani's phone rang.

'Inspector, Senior Willans, St Kilda, your daughter Lizzie's here, brought in by officers.'

'Found where?'

'The parade, boss. With a group.'

'She's okay?'

'Um, speak freely, boss?'

'Yes.'

'Off her face, boss.'

Fifteen years old. The child in her arms in the armchair wandering the hard streets of St Kilda. How had Laurie allowed this to come to pass?

'Okay. Hang on to her, be there soon as I can.'

'Boss, she's a handful, there's nowhere, just the cells . . .'

The cells.

No liquid known, not carbolic acid, not citric acid, not all the tears of the risen Christ could cleanse the holding cells of their perfume of sweat, blood, vomit, shit, snot, spit, semen, piss and fart and phlegm.

His daughter taken to the holding cells, on her father's instructions. He should phone Corin, get her to fetch Lizzie. No, he
couldn't do that to Corin: call her away from dinner at Epigram
with her young Trinity College smartarse and his millionaire
lawyer father to fetch her freaked-out fifteen-year-old sister from
the St Kilda police station.

Winter glanced at him. They were almost there. Jesus, what a
time for crap like this to happen.

The cells wouldn't hurt Lizzie. What the hell, give her a taste
of what came from hanging around with shitheads, doing
drugs.

'Put her in a cell,' Villani said. 'Alone, mark you.'

'Boss.'

They went in the long way. A cop in overalls waved them
through a construction-site gate, they parked beside a crane. A
woman from surveillance led him and Winter up rough stairs, the
damp, sour, heady smell of new concrete. Outside a shadowy
doorless chamber Birkerts stood. Inside, two people sat at the
blocked-out window holes, one behind a camera, one with night-
glasses, looking through a slit.

Kidd's building was on a shrouded monitor. The woman gave
him headphones with a throat mike. He was adjusting them when
Jerry the tech, kilometres away, said, 'Incoming. Mobile.'

In the dark room, looking at the windows on a monitor, they
listened to a phone ringing. It went on, on, ten, fifteen seconds,
it rang out, became a buzz. It began again, ringing . . .

Yeah?

Wake-up call, mate.

Fuck off.

Listen, listen, some worries. Serious.

What?

Old girl's, call you on that in five, okay?

Yeah, okay, right.

Clicks.

'What's that about?' Kiely's voice.

'Got the caller?' said Villani.

'Mobile,' said Jerry. 'Won't get anywhere.'

The voice in Villani's head.

Old girl's, call you on that in five, okay?

Old girl? Old girl?

Kiely said, 'Laser'll be . . .'

'Kidd's aunt,' said Villani. 'Mrs Hocking. Run her for mobiles, the hotline.'

'Right.'

They waited.

The sitting room lit up.

A big naked man in the room, scratching his scalp with both hands, then his chest, his right hand went to his groin.

Birkerts said, 'Himself. The target.'

The man was going to the kitchen counter, they saw his body-builder's wedge back, the muscular canyon of his spine, he was turning, they saw him side on.

'My Jesus,' said Birkerts. 'Like a low branch. He's dialling . . . do we have this?'

'No,' said Jerry.

Villani said, 'The fixed line, Jerry?'

'Too far away.'

'I understood we'd have the laser by now,' said Birkerts. 'The highest tech known to man.'

'Mr Kiely?' said Villani.

'Check that,' said Kiely. 'Want me to brief Mr Colby?'

'Just get the fucking laser here. The Prado's tagged?'

'Elephant on the move,' said Birkerts.

Kidd leaving the room.

'Small arse,' said Birkerts, thoughtful.

Three seconds, bedroom light, the vertical blinds opened, they saw Kidd sliding a window.

'But a jockstrap designed for Phar Lap,' said Birkerts.

Vision sliced by blinds, they watched the man moving around, pulling on clothes, sitting on the bed, shoes going on.

'No shower,' said Birkerts. 'This isn't date behaviour. Prado wired?'

'Inspector Kiely to confirm that,' said Villani.

It was dawning that this was a bad mistake. Colby and Kiely were right. He should have sent in the SOGs. If they lost Kidd now, it would be his fault, his alone.

Kidd up, leaving the bedroom.

'Brush teeth, take a piss,' said Birkerts. 'I would . . . Jesus Christ, who's this?'

A figure in the sitting room, slim, long hair.

Going to the kitchen, ducking behind the counter, just the top of his head visible.

'Flatmate?' said Villani. 'Boyfriend?'

Standing up, T-shirt, coming around the counter, hands behind his back, torso wriggling.

'What's he doing?' said Birkerts.

'Could be a piece,' said Villani. 'Inside-pants holster. Here's Kidd.'

Kidd and the man talking, Kidd's right hand in the air. The second man had a long nose.

Villani became aware of someone else in the dark room with them. Tomasic.

Kiely's voice. 'Problem with the tag. Some misunderstanding.'

'Misunderstanding?' Villani said. 'What the fuck's to misunderstand?'

'Didn't quite get the urgency.'

'Jesus Christ.'

It was too late but this was the moment.

'I want the SOGs now,' Villani said. 'Highest priority.'

'Well, that's a . . .'

'Just do it, inspector. Now.'

'These blokes might be going out,' said Birkerts. 'Are we ready for that?'

'Inspector Kiely?' said Villani.

'They say they're stretched, thought they had more time.'

Villani said, 'Three dead's not a priority? I'll personally kill every last cunt if we lose them.'

The second man left the room. Kidd silhouetted against the kitchen light. His head slightly turned, they could see his profile, the heavy ridge above his eyes. He was talking on a mobile, putting it away, crossing the room, sliding open the balcony door, going to the railing, looking at the street, putting his hands behind his head, moving his torso from side to side.

'Go down,' said Villani.

The street, nothing moving.

'Up.'

Kidd rubbing his face with both hands, his scalp, looking at his watch, going inside, closing the door, leaving the sitting room. Out of sight.

'Not going out, I'd say,' said Birkerts.

They watched the empty rooms. Villani felt the tightness in his scalp, around his mouth. Something wasn't right.

'Don't like this,' he said.

They waited. A minute. Two.

Villani knew. 'Fucking gone,' he said.

Just walked out their own front door and no one there.

Get there before the Prado took off, that was all they could do.

'Have to be our own SOGs,' he said.

He went for the door, for the stairs, heard Winter and Tomasic behind him.

THEY CROSSED half a block down.

He sent Tomasic to go around the block, stopper the lane. Winter following, he walked down the street, ran up the narrow driveway of Kidd's building, stopped before the corner, looked around it, one-eyed.

Two security lights lit the small parking area, perhaps a dozen cars, the Prado at the end, a high wall at the back.

Not gone. They were still in the building.

Villani drew the Glock. His mouth was dry. 'I'll take the door,' he said. 'You take the fire escape.'

Winter said, 'Boss.'

Villani went to move and then the back door came open and a figure jumped the three steps, a big man, big upper body.

Kidd.

Villani shouted:

'POLICE! DON'T MOVE!'

Kidd turned his head, kept going, Villani sighted on him, two hands.

Greg Quirk came into his mind. He didn't fire.

A gun in Kidd's hand, left-handed, that had not been noticed. Scarlet-violet muzzle blinks, two, three, whines off the wall above them, Villani was off balance.

Kidd running across the space, moving lightly for a big man, Villani tried to sight on him again, he was heading for the lane, changed direction, made a clean jump onto a car bonnet, seemed to trampoline, put both hands on the top of the wall. He heaved himself up, got his right leg over.

Gone.

To Winter, Villani said, 'Tell them target over back wall, we're following.'

He ran, holstering, climbed onto the bonnet of a VW, it was Laurie's model, he registered that, clambered onto the cab.

Madness. Not the movies, this was SOG work.

He jumped for the wall, pulled himself up.

No Kidd.

A narrow back yard, a wall of glass, no light in the house, a long lap pool, it glowed the green of the inside of a high-summer wave.

Go over?

He was scared. But he had fucked this thing up and all that remained was not to show fear.

Never take a backward step, son. Bad for the soul.

Kidd wouldn't be hanging around, Kidd would be running, trying to get as far away as possible, pick up a car, there was nothing to fear here.

Villani swung over. He hurt his balls, hung, dropped a good metre, hard landing, his knees gave, he lost balance, fell over backwards, rolled, the gun pressed into his lower ribs.

He got to his feet, took the gun out of the spring clip, went along the pool edge. How did Kidd get out of here? The building occupied the whole block, wall to wall, there was a roll-up door to the right, that would give access from the street, a garage with doors at each end.

A slightly open steel door to the right of the garage. There was a way out.

Villani ran for the exit, knelt against the garage wall and pulled the door open, tensed against the bullet.

A lane, another door at the end, open. Twenty strides and he was out onto the pavement.

A leafy street, jammed with parked cars, lamplight in ragged-edged puddles. Left, right? He went right, crossed the road, ran, heard the roar and squeal of a car around the corner, not far away.

He got there. Taillights, brake lights, a vehicle swung right, it was too dark to identify, he heard more tyre complaints, it had turned again.

Someone running. He came around the bend, gun drawn. Tomasic.

'See it?' said Villani.

'Ford,' said Tomasic. 'Two men.'

Winter came up behind Villani, gun in one hand, radio in the other.

'Tell Inspector Kiely we want a chopper,' said Villani. 'Highest priority. Two males, armed.' He gestured to Tomasic.

'Ford Mark 2,' said Tomasic. 'XR6, spoiler, dark colour. Travelling west.'

They walked back, Winter talking to control.

Career-destroying moment, Villani thought. At least he'd gone over the wall after Kidd. They couldn't say he'd shirked it.

IN THE communications vehicle, they watched the monitors. Grey highway vision from the helicopter: four lanes, Western Ring Road, six or seven vehicles visible.

Target behind two semis, he's not in a hurry. Skyeye Two falling back now.

The Ford and two early-start truckies travelling together. Receding vision.

The helicopter said:

Pursuit vehicles entering freeway.

Two cars on the entry ramp.

Static. Radio:

Control to CV, support vehicles on Deer Park ramp await instructions, please.

They looked at him.

Villani said, 'Proceed, stay ahead, do nothing, we are accompanying target to Darwin if necessary.'

The operator repeated his words.

Copy that, Control.

Skyeye Two. Target in sight. He's coming out . . .

The Ford pulling out, not fast, just overtaking.

Level with the back truck.

Deer Park exit approx one kilometre, CV, Control.

The Ford level with the front semi.

He's picking up speed, left lane, could be looking to exit . . . Jesus, that's grunt . . . Jesus . . .

The Ford seemed to jerk left, right, the driver losing control, it crossed two lanes, came back inside, fishtailing, seemed to be braking . . .

He's lost control.

The Ford hit the left guardrail, a massive impact, the bonnet opened.

A puff, grey, like soiled cottonwool.

The semis passing the spot.

Fuck.

A fireball.

Target's exploded. Like a bomb.

Control to all cars, this is Red, repeat Red, pursuit vehicles cordon freeway scene, we need medics . . .

The chopper went in low, hovered over the flames. There was no recognisable car. The engine block lay three metres from the drive shaft, the highway was littered with smoking pieces, the steering wheel a ring of flame, the back seat burning by the roadside. Beside it lay the upper half of a body.

In the van, hair wet with sweat, listening to the radio traffic, Villani watched the pursuit cars arrive, block the highway, apply the emergency drills.

Five dead now.

He said to the operator, 'Tell them weapons in the car, that's the priority.'

EYES IN sockets of gravel, Villani stood in Kidd's kitchen. His mobile rang.

'Stephen, Lizzie, what?' Laurie.

'Okay, yeah. Found her.'

'Where is she?'

Hours ago, how many? His skin felt tight, as if he were expanding.

'Ah, picked up on Beaconsfield Parade with these streeters, shitfaced. She's at the station, I've been tied up, I was on my way . . .'

'Police station?'

'Where are you?'

'On my way from the airport. She's where?'

'St Kilda. They're hanging on to her.'

'Quarter to two, how long's she been there?'

'A while, yeah. Hours. Can you collect her? Bad night for me, I'm not quite done.'

'This is your daughter we're talking about,' said Laurie. 'You miserable fucking bastard.'

End of call.

Colby came in, slit-eyed, slicked hair, hands in windcheater pockets, looked around like a man hired to fumigate the premises.

'Up early, boss,' said Villani. 'Or late.'

'Complete cock-up here,' Colby said.

'Can't argue.'

'No. When did this fucking death wish grip you?'

'I'll say, I'll say there's interesting stuff on the tape.'

Colby stared at him, blood in his eyes, deep lines from his nose. 'Need a leak,' he said. 'Take a piss at your crime scene? Piss in a plastic bag?'

'Down the passage, second left,' said Villani.

He waited, dull mind, watching the fingerprint techs. He felt the weight of his body, the ache in his shoulders, his calves, felt the time since waking.

Finucane at his shoulder. 'Boss, they say ID is going to take time. There's near nothing left of the blokes. But they've got two guns.'

Colby came back. Finucane retreated.

'Putting it mildly,' Colby said, 'you are in damage control big time. Forget about interesting stuff on any fucking tape, that's in lock down. Fucking can of worms.'

'Why?'

A Bob Villani look, the *Jesus, how often do I have to show you?*

'Consider,' said Colby, 'how many people are inside this. The tollway people who told you. Your own holy mob. How many heard the name? Barry's office. Me. What about me? Maybe I'm your dog.'

'So?'

'You tell your people they say a fucking word to anyone about interesting stuff on the tape it's career over. Okay?'

Colby's assistant arrived, spoke to him in a whisper.

'Hyenas are here,' Colby said. 'Courtesy of Searle's meerkats. I'm out the back. Need advice on what to say?'

'No, sir.'

'Don't tell me you've learned something? Don't fucking shock me.'

Villani waited a while. Finucane waited, hands in pockets. They went down, crossed the narrow yellow-tiled space to the glass doors, a uniform opened one. The line was a few metres away, three cops, lights, cameras, fat microphones, scruffy techs.

The talent dropped their cigarettes, stepped up, third-string talent, hair stiff with chemical preparations.

Villani went to the pack, blinded for a few seconds.

'Good morning,' he said, waited.

The Channel Nine youth raised a hand, said, 'Inspector, the Oakleigh killings, this is, we're told, can you confirm . . .'

'No,' said Villani.

'It's not the Oakleigh killings?'

'All I have to say is this is a search of premises in the course of an investigation.'

Silence. This was not the script.

'Inspector, the shots fired . . .'

'It's an attempt to interview someone of interest who left the scene before that could take place,' said Villani. 'Now if you'll excuse me, I have some work to fit in before dawn.'

A woman said, 'Inspector, don't you think we deserve . . .'

Villani wanted to say Channel Seven deserved whatever it got, but he said, 'I can't say anything more because there's nothing to say. Thank you.'

Finucane went ahead, the crowd parted, they walked in the street to the car, halfway down the block. Finucane did a careful U-turn.

'Home, boss?' he said.

'What's that again exactly?' said Villani. 'And where?'

Laurie's VW was in the drive, the passage light on. In lead shoes, Villani walked down the path, stood before the door, looking for the key.

It opened.

Laurie.

'Well, hi,' said Villani. He went to kiss her, a reflex, but she moved back, said nothing.

'Listen, I'm sorry,' he said. 'Very bad day for drama. You got her?'

'No,' she said.

'What?'

'I was parked down Chapel Street. We walked together, I had my arm around her. When we got to the car, I went to my side and she went around to the other side and then she ran away.'

'Jesus Christ.'

'She looked at me and she said, Mum, I can't come home, and she ran off, around the corner.'

'You follow her?'

'I got in the car and drove around the corner. She was gone, she could have been hiding.'

'Tell them at the station?'

'They said they'd put out an alert for her.'

'What the hell have we done to deserve this?' Villani got out his mobile, walked through the house into the back yard, stood in the gloom, made two calls.

Laurie was in the kitchen. 'Anything?' she said.

'Everybody's looking for her. If she's walking around, they'll find her.'

'What?' Corin in the door, in pyjamas.

'I went to pick up Lizzie at St Kilda police station,' said Laurie. 'She ran away.'

'When?'

'Oh, half an hour ago.'

'How long was she there?'

'Hours,' said Villani. 'I had a lot on.'

'Jesus, Dad, why didn't you ring me? I'd have picked her up.'

'Didn't think a bit of reality would hurt her,' said Villani.

'You stupid bastard,' said Laurie. 'Call yourself a father?'

He felt no anger, just a variety of contempt. 'Listen, if you didn't spend half your life in Queensland fucking bloody cameramen, this wouldn't have happened.'

Laurie turned to Corin, 'Go to bed, darling.'

Corin looked at Villani, held up her hands, 'Dad, I said I'd look after her.'

'I know,' said Villani. 'I know.'

'If they find her, wake me,' Laurie said, disgust on her mouth. 'If you can be bothered.'

Villani went to Tony's room in the back yard, had to wrench the door. The room held the smell of a cigarette smoker's kiss. He felt his way to the bed, clicked the lamp. The bulb fizzed, electrocuted itself. He took off his clothes, lay on the bed naked, chest tight.

Think about something else. The smoke, it dated from the night Vic Zable got it in the carpark at the Arts Centre, the day Cashin's brother tried to kill himself. How long ago was that? Six, seven months? It was winter. Cashin slept in this room. But before that they drank two bottles of red, both given the smokes away, smoked most of a packet, talked about the job, life, the choices, the fuck-ups ...

He woke, sat upright, no sense of place, put his feet on the floor.

Where?

He remembered, and he lowered his forehead into his hands, rubbed his eyes with his thumbpads.

It was 7.15. He went into the day, hot already. Laurie's car was gone. Corin was gone, bed made. He showered, shaved, dressed, packed his bags, took everything he still wore, threw the rest in the big bin. Then he drove away, stopped at the milk bar to buy cigarettes.

'Smoking again?' said the owner. 'Work getting ya?'

'Not at all,' said Villani. 'Having so much fucking fun it makes me want to smoke.'

In the car, smoking, no joy in it, he rang Kiely's mobile.

'They get anywhere on IDing the second bloke?'

'Not yet,' said Kiely. 'Got his prints from Kidd's place.'

'Shit,' said Villani. 'Anyway, someone gave Kidd up. So first we need to scope ourselves. Every last person who could have done that. All calls out from the time Tracy ID'd him. That's home, wife, children, the girlfriend, the boyfriend, the lot. Put Burgess to work.'

Kiely coughed. 'Ah, this'll take a while.'

'Of course it'll take a while. Everything takes a fucking while.'

He felt Kiely's hatred enter his ear like warm olive oil.

. . . two still unidentified men died when their car crashed and exploded on the Western Ring Road just after midnight this morning . . .

He headed for Essendon.

IN THE big dim corrugated-iron room, light from the dirty clerestory windows, people skipping, on the bags, in the ring, Villani warmed up shadowboxing at the mirror, no skipping, he could not do that, he could not bear the jolting of the flab. He went on to the speedball, the double-end bag. Stopping, he felt weak in his legs and arms, his hands and elbows and shoulder joints hurt.

He caught the eye of Les in the ring, big sparring gloves on the rope, a tall, white, tattooed kid was getting out, blotches on his arms.

'C'mere,' Les said, beckoned with a glove.

Villani went across the cracked concrete, it held the sweat of sixty years.

'Where you bin?' said Les. 'You look like shit.'

'Work,' said Villani. 'Work and sleep.'

'Fucken tub of lard,' said Les. 'Lookit your legs, fucken cellulite.'

'Just two, three kilos,' said Villani. 'Drop it any time I like.'

'Get in here, drop it with me,' said Les. 'Let's have a little touch-up, sixty-six next birthday, how's that suit you? A bit young for you, cop bastard?'

If he invited you, you had to. Otherwise the place became less welcoming, you had to think about another gym, but there were no other gyms like Bombers except a place in Richmond that was even more clubby, it didn't welcome refugees from Bombers.

Les's amateur record was fifty-one fights, thirty-eight wins, a lightweight, eleven TKOs, he never knocked out a single man, he didn't have the punch, but no one ever knocked him out either. He was a no-nonsense fighter, he wasn't a dancing fool or a slapper. In the pros, his career was short: eleven and four, lost his last three, knocked out twice in a row. The second time, he woke up in the ambulance. And he then showed that he wasn't stupid. He gave it away and began another life: a stablehand, track rider, assistant gym manager, trainer, up at four, bed by nine.

Villani put on a headguard, approached the ring, bugger mouthguard, he wasn't going to be hit in the mouth.

Les pointed at his mouth. 'Got the falsies now? Don't need teeth?'

Villani went to his bag, found the guard, God knew what germs it harboured.

Once, in the early days, he watched Les sparring with a man thirty kilos heavier, a full head and shoulders taller, a North Melbourne football star, a man who fancied himself as a fighter, now a legend, you heard him on the radio talking about the good old days, how tough it was, the blokes he'd flattened. Les was hitting him at will, not hard, stinging him. The man lost control, the red mist, forgot about boxing and went for Les, tried to grab him. Les moved back, stood flatfooted. He hit the man in the face two or three times, then in the ribs, both hands, four or five punches so fast you couldn't distinguish them.

The man dropped his arms, sagged, staggered away trying to breathe, hung onto the rope to keep upright, dry-retched.

'Don't open up like that, mate,' said Les, 'somebody'll hurt you.' He beckoned to his next partner.

In the ring now, Villani went straight for the small lean man, Les had contempt for any messing about, had no time for circling and waving. 'Save that for when you're in the shit,' he said.

Les stood, perfect stance, thin white legs, little white socks, hands not moving, mouth running, *watch me, watch me hands, jeez you're lookin slow, sonny, so fucken slow, watch me . . .*

They exchanged feints, Villani got caught in the face, not hard, *get yer hands up, not fucken Ali,* picked up his hands and took a left and a right in the bottom ribs, it hurt, Les started taking him right, not his good side, he never had a good side, he got a left hand in, Les blinked – *hey, hey, hit an old man, typical fucken cop.*

He met Xavier Dance at Bombers, he would have been nineteen then. Dance was a year or two older, a good boxer, stylish, but he had rushes of blood to the head, lost his concentration. Also he didn't like being hurt. There was still cop boxing then, they fought for the cop title twice, one–all, Villani thought he'd done enough to win the second one. Matt Cameron, the boss of the Robbers, was there that night, he came around and said, 'Ever think about the Robbers? You might be a handy bloke.'

'C'mon,' Les said. 'The right, fatarse, all you ever had.'

'Fuck you.' Villani pushed a few, Les blocked, backed off, stepped in, jab, jab, jab, then his right hit Villani in the face.

Being welcome at Bombers meant being serious about training and boxing and not minding being told by Les what you were doing wrong, why it was he was able to hit you so easily, you fuckhead. He walked you around, smacked you a bit, it didn't hurt much but it was tiring and, even when you were smart to it, after a while it upset your feet, you lost balance, and then he gave you his left hook to the head, to the body, a good punch, not weakening much as the years passed.

'So fucken slow, fatty,' he said now.

They feinted and feinted, Villani went forward, kept his elbows tucked in, tried to push Les back, Les darted left, Villani followed, gave him a flurry of punches, all blocked, Les fooled him, came in, poked him in the solar plexus with a short right hand, hit him in the ribs with a left, pain.

'Jesus,' said Villani. 'Take it easy. I'm tired.'

'You girl,' said Les. 'You cop girl.'

It wasn't amusing. He stalked Les, legs heavy, breathing hard after less than a minute. He never caught him, made a few swipes, lost concentration, tried to take his head off.

'Jeez, we're a fighter now?' said Les. 'Wasted my time. Technique, sonny, technique or you're just an arsehole in a pub.'

Villani started boxing because he wasn't brave, because his father always acted as if his oldest boy was brave and his oldest boy knew he wasn't. That haunted him. He thought boxing might give him courage. It didn't but he loved it from the start – the exercises, the drills. And most of all the sparring, the fighting. In the ring, in the thrall of adrenalin, looking over the fence of your fists into the stone eyes of the other man, a great calm took you.

There was nothing else, a world stopped. Just the two of you, the smell of glove leather, of resin, of the salve, you were in a dance, hypnotised by each other. In the ring, time became elastic, it extended, contracted, extended. You felt alive in a way you never felt otherwise. There was a sense of order, there were rules, there was clear intent, ways and means, there was discipline and power. You felt little pain, your concentration on your opponent was total. He was your universe. He was you and you were him.

Les stopped walking away, came at him, at his face and body, up, down, four, five, six, seven punches, a sequence done ten thousand times, Villani covered, going back, flat-footed, hands too high for a second, just off balance.

The left hand dug into his right armpit, a sharp pain went through his body, Les's right banged into his head, water in his eyes.

Villani shook his head, dropped his hands, panting, nauseous, spat his guard. 'Happy, gramps?' he said. 'Let you hit me a few. Nanna-nap time now?'

Les patted him on the arm. 'Not too bad,' he said. 'For a fucked old cop. Still got a good right, feet work a bit.'

Out of the ring, Les said, 'You want to train here, it's two days a week minimum or fuck off. And don't shit me about work. On the television, all bloody actors, that's what you cop pricks do.'

In the car, his mind went to the Prosilio girl. Her body already so marked by life. Did she start out like Lizzie, a loved child? Who would tell her father his little girl was dead? Fucked to death in a palace.

Lizzie.

Prim little girl with pigtails, she sat on the couch in the old sitting room, before the renovation, didn't watch television, she drew pictures in her big book. He remembered putting her to bed when she was little. First the dolls had to be put to sleep, one at a time, she had about twenty. It took so long he couldn't bear it, he called for Laurie to take over.

Fussy child, she wouldn't eat meat, wouldn't eat fish, didn't like foods mixed on her plate, lifted her upper lip in distaste, showed gum, tiny white stubs, provisional teeth.

It always pissed him off. Corin and Tony had eaten everything.

Jesus, Stephen, don't make an issue of it. It's a phase, some kids are like this.

Not in my day.

Well, maybe trained killers aren't the best role models for parenting. Not a barracks we're living in here.

Knockout punch. He couldn't defend his father, his own upbringing. He wouldn't know how to begin. He'd never thought of Bob as a father, more a dominating older brother, a much,

much older brother who could stop you dead with a look, move a hand in a way that suggested he could backhand you into oblivion. He never did that, he never hit any of them. He didn't have to.

Paul Keogh's grating voice on the radio:

. . . *Keystone Cops events in South Melbourne late last night ended in two dead on the Western Ring Road. I'm reliably told that the prime suspects in the Oakleigh massacre escaped from a block of units in Roma Street while police watched. Yes, people, the place was under high-tech surveillance. Brilliant or what? On the line, we've got the head of police communication, hello Geoff Searle.*

Morning, Paul.

This South Melbourne thing, that's a major cause for concern, isn't it?

With respect, Paul, things happen in police operations no one can control, this was a . . .

Suspects escaped while you watched, that's it, isn't it?

I can't comment on what happened except to say that our officers behaved with the utmost professionalism and . . .

C'mon, Geoff, how sick are you of serving up that old line? Utmost professionalism my bum, not to put too fine a point on it. Two murder suspects escape while you're watching and then they die as a result of a high-speed pursuit . . .

Paul, there was no high-speed pursuit, that's just wrong . . .

I can't expect you to come right out and say what you and I both know, can I? That this South Melbourne cock-up is par for the course, isn't it? What do you say to the rumour that the suspects were tipped off from inside the force?

I say simply ridiculous, Paul. Simply ridiculous. There is absolutely . . .

Let's see what the listeners think, Geoff, let's open the lines and . . .

With respect, Paul, I haven't come here to take part in talkback, I have no authority to do that.

Oh sorry. My mistake. I thought you spoke on behalf of the force? Haven't you just been speaking on behalf of the force? Who exactly do you speak for, Geoff?

COLBY WAS at the window, he went back around the desk. He moved like a young man, he behaved like one too, lived in a high-rise in Docklands with his new wife, a real-estate agent, young, blond, pregnant, it was said.

'Terrible shitstorm this,' he said. 'Hear that fucking Keogh?'

'Yes.'

'That kind of thing is not what the leadership wants to hear around election time.'

'What leadership is that?'

'All the leadership. I thought I was giving off the signals last night. To a bloke knows me a bit. Sit.'

Villani said, 'I listen to advice and I use my judgment.'

'With shit like this,' said Colby, 'you would say the sensible go is call the Soggies, they remove the back wall, simultaneously doing their rope trick, what's it called?'

'Rappelling.'

'Yes, that crap. They grab them, excellent, Oakleigh massacre, men held. If they kill the targets, right pricks, wrong pricks, it's their fault, you walk away blaming gun-crazy gymrats.'

'Over the years,' said Villani, 'I've gained the impression Homicide's business is catching people who've killed other people. Putting them on trial.'

Colby put his hands behind his neck, rolled his head on the thick trunk, eyes on the ceiling. 'Right, well, there's Homicide's saintly business and then there's your career,' he said. 'Mr Barry this morning, 6.45am, I'm just back from my twenty-k run, you understand. Feeling perky. He says Gillam rang him and expressed his happiness about Homicide. And guess who rang fucking Gillam?'

'Yes?'

'To be clear here,' said Colby, 'your thinking was, we'll just sit and watch, the whole thing will open like a flower?'

Villani said, 'You know what my thinking is, boss. They should worry about who gave up Kidd and his mate. That's what they have to worry about.'

'It's you I'm worrying about,' said Colby. 'Sucked in by this high-tech crap, Crucible bullshit. Ten million hours of fucking phone taps, you can sit there watching exciting vision of arseholes in cars, scratching their balls, doesn't matter that it adds up to a pint of warm piss.'

Villani had nothing to say because to some extent it was true. The new world of surveillance was intoxicating, seeing the city from on high, zooming in on alleys and back yards, following pursuits as they happened.

'And at the end of it,' said Colby, 'we say fuck to the high-tech, we go jumping over walls and running after a certified ex-SOG psycho who's quite happy to shoot cops. Fucking pig-stupid or what?'

Eyes locked.

Villani said, 'I'm sorry. Had some really bad examples to follow. Dumb turkeys jumped on moving cars.'

Colby's phone murmured. He agreed with the caller five or six times, deferential, hard gaze always on Villani, marbles expressed more meaning. He said goodbye, put the receiver down.

'There's a feeling you should be less visible on Oakleigh, Metallic, for a while,' he said.

'Whose feeling is that?'

'Just accept it.'

'I'm guilty of something, am I? Fuck that.'

Colby pulled an ear, a dried apricot. 'Think, son. Strategise. We are in a delicate phase. The present lot are now dying fish, Orong's eyes are glassing over. But they're still hoping, still paranoid about bad news. On the other side, Mrs Rottweiler Mellish's got her whole kennel out sniffing for damaging shit.'

He gazed at Villani. 'You, for example, are damaging shit.'

'Damaged,' said Villani.

'Yes. Both. Second, Gillam's going to the feds, heaven help the fuckwits, average IQ drops even lower. Mr Barry steps up, acting chief commissioner. I hear that. But not until after the election. So the mick's got to suck both sides of the street.'

'I'm slower than usual,' said Villani.

'Why's Barry holding your dick, taking you to meet the glitterati?'

'Tell me, boss,' he said.

Colby held up his hands, meshed fingers short and blunt, set like a cactus. In the squad offices, Villani once saw him pick up an armed robber and throw him across a desk into the wall. An old calendar fell down, draped itself over the man's head.

'The farmer's wife wants O'Barry for Pope,' Colby said. 'Cleanskin, untainted by the culture. But the boyo himself, he knows it's a moon landing. The twat's walking around in the big boots, fucking fishbowl on his head. Knows zero plus buggerall about the place he's in. At. On. Whatever.'

'Yes?' said Villani.

'So he wants a mate,' said Colby. 'He badly needs a mate. Smart person done the shit from the street up, done all the work, fired upon by the scum, a brave and loyal member, no one has a bad word.'

'Heard about Quirk?' said Villani.

'Hear everything,' said Colby. 'Anyway, Barry's the fat kid sucks up to the tough boy. Buys him the Mars Bars.'

'Me?'

'Absolutely.'

'He's got a tough boy. He's got you.'

'No, no, mate, he can't trust me.'

Villani shook his head, he had no idea how this worked, he didn't care much either, partly lack of sleep, partly the stupidity of going to the gym. He could feel every punch Les had landed.

'I'm slow here,' he said.

'Well, you, it worked, you'd go straight to crime commissioner,' said Colby.

'Me?' This could not be right.

'You.'

'No. Anybody ever done a jump like that before?'

'Look around, son. Just traffic deadshits, long-lasting legacy of our lady Fatima. You now stick out like a hardie in the convent showers. Proper cop.'

'And you?'

'Well, roll the dice,' said Colby. 'I'm happy to take a package. Anyway, the mick wants you below the parapet for a while. Racing with cover.'

'And Kidd?'

'I've heard the tape. There's nothing there.'

'He was going nowhere before he got that call,' said Villani. 'Then he takes another one on his auntie's mobile and they're off. And not in the Prado.'

'Pure fucking supposition. Anyway, assuming he was dropped, there's no way we can find the dog. Yes?'

'We can try.'

Colby blew like a horse. 'Mate, mate, don't dial-a-turd here, the job leaks from the minister to the fucking typists. Who'd you give the name to first? Mr Barry?'

'My recollection, yes,' said Villani.

'In that case, my advice is forget it. What we want is ballistics matching Oakleigh to the dead blokes. Then we can close the door on this shit. Be grateful people are looking out for you.'

Villani did not feel grateful. 'I'm grateful,' he said.

'Yeah. Searle's the worry here, he'd like to see me buried. Whole Searle family'd have a wakey. My distinction is, I punched out two Searles in one fight, this cunt's old man and his uncle, two weaker dogs you never saw. Know that?'

'Yes, boss.'

Everyone in the job knew it, it was legend. From never speaking of it, Colby had now told the story five or six times in the last year. Not a good sign.

'Collingwood, of course,' said Colby. 'Fucking over the slopes, that was the Searle speciality. Kings of Richmond, lords of Saturn Bay, there even the mozzies obey them and the tradies build their houses out of stuff stolen off building sites.' He coughed. 'I gather you've carried on Singleton's policy of treating Searle like dogshit.'

'He is dogshit.'

'No argument on facts, your honour. The point is I hear the squatter's wife's told the vermin he's her pick for media boss. Subject to performance. You with me?'

'Boss.'

Pointing. 'What's that red?'

'Old bloke hit me,' said Villani.

Colby blinked at him. 'Not still doing that shit?'

Villani shrugged.

'Why don't you go for a fucking walk in King Street? People will hit you for nothing.'

HE TOOK his seat, clear desk, looked at the big room outside. It was more than two years since he'd taken charge, the day of Singo's stroke. Even if you thought you didn't deserve to be the boss, it grew on you. After a while you didn't think anyone else could do it better.

Kiely came out, touched his oiled hair, walked around the room, people ignored him, came to Villani's door.

'Instructions?' he said.

Villani said, 'Found out who sold Kidd yet?'

'I'd like to say,' said Kiely, a little liplick. 'I want it on record that I think this squad should be managed in a professional manner. Not like a bad restaurant where the manager also wants to do the cooking.'

He would have to die. Villani felt the pressure in his head, considered letting go, saying, *Take over, I've got flu coming on*, going home, the old couch in the back room, sleep, sleep.

The old couch was long gone. And it wasn't his home anymore.

'Is that walking away from your fuck-ups?' he said.

Kiely's eyes wide. 'Excuse me, nothing last night was my responsibility.'

'I mentioned the full weight of the surveillance state, didn't I? No laser, no tags, we let the prick run out of his back door, fire at me and Winter and then bloody vanish. Want more?'

'All irrelevant to the outcome. Which wouldn't have been the outcome if my advice hadn't been sneered at. That's on record, my word.'

'What record?'

'Memos to command.'

'Ah, the Kiwi way,' said Villani. 'Here, that's called being a dog.'

Kiely tried the Singo look.

Villani said, 'Staring at me?'

'Moving on, it's also my opinion that Weber should take over the Prosilio matter.'

'What's wrong with Dove?'

'Not ready for responsibility. Shown that, hasn't he?'

'Told him that?'

'Not yet.'

Villani looked, saw Dove waiting, bony figure sitting on a desk edge, shoulders slack, head down, light reflected on his scalp.

'Jesus, mate,' he said. 'He took a bullet. These days they take a love-tap, they go on sick leave, stress leave, next it's full disability for life. But this bloke actually comes out of hospital, he reports for duty. Give him a fucking break, will you?'

Kiely shrugged, blinked. 'Well, made myself plain. That's my responsibility.'

'Metallic. Tell the ballistics pricks we want a yes or no on the Ford guns and Oakleigh in hours.'

Impassive, Kiely left.

Villani found Dove's gaze, nodded. Dove crossed the room, file in hands, stood.

'Nobody told me this bloke Kidd's name,' he said. 'Am I on some blacklist?'

'Remarkably bad time to fuck with me, son,' Villani said, he held his iron face.

'Sorry, boss,' said Dove. 'Alibani? Prosilio . . .'

'I remember,' said Villani. 'I'm paid to remember.'

'Right. Well, in looking over the family unto the thirteenth cousins, I find that he owns a house in Melbourne. Preston.'

'It's him?'

'Well, the address for rates is an accountant in Sydney. He says Alibani has been gone for years, hasn't heard from him, but he left money to pay the rates on three properties. Rates and other bills, they come to the bean counter.'

Villani thought about his pledge to stop interfering, stop taking charge. 'Get a car,' he said.

THE SKY was old bottle glass, smoke in the air. Villani slumped in the passenger seat, another air-conditioner that didn't work, the car smelled of cigarette smoke and chemical aftershaves, deodorants.

They drove up the spine of the clogged city, Dove cautious, bullied by reckless Asian taxi-drivers, black BMWs, Audis, drivers quick to hoot, force an entry.

When he looked up, they were in Russell Street.

That long-ago day, he came out of the old stone magistrates' court, he was there to give evidence, it wasn't going to happen until after lunch, half a day wasted, the woman was genetically programmed to steal stuff, you might as well imprison dolphins for leaping out of the sea. The next day was Good Friday, he was off, thinking about going surfing, hungry, he was waiting to cross to the Russell Street station, standing on the La Trobe corner. You could get a decent ham and cheese sandwich from the canteen, there was a woman cop crossing the road.

The world went orange, a massive impact knocked him over, his head hit the tarmac, something landed on his chest, he grasped it in both hands, mind blank, registered more explosions, people screaming. He got up, vision blurred, no idea of what had happened, his nasal passages were full of burnt rubber and hot dust. He focused on what he was holding. A hubcap, folded, like a pastie.

He sat down, feet in the gutter, head on his knees, feeling tired, unsure of mind, have a little rest. Then the thought rose in him:

You're a policeman. Get up. Do something.

He got up, not at all steady, he brushed himself, there were dark marks on his shirt, he nodded at them and stepped into the street.

The policewoman he saw crossing the road died of burns. She was about his age, he knew her by sight. Much later, he worked with cops who knew the men sentenced to life for killing her, for injuring all the others, they were armed robbers, they hated cops, turning a lifted Holden into a gelignite bomb was a very funny thing to do, an outlaw thing.

Livin on the wild side, mate, stick it up their fucken arses, park it outside the fucken front door, how's that? Cop fucken HQ. Middle of the fucken day, all those fat cunts in there talking on the radio to other cop cunts, Read you, car fucken fifty-one, over and out, then it's fucken KABANG!!!

They could have murdered any number of people, just luck a group of cops wasn't passing, the SOGs from around the corner, cops coming out of the station. Him. That day he grew up, he realised just what it meant to put on the uniform.

Lizzie.

A teenage druggy who didn't give a shit about her family.

Laurie's family were nothing to write home about. Her old man, Graham, big-nosed Graham, he worked for Telecom all his life, not so much a job as an explanation for being away from home in daylight. Her mother was pretty, a self-taught bookkeeper for a Fitzroy leathergoods factory that went under in the nineties. She did a lot of overtime, Graham often said that, fake smile. Villani took it to mean she'd been fucking the boss.

Whose fault was Lizzie?

After Rachel Bourke, Tony's friend's mother, things went badly sour. He met her when he went to watch Tony play hockey, she was a mistake but she'd stalked him, he hadn't looked for it, didn't cross the street for it. Anyway, it was weeks, six tops, four or five fucks, that was it. Laurie knew, she had no evidence but she knew, women knew, she read it in his body, his voice.

'Not exactly sure where we are, boss,' said Dove. 'The GPS isn't working.'

Villani looked around. They were in Plenty Road. 'Jesus, how'd you get here?'

'A bit new to me, this part.'

'Cops don't get lost,' said Villani. 'They study Melways at night, they study it before they get in the car. Don't need a degree to learn the Melways. No wonder the feds use a GPS to find their dicks.'

He gave directions. In time, they crossed the railway line, found the street, the number, parked opposite. The house was behind a two-metre-high corrugated-iron fence, just its tiled roof visible. They walked over. A padlock and chain on the double driveway gates. Villani looked through a gap. He could see little.

They shouted, banged on the gate.

'We need a warrant here,' said Villani. 'Going by the book.'

'What book is that?' said Dove.

Villani made the call. They sat in the car. He offered Dove a cigarette. A time passed, his view was north-east, the sky was dull yellow-brown, a huge diatomic bloom caused by dust and smoke. From the hills, the city would be wobbling in its own heat.

He rang Bob. It rang out. Again.

'Villani,' said Bob.

'Me. What's happening?'

'Nothing. Come up to Flannery's last night before the wind shifted. Still in the north-west. We should be all right.'

'And Flannery?'

'Some burnt mutton. Now shot and that's fucking expensive. He had the CFA on him to move them yesterday, won't listen. Man's gaga.'

'What do they say about you?'

'Mate, the dickheads know me. Keep their mouths shut.'

Coughing, throat clearing. 'Listen, the doctor's wife rang. Last night.'

Karin. Mark's wife number two. Number one was Janice, a nurse from Cobram, pregnant when they married just after he started specialising, she lost the child early. They broke up inside a year.

Mark went up the medical scale, Karin, a researcher, something to do with blood, her father also knew blood, he was one of Mark's teachers, Mr David Delisle, all-purpose surgeon, cut anything needed the scalpel. Villani met him at the civil ceremony in Kew, a brick mansion, wrought-iron gates. Mrs Delisle gave him the eye, handsome in a Botoxed stringy gymrat way. The knife man was poreless, silky hair, like a greyhound somehow but without the nerviness.

Right from the handshake, Bob Villani and David seemed to have some joke going. Perhaps they recognised each other as born killers. Karin got on with Bob too, a pony-club girl, besotted with horses, couldn't keep her hands off them. Before the pregnancy, she drove up to the farm on her days off, stayed over. It occurred to Villani that she was in love with her father and she put that on Bob. The men had the same stillness, the appraising stare. They gave the impression that, if circumstances required, they could do an appendectomy in the dark with a reasonably sharp Joseph Rodgers Bunny Clip and Castrator. Working purely by feel.

'What's she say?' said Villani.

'Well, makes out it's about the fires. Then it's tears, Mark's gone off her, out late all the time, no-show for the kid's birthday party. And so on.'

'Tragic,' said Villani. He wasn't going to tell Bob about Lizzie.

'Talk to him,' said Bob. 'Have a word with the doctor.'

'Be reasonable,' said Villani. 'You can't talk to blokes about that stuff.'

'Not a bloke, he's your brother. He'll listen to you.'

'What, the boss manner?'

'Something like that. Kick his arse.'

'The boy may be in need of emotional support,' said Villani.

'Yeah. Kick his arse.'

'Know a Danny Loneregan? From Vietnam?'

He thought he could hear birds.

'Who wants to know?'

'His son. He's a cop. Asked me to ask.'

'What's he want to know?'

'Just about him. Didn't know him.'

'Tell him his dad was a good bloke. Had guts. Used to show anyone who'd look his boy's picture.'

'Do that then.'

Cough. 'Talk to Mark, okay?'

It was forty minutes before the van came down the street. Two men in overalls got out. Villani crossed the street.

'The gate, Gus,' he said. 'Then possibly the front door.'

'This a legal entry?'

'I'm an officer of the law, yes,' said Villani.

The offsider cut the chain with boltcutters, a hard snick. Dove pushed a wing open and they entered.

The house was small, an ugly yellow brick-veneer in the centre of its block. It was partly obscured by gum trees, weedy splitting things, the result of some misguided arboreal instinct. To the left, the high unbroken wall of a sheet-metal fabricator shadowed the driveway. On the other side, beyond the high fence, a brick building of no obvious purpose showed dirty windows.

They went down the concrete drive, walked by a window covered by a metal roll-down security blind. Villani climbed a step to a brick verandah. Two new padlocks secured the steel front door. Attempts had been made to jemmy it.

'Got replacements?' said Villani.

'Pope Catholic?' said the offsider. They were civilians, had no respect.

The pair wheeled in a buggy with a gas bottle and cut the locks in minutes. 'Bunnings shit,' said Gus. He went to the van and came back with three new locks and a length of chain. 'Bloody waste of quality,' he said.

They left.

'Little sniff before we go in,' said Villani.

He pointed Dove to the left, stepped off the verandah and went to the right, past the other shuttered window. There had once been a flowerbed along the house, a strip of dirt marked out by bricks on the diagonal. Now it grew only plastic bags, cigarette packets, beer bottles, mixed-drink cans, chicken bones, unidentifiable bits of cloth, a pair of nylon underpants, a denim skirt, one cup of a bra, the fabric peeled back to reveal a grey cone of foam rubber.

The alley between the house and the fence held more of the same, plus pale condoms and turds coated with baize-green moss. Two windows had been sealed with unmatching bricks.

The small backyard had all these things and much more. The bodies of three pillaged cars, crowpicked, bled rust into the concrete. Their unwanted innards lay in oil stains.

'Recycling,' Dove said. 'That's nice. Power's on, the water meter's ticking.'

The back door was steel, blank, internal bolts. Serious attempts to open it had failed. The windows were high and small, broken but negotiable only by cats.

They went back. Villani opened the steel front door. There was another door behind it, of delaminating plywood. He opened that, went in first, that was his prerogative and his duty.

He stood in a passage: dead air and the gas given off by cheap carpets and the foam beneath them. Something sweet and sour, too, like the sweat in old intimate garments.

The light didn't work.

Dim sitting room. Dove wound up the metal blind. It groaned, it had been a while. Sixties furniture, glass coffee table, a kidney shape.

'Coke,' said Dove, pointing.

Villani looked, saw the smears, walked around sniffing, went down the passage and into the bathroom. Nothing on the rails, nothing in the cabinet above the basin.

'Do that room,' he said to Dove. 'Don't touch.'

The first bedroom had a bare single bed. He opened a wardrobe by tugging on the bottom of the door. Empty.

In the kitchen, the small fridge was running, freezer iced up. Empty.

Who paid the power bills?

'Boss.' Dove.

Villani went to the back bedroom, stood in the door.

'Nothing here,' said Dove, eyes on the carpet next to the stripped bed. 'But there's this.'

Villani crossed. On the cheap dark carpet, a darker stain, large.

'Another one here,' said Dove.

'Well,' said Villani. 'We should ask the question. Get them. Prints, DNA, the lot. House search. Under the floor, roof, everything.'

He left Dove to wait, drove out of the street.

HIS PHONE rang as he was parking in a small shopping centre carpark, directly across from the arcade that ended in his brother's consulting rooms. It was Kiely.

'There's no Metallic match with the weapons in Kidd's car, the Ring Road one. That's one hundred per cent sure.'

'Bugger,' said Villani.

'And the vehicle. Genuine plates. It's registered to a man not seen for nearly ten years and was sixty-eight then.'

'Bugger again.'

A big man with long greased hair in a ponytail came out of the arcade and stood at the kerb. He took sunnies out of his denim jacket, big wraparound glasses, put them on, looked around, lit a cigarette.

Villani knew him. His name was Kenny Hanlon, they brought him in for questioning over a man called Gaudio, a minor drug figure. Gaudio's biggest impact on society was to block a storm-water pipe in Melton. Someone, possibly Kenny Hanlon, had bound his hands and feet with no. 8 fence wire and stuck an apple in his mouth. Then a heavy vehicle had driven over his head, several times.

He watched Hanlon cross to a black Holden muscle car parked tight against struggling hedges in the far corner, get into the passenger seat, vanish behind the dark window.

Villani waited for the Holden to leave. Waited.

Mark came out of the arcade, white shirt, open-necked, he

stood where Hanlon had stood, looked around, turned left. Villani lost sight of him, then he came through the ragged hedge in front of the Holden, went to Hanlon's window, blocked Villani's view.

The urge was to look away, start the car, drive off. Get on with the business of the day. But he looked and his throat was tight and his mouth was dry. The dark window came down. Mark Villani leaned his forearms on the sill, head almost in the car.

In less than a minute, Mark straightened, tapped the roof of the Holden, went back the way he had come. The machine woke, the driver made it growl, it backed, went forward, backed again until a wheel mounted the kerb. Then it escaped its lodging, came past Villani, slowly, eight-speaker sound system threatening to break windows, dent cars, blow the infirm and their shopping carts back into the supermarket. It had three short backsloping coil aerials on the roof.

Villani went to his brother's surgery. An old man, two women and a toddler, a girl, were waiting, sitting on white plastic chairs. 'His brother would like to speak to Dr Villani,' he said to the receptionist, a thin woman with dyed black hair and pencilled eyebrows.

She picked up the phone. 'Your brother's here, doctor. Okay. Right.' She smiled at Villani. 'Doctor will see you next.'

Villani sat as far away from the others as possible, hands in his lap. He closed his eyes, tried to think of nothing, failed. He opened his eyes. The child was looking at him. She took off towards him, plodding and uncertain steps.

'Dadda,' she said. 'Dadda.'

'Shayna, leave the man alone,' said a young woman in a man's leather jacket. She had a tattoo around her neck below the Adam's apple, a strand of blue barbed wire. The child ignored her, eyes fixed on Villani, took another step, held out her dimpled arms.

Villani looked away. How had the budding neurosurgeon ended up in this sad dump?

'Dadda,' the child said.

The old man made a popping sound like a failing two-stroke ignition. It might have been a laugh. He pointed at Villani. 'Nailed yer, mate,' he said. 'Nailed yer.'

'Shut yer fucken mouth,' said the woman. 'Stupid old cunt.'

'Fuck you too,' said the man. 'Seed you got two more in the car. Three fucken dads no doubt.'

'Mr Stewart, kindly be quiet or wait outside,' said the receptionist. 'And you'll wait all day.'

The child took another step towards Villani. 'Dadda,' she said.

The woman came out of her chair, wrenched the child away by the arm, sat down holding her tight. The child began to whimper and tears rolled down her fat cheeks. Her eyes never left Villani.

The door opened and a pimpled teenage boy came out, perhaps sixteen, olive-skinned, Elvis hair. He looked straight ahead, walked. Mark Villani stuck his head out. 'Steve,' he said.

The consulting room had a temporary look, a chipboard desk, a cheap computer, an examination table covered with a sheet, not sparkling white. The calendar was for 2009.

They sat.

'Been meaning to call you,' said Mark. He had grown his hair, grown a little goatee, a ring in an earlobe.

'Saw you outside,' said Villani. 'At the black Holden.'

Mark lifted his chin, blinked twice, looked down at the desk pad, wrote something. 'Patient left his prescription behind.'

'I could see you knew him.'

'Of course, I know him. He's a patient.'

'Could have sent the receptionist.'

Mark looked up. 'You here to tell me how to run my practice?'

'He's not a model citizen, your patient. Know that?'

Mark shook his head. 'Steve,' he said, 'I actually don't ask sick people to present character references. Feeling crook is enough.'

'What's wrong with him?'

'I also don't discuss my patients with other people. That's a principle among doctors. Not heard of it? I suppose you're in the pub telling the drunks about who murdered who?'

Villani waited, looking at his brother. Mark looked back, tapped a finger.

'Nice of you to drop by,' he said, 'but I've got patients waiting. I'll call you, find a time.'

'Hellhounds,' said Villani. 'You're associating with Hellhounds.'

Mark raised his upper lip. 'Steve, don't come the cop with me. The bloke's a patient, he rides a Harley, I've got a Harley, we talk Harleys.'

'Go round the clubhouse, do you?'

Mark picked up his ballpoint, clicked it, kept clicking it. 'As I understand it, it's just pool tables and beer fridges and a work-shop.'

'Are you fucking naïve or what?'

'Listen, don't tell me who I can talk to. Got fuckall to do with you, okay?'

'No, it's not okay,' said Villani. 'You've got something to do with me. I think that.'

'Can we have this conversation some other time? I'm busy, I don't have . . .'

Villani said, 'So the golden boy's now giving the wife and

kids the arse, got a little beard, little earring and he's associating with murdering bikie scum?'

Mark placed the ballpoint on the blotter, looked at his hands, opened and closed his fists. He had big hands, wiry hair on the backs. 'Anybody punched you recently?' he said.

'Don't give me tough, sonny,' said Villani. 'I'll put you on your arse. I'm your brother. I'm telling you what you don't want to hear.'

'How's your happy family?' said Mark. 'You still fucking everything in a skirt? You think Laurie doesn't know? I've had enough sanctimonious crap from you.'

'Fuck you.' Villani got up. He had handled this badly, he was handling everything badly.

'Sit down,' said Mark. 'Sit down, Steve.'

Villani sat.

'Jesus, you're a bully,' said Mark.

'People are telling me that,' said Villani. 'A boss manner, they say.'

'Bullied the life out of me and Luke.'

Villani wanted to say, *You're only a doctor because I was a bully,* but he said, 'You'd both still be fast asleep if I hadn't kicked you out of bed.'

Mark's eyes were on the desk. 'You were like a god, y'know? Always in charge, always knew what to do, so fucking cool and calm. I wanted to be like you. I wanted you to like me. You didn't like me, did you? You don't now.'

Villani felt unease, looked around. 'Yeah, well, you're my brother, like doesn't come into it. I don't want to see you fuck up your life. What's wrong with you? There's shit, right?'

Mark held his eyes, defiant.

Villani waited, folded his hands and waited, didn't blink, didn't shift his gaze.

Mark tossed his head and then he misted, blinked, and he put his arms on the desk and lowered his head, said something Villani couldn't make out.

'What? What?'

Mark looked up, more blinking. 'I'm under investigation.'

'By?'

'Practitioners Board.'

'For what?'

'Prescribing and other stuff. They want me to suspend myself.'

'Prescribing?' He noticed for the first time that Mark's eyes were a soft brown, not the glossy black olives of Bob Villani.

'The pressure's huge, you have to be in the game to understand, you . . .'

'The game? This's a game, is it? You're saying you've got a habit, don't fuck with me.'

'It's under control, Steve. Under control. I am coming out of a bad time, but, yes, it's now under . . .'

'What's the stuff in this prescribing and stuff?'

'Well, they have some, they have someone saying I treated someone for a wound. Gunshot wound.'

'And that's right, is it?'

'Don't look at me like that, just don't look at me like that, okay, it's not a fucking major offence, it was an accident, blokes buggering around, a gun went off, it's not like the person was shot by . . . by someone like you. No.'

A coldness in him, Villani got up. 'So you're the Hellhounds' tame fucking GP,' he said. 'You're the smacked-out medico patches up these cunts, prescribes what they can't make.'

Mark stood up. 'Stevie, it's over. I swear that, I swear it is over, it is under control, I am taking back my life, that is . . .'

'You're a disgrace,' said Villani. 'Bob, me, all the fucking effort, we thought we had a thoroughbred in the stable, a surgeon. You blew it, you weak dog, you fucking waste of space.'

He left, passed swiftly through the death-ray eyes in the waiting room, went down the shabby arcade, crossed the parking lot. In the car, he sat for a moment, composed himself.

VILLANI AND Dove sat in the car eating salad rolls bought by Villani on the way back to Preston, he could not trust Dove not to get lost.

A car parked behind them. Birkerts. He got in the back.

'Coming past,' he said. 'Heard you were here. Mr Kiely's given me Burgess.'

Troy Burgess had been Villani's first section boss in Homicide. Why Singleton took him from the CIB was an enduring mystery. He was work-shy, a heavy drinker, spent most of his day on his gambling, his domestic problems, two ex-wives, four children, one with time for drugs, one married to a violent crim shot in the back by an associate, a succession of demanding young women met in strip joints and pubs, at the races.

'Off the piss, Burgo,' Birkerts said. 'The punt too, they say. Become a bit of an advisor to Mr Kiely. As an elder of the force. Explaining the history and quaint customs.'

'God help us,' said Villani. He had no high ground on the punt, it had come so close to bringing him down.

'Waiting,' said Dove. 'I never realised how much waiting there was.'

'It's television,' said Villani, chewing. 'These techies now see themselves as the band. We're just muscle, the roadies.'

'Can we be told why the boss roadie himself isn't running Metallic anymore?' said Birkerts. 'Or is that impertinent?'

'Mr Kiely deserves a turn.'

'Great timing. What's the charge?'

Villani didn't want to talk in front of Dove. 'Men now dead escaped while under surveillance,' he said. 'They think there might have been a better way.'

'What way?'

'When they tell me, I'll tell you.'

A hot wind had arrived, moving the ragged, forgotten trees. Two youths in overalls, a tall and a short, came out of the factory next door, stood smoking, looking at them, one said something, they laughed.

'Only the truly ignorant are truly happy,' said Birkerts. 'My dad.'

'Penetrating,' said Villani. 'An old Swedish saying?

'Don't know Swedish sayings from fucking Ukrainian,' said Birkerts, rubbing his face with both hands. His mobile rang. He had a short conversation, put the device away.

'So what's on here?' he said.

'We have no idea,' said Villani, chewing, looking at the youths, at the house, waiting for some sign.

Birkerts sighed. 'Three highly trained operatives in one car. With no idea why.'

A man in overalls in the front door of the house. He raised a gloved hand.

'Like the fucking Pope,' said Villani.

'I'll be on my way then,' said Birkerts. 'See you later, roadies.'

'Tell you the Ford guns don't match Oakleigh?'

'Mr Kiely did.'

'I want the Oakleigh gun,' said Villani. 'I want the satisfaction of the Oakleigh gun.'

'Do anything to satisfy you, boss.'

Villani and Dove crossed the street, went down the path, filed through the front door, stood in the dim house. A woman was mixing fluids in a pump spray, the sickening smell of peroxide.

'The big stain,' she said. 'And there's others. Have a look at a bit of the big one. Not to bugger the DNA.'

A man edged around them. 'Tape it?' he said.

'No,' said the man in charge. 'Shutters down, Wayne.'

Wayne wound away the light. A torch came on, lit the room.

The leader said, 'Yeah, dark enough. Gerry.'

Gerry sprayed the carpet.

'Off.'

Click. They stood in blackness, blind.

A small piece of carpet began to glow, luminous blue.

'Oh yes,' said the woman, cheerful. 'Blood. That's lots and lots.'

VILLANI WENT back to the car, made calls about Lizzie. She was on all the keep-a-lookout-for lists. He put the phone away and leant back, slept for ten minutes until his head lolled. He sat up, dry-mouthed, thirsty.

It came into his mind: the faraway Thursday in winter, the long drive on the snow road, Singleton and Burgess in front, Burgess's terrible jokes. He didn't understand why Singo could be bothered, remembered wishing he had never transferred to Homicide, aching to be back in the Robbers, they did not drive for hours. The day was dying behind the mountains, steady drizzle, when they saw the divvy van at the side of the highway. The cop, stoic face, waved them onto the track, they went about two hundred metres.

She was naked, she was small, pitifully thin, prominent ribs, a long neck. The corners of her mouth had been cut by something. It took weeks or months to identify her, he had moved on, she wasn't local, that was all he remembered. Darwin, somewhere far away . . .

His phone.

'FYI, the second man is a Raymond Judd Larter, age thirty-eight,' said Kiely. 'Unfortunately, he turns out to be ex-Special Operations Group too. He quit six years ago to join Special Air Services, time in Afghanistan. Discharged two years ago.'

'Why?'

'I've asked the question. We're trying to find him on other bases.'

'We are obliged to warn Searle about impending shit,' said Villani. 'Need to find the gun. Get the Prado X-rayed.'

The girl on the track, Burgess would know what the outcome was. No conviction, that was certain.

Phone again.

'Lizzie,' said Laurie. 'She says she's okay.'

Instant anger. 'Where the fuck is she?'

'It was noisy, street phone, she said, Hi Mum, I'm okay, talk to you later. That was it.'

'You want them to keep looking for her?'

'Of course. Yes.'

'Right, okay. This really pisses . . .'

'I see you've taken your clothes.'

'Any reason I shouldn't do that?'

'No, not a single one. Goodbye.'

You could not slam down a mobile. He was looking at it, clenching it, when it rang.

'Need a chat, mate.' It was Dance. 'How's the old spot suit? Five-thirty?'

'See you there.'

Villani got out, stretched, tried to touch his toes, felt eyes, saw a worker looking at him. He crossed to the house, walked around it and sat on the back step. He watched Dove walking around the yard. His suit wasn't a Homicide number, the jacket didn't have the poncho fit. He had never had a good look at Dove. Until you watched people from a distance, you hadn't really seen them. You had to register the way they walked, held themselves, moved their arms, their hands, their heads. You could learn things by doing that, observing, some mothers could read their kids from half a block away, know what was going on in their heads.

He remembered sitting outside Brunetti's in Faraday Street that day, seeing Laurie from a long way, waiting at the lights. He watched her come, jeans, black leather jacket, jinking through the walkers, he realised she'd lost some weight, slightly different haircut, shorter, she was walking in a more confident way. Their eyes docked when she was ten metres away. He was the one to drop his gaze.

She touched his shoulder, the long hand, she kissed his forehead, perched on the chair, straight back. 'Haven't been here for yonks, got a meeting in half an hour.'

Villani said, 'You're having an affair.'

It was not what he had planned, he had wanted to hint, to force her to say the words.

She moved her head, looked at him over her nose. Now he held her eyes. She blinked, moved her mouth, revealed a tip of pink tongue.

'I don't think this is the place to talk,' she said.

Blood in his face, in his eyes, he said, 'Well, we don't have to talk at all, piss off. Fuck meeting with the boyfriend, is that it?'

She rose and walked, a few quick paces, turned and came back, stood over him, loomed, made him look up, his spine cracked.

'I'm not having an affair,' she said. 'I'm in love with someone. I'll move out today.'

'No,' he said, anger dead, ashes. 'You stay, I'll go.'

'Don't come the victim with me, Stephen,' she said. 'After what I've put up with, your whoring, the gambling.'

But he didn't move out, she didn't. For a long time they passed in the house like boxers before a fight.

The forensics boss came around the corner, clipboard in hand. 'We're done,' he said. 'Lots of everything. I'll be in touch.'

'The blood.'

'There's a trail down the passage to the kitchen. I'd guess the body dragged.'

'The Prosilio woman,' said Villani. 'She might have been here.

Need to know that as a priority. Then we want to run all prints as fast as possible.'

He wrote on the clipboard. 'Action that.'

Villani's mobile rang when they were in Flinders Street.

'Anna,' she said, the throaty voice.

'Yes,' he said.

'Are we speaking? As in, do you wish to speak to me?'

'I think so, yes.'

'Good. Saw you at Persius with the rich and the famous. Looked right through me.'

'Dazzled by the light.'

'Well, I thought I was a bit teenagey the other night. Perhaps less mature than a person like myself should be.'

'Maturity's not all it's cracked up to be.'

Not her big laugh, not the one that made him look across the room that night at the Court House and find her eyes and the switch tripped, the current ran, the crystal moment. He had dropped his gaze and, when he looked again, she was still looking at him.

'Eyeballing my sexy friend,' said Tony Ruskin. He was the *Age*'s crime man, on the cop drip, Villani had known him since he was a junior reporter, the clever son of a clever cop named Eric Ruskin, who chucked it in and stood for parliament, ended up as police minister. They met at Matt Cameron's Christmas barbie for Robbers and friends, around the pool in Hawthorn on a Sunday, noon to loaded-in-taxi-after-puking-in-rose-garden.

'I don't eyeball,' said Villani. 'Sometimes I stare.'

Anna Markham left the room, came back, detoured to put a hand on Ruskin's shoulder. 'Bit public this, isn't it?' she said. 'I thought you had these meetings in underground carparks.'

'Hide in plain view,' said Ruskin. 'Anna Markham, Stephen Villani.'

'I know the inspector by sight,' she said.

'Ditto,' said Villani.

She joined them later when they had eaten, drunk a glass of red.

'My bedtime,' said Ruskin. 'Unlike some, I need to think clearly in the morning.'

They all made to go, then Anna said, 'Actually, I wouldn't mind another glass. What about you, inspector?'

Ruskin left, he knew. They had another glass, another, laughed a lot. Outside, in their coats, waiting for cabs, breathing out steam, Anna said, 'You don't associate the Homicide Squad with laughing.'

'We laugh a lot. We chuckle all day long.'

He wanted to make the move, but he didn't, he was in a guilt phase. She wrote her number on a blank card. He never called. Every time he saw her on television he considered it but he was not an initiator. That was what he told himself. That was his defence.

Now, Anna said, 'Can we pursue this conversation somewhere?'

'Name a venue.'

'Cité. In Avoca Street. Know it?'

'Oh yes, major cop hangout. Pot and a parma, ten bucks, half-price happy hour four to nine. That's in the a.m.'

'The place that forgot time. I'll be there by eight. From eight.'

First there was the Dancer.

ARCHITECTS HAD worked over the old bloodhouse, knocked out walls, exposed bricks, it was now all black wood and smoked glass, a wall of wine bottles. In the big open room, a dozen people were drinking and eating. A flat screen behind the bar was showing news.

Dance was in a corner, needing a hair trim, dark pinstriped suit, no tie, dipping bread into olive oil. A waiter finished pouring red wine into two glasses.

Villani sat.

'Like this, you and this place,' he said, showed the crossed fingers. 'Mine?'

'I'm not drinking two at a time. Nice little Heathcote shiraz. Nice suit too.'

Villani sipped, he rolled the wine. 'Definitely wine. When did you move on from Crownies?'

'Stella, mate, that's what you drink when you drink beer,' said Dance. 'Only you morgue blokes still drink Crown.'

Dance looked around the room, long face of a Crusader, God's soldier, handsome, growing old, tired, loved the Lord, loved himself, and loved a lot more besides.

'You know, I wake up,' he said. 'Three, four in the morning, it's like it's wired in me. Utterly knackered, lie there, think about the old days.'

'Everybody's talking about the old days,' said Villani. 'What did I miss?'

'What I miss, it was simple. Us against filth with guns. Outlaws. Taking stuff that wasn't theirs. Terrorising innocent citizens. You shake the cunts, it's a public service. Ends justify means, nobody cared. Pest exterminators. You got some respect.'

Two young women came in, sleek, laptop bags. They sat nearby and feigned exhaustion, closed their eyes, rolled their heads, moved their shoulders.

'Now,' said Dance, 'I'm supposed to do something about crime networks. The fucking Rotary Club is a crime network, blokes doing deals, they make stuff, they sell it to middlemen, it gets retailed. It's called commerce. Exchange of goods between willing sellers and willing buyers.'

'You learn this at the gym?' said Villani. 'Not going to uni part-time, are we?'

'I'm growing up,' said Dance. He offered the bread fingers. 'You dip it in the oil.'

'Really? That's so weird.'

'Fucked up big time last night, you lot.'

'We're pretty happy about it.'

'Pity you didn't call in the sons to take them out. Been like World War Three.'

'Why?'

'Why? Well SOG on SOG, that's cage-fighting with guns.'

'Where'd you hear SOG?' said Villani.

'The ether, mate.'

'Ah, the ether. Know them?'

'Not on our books. Tied them to Metallic?'

'Just the vehicle,' said Villani. 'Got two guns out of the wreck, no match.'

'Now that's truly unfortunate. You want the ballistics.'

A waiter slid by, plumpish, thirties, oiled hair, he knew the women, he said, 'Chill time, guys. Let me guess? Morettis for openers, duck clubs, no capers. And we drink the Oyster Bay.'

'Fold,' said the short-haired one, sallow, deslanted eyes. 'Why are we so predictable, Lucy?'

Lucy was finger-combing her hair. 'I'm over duck, PJ. Make it the crab cakes.' She turned her head and looked at them, appraising.

'Anyway, this little talk,' said Dance. 'Lovett.'

'What am I supposed to do?' said Villani. 'I've got no clout.'

'Well, we need to consider,' said Dance. He looked around the room, drank wine, turned the cold blue eyes on Villani. 'Saw the tape today. The cunt said this stuff the first time, we'd still be giving blow jobs in Barwon.'

'What's he say?'

'I shot Quirk in cold blood. Executed him. Says Vick brought Quirk's gun.'

Villani felt the air-conditioned chill on his face. 'What's he say about me?'

'Lied in your teeth.'

Dance closed his eyes, showed his long dark lashes. The day in the shopping-centre carpark, waiting for Matko Ribaric to come back to his car, he told Villani he had put a much older cousin in hospital for calling him a pretty boy.

'Vickery says the drugs,' said Villani. 'Delusions.'

'Drugs,' said Dance. 'Blamed for everything. Personally, I wouldn't put my balls on that horse.'

'How's he on the tape?'

'Looks like shit, but all the marbles. Made up lots of details.'

'And Mrs Lovett, what's she going to say?'

'The divine Grace,' said Dance, drinking wine, eye contact with the Asian woman. 'I was just a boy.'

'Aged thirty. Sensitive boy cop sexually abused by fifty-year-old colleague's wife,' said Villani. 'You should lay charges, that might help. What's Grace going to say?'

'No statement. As I understand it. Not in the pink herself.'

'What, just sent the DPP the tape?'

'To Lovett's brief. The prick tried on a compo for years. Non-smoker forced to endure smoke in confined spaces, et cetera. He never stopped crapping on about smoke, his asthma.'

'Eating with us, guys?' said the waiter, come from nowhere.

'PJ,' said Villani. 'That's your name?'

He didn't look at the man, looked at the long-haired woman, she parted her lips, red as the rose beside Ma Quirk's gate.

'Certainly is,' said the waiter.

Villani turned on him the full stare. 'Two more, PJ. But not the nine glasses to the bottle.'

Lips licked, glasses collected. 'Two Cold Hills coming up. Sir.'

The waiter left, he caught the women's eyes and he made a small gesture with his hips.

'I love it when you turn up the charm,' said Dance.

'The tape's where?'

'DPP.'

'She's the only witness to the taping?'

'As I understand it,' said Dance.

'Video allegations of a man now dead about events fifteen years ago. Man saying he committed perjury then, now wants justice for Quirk.'

Dance looked at a palm, long fingers, deep lines. 'They reopen, it's not about justice. It's politics.'

'Yeah?'

'I talked to a man who talked to a man knows the AG by sight. The word is DiPalma won't reopen. But the Libs come in, they can skin a whole cage of furry animals at once. Cops in general, the old culture, corruption, Crucible. And Vick. They hate Vick.'

You, on the other hand, you'll be collateral. No one hates you much. Just a select few. Like Searle.'

'Add this waiter,' said Villani.

'Loves you, pants on fire. So fucking butch. We need serious thought.'

The waiter arrived. He landed glasses. 'Brimming, sirs,' he said. He put down a plate of six butterflied sardines, crumbed, grilled. 'Enjoy.'

They watched him go.

'Free food,' said Villani. 'That's like the old days, that's what I miss.'

'Oh, I don't know,' said Dance. 'I hear you were grazing on the little Wagyu burgers, Mr Barry's showpony at Persius. Chatting to Max Hendry, our beloved Mr Cameron, world's richest ex-cop.'

'He's lonely, Barry,' said Villani.

'Not the way I hear it.'

'No?'

'Ms Cathy Wynn gives comfort.'

'What? Barry and Searle?' said Villani.

'No, not Searle. Searle's an enabler. The boy tells me Ms Mellish wants Barry for El Supremo. Had him over at the house in Brighton for the little chat, meet the bluebloods.'

'Swapping playlunch with Searle now?'

'He tells me stuff. I don't know why.'

'To keep being your little friend.'

Dance fed himself a sardine, added olives, chewed for a while. 'Let's be clear what the position is,' he said. 'Shake one of us loose, we all get blown away. Lovett was a deranged person on the way out talking complete shit.'

'That's what it seems,' said Villani, not easy.

'It is so exactly. Something else. You remember Lovett tried to stiff me and Vick, that's a year ago. Hundred grand or he leaves a shitbomb.'

Villani couldn't look at Dance, he finished the wine, eyed the last stiff fishlet. 'Want this?'

'No.'

Villani ate the sardine, crunchy, hint of chilli.

'Did I tell you then?' said Dance. 'I thought I did.'

'Don't quite remember that.'

'Well, think about it,' said Dance. 'Dwell on it.'

The moment of their eyes.

'Life's short enough, Stevo,' Dance said, 'without two dead pricks fucking up what we've got left. We do what we have to, right?'

'I see the force of that,' said Villani.

Dance's eyes flicked the room, he emptied his glass. 'Up for it, this japanoid sheila,' he said. 'The place in Docklands, the sumo bed, the spa. Pity I'm so fucking pressed. Need a piss. You?'

'No. Cameras in there.'

Villani watched Dance go, the women watched him, a long frame, held himself like Bob Villani, stick up his arse. He found the waiter's eyes and made the sign. The man swept across.

'Please be our guests, sir. You and Mr Dance.'

A worm moved under Villani's scalp. 'Thank you but no,' he said. He found two twenties. 'Change to the guide dogs.'

Dance returned. They went out. At his car, Dance offered a smoke. They stood, the traffic zipping metres away. It was dusk at ground level now, the light was yellow stained-glass panes between the buildings.

'So the Mellish bitch,' Dance said. 'She needs to grasp something. You don't make three senior officers walk the plank, then it's back to the captain's cabin for a fucking G and T.'

'No?'

'No. The officers will take HMS fucking Liberal Party down with them.'

'I'm the man to tell her?'

'Mr Barry. He needs to tell them he wants a clean slate. Ground Zero. Not putting on a backpack loaded with ancient shit. Heritage issues. That kind of thing.'

Villani's mobile.

'Boss,' said Dove. 'A bloke wants to talk to you. Just you, he won't come in. He says he can do it now.'

'About what?'

'Prosilio. The girl.'

He saw Dance arc his half-smoked cigarette into the traffic, it hit a taxi wheel, sparked like a metal grinder.

'Tell him the Somerset in Smith Street, half an hour,' said Villani. 'Pick me up across from the Grenville Hotel, that's South Yarra. Both addresses in Melbourne. Reckon you can find them?'

'Up all night studying Melways. Boss.'

Dance said, 'Your old man okay?'

'Good, yeah. Up there waiting for death by fire.'

'Top bloke, Bob,' said Dance. 'Wish I'd had a dad like that.'

THE PUB wasn't crowded, a dozen or so drinkers at the long bar, a few sad cases, a game of pool in progress. A man in a grey suit came in from the toilets and looked around the room, uneasy, black-framed glasses, not a pub drinker. He was in his thirties, ordinary height, balding neatly.

Villani lifted his beer, stood back. Their eyes met, the man's mouth twitched, he walked around the pool table, found his beer bottle on the counter, came up.

'Are you . . .'

'The man who wants to talk to me,' said Villani. 'Let's stand at the window.'

They went to the alcove, Villani made sure the man was facing outward so Dove could get a clear view of him.

'I didn't think this would happen,' said the man. He had a snub nose, cupid lips, some older women would find him attractive, some men too.

'What?'

'You coming out to meet me.'

Villani drank beer. 'We take things seriously,' he said. 'Also we take serious revenge on people who fuck with us.'

The man smiled, a smile that wanted to be confident. 'I didn't want to talk to underlings,' he said. 'I'm no stranger to the bureaucracy.'

'Talk about what?'

'Confidentiality guaranteed?'

'You're a bloke in a pub, never seen you before,' said Villani. 'What's your name?'

The man touched his upper lip, he hadn't thought about this. 'Need my name?'

Villani closed his eyes for a few seconds.

'Okay. Don Phipps, that's my name. But I don't want my name attached to this.'

'If you're not involved in anything, that's not a problem.'

'I'm not. I worked for the state government, an advisor to Stuart Koenig, the infrastructure minister. Until last week.'

'Yes?'

Phipps had a sip from his bottle. 'Something happened about two weeks ago.'

'Yes?'

'I stayed at work late to finish a briefing paper for Stuart, it was a rush job, we were facing questions in parliament the next day. I thought I'd drop the brief at his place in Kew, he's got a townhouse he stays at during the week. Put it in the mailbox, it's a secure box, and ring him in the morning so he could have a look at it over breakfast.'

'Love suspense,' said Villani.

'Sorry. Well, I had to park across the street down from the house and walk up and I was near the front gate when it opened and a woman came out.'

'Yes?'

'I got a good look at her. The woman on Crime Stoppers. Described as a Caucasian woman.'

'How good's the light there?'

'Well, Stuart's got an elaborate security set-up,' said Phipps. 'I'll go so far as to say he's paranoid. Not without some reason, I might add, he had a . . .'

'Mr Phipps, I have things to do.'

'Right. Well, he's got cameras on both gates, the driveway, you drive into this bay, you press a button, and then you're told to wind down all your windows so the cameras on both sides can see everyone in the car.'

'You saw her clearly.'

'The security lights were on. It's like daylight. She got into a black BMW. Tinted windows.'

Villani felt the pulse, but you didn't want to excite them. They thought they'd seen things, if you took them seriously, they became more convinced.

'Mr Phipps, people phone in with stuff like this all the time. They identify their ex-best friends, their in-laws, people who give them shit at the supermarket.'

'No, no, I've got the Crime Stoppers on tape, I was recording, a bit serendipitous really, I wanted the program after it. I've looked at it over and over.'

Villani looked at the room. Dove's sallow face was partly visible behind a pillar.

He found a card, gave it to Phipps. 'Name, address, contact numbers.'

Phipps blinked rapidly, got out a pen, a fountain pen, took off the cap and mounted it on the back.

Villani took the paper. 'Why'd you wait so long?'

Phipps drank, a bigger drink. 'Well, you have doubts. I considered going to Stuart . . . just mulled it over really.'

'You didn't go to Koenig?'

'No.'

'How long did you work for him?'

'A year. I was on a contract.'

'Not renewed?'

'People want change, new ideas. My replacement's a woman.'

'Meaning?'

'Nothing really. Well, I think Stuart'll be happier with a woman.'

'Why's that?'

Uneasy look. 'I shouldn't talk about him. He doesn't like being stood up to. A bully actually. And women. It's my experience, they'll put up with a bit more.'

'You're trying to shaft him?' Villani said.

'God no, I'm trying to do what a citizen should do. A person missing.'

'Dead.'

Phipps showed surprise, square teeth. 'It didn't say that.'

'When you saw her at Koenig's, what did you think she was doing there?'

'No idea. Visitor.'

'See the driver of the BMW?'

'No.'

'How far from her were you?' said Villani.

Phipps pointed at the bar. 'Here to there. What, three metres? She looked at me, that's why I'm sure.'

'The cameras. Koenig would have vision of this?'

'That's the point, isn't it?'

'Date and time?'

'Just after ten, two weeks ago, Thursday.'

'Koenig was there?'

'His car was there, lights on in the house.'

'Someone can confirm your movements?'

'When I left the office, yes. And when I got home.'

'The document, the briefing? Leave it in the box?'

'Oh yes. Three copies stamped, time and date.'

'I'll be in touch, Mr Phipps,' Villani said. 'We'll need a proper statement. Meanwhile, don't tell anyone you've talked to me, that's important. Okay?'

Phipps nodded, leaned. 'Can I ask? Is that your photographer or some student doing a documentary on pubs?'

Villani didn't look for Dove. 'Student. They're everywhere. Menace. Thanks for your public-spiritedness.'

In the car, he said to Dove, 'The trick is they don't see you. Look at the screen not the target.'

'Saw me?'

'Blind Freddy could see you.'

He told Dove about Phipps. 'Makes a ringing sound to me.'

'So I should . . .'

'See the minister tomorrow,' said Villani. 'Ask for an appointment as a matter of urgency.'

'Is that me or . . . ?'

'Want to do it? You and Winter?'

Dove didn't look at him. 'Not especially, boss.'

'Okay. Me and you. And on Preston, you want everything run against Prosilio.'

'Done that. Given that instruction.'

They drove in silence.

'I'm beginning to see the outline of the job now,' said Dove. 'Boss.'

'This job or the whole job?'

'Whole job. The full horror.'

'Beginning of wisdom,' said Villani. 'Still time to make a run for it. Why'd you become a cop?'

'To spite my father,' said Dove. 'He hated cops.'

'That's a good spite,' said Villani. 'That'd hurt him. I'm going to Avoca Street. Know where that is?'

'Is that Highett, Yarraville or Brunswick?'

'Let's try South Yarra, please. Go down Punt.'

Crossing the Yarra, Villani said, 'Why'd your dad hate cops?'

'Bashed by cops,' said Dove. 'In Sydney. A number of times.'

'Why's that?'

Dove looked at him, dark eyes. 'Same colour as me. The wrong colour.'

'He forgiven you?' said Villani. 'I wouldn't forgive you.'

'He thinks being shot's my punishment,' said Dove. 'He thinks we all get punished for our sins. In time.'

'He may well be right,' said Villani. 'And my time is now.'

AT THE end of the night, a sound from the street woke him, rubber shriek, a hoon, they were naked, sheet thrown aside, a light from the unclad window lay upon them. She was on her spine, face to him, denied by a page of hair, her hands folded at her throat, her hipbones jutting, the dark in her delta.

Sleep gone, a new day but the old day in his mouth – old day, old week, month, year, life. A middle-aged man with no address, his possessions in the boot of his car.

Villani slid from the bed, stood, moved to collect his clothes.

Anna stirred, turned onto her right side.

In the weak soiled light, he waited until she had settled, looking at the sweet line of her body, a sadness in him, he went silently to the bathroom, showered in the big slate stall, thought about his feelings for her, the stupidity of it, the pleasure of being with her, talking to her, the looks she gave him. He had not been looked at that way since the first months with Laurie.

I'm in love with her.

In words. Stupid childish thought. He shook his head and shuddered as if that could dispel it.

At some point in the night, body cooling, eyes on the ceiling, the curtains were open and lights from outside played on it, he said, 'The men in your life.'

A long silence.

She said, 'The men, the men, oh Lord, where should I start? With my dad?'

'Only the good memories, please. No abuse. That's reportable.'

Her right arm across him, her mouth close, he felt her breath. 'Bastard. Why do you want to know?'

He knew what she was asking. He had no true answer.

'As a cop,' he said, 'I have a need to know.'

'Well, I confess to not a lot of luck with men,' she said.

'What's luck look like?'

'Your older brother and father combined. But not related to you.' She brushed his throat with open lips.

'This is hard,' he said. 'We can try the photofits, the DNA, might turn someone up.'

Anna bit his shoulder, soft cat-bite.

'So in the absence of cloning your family,' said Villani.

She shifted, turned, arranged herself, head on his chest.

'A mixed bag,' she said. 'The longest, a uni professor, estranged from beautiful wife, I was led to believe. I wanted to believe, I was twenty-one, I had a strong moral sense then. Six years, on and off, I was such an unbelievable dickhead. Then he left for the States, his new PhD candidate in the luggage.'

Pause. 'You don't really want to know this stuff, do you?'

'I asked.'

'What happens when I ask you?'

'Wife, three kids.'

'No, mate,' she said, 'that's not the answer, that's the alibi.'

They lay in silence.

'No saint,' said Villani. He wanted to tell her he had left home, had his suitcases in the car, but he couldn't. It would mean telling her about Lizzie and she would see Laurie's point of view, see him for what he was. Also it would sound pathetic, as if he were asking to be taken in, given a home.

'You knew that night with Tony Ruskin, didn't you?' said Anna.

'Knew what?'

'That I was available. Only had to blink.'

'Well, no. I thought you liked me as a friend.'

'Lying bastard,' she said.

'Moving on,' said Villani. 'The men.'

'A lawyer, a journo, a few journos. Two lawyers actually. And rougher and rougher trade.'

Tony Ruskin. He would be one of the journos.

'And now, rock bottom,' said Villani. 'The bedrock. Cop.'

She kissed his collarbone. 'Cop is not rock bottom,' she said. 'Ex-Collingwood footballer is rock bottom. I still shudder. I'm happy to say you're not too bad in the bottom department, though. Rockish bottom.'

'Careful,' he said, 'I'm easily aroused.'

'Is that dangerous?' Her right hand was moving down his stomach.

'Not so much dangerous,' he said, 'as potentially disappointing.'

'Every minute of every day, I risk disappointment,' said Anna. She slid onto him.

It went on for a long time. Villani had forgotten that sex could last this long and feel like this.

Done, sweaty, they lay in silence until Anna sighed, said, 'Well, you take a punt, some come off. Is this half-time?'

'Full, I think,' he said.

'The bruises. Is that work or pleasure?'

Villani looked. The first faint signs of Les's pounding. 'Boxing,' he said. 'I don't know why. Don't ask.'

She laughed, got up. By the passage light, he saw her body, its sway, the sheen on her flank. He turned his head on the pillow and he could smell her perfume.

She came back with two big glasses of water, lime slices floating. He sat up. They drank. She lay down.

'Your old man,' said Villani. 'What does he do?'

'He was in finance.'

'Like a mortgage broker?'

'No. Investment banking. He got the sack a few years ago. The sub-prime crash. Went from being a genius to being a dill in two months. He aged about twenty years.'

'And your brother?'

'Advertising. He's still a genius. For the moment.'

'So it's safe to say I'm not like him.'

'Not remotely,' said Anna. 'Which is sad. I've been listening to Paul Keogh giving the force a hard time.'

'We're waiting for him to call triple O, home invasion by lesbian bikies. Put him on hold for two days.'

'You know Matt Cameron.'

'You too, I saw.'

'Through work. Attractive man.'

'Not so much to me. But.'

'He says you've got a future. He's not flattering about the upper levels of the force.'

'Discuss me, did you? Why's that?'

'I have a small interest in you. Perverse interest. You probably haven't noticed that.'

'What's your name again?'

'My little friend Gary Moorcroft asked me if we were an item.'

Moorcroft was the channel's crime reporter, a man with a pointy nose.

'What's Pinocchio's interest?'

'Just unnaturally curious.'

'What did you say?'

'I said I was over married men.'

'Right. Is that over as opposed to under?'

She bumped him with her thin shoulder. 'Too smart by half. At least you haven't told me lies about your marriage. That is unusual in a man.'

That was the moment to choose another life. Start another life with her.

In the street now, the night wind had brought the smoke from the high country, mingled it with the city's smells of petrochemicals, carbon, sulphur, cooking oils and burnt rubber, drains, sewers, hot tar, dogshit, balsamic nightsweats, the little gasps of a million beer openings, a hundred trillion sour human breaths.

He thought about the dawn walks with Bob when he was a boy, after the trees were in, the silence of the world, the chill air you could drink. Last thing on Saturday nights, Bob in his chair with his book, his glass of whisky, Villani always said, 'Trees tomorrow, Dad?'

And Bob always said, 'I'll be in that. Wake me.'

In memory, Bob never kissed him goodnight, goodnight or goodbye or good riddance or anything else. He always kissed Mark and Luke, pulled them to him, rubbed their heads. On Sunday mornings, Bob would come into his room before the alarm went, touch his shoulder, and Villani would sit up, already moving his legs off the bed, smelling the alcohol on his father's breath, rubbing his eyes, his head, for a moment he didn't know what day it was.

Across the sloping paddocks in the grey silent day, man and boy, through the ancient lift-and-drag gate, Villani left the rifle there. They walked the forest, pulling out the dead and dying, to be replaced. They didn't lose too many. In the first years there were sodden winters and, in summer, every weeknight, Villani gravity-fed part of the forest with water from the dam, running it through hundreds of metres of old playing-field hoses Bob found on the tip. It wasn't easy moving them, the hoses had to snake, they tangled because the trees weren't planted in rows.

When they began planting, he asked about this. 'Not a plantation,' said Bob. 'They clearfell plantations. We're planting a forest. No one's going to cut this down.' He looked at Villani, the long weighing gaze. 'Not in my lifetime and not in yours. You promise?'

'Yeah.'

'Say I promise.'

He said the words.

At the end of every walk, Villani collected the Brno at the gate, it was a bolt-action .22, cheekworn stock, little five-bullet magazine never inserted until needed, his father's orders. He went down the gully that wandered to the road, sat still for a minute and picked off a few rabbits for Bob's stew, the high point of the week, made on Sunday afternoons, carrots and onions, tomato sauce, curry powder, vinegar and brown sugar. It cooked for hours, they ate it for tea with rice. Bob had a taste for rice, he could eat rice by itself with tomato sauce, and they all went that way.

The rabbits were healthy, there had never been myxo on the property.

'No logical explanation,' said Bob. 'Nature's way of telling us something.'

The rabbits stayed manageable without massacres. Other animals did the work, the feral cats and foxes. They shot them but Bob wouldn't allow fox-shooters on the property. One Saturday, they were eating the stew, a vehicle hooted outside, long blaring hoot, two short ones, another.

'That's rude,' said Bob. 'See who it is, Stevie.'

Villani went down the passage, out the front door. A truck in the drive, on the front path two big red-headed men, fat, dirty clothes.

'Get yer dad,' said the older one, balding freckled head, a comb-over.

Villani didn't have to call Bob, he came out, he was rolling a cigarette one-handed, the screendoor banged behind him, a flat smack.

'I can do what for you?' Bob Villani said.

'Had it with your fucken vermin,' said the older man. 'Told you at the servo then, you don't fucken listen. Last night it's six lambs.'

'Don't swear in front of my boy,' said Bob, quiet voice.

The man scratched his head, displaced the strands. 'Yeah, well, fuck him'n you, you kill em or we'll fucken do it, six of us and the dogs, lots of dogs.'

Bob took the Zippo out of his top pocket, flicked the lid, made the fire. He drew on the cigarette, picked a strand of tobacco off his bottom lip.

'What's your name again?' he said.

The man twisted a boot. 'Collings, fucken told you my name.'

'Collings,' said Bob. 'Collings. Well, Mr Collings, you go for your life. Shoot an animal on my land, I shoot ten on yours. Beginning or ending with you two, I don't mind which.'

Villani remembered the silence, Mark and Luke behind him, pressing on him, their hands, his father looking at the men, his father taking a drag on the smoke, blowing a single ring, perfect, it grew in the still autumn air, it hung, it rolled.

And then his father flicked his cigarette past Collings' face, missed by a hand span, and he said the words, 'Maybe you'd like to settle it now, Mr Collings? Why don't you step back a bit, then you can both have a go.'

A few moments, then Collings said, 'Give you your fucken chance,' and the men walked off. In the truck, the father shouted, 'Fuck you!'

A wheel spin, it sent up dust.

Heart beating in his throat, Villani said to Bob, 'Would you've done that?'

'What?'

'Fight them both.'

Bob looked at him, the little smile. 'My word,' he said.

For weeks, alone with the boys, Villani froze every time he heard a vehicle. But they never came, the men and the dogs, they never came.

DRIVING BENEATH the cliffs, the dark still high on the city walls, blocking the lanes, the doorways, held in the street trees, Villani kept an eye out for Lizzie, glancing down the alleys. He was being a cop, cops didn't see the world like other people. They saw everything and everyone as suspicious until proved to be otherwise.

Two boys crossing the street, baggy clothes, the smaller one was limping, the other one had his hood up. How old? Ten, twelve, not much more? In the CBD at dawn. Where had they slept? They were like foxes, both hunters and prey.

He thought about himself at twelve. He knew many things by then, but he knew little of the intimate physical world of adults, he had only glimpsed the violence. Now, some children that age had seen every last sexual thing, every thrusting sucking beating strangling act, they had seen violence of every kind. Nothing was strange or shocking, they were innocent of trust, honesty, virtue.

What they had was existence in all its careless, joyless horror.

Lizzie. Chucked away her home, the comfort, her mother's love. For what? Did she not grasp how precious was a mother's love?

Bob gave Villani the letter on a Sunday not long after fetching him and Mark from Stella Villani's house and taking them to the farm. It was written in ballpoint on thin paper with pale-blue lines torn from an exercise book.

My dearest boys,

I am writing to tell you how much I love you and how much I miss you. I have been ill for a long time but I am feeling a lot better now. Soon I hope to be home with you. Please be good and work hard at school. My darling Stephen, you must take great care of my darling Mark. Tell your Dad if there is anything he should know about from school. Remember that I love you always and forever.

Your Mum.

For the first time, Villani asked his father the question.

'Dad, what kind of illness has Mum got?'

Bob looked away. 'Something wrong in the brain,' he said. 'They don't know exactly what.'

Villani never asked about her again. He folded the letter and put it in his tin toffee box under the two photographs of his mother. He never read it again and he never forgot a word of it.

Going east on Victoria Parade. Too much thinking about what you couldn't change. He should be with Bob, waiting for the fire, the two of them, they would not say much, think about what was undone, what was always beyond doing.

You could truck the horses out, you could try to save the house, the farm buildings. But their forest. If the flames came over the northern hill, if the wind blew the superheated air down the valley, you could not save the forest. Every leaf would shrivel, the eucalypts would explode. Once it was thought they were born to burn and live again. Jesus trees, Bob used to call them. But that was before Black Saturday. They would die too and take everything with them. The oaks, the understorey, every last living creature. Marysville, Kinglake, nothing was the same after that, you could never think of fire in the old way again.

He turned into Hoddle Street, light traffic, people beating the jam, start early, leave early, the tollway gave the car slaves a few minutes of pleasure, they cruised along at a hundred, then they hit the wall, crawled into the CBD. The city badly needed Max Hendry's AirLine.

He remembered the square envelope, delivered to the desk downstairs on Tuesday. One thick creamy page.

Victoria Hendry,
Capernaum,
Coppin Grove, Hawthorn

Dear Stephen,

It was such a pleasure to meet you the other night. If you can make the time, Max and I would love to have you over for the Hendry Friday barbie. (It's a bit of a summer tradition, just a few people around the pool, kicking off around six.)

We'll expect you when we see you. Do come.

Best,
Vicky H.

Villani saw the public swimming pool, glanced at the spot on the other side of the road where, from behind a billboard on a cold evening in 1987, a young misfit, sacked army cadet, a little knot of incoherent rage, began to fire on the passing traffic. He hit a windscreen, the woman driver stopped, puzzled, got out. He shot her. Cars stopped and two men ran to her. Villani remembered the interrogation.

The first one fell onto the road, and then the second one, I don't know where, where he came from, but I dropped him as well.

Now, did they appear to be dead, when you . . . ?

The one that fell back on the road wasn't.

What happened then?

Oh, I let off another two rounds.

For what purpose?

Finish her off.

They were leaving a house in Footscray, he and Dance, when the call came.

. . . all units, all units, we have shots fired and bodies down, possible fatal. Repeat, several shots fired and the offender still on the loose, any unit in a position to attend the Clifton Hill railway station...

By the time they got there, the shooter was gone, Hoddle Street looked as if it had been strafed, cars everywhere, a motorbike on its side, seven people dead or dying, nineteen wounded.

For a while, no one could believe it was the work of one shooter, the radio spread alarm, householders panicked, the helicopter chopped over the law-abiding streets of North Fitzroy, its spotlight turned night to yellow day, the SOGs ran through houses in full combat gear, a woman later made a claim for a broken vase.

And then it was over, the worthless creature had given himself up, shouting, *Don't shoot, don't shoot,* terrified.

Villani took the turn for Rose's suburb, stopped at a newsagent and bought the papers, read them in the car.

The *Herald Sun* front page had pictures of Kidd and Larter, mug shots, the lagophthalmic psycho child-molester serial-killer look all men had when their driver's licence photographs were enlarged six hundred per cent.

EX-COPS DID TORTURE KILLINGS

The writer, Bianca Pearse, convicted the men of Oakleigh. A run-through, her police sources said. Renegade ex-SOGs ripping off vicious armed robbers, torturing and killing them for fun. Probably drug-fuelled. Searle had worked her over on the high-speed pursuit. No police vehicle near, driver lost control, so they killed themselves. A good outcome all round, really, world a better place.

Tony Ruskin's *Age* story ran across the bottom of the front page, same pictures.

Elite cops link to torture killings

Ruskin knew much more about the careers of Kidd and Larter than he should. He said Larter had been involved in a covered-up incident in Afghanistan where four civilians were killed. He was also up to speed on the Ribarics and Vern Hudson, suggested that they'd been betrayed by other filth. It couldn't have been done without Ordonez. But Ruskin had always had a better class of leaker, he was on a quality drip. In parliament someone once said his father Eric had not only been the minister for police, he was also the minister for the police, to the police, up and under and behind and on top of the police.

Without saying so, Ruskin suggested the Homicide Squad had done a remarkable job in identifying the Oakleigh killers. Unspecified acts of personal bravery by Homicide officers followed. The death crash meant the squad, through no fault of its own, was cheated of seeing the killers in court.

Barry, Gillam and Orong would be pleased. Now all that was needed was a weapon.

Rose Quirk's street was jammed with cars, he had to park a block away, walked down the street, having a little squiz. Rose was on her verandah, pink tracksuit.

'Stickyin,' she said. She drank tea out of a glass beer mug. 'Where the hell you bin?'

'Few things on,' said Villani. He opened the gate, closed it, the latch needed fixing. 'Going all right?'

'All right's history, mate. Back's gone. Had this massage, the cow touched somethin, musta learnt the trade on horses. Pain like you never seen. Into me head, down me legs.'

In the beginning, Rose's street was mostly pensioners, everything spent on rent, cigarettes, the pokies, living on mince and battery-chicken pieces, the single mothers ringing for pizzas, drugging their children with sugar and salt, Coke, bar-becue chips and chemical ice cream. Then one day Villani took notice and the street was *Location, Location, Renovator's Opportunity.*

The cars changed. The rusting Commodores, Falcons, faded Renaults and Jap cars, all with skun tyres and chipped windscreens, coat-hanger aerials, wrecking-yard doors the wrong colour, all standing in oil stains that flashed iridescent on rainy days, they gave way to Subarus, VWs, Saabs, Volvos.

On a day, Villani counted twelve tradesmen's utes and seven skips in the narrow street, the bins overloaded with ripped-out carpets and lino, baths, sinks, shower stalls, formica-topped kitchen cabinets, plastic light fittings, cattledog-brown gas heaters, embossed purple wallpaper, torn sheets of fibreboard, chipboard cupboards, tin pelmets, water heaters, dismembered Hills hoists, rotten fencing. On top of one skip sat an old dog kennel, neatly made, tin roof, the dog, the maker, the tools, the love, all gone, dead and gone.

Now he saw the beans he had planted broken, collapsed, as if an animal had been through them. 'Jesus, what's this?'

'Number 17's boy,' said Rose. 'Bit of a brat.'

The tomatoes. 'Eating a lot of cherries, are you?' he said.

'Across the road. Sophie and someone. They come and intro-duce themselves. My fault, I said help yourself.'

Hands had also plucked miniature carrots, extracted potatoes, his Kennebecs and King Edwards, from the drum. They would still be pale balls no bigger than king marbles. He heard a car boot clunk across the street, a man with a polished bald head waved, his glasses caught the light like flashbulbs.

'That's David,' said Rose.

'Why don't you get the prick over to do some gardening?' Villani said.

'You got the look,' said Rose. 'What's wrong?'

'Not thrilled about providing Audi drivers with free vegies.'

Rose squinted at him. 'Well, who said you bloody had to? Never worked out what was in it for you anyway.'

'Nothing,' Villani said. 'Not a single thing.'

He had never spoken to anyone of his visits to Rose's house. Laurie wouldn't understand. His colleagues would think he was mad. He didn't understand either, except that in the beginning he felt he owed her something and later, when he knew her, it was like being at his grandmother's house, his only real childhood, the time before he carried the weight of Mark, Luke, the animals, no hour without a duty or a care until Bob came home. And always, every hour, every day, always the fear that one Friday Bob would not come home, he would stand outside in the closing day and wait for the sound of the big rig on the hill and for the airhorn and the world would fall dark and Bob would not come home, he would not be coming back that night or ever.

'Lookin a bit pinched, son,' said Rose now. 'Want some brekkie? Got eggs from down the road.'

'Down the road?'

'The lezzies got chooks. I give em some vegies, I give em somethin, I forget.'

She wouldn't meet Villani's gaze.

'Brekkie'd be good,' he said. 'What about bacon? The lezzies keeping pigs too?'

'You're such a smartarse.'

She touched him as she went by, ran a hand up his arm to the shoulder, stroked him as she would a cat.

THE MINISTER was a big man, early fifties, jowled, a chin-down pugnacious air. He sat behind a standard public-service desk, top of glass, bare except for his mobile.

'What's this in aid of?' he said. He didn't much resemble the jovial man talking to Paul Keogh at the AirLine launch,

Villani said, 'We're from the Homicide Squad, Mr Koenig.'

'That's clever? I know where you're from.'

They were in an interview room, well away from the parliament, a room with a view of a grey rendered wall.

'It's about Thursday the eleventh, fortnight ago. The night of. Were you at home then?'

'Why?'

'We'd appreciate your cooperation.'

'I don't give a fuck what you'd appreciate. What's the point of the question?'

'A murder investigation. Your name has come up.'

'Bullshit.'

'Distant connection,' said Villani. 'But we need your help.'

Koenig looked at Villani for a good while. Villani looked back. Koenig picked up his mobile and used his thumb, put it to his head.

'Diary for eleventh of February. Evening. Where was I?'

He waited, he looked from Villani to Dove and back, looked hard, he was a man used to intimidating people.

'Okay,' he said to the phone, put it down. 'I was at home in Kew.'

'Any visitors?' said Villani.

Koenig knew this was coming, he had always known, he didn't need to have his diary checked.

'I don't understand the question,' he said.

Villani said, 'Tell us about the woman, Mr Koenig.'

'What woman?'

'The one who visited you.'

Koenig's eyes said he knew he was stuffed.

'A whore,' he said. 'Just a whore.'

'Expensive?'

Some people you enjoyed asking for humiliating details.

Koenig said, 'What do you call expensive? On your wages? Fifty dollars?'

'How much did you pay, Mr Koenig?'

'Five hundred, from memory.'

'Is that with the extras?' said Dove, head down, round glasses glinting, writing in his notebook, he was the note-taker.

Koenig pinkened. 'Who the fuck are you, sonny?

'Who delivered her?' said Villani. 'She was delivered.'

'I have no fucking idea,' said Koenig. 'She came, she went. Where'd you get this from? Who told you this?'

'How did you arrange the visit?' said Dove.

Koenig said, 'I had a number, I forget where I got it.'

'We'll have to ask you for that,' said Villani. 'You're not curious about who's dead?'

'Well, I'm assuming it's her. What else could you assume? Am I wrong?'

'Where were you last Thursday night, Mr Koenig?'

'What is this shit? I was at the beach house in Portsea.'

Silence, the muted sounds of people passing in the corridor.

'Are we done?' said Koenig. 'I'm a busy man.'

'Not done, no, not at all,' said Villani. 'But we can conduct this interview in other circumstances.'

'Is that, we can do this here or we can do it at the station? Jesus, what a cliché.'

'That's what we deal in,' said Villani.

'I'm a minister of the crown, you grasped that, detective?'

'I'm an inspector. From Homicide. Didn't I say that?'

Koenig looked at the ceiling. 'What?'

'Did you see the news last Saturday night?'

'No. I had meetings in Canberra. Went up on Saturday morning. Want to check that?'

Villani thought that it would be a pleasure to arrest Koenig, tip off the media, have them waiting. 'Let's start with how you arranged for the woman,' he said. 'Who you had dealings with.'

'I think I need my lawyer,' said Koenig.

'Of course,' said Villani. 'We'll interview you in the presence of your lawyer. Would you like to give me a time today? St Kilda Road headquarters. Give your name at the desk, someone will come down.'

'I rang a number someone gave me. I said I wanted a certain kind of woman. The person told me the price, cash, in advance. I said okay, gave the address. She arrived. I paid her, she went out to a car, she came back. Later she left.'

'You had the cash?'

'Well, I didn't pop out to a cash machine, I can tell you.'

'A certain kind of woman. What kind?'

'None of your business.'

Villani looked at Dove, blinked at him, *Take him on.*

'Tell us about her, minister,' said Dove.

Koenig's mobile rang, sharp buzzes. He listened, said Yes a few times, then No twice. 'Tell him I'll get back to him ASAP.'

He ended the exchange. 'I don't have all day,' Koenig said to Villani. 'Can we get this over with?'

'The woman.'

'Young, long hair, ten words of English. Very pale. White.'

'Caucasian pale?' said Villani.

'Oh yes.'

Dove said, 'So you specified a non-Asian?'

Koenig stared at him. 'Not in a fucking SBS crime show, sonny. You could quite soon find yourself liaising with your drunken brothers in Fitzroy. Sharing a cask.'

Villani looked around the room, nothing to look at. 'I take that to be a racially offensive remark, Mr Koenig,' he said.

'Really? My, my, how could you conclude that?'

'The number you rang,' said Villani. 'That would save us some time.'

'Meaning?'

'You can give it to us, Mr Koenig, or we can seek to get it by using the powers given to us under . . .'

Koenig raised his right hand, rose and went to the window, put his bum on the sill, hands in his pockets. His belly rode over his belt. In a smart bar in Prahran, he had once pushed and shoved and grabbed by the ears a much younger man who gave him cheek. The next day there had been a stiff-jawed public apology.

'Let me get this clear,' he said. 'I can't be a suspect in a murder investigation. I can account for all my time. That's an alibi in the correct sense of the word, which you probably don't know.'

Dove put up his right hand. 'Sir, sir, I know, sir!'

Koenig didn't take his eyes off Villani. 'Shut up, sunshine,' he said. 'You're dead in the water. So, although I have no involvement in anything, Homicide is threatening me with a warrant to look at my telephone records. Is that right?'

Villani thought about how sensible it would be to say that Homicide had not intended to give any such impression, Sorry, Mr Koenig.

'Not right,' he said. 'We make no threats. You may wish to take advice about the rights and obligations of someone who possesses or is reasonably believed to possess information material to an investigation.'

'I don't have the number anymore. I threw away the card.'

'Why's that?'

'Possibly to avoid temptation.'

'The person you spoke to last time . . .'

'A woman.'

'Accent?'

'Australian.'

'Who gave you the number?'

'I forget. I said that. I've said that.'

'How many times have you called it?' said Dove.

'You can call me Mr Koenig. Show some respect.'

'How many times, Mr Koenig?'

'None of your fucking business.'

Villani said, 'I'll repeat myself. Reasonably believed to possess . . .'

'Twice,' said Koenig. 'The first time they didn't have anyone available.'

'Talk to the same woman?' said Dove. 'Mr Koenig.'

'I really don't know.'

'Tell us about marks on the woman's body, Mr Koenig,' said Dove.

In that instant, Villani knew that Dove was not a mistake. He was a smart aleck but he was not a mistake.

'Marks?' said Koenig.

'Marks.'

'An appendix scar, that's all I saw.'

'Sure about that?'

'I know an appendix scar when I see one. I've got an appendix scar.'

Oh, Jesus.

Villani stared at Koenig for a while. 'Sure we're talking about the same woman here, minister? Not some other visitor to your house?'

'Fuck you. I couldn't be more sure.'

Phipps had made a mistake. This was a major error. He didn't look at Dove – they couldn't back off.

'We need to know who gave you the number,' he said.

'A bloke at a party gave me the number, wrote it on a card.'

'His card?' said Dove.

A hesitation. 'No, mine,' said Koenig. 'I gave him my card. He wrote it on the back.'

'A bloke you know?'

'No. Big party, we'd all had a few.'

'Whose party was it?' said Dove. 'We can go down that route.'

Koenig licked his lower lip, an unhealthy tongue, spotted. 'Now that I think about it,' he said, 'It was at Orion. Or Persius, maybe Persius. Could have been the snow, though. Yes, might have been at the snow last winter.'

Dove said, 'I suggest you know who gave you the phone number, minister.'

'Really?' Koenig said. 'I suggest you pull your fucking head in, sunshine. And you, Villani, you've made a very bad career move today, you and this clown of yours.'

Villani said to Dove, 'Record that at this point Mr Koenig made what appeared to be a threat to Inspector Villani, with the words, quote, You've made a very bad career move today, you and this clown of yours. Unquote.'

Dove wrote, slowly. Villani watched him. He didn't look at Koenig until Dove was finished. Then he said, 'Mr Koenig, we'll probably want to take a formal statement from you. You might want to bring your lawyer with you. In the meantime, we'd be grateful for the security system vision.'

'I've wiped the tapes. I wipe them once a week. That's part of my Sunday-night routine.'

Villani rose, Dove followed.

'Thank you for your time, Mr Koenig,' said Villani. 'We'll be in touch about the statement.'

'You think this up on your own?' said Koenig.

'No idea what you mean, minister,' said Villani. 'Good day.'

Outside, going down the steps, Dove said, 'I think there's been a mistake. Putting it delicately.'

Villani was putting on his sunglasses. 'You're the designated thinker here,' he said. 'I take it then you and Weber didn't just forget to mention the appendix scar I didn't notice on the Prosilio girl?'

'No, sir. There's no scar.'

'Well, then the way I'd put it, delicately, is our careers are fucked. For the moment.'

'So what now, boss?'

'Every call the prick's made in the last two months. But that's only me.'

'Can I ask why?'

The question hung, they came to the vehicle, Dove was driving. In the traffic, Villani said, 'You'll never hear me use the term fishing trip. We do things by the book.'

'I respect the book,' said Dove. 'The book is the way and the life.'

'Pity Weber's married,' said Villani. 'You have much in common.'

'What grounds do I offer?'

The radio:

. . . day of total fire ban for the state, another scorcher and no sign of a change. Firefighters are pinning their hopes on a wind shift in the early afternoon. Householders in the fire path have been advised to leave but some . . .

There was no doubt about the identity of one person in the *some* category. No, two. Gordie would drive straight into the fire with a waterpistol and wearing only a flameproof jockstrap if Bob thought it was a tactic with potential.

At the Swanston Street intersection, a wasted kid, chewed-string hair, weaved between the vehicles, tripped over the kerb, fell forward and lay still. His shirt was pulled up and his birdlike ribcage showed beneath his milky skin. People walked around him, a man kicked him by accident, jumped sideways.

The boy moved his head, got to his knees, levered on stick arms, looked around, big eyes. He stood, unsteady, took three paces to the wall, put his back against it, slid down, legs giving way.

On the station steps and on the pavement, other kids stood, sat, restless, hanging, some out of it. Two young cops were talking to three males. One was talking back, animated, changing feet, pulling at his singlet, tossing his head, sniffing. The one next to him ran fingers through his long hair, ran them over and over again.

Dove coughed. 'Koenig's calls, boss.'

'You want them as a matter of urgency,' said Villani. 'On the grounds that he is a person of interest in a murder inquiry.'

'Try that, then,' said Dove. 'That porky.'

'Only a porky if you believe every word he said. If you act in bad faith. You wouldn't do that, would you?'

'Not knowingly, boss.'

'Good. You'd also want a result today.'

'Today, certainly, boss.'

'And then we could have a talk.'

'Boss.'

This was terrible police work. It was work to be ashamed of.

The lights changed, they turned left, crossed the bridge and drove down the grand avenue. Dove dropped Villani in the street beside the police building. He rose alone in the lift, tried not to breathe the air of synthetic pine and lemon.

Lizzie. Where the hell was she? Not on the streets, cops were looking out for her, someone would see her, see the dreadlocked man. He should have had her taken home, rung Corin, told her to be there. Neglect. He did not see to her. It was his responsibility to see to her. Careless father. Bad husband. Short-term head of Homicide.

In the office, he went to his box, put on the radio, Paul Keogh's station, a woman's voice:

. . . Paul, talk to people in the rural areas, they've had enough, I can tell you. They feel betrayed, disenfranchised. This city's now a city-state, it's like Venice once was and, dare I say it, just as . . . no, I won't say it.

Is that the c-word? Corrupt?

You said it, not me. But the betrayal's also felt in the outer suburbs. Public transport's a joke, two-hour wait to see a doctor who doesn't speak English in one of these medical superpractices, one police officer for every 30,000 people, childcare's a disgrace, it's safer to leave your kid with the junkies in a park. This downturn has shown these people up for what they are – political opportunists and hacks.

Please don't hold back, Ms Mellish. My guest is Karen Mellish, leader of the Opposition. Any other things you admire about this government?

Birkerts was in the door, sad, eyebrows in a pale chevron.

Paul, even before this government took the federal recession-panic money and blew it, they were making spectacularly bad moves. Billion-dollar pipelines that are empty, the world's most expensive desalination plant, it's cheaper to bring bottled water from France. They've handed bushfire-reconstruction projects to mates, they tolerate public-transport operators who couldn't run a model railway, the tollways have seen five major tunnel shutdowns in ten months.

The police minister was on earlier talking up policing successes . . .

I heard him talking rubbish. Didn't he read the papers this morning? Two ex-policemen involved in the Oakleigh murders. We have his seat squarely in our sights, he's done his last tawdry little branchstack. What Mr Orong needs to explain to voters is why the so-called police taskforces against organised crime and drugs have achieved nothing, why the CBD is becoming more frightening than Johannesburg, kids everywhere wasting their lives on drugs. Remember the Saturday night shock-and-awe tactics?

The Humvees.

Indeed. And we now apparently need bombproof battle trucks. Overall, this city is now up there with the most violent in the world and it's not the fault of ordinary stressed police officers. The force is under such duress, it's no wonder so many are on sick leave . . .

Villani tapped the Off button.

'Ordinary stressed police officers,' said Birkerts. 'Love that. OSPO.'

'You'll love serving out your years under Kiely.'

'I can serve anyone.'

'Service, maybe. Mr Kiely thinks your manner is highly disrespectful. I think so too but I don't care as much.'

'The X-ray's at Kidd's in an hour. Want to take another look?'

'I thought the techies'd taken a girl look? What else can you offer?'

'Pitstop at Vic's. Raisin muffin.'

'Suddenly a window in my day. Dirty little window.'

THEY SAT in the car, engine running, air-con on, looking at the sluggish sea. Two silver cats on leads drawing a woman came into view on the damp edge of the continent. She wore shorts and a muscle shirt that revealed no trace of what it was meant to display. The cats minced, offended by the moisture beneath their paws.

'Just a massive sandbox,' said Birkerts.

Villani finished his coffee. 'Good, this bloke,' he said. 'Reliable.'

'His ex lives in Tassie,' said Birkerts. He was eating a banana muffin. 'She had the kids for a holiday, won't send them back. He says he might have to move.'

'Ask the pointyheads to give her a fright,' said Villani. 'Can't lose a decent barista. You the one filled in Tony Ruskin on Kidd and Larter? He knows more than I do.'

'Don't look at me. We get the arse from Defence but somebody tells Ruskin about this killing of four Afghan civilians stuff. Since the discharge, Larter's a ghost. Possibly on a mountain in Tassie eating possums. Live. Popular among your returned killers.'

'And the guns?'

'Nothing shows. Bikie imports.'

A group of joggers crossed their vision: old men, creased, humped, silent. Heads down, they shuffled by.

'In step,' said Birkerts. 'How is that?'

'Got the same tune on their iPods,' said Villani. 'Colonel Bogey. Finished at Oakleigh?'

'Going out after this. Want to come?'

'Why not? Got all day, all night too since I don't have any-where to live.'

'Live? Why?'

'Marital dispute.'

Without smiling, Birkerts took on an amused look. 'This is sudden?'

'When it happens,' said Villani, 'everything is sudden.'

'Stay at my sister's place if you like. You met Kirsten.'

'I did. At your barbie that day. The charcoal went out. Died. Where's she gone?'

'Italy. Successful divorce, skinned the bloke. Now she wants to be an artist.'

'Her place where?'

'What? Picky?'

'There are places I won't live, yes,' said Villani.

'Fitzroy. In your zone of acceptability?'

'I can handle Fitzroy. Parts of Fitzroy. What else about Kidd?'

'After the SOGs, he went overseas for eighteen months. The suggestion is private security in Iraq. Then a couple of months with GuardSecure, sacked for putting a bloke in hospital, case pending. Since then he's a ghost too. One bank account, about eight grand in it, there's cash deposits, like five, six hundred bucks. He's got two credit cards, not a big spender, ordinary stuff. He pays it in full.'

'And the Prado?'

'Bought in a yard a year ago. Car City. He traded in a Celica, balance cash.'

'Well, let's have a look then.'

Birkerts made a call. 'They're on the way.'

They had just parked behind the building in Roma Street when the van drew up. Two men in overalls got out, took two black rubber cases from the back. Birkerts led the way upstairs.

Kidd's unit was stifling, the heat amplifying trapped cooking smells: fried onions, meat. Passing the bathroom, Villani smelled talcum powder. He hadn't smelled it on the night.

'Talcum powder?' he said. 'Men?'

'Jock itch,' said Birkerts.

They went into the big room. One tech took the device out of its case, it was like a big fox-hunting spotlight but blind. He ran a hand over it.

'Fond of it?' said Birkerts. 'Like a pet?'

The man said nothing, unclipped a tight coil of yellow cable. On the kitchen bench, the other man opened his case, a computer monitor in the lid.

Villani left, looked into Kidd's disordered room, moved on, opened the sliding door to the back bedroom. No more than a big cupboard with its own built-in cupboard.

Ray Larter slept here. In the built-in, a pair of denims on a wire hanger. He found the label: waist 34, leg 44. A tall man and slim, Ray Larter. His sports bag had been on the floor beside the bed, it told little – T-shirts, underpants, clear toilet bag with toothpaste, disposable razors, tube of shampoo. Ray was neat, unlike Kidd.

Villani thought about his father's bare bedroom on a Monday morning, bed stripped, blankets on the line, sheets and dirty clothes in the machine.

He went down the passage and onto the balcony, looked down at the street, the trees, a woman in a tight red skirt standing beside a parked car, talking to the driver. She sucked a cigarette, waved it. A hand came out of the window, she passed the cigarette, the taker flicked it into the street. She slapped at the hand, missed.

Anna.

She came to mind in all the interstices of the day, other women had not done that, not since the early days with Laurie. What did she see in him? Some women had the cop thing, early on in the job you heard the stories, the jokes. There was truth in them. Even the ugly cops got the chances, the eyes, the offers. He was clean there, he never went back to a single-mother's place to see if everything was all right, part of the service to give you a fuck. Comforting fuck.

On the job, something always said No. It was when he was not on business that something said Yes.

The *Herald Sun*'s crime journo got off on cops. Bianca Pearse. Bianca wasn't a starfucker though. Just as soon root a constable as a commissioner. Just a copfucker. Birkerts had been there, he was pretty sure of that.

It didn't feel like a cop thing. Anna didn't ask questions about the job, they always did. She seemed interested in what he thought, happy to be with him.

This was pathetic. He was too old to let this take him over. This was for your twenties, when an ignorant country dork could be flattered if Miss-Private-School-My-Father's-an-Investment-Banker took a fancy to him.

He looked at Kidd's barbecue in the corner of the balcony. Narrow, rusty, the grill crusted with charred grease and tiny welded-on lumps of meat. Not the Ozzie Grillmaster Turbo. Did they have a barbie on the night? Few beers, burn a couple of steaks, press them, see the pricks of blood, then the watery red ooze. Did they talk about what they were going to do to the Ribaric boys? Talk about lighting the Ribs' hair, first the pubic. Full of oil, it would frizzle.

Then the hair on their heads. But first slit their nostrils. Then light the hair on their heads.

Hair full of chemical shit. Product. Click the lighter in Ivan's face. Look in his eyes. Take a moment. Enjoy it. Lift the flame over his forehead. Slowly.

Whoosh.

Under the gas burner sat a foil tray, half-full of fat set solid, grey, mottled like marble, the drippings from the burning altar above.

Birkerts came out, hands in pockets.

'Well, bedrooms clean,' he said. 'Doesn't leave much.'

The techs came into the kitchen, had a discussion. The shorter one shrugged, knelt and pointed his device at the side of the kitchen bench. The other one looked at the laptop screen.

'You can see why they joined,' said Birkerts. 'Adrenalin junkies.'

'Kirsten's place,' Villani said.

'Got the keys in my car.'

'Take me around when you knock off?'

'I think I'll just give you the keys,' said Birkerts.

They smoked Birkerts' cigarettes, watched the techs go around the kitchen bench. When they'd finished, the taller one came out.

'Nothing, boss,' he said. 'Anywhere else?'

'Check around the bath?' said Villani.

'Yup.'

'Bugger,' said Villani.

'That's it,' said Birkerts. 'Thank you.'

The men packed up, snapped their cases, waved, left.

THEY WERE on their way to Oakleigh, passing the Albert cricket ground.

'What's the rent?' said Villani.

He didn't care. He had not lived alone since he was twenty-two. This was a bad time to change that. He and Laurie had always slept in the same bed. When all was gone and lost, when they no longer touched, they still shared a bed. The last person in it made it, that was the rule, from the start.

He often dreamed about sex with Laurie. She was always the same age, the quick-handed girl in the sandwich shop who layered the basics on the white slice, the slivered iceberg strands, the pale discs of tomato, the bleeding beetroot, the square of factory cheese, the cheeky girl who looked at him and said, 'What else can I give you?'

The first sex with Laurie was on her friend Jan's futon. Laurie picked him up after his shift, they ate at the Waiters' Club, the small rooms packed with the late-night hungry, and went to the student house in Clifton Hill. It smelled of dope, that made him uneasy.

'Pay the bills, that'll do,' said Birkerts. 'Left two weeks ago. I said I'd clean out the fridge. Be full of rotten stuff. You can do that.'

'How long's she gone?'

'Six months, she says. There's a new man, some mystical lawyer arse she met in Byron Bay. At a wellbeing spa.'

'Wellbeing spa,' said Villani. 'Just trips off your tongue, doesn't it? What the fuck is wellbeing?'

'Respect your body. Think positive thoughts. Live in the moment.'

'What if the moment is absolutely shit?' Villani said. 'What if you have no respect for your flabby fucked-out body? What's the other one?'

'Positive thoughts,' said Birkerts, eyes on the road. 'You think positive thoughts. I don't think you're thinking positive thoughts now. At this moment. I feel that.'

'How wrong can your pathetic instincts be?' said Villani. 'I'm thinking positive thoughts about finding the gun. I'm thinking if we don't then my whole . . .'

It came to him.

'Turn around,' he said. 'Back to Kidd's.'

Birkerts said nothing. He turned right on Roy Street, right again on Queens Road. They were turning into Kidd's street before he spoke.

'Forget something?' he said.

'Remembered something,' said Villani. 'Park in front.'

Birkerts parked. 'Need me?'

'Oh yes,' said Villani. 'Gloves?'

'Like that, is it?'

Villani went in first, down the passage, into the sitting room, waited for Birkerts.

'Put on the gloves,' he said.

'Me?'

'I don't do this kind of thing. I'm the boss.'

The rubber gloves made the whispering, hissing sound, Birkerts held up pale blue hands. 'What?' he said.

Villani went onto the balcony. Birkerts followed. Villani pointed.

Birkerts held the foil tray over the grill, turned it over, twisted.

Nothing happened. He shook it.

The cake of solid fat fell to the grill, stayed intact.

'Well bugger me,' Birkerts said.

'HOW LONG?' said Villani.

He saw Kiely come out of his door, cross to Dove's desk, lean over it, lecture Dove about something.

'Being redone now,' said the ballistics man.

'What's the first time say?'

'Can't say.'

'Fired recently?'

'Can't say that either. Say it hasn't been cleaned.'

'Dirty?'

'Well, just not cleaned. Not dirty, no.'

'The husband's defence,' said Villani. 'Call Tracy when you've got a strong opinion, will you?'

He watched Kiely coming his way, the buttoned suit jacket, where did he think he was?

'BUL M-5,' said Kiely. 'Unusual weapon.'

'Israeli. Every second Afghan's got one. Handgun of choice.'

'They sell arms to Afghans?'

'Don't discriminate, your Israeli arms dealers. Sell arms to anyone. Make guns in New Zealand?'

'No,' said Kiely.

'Probably just as well.'

'The crash people say explosions in Kidd's Ford.'

'Brilliant,' said Villani. 'Went up like Krakatoa.'

'Not fuel,' said Kiely. 'They say two explosions before that, the second one, the big one, that blew the driver's legs off. Then the fuel caught.'

Villani felt his scalp itch, he did a circuit on the chair. 'So not high-speed pursuit crash, driver lost control?'

'You should talk to them.'

'My word.'

'Tanner's the man's name. Glen Tanner.'

He had a call made.

'That's right, inspector,' said Tanner. 'We would say two charges, possibly some mechanism triggers the first, which damages the steering, the driver loses control. Then there's the impact. And then the main charge goes off and it's big and the fuel ignites.'

'No chance it's just fuel?'

He heard the sniff of contempt.

'Not unless it was a stunt for a movie, that exploding-car rubbish. Low-pressure fireball is possible when fuel escapes and ignites, yes. But not here.'

'Obliged to you,' said Villani. 'Also if you keep this in-house until we've got somewhere.'

He thought about watching Kidd, hearing the call.

Listen, listen, some worries. Serious.

What?

Old girl's, call you on that in five, okay?

How was that conversation to be explained? How was Kidd not using the Prado to be explained? Where did the Ford come from, a street rod with genuine plates and a missing owner aged seventy-eight?

Tracy.

'Boss, ballistics rang,' she said. 'That's positive. A match with Metallic.'

The weapon in the slab of dripping had executed the Ribarics. The BUL M-5 had been in the hand of Kidd or Larter.

OAKLEIGH buttoned up. Something to be happy about. Colby would be happy, Barry would be happy, Gillam would be happy. Orong would pat Gillam. Orong would tell the premier.

Villani rang Colby.

'Got the Oakleigh gun, boss,' he said. 'Ballistics match.'

'Sure?'

'As science can be.'

'Where?'

'Kidd's place. Under our noses.'

'Techs find it?'

'No. Me.'

'You?'

'In the barbie fat tray. Kidd's barbie.'

A moment.

'It takes a certain kind of sick arsehole to check the barbie fat tray,' said Colby. 'You're an example to your men. Women.'

'Don't have any women.'

'Keep quiet about that,' said Colby. 'A fat dyke'll have your job in a minute. Promoted from ethnic transgender liaison squad.'

'Sir.'

'Now Mr Brendan O'Barry, emphasise he's first cab, be breathless. Pant a lot. Then he can tell the ranga, Gillam can tell Orong. At some point, someone will tell me, I'll be so stunned. Searle and his new slapper can then feed shit to all and sundry about how wonderful Homicide is.'

'Sir.'

'We now want to close the book on Metallic. Gone, finished. With me?'

'With you. Yes.'

'You might still have a career,' said Colby. 'In spite of your fucking self.'

Villani rang Barry, told him the story.

'Excellent,' said Barry. 'I'll inform the chief immediately. We have closure on Metallic. Much to be explained but killers identified and, by their own hands, deceased.'

'That's it, boss. More or less.'

'We need to have a little talk soon.'

'When it suits you, boss,' said Villani.

DOVE OPENED the folder, gave Villani pages.

'Calls from Koenig's Kew house, fixed line, the mobile in his name,' he said. 'Taken out his staff, pollies, family. Also now have the Orion guest list by unofficial means. I'd like to put that on record.'

'You can't,' said Villani. 'Unofficial doesn't go on record.'

'I can see the logic. Boss.'

'You could be approaching take-off speed in this job. Flying a Piper Cub, mind you.'

'It's calls in the past two months, ranked by number, from the bottom.'

Twenty-odd names. Villani knew some of them from the newspapers, television.

Mervyn Brody, Brody Prestige, expensive German cars, second-hand, also a racehorse owner. Brian Curlew, criminal barrister, defender of the high-end scum, they said the first consultation was free, the second one cost fifty thousand bucks, some cash, some declared for tax. Chris Jourdan of the Jourdan brothers, owner of restaurants and bars. Daniel Bricknell, art dealer. Dennis Combanis, property developer, Marscay Corporation. Mark Simons, insolvency expert. Hugh Hendry.

'Mr Hendry junior,' Villani said.

'At school together,' said Dove. 'St Thomas College. Also Curlew and that Robert Hunter. All in the same year.'

'That's important?'

'I don't know what's important, boss.'

'I like an open mind. Empty mind is what worries me. Who's Hunter?'

'Headmaster of St Thomas.'

'Yes?'

'Brody and Bricknell and Curlew and Simons and Jourdan are all on the casino party list.'

'No doubt many people on the chief commissioner's speed-dial were there too,' said Villani. 'A-list people. Saw some of them at Persius the other night. What do you want to make of that?'

Dove touched his chest, under the right pec, a finger, a small, gentle rub, he would do that for the rest of his life.

'Can we get their phones?' he said.

'On what grounds?'

'Well.'

'That's the fed approach,' said Villani. 'Any phone, anybody, any time, any reason, no matter how pissweak. No, son. Here the magistracy takes the view that murderers should walk free rather than a single innocent person's phone records be examined.'

'What's your view, boss?' said Dove.

'I don't have a view. Anyone in Homicide misguided enough to use unofficial channels, it's their marching ticket. Birkerts has been suspected of doing this shit.'

Dove smiled. 'Is that so?'

'It is so. I think what we've established is that Koenig likes whores,' Villani said. 'Mr Phipps saw one who happened to look like our girl. So what we are engaged in is a wide-ranging investigation that goes down some dead-ends. Inevitably. It's in the nature of wide-ranging investigations.'

'Yes?' said Dove.

'In the course of investigations, information emerges that's not helpful but can be embarrassing for some people.'

'Yes?'

'That information goes in the vault. Is that clear?'

Dove looked at the ceiling, interested, like a man observing the heavens, a student of stars. 'Could not be clearer, boss,' he said.

A knock, Weber came in, bunny-eyed, awkward, shifted his feet.

'Welcome,' said Villani. 'Haven't seen you for a while, detective. Speak freely to us.'

'Been out there, boss. Talked to everyone in Prosilio over the time. Nothing. Also the staff records. Clean, just speeding, some juvenile, that kind of thing.'

'That's promising,' said Villani. 'That's marvellous.'

Guilty, contrite, Weber looked at the grey public-service carpet.

'What about the owner of the apartment?'

Weber looked at Dove.

'Just getting there,' said Dove. 'Shollonell, this Lebanese company, bought it six months ago. Directors are Mr and Mrs Ho from Hong Kong. In their late seventies, Mr Ho is in a wheelchair. Prosilio housekeeping now remembers they got everything ready then, beds, the champagne, in case they arrived without notice. But they've never arrived.'

Villani became aware of the dullness of his mind, the ache in his ankles, his knees, his shoulders, his neck. 'I'm inclined to rule the Hos out. Just instinct.'

The phone.

'Chief Commissioner Gillam for you, inspector.'

'Yes.'

'Stephen?'

'Commissioner.'

'Good result on Metallic, yes. Turned out well. Possibly better than a SOG move on Kidd's premises would have produced.'

'The possible gun battle,' said Villani. 'The possible loss of officers' lives. The possible collateral damage to the innocent.'

Gillam coughed. 'That sort of thing, yes. So, well done. The minister will be pleased.'

Villani put the phone down, looked at his watch. 'I'm leaving the building now,' he said. 'My day is over. I leave you with the thought that we, that's the three of us and by extension the whole fucking squad and the whole fucking force, we have failed the little Prosilio girl.'

The men both looked down, Weber nodding.

Singleton would be so proud.

'And see if the Hos have kids. Junior Hos. And grandchildren. Concentrating on the male line.'

THE APARTMENT was in a redbrick building a few streets down from Brunswick Street, Villani knew it from when he was eighteen and it was standing empty, boarded up. They went there early one morning to evict squatters, he remembered sleepy, spunky women and dirty-haired men holding at least two guitars.

The removal people carried out a remarkable number of amps. Fender, Vox, Marshall, they looked as if they had been dropped and kicked many times.

The parking garage was off a pissed-in, puked-on lane, through a graffitied roll-up door Birkerts opened with a remote. Concrete stairs led to a steel door, opened with a key.

Villani followed Birkerts up more concrete stairs to a long landing, they turned left. The apartment's front door was steel too, studded. Beyond it was a long room, high ceiling, done over in jarrah, granite and stainless steel, a sitting-down area, a television-watching area, a cooking and eating area. The table was made from ten-centimetre thick gum slabs, it could seat twelve, provide shelter from a missile attack.

'More than I expected,' said Villani. He went to the window, looked through treetops to the city's towers, vague in the smoke.

'She wanted a cash payout from the boy,' said Birkerts. 'He offers one mill. Take it, says her brief. I said, the family home plus new car, plus five hundred grand. As of last valuation, recession and all, the settlement's now worth one point eight mill.'

'Amazing,' said Villani. 'The foresight.'

'Long ago, my old man said, inner city, never mind price. Always on the button, my dad.'

'I recall he also said only the truly ignorant are truly happy,' said Villani. 'Does that include the truly ignorant about real-estate opportunities?'

'I wish I'd never told you that,' said Birkerts. 'You forget nothing, you wait. There's bedrooms at each end. With en suites.'

'I'll find one.'

'Okay. I don't want to look in the fridge. Chuck out the dead stuff, will you? There's booze in that cupboard.'

They went to the door. Birkerts gave him a key ring. 'Buzzer, keys. Garbage instructions on fridge.'

'Appreciate this,' said Villani. 'But don't expect any favours.'

'Bugger,' said Birkerts, 'I had hopes.' He looked around. 'Got a bit of domestic drama on myself.'

Villani didn't look at him, that encouraged confession.

'Job's a breaker, no question,' said Birkerts. 'Ever ask yourself why you do it?'

A moment between them.

'No day passes,' said Villani. 'Just don't curl up.'

Just don't curl up.

Bob Villani's instruction. Bob and Cameron and Colby and Singo and Les, the men in his life, they'd all given him plenty of instructions.

Had Bob ever curled up? On his own in Vietnam, a lone operator in a strange place, strange people, so far from home, had he crunched up in his sleeping bag, whimpered? Even once? One tiny whimper?

Not likely.

'Curl up?' said Birkerts.

'You feel so sorry for yourself, you lie down and curl up,' Villani said.

'You done that?'

'No day passes. See you in the morning,'

Alone, he chose a bedroom. It was the size of a double garage, white walls, no decoration. The bed was made. He put his clothes in a walk-in closet, a room, went back and inspected the fridge: solid milk, limp coriander, two flaccid cucumbers, no meat.

Dozens of bottles of wine, spirits, mixers in the drinks cupboard. Whisky and soda. There was ice. He sat in a leather armchair, tinkled the ice, drank, listened to the building, the street, beyond. Faint music, piano.

Tired, nodding off, he should eat something. When had he eaten? Breakfast with Rose. Terrible bread but good everything else – the scrambled eggs, his cherry tomatoes done in the pan, popped, the juices.

Lizzie. Why had he cut her out so early? Felt so little for her? Even now, his strongest feeling was resentment, betrayal. Why didn't Tony cross his mind more often? Tony got the best he had to give. He found time for Tony, he had been a decent father. In a way.

He began taking Tony to Carlton home games when he was tiny, carrying him in a backpack. He was Fitzroy, but it had never been serious and he'd drifted into supporting the Blues when he was stationed at Carlton. You had to have a team. You couldn't say you didn't care. Cashin came to the football with them. He was Geelong but he came. Sometimes Laurie came, it was just to please him.

Bob Villani didn't care about footy, they didn't talk football when he was a kid, they didn't have a family team. One day, Villani asked him.

'Who do we go for, Dad?'

Bob was reading his book, *The Faber Book of 20th Century Verse*, brown-paper cover with big grease blots, he took it with him in the rig.

'Go for?'

'Footy. They ask me who we go for.'

'Fitzroy,' his father said, he did not move his head.

'Why, Dad?'

'Need all the help they can get.'

He didn't know Bob had played football until he found the photograph of the 1960 Levetts Creek Football Club Premiership Team, fifteen men and three boys. Twenty-odd years later, they went up there for a girl, throat cut, it was a hard little town, all mullets, feral utes and punched women, beer cartons blown flat against the fences. He saw the faces in the picture, the sons and grandsons. They would have been woodcutters or sawmill workers then, the man holding the ball was two fingers short on his right hand.

On the back, in violet pencil, someone wrote: *Robert Villani (centre half-back)*.

Perhaps sixteen, short hair, chisel chin, long upper arms, bruise on his right cheekbone, as tall as the men in his row and half their thickness. And the eyes, they caught the light.

One bitter Saturday when Tony was seven, he put the navy-blue scarf around the boy's neck, they went to Princes Park to see Carlton play the Bombers, met Cashin there.

In the queue, Tony said, 'The Bombers, they're my team.'

They looked at him.

'The Blues are your team,' said Villani.

'No,' said Tony. 'The Bombers.'

He took off his scarf. 'You wear this, Dad.'

Villani could never have done that to Bob. He could not do

that to Bob now. It was a kind of bravery. Why didn't he ever tell Tony that?

Pointless. He wouldn't remember it. It would have no meaning for him.

Why didn't Tony ever ring him? Scotland, he was in Scotland, a Scottish island. What would Scotland be like? The heather on the hills. What was heather? What was it like to be an nineteen-year-old Australian boy in Scotland?

He was eighteen when he took his first walk in uniform after the course, a country boy, open-mouthed, thrilled. Not dangerous the city then. Dope was the street drug, some smack, cocaine seriously sophisticated. Around midnight, the nightlife ended. You could drive home drunk, needed to ram a cruiser to be blood-tested.

The cop talk was all marijuana busts, armed robberies, illegal gambling, wogs fighting to control Victoria Market, wharfies fighting over who was allowed to steal what on the docks.

You didn't notice the job change. More people on the nod, shooting up on the street, shopping centres, stations, parks, churches. More dumb burgs, brain-dead robberies, kids selling themselves to anyone for anything, dead in alleys, railway stations, tunnels, sewers, on the grubby beaches.

Villani remembered when the CBD was still safe enough to walk across on a Friday night. But once the chemicals took over, spread into the suburbs, cops regularly began to see things once rare – teenagers bashing old people, women and children beaten, the punching and kicking and stabbing of neighbours, friends, cab drivers, people on trains, trams, buses, strangers at parties, in pubs and nightclubs, the hacking at people with swords, road-rage attacks, bricks hurled at trams, train drivers.

Then they got rid of the old liquor laws. Civilising move, they said. Australia's most European city needed more relaxed liquor laws.

In a short time, hundreds of all-night clubs and drinking barns opened in a few dozen blocks in the CBD, most of them owned by the same people who ran the poleholes and titmarts.

At weekends, thousands upon thousands of people flowed into the city, very European to come in from Donnie and Brookie and Hoppers with your mates, half wasted to begin with, swallow anything, get totally munted, walk around, no fucking fear, mate, the ice fever made you fight your mate, any cunt looks at you, take a spew, take a piss, take a shit, anywhere.

Mobile.

'This a good time, boss?' Dove.

'Depends on what you say.'

'There's nothing at Preston. That's prints, DNA. Nothing. They report signs it's been wiped.'

'This is not a good time,' said Villani.

DEEP IN the freezer, he found a pizza encased in shrinkwrap. He microwaved it and sat at the monks' table to eat. It tasted like food found in a glacier, locked in the ice for a hundred years, a memory of a pizza in which all the good parts were forgotten.

He stood in a large porcelain saucer to shower. On a hook beside the door hung a man's thick white towelling gown. The property of the mystical lawyer arse from Byron Bay?

Naked, he crossed the dressing-room and lay on the low bed, a rock-hard mattress, probably a futon. Futons. Did they still sell futons? He studied his body. It did not please him. He touched the dirty marks, the purpling where Les caught him in the bottom ribs, a good place to catch someone, bend the rib into the cavity.

Anna hadn't called.

Should he have left a message? There was a pad beside her telephone in the passage, he could have written a few words.

I love you. Stephen

He could have passed it off as a joke. Or not. If the response was favourable. Probably not. Definitely not.

What a stupid teenage prick he was.

Lizzie. They would call him if they found her, they had the instruction, any time, twenty-four hours. Somewhere with the streeters? In some crevice in the city, a tunnel, a half-built highrise, sleeping on the raw concrete? They found dead people in these places every day.

The Prosilio child.

The truck stop on the Hume. Swooshing highway, a hot night, airless. As you opened the car door, it would hit you: petrol, diesel, heated rubber, exhaust gases, chip-fryer oil, the smell of burnt meat. Overweight truckies coming out of the ablution block, wet hair, men shat, shaved, showered, shampooed.

The sounds of engines ticking, air-conditioners and extractor fans humming.

A girl coming out of the toilet block, Caucasian girl, speaking to a man in her own language. Not English. On her way to Melbourne, to the ugly fortress in Preston, perhaps a cheap nylon suitcase in the boot, hookers' clothes, sexy bras, pants, suspender belt.

To have her life taken in the rich people's building. They had not made one centimetre of progress towards finding her killer. They had been toyed with by the building's owners. They had pointlessly made an enemy of a powerful man. They looked like idiots.

Mobile again.

'Boss, I also wanted to say,' said Dove, 'I got the water usage there. No water used for the month leading up to that sighting on the Hume. Then it's average for four people, a bit higher.'

'Four people?'

'Perhaps people who need to shower often.'

There was much more to Dove than extraordinary clotting power.

'That's a bit of a pattern,' said Dove. 'Over the last three years.'

'Well, it's interesting but it's not taking us anywhere.'

'And boss, that number, I've got . . .'

'When I see you,' said Villani. 'Face to face. I like to observe your body language.'

'In the morning then.'

'Yes. Go home. Got a home?'

Why did he ask that? Stupid.

'Got the bed, yes,' said Dove. 'The shower.'

He didn't know anything about Dove's life outside the job. Singo knew everything about people's lives, he knew your kids' birthdays, he could drop a reference to your wedding anniversary, show you that he knew. But Singo didn't care.

Son, life's got layers, the work layer's on top. That's my layer, that's my business, that's my duty. Under that, it's personal, it's your business. I don't want to know. It's not that I wouldn't care. I would care. That's the problem. So I just don't want to know. See the sense?

Villani had seen the sense.

'Breakfast meeting,' he said. 'Know Enzio's? Brunswick Street?'

'I can find Enzio's.'

'Seven-fifteen. Back left corner.'

Villani fell asleep and he dreamed of Greg Quirk, of crossing the filthy unit and seeing Greg squirting blood, of looking up and seeing Dance with the gun in both hands, smiling his canine smile.

VILLANI WOKE just after 6am, dull-headed, knowing where he was, full of dread in the way of the early Robber days. He lay, unwilling to get up, cross the threshold of the day.

The smallholding in the valley near Colac where Dave Cameron lived with his girlfriend came into his mind. Dave had put up a fight, the kitchen was chaos, blood everywhere, table overturned, crockery on the floor. He had been hacked with something, a big knife, a sword, deep cuts to his arms, shoulders, neck, head, before he was shot. Twice with an unknown weapon, twice with his own service weapon.

His girlfriend had been shot in the head, three times, with Dave's weapon. She was found to be pregnant, Dave's child.

They threw everything at it, the whole force, other investigations went on hold. They didn't see Matt Cameron for weeks. Deke Murray, the SOG boss, was made head of the taskforce, he had started with Matt, they were like brothers, their careers marched together, they both became Robber legends. They even looked like brothers.

Deke had gone to the SOG before Villani arrived, but he came to Robber piss-ups, to Cameron's parties, sometimes showed up on a Friday night at the pub. Matt quit the force when his wife Tania committed suicide, he had no family left. Deke quit soon after. The prime suspect, a hard case called Brent Noske, twice arrested by Dave Cameron in the months before the murders, killed himself, shotgun in the mouth. Noske was a cop-hater, they narrowly failed to get him for firing on a Geelong cop's house with an M16.

What happened to Deke? He'd resigned. Where had he gone?

Villani shook the thoughts away, rose, showered, dressed, went into the big room and switched on the radio.

Bruce Frank, the morning man on the ABC, was talking his usual drivel, he had a voice that shifted in tone, from gruff to shrill in the same sentence. Villani sat in an armchair with the battery razor, head back, eyes closed, the machine wasn't up to the task but it was soothing.

He registered the word *police* and thumbed the shaver off.

. . . leader of the Opposition Karen Mellish on the line, she's called in. Up bright and early, Ms Mellish.

I'm a farmer's daughter, Bruce. And a farmer's wife. We don't loll around in bed. There's work to be done.

A case can be made for a bit of lolling in bed, surely? I mean the birthrate isn't what it should . . .

No frivolity please, I'm ringing about your caller's comment that my party takes pleasure in knocking the Victoria Police. That is absolutely and completely wrong and . . .

You've said a few hard things about the police recently, haven't you? Bit more than a few.

Bruce, our job is to speak out against incompetence where we see it. And we see it everywhere under this shoddy government. But take pleasure in denigrating the police? Never. No. We want to see our police force given the numbers and the leadership to do what they are quite capable of doing, which is to make this city and this state the most inhospitable place on earth for violent hoons, drug dealers, career criminals . . .

A big ask that. I have no doubt the government . . .

To wake without the hangover feeling took a holiday of at least a week. The first two or three days were detox, twitchy, irritable, aware of feeling tight in the shoulders, in the neck, in the back. The second week, he lost interest in organising.

Two weeks? Not since Corin was fifteen.

Surfers Paradise was going to be a week alone, the two of them, kids in safe hands. He thought they could patch things up, start again. That Laurie suggested going was hopeful, the matter of Tony's friend's mother was still close.

Catering customers, television people, offered their holiday unit. Laurie's company was by then catering for lots of shoots.

She went ahead. Villani remembered almost missing the plane, falling asleep before take-off, finding a taxi, standing on the narrow balcony of the beachfront tower looking at the sea, the beach far below in deep shadow, lace-frilled waves unrolling, people walking on the wet sand.

He fell asleep on a sofa in the sitting room while Laurie was on the balcony, talking on her mobile. In the small hours, a cramp in his left calf woke him. He could not believe the pain. He thought: the deep-vein thing. He put his feet on the floor, frantically massaged the muscle, pummelled it, tears came to his eyes, he stood up, shook his leg, stamped his foot.

The pain gave way to numbness. He slept for a few hours, woke in the dawn, hungry. Nothing to eat in the place, he smoked a cigarette on the balcony. There were a few dozen surfers out, scattered, it was playschool, the wind in the south-east, nothing happening, two-footers.

Villani took the lift down, left his shirt and towel on the sand. Walking out through the warm shallows with two young women surfers, girls, he eyed himself unhappily, pale chicken-breast skin, flab on his hips. It was a long swim to where he could catch a wave, the girls were ahead of him, paddling, in no hurry.

He wasn't the world's greatest swimmer and he hadn't been to the gym for a while. He had to push himself, the girls looking back at him – pityingly, he thought. When he reached the deep water, he was winded. Hundreds of thousands of people swam off this beach every year and he found himself alone.

Joe Cashin taught him to surf. Cashin was junior to him, a reserve about Cashin, a little smile, no friends among his peers. At Carlton, they became friends, both much smarter than most of the people around them. When they were not working in daylight, they went to Rye or Portsea in Villani's Falcon. It was tame for Cashin, he'd surfed since he was a kid, he mucked around, walked up and down on his board, turned his back to the shore. But he put up with it until Villani was ready for proper surf, ready to be trashed in the breakers at Bells.

At Surfers, Villani floated on the swells, back to the shore, trying to get his breath, then he saw the first wave of a set. He rose with it, with the bigger second one, turned and swam for the third. Head down, arms threshing, he caught it, hunched his shoulders. He felt its power take hold of him, enter him, he was not propelled by the wave, he was the wave, he was the power, arms tucked in, body arched, he was the lovely bouncing force.

Then the wave obeyed some secret command, betrayed him. It hollowed, it dumped him, his forehead hit sand, he thought his neck was broken, the force rolled him, rolled him, tumbled him, pulled down his Speedos, he swallowed water, water went up his nose, he did not know where up was, he was drowning.

His head broke water and it was over, nothing special, he was in the foam, bodysurfers copped dumpings like this as a matter of course – they snorted out half a glass of salty snot and swam out for the next round. But he was done.

He walked in, looked down and saw the blood drip from his chin onto his chest, into the sand stuck to his shiny black stomach hairs. Putting on his shirt, he saw the bleeding burns on his fore-arms and elbows.

Laurie was up when he got back.

'Jesus, what happened to you?'

'Nothing. Got dumped.'

'You need something on that.'

No concern in her voice, she knew blood, she ran a big cater-ing kitchen, they cut themselves all the time, bled into the yellowfin tuna, the Wagyu beef, the swimmer-crab meat, the twice-cooked duck, they added blood of all groups to the finger food, an exquisite coin-sized portion cost five dollars.

In the shower, he studied his knees, his forearms, his elbows. He found antiseptic cream in the medicine cabinet, put it on, winced.

They had breakfast at a café – cold scrambled eggs, cold bacon, cold toast, lukewarm terrible coffee. They read the papers, talked about the kids in a listless way, he remarked on things, she wasn't interested in his views. She had been once. He tried to remem-ber when that was. They bought food at a supermarket, at a delicatessen. Laurie suggested the beach. He said no. One humiliation a day was enough.

She changed, went down, and he sat on the balcony and switched on his mobile – a dozen messages. It took more than an hour to sort things out. He switched off, dozed in a chair.

Laurie came back in the early afternoon, she hadn't taken a key, she rang. He opened the door. She was in shorts and a T-shirt, skin pink beneath a film of sweat, oil, nineteen again.

She looked and his right hand moved to her cheek.

She pulled her mouth in distaste. 'God, you look like you've been in a fight,' she said.

As his hand fell, he knew to the millimetre how far apart they were.

He turned away. The afternoon passed. Laurie went out twice, made calls. They started conversations several times, her mobile rang.

'For Christ's sake,' he said. 'If I can, you can kill that fucking thing.'

'You think I don't want to?' she said. 'Chris's got the flu, Bobby's on a job, there's no one there knows what to do.'

In the hot, still afternoon, a north-easter came up, the horizon vanished and rain came in short, violent bursts.

He went out, walked along the beachfront, got wet. On the main strip, he found a gambling barn – half-pissed young men in board shorts and T-shirts, bead necklaces and gold chains, budgie-eyed old men, brown-bread ruined skin, caps and long socks, they all sat in the flickering air-conditioned gloom reading the screens: Murray Bridge, Kembla Grange, Darwin, Alice Springs, Bunbury, New Zealand. He boxed favourites with no-hopers, the longer the better, threw money away. A young man with long tipped hair tried to strike up a conversation. Villani didn't give him any help. He persisted. Villani gave him the long fuck-off look, the man went away.

At the unit, towards evening, bored, twitchy, on his fourth beer, he switched on his phone, looked in cupboards.

'Scrabble,' he said. 'Want to play?'

Laurie was lying on the couch, flipping a magazine. 'Not really,' she said.

'Come on. I'm stir crazy.'

His father taught him to play. For Bob, it was a game of speed, you put down the first word that came to mind, there was no rubbish about trying for maximum possible scores.

That hot dripping late afternoon, in the box in the sky, he lost patience after fifteen or twenty minutes. He began to nag Laurie. 'Let's get a move on here, can we, haven't got all day.'

She said nothing, concentrated on her letters, earned big scores.

He kept at it. 'Come on, come on, get on with it, will you?'

Without warning, she rose, tipping the board on him, letters fell on him, went everywhere, she said, quietly, in control, 'You stupid bully, it's just a game. Ever asked yourself why Tony wouldn't play anything with you?'

Villani put the board back on the table, squared it. He looked down, saw the letters on the carpet, the perfectly smooth pale wooden squares on the green nylon. He pushed back his chair, went down on his hands and knees.

His mobile rang. He answered without getting up, kneeling on the floor.

'Villani.'

'Steve.' Singo, soft voice. 'Bit of shit here.'

'What?'

'Cashin and Diab. Bloke rammed them. Diab's dead, Joe's touch and go. Life support.'

'Jesus, no.'

Laurie said, 'What, Steve? What is it?'

To Singo, Villani said, 'I'll get the first plane, boss.'

'Ring with the number,' said Singo. 'Somebody'll meet you.'

Villani closed the phone, put it in his shirt pocket.

'What?' said Laurie. 'What?'

'Joe,' said Villani. 'On life support.'

'No,' she said. 'My God, no.'

They flew home together on the last direct flight and they spoke no more than a few dozen words then and on any given day thereafter.

. . . intelligent leaders and enough troops, Bruce. Together they move mountains. And intelligent leaders come first. Can I say here, can I commend the Homicide Squad over their work on the Oakleigh killings? Not every day does a senior officer, he could be sitting behind a desk, he goes out and puts his life on the line. We salute him.

Sorry, not up with this, that's a bit of a personal Oops, who are you . . .

Inspector Stephen Villani of Homicide. I'll say no more.

Yes, well, on another tack, Max Hendry's AirLine project, where do you . . .

I love Max. Only Max could try to get away with something like this, with not putting any figures on the table. His major problem in getting AirLine to fly is Stuart Koenig, the infrastructure minister. Koenig's told the Labor caucus the sky will be dark with pigs before Max Hendry gets government support . . .

On the snow that cold, misted evening, they watched the men slide a stretcher under the sleeping girl, two men carried her to the vehicle without the slightest strain, she could have been a dog, a greyhound.

Curled up. She was curled up.

VILLANI TOOK a used *Age* from the basket, sat at the corner table. The waiter was with him in seconds. She was Corin's age, student labour.

'Two sourdough toasts,' he said. 'Still got the little Italian sausages? With fennel?'

'Certainly do.'

'Two. And a grilled tomato. Long black, double shot. That's after.'

'You know your own mind,' she said.

'Together a long time,' Villani said. 'My mind and I.'

'That's like a lyric.' She sang, softly: *My mind and I, it's been a long, long time.*

She was older than Corin. Mature student. Post-graduate student.

'How do you know I'm a talent scout?' he said.

'Your hands,' she said. 'Strong but sensitive talent-scout hands.'

'I don't have a card on me.'

'I'll give you mine.'

He had finished, plate taken, sniffing the coffee when Dove came in carrying a briefcase, on time to the minute. The waiter followed him to the table.

'Breakfast?' she said.

'No, thanks. Long black, please.'

When she'd gone, Villani said, 'Be clear, stuff like this, it's not on the phone, not in the office.'

'Sorry, boss. Had a go at some phone data last night. It's six months of calls, it's a mountain.'

'You didn't put it in the system, did you?'

'No, no, I did it at home.'

'You've got the program at home?'

'Well, not the big one, no. But enough. I did this in the last job. All the time.'

Dove didn't want to say the word *feds*.

'And?'

'I had it look for clusters. It's called unsupervised learning.'

'I know that,' said Villani.

'Sorry. Boss. Turns up many clusters, big and small. Three around Mark Simons. Of Simons & Galliano, the bankruptcy kings. And they twin with calls to a Ryan Cordell. He's some kind of account-ant, financial advisor. When it starts, it's like a feeding frenzy. He calls Curlew, Curlew calls Hendry, Bricknell, they call others, some then call Cordell, it's back and forth.'

Dove's coffee came. She pointed at Villani's glass. He made the short sign.

'This is helpful?' said Villani.

Dove reached down to his briefcase, put a folder on the table, opened it.

'Not that, no,' he said. 'On the night, the Prosilio night, Bricknell, Curlew, Simons, Jourdan, Hendry and Brody all made and received calls from the casino LA. At 11.23, Bricknell calls Koenig. At home in Portsea. That home. Then, 11.29, Bricknell calls a mobile, pre-paid, so that's probably a dead end.'

Villani could see where it was going.

'At 12.07,' said Dove, 'Bricknell calls the number again. At 12.31, the number calls him. At 1.56, he calls the number again. At 2.04, it calls him.'

'Pause here,' said Villani. 'This is a very small cluster. Cluster of two.'

'Yes.'

'So what then?'

'I'm still looking at that.'

'Well, Bricknell calls Koenig. They're friends. Later he repeatedly calls someone who's on a pre-paid in the name of a cat. The person calls him back.'

'That's right.'

'So fucking what?'

Dove kept his eyes on his notes. He drank half his coffee.

'Got a theory?' said Villani. 'Want to tell me your theory? Koenig and the St Thomas boys? What?'

'They go to the gym together,' said Dove. 'To Rogan's in Prahran. Same workout group. Bricknell, Simons, Brody, Curlew, Hendry. And Jourdan.'

'How do you know that?'

'Sniffed around.'

'You're suggesting that although we latched on to Koenig by mistake . . .'

'I've been thinking. Maybe it wasn't a mistake. Maybe we were being pointed at Koenig.'

Villani ate, considered. 'Phipps?' he said.

'Not answering the phone. Not at home. Neighbour says she hasn't seen him for a while. But that's not unusual, she says.'

Dove put his hand in his jacket, took out his phone, slid it, talked, yes, no, yes, okay. He put the phone away.

'A woman rang Crime Stoppers last night,' he said. 'She's in a building across the road from Prosilio, just come back from somewhere, she's been away. Saw something.'

Villani found the waiter's eyes, made the sign. She glided through the tables.

'It's taken care of,' she said.

'How's that?'

'Jack Irish sends his regards.'

She pointed to a man sitting in the window, he was reading a newspaper.

They rose. Dove took the direct route, Villani went via the man.

'Can't be bought,' he said.

'I always knew you were cheap,' the man said. 'But free? That's undercutting your fellow officers. Still using the no-bruising wet towel method?'

'They want to confess. It's a relief for them.'

'Think about going into private practice. Help the guilt-haunted get closure.'

'People like you. Killed anyone recently?'

Irish smiled. 'You'll be the first to know. Well, the second probably.'

DOVE SPOKE to the woman from the desk in the foyer. Her name was Keller. The security man went up to the sixth floor with them, walked to the last door in the corridor, pressed the buzzer, looking into the camera eye beside the door.

'Security, Mrs Keller,' he said.

The security door slid into the wall, the second door was opened by a Eurasian woman with short grey hair, perhaps sixty, handsome, high cheekbones, dressed in black from throat to toe.

'Thank you, Angus,' she said, very English. 'Come in, gentlemen.'

They followed her down a passage hung with paintings into a big sitting room, grey carpet, three white walls, a wall of glass, three big paintings. The furniture was chrome and black leather.

Dove did the introductions.

'The head of Homicide,' she said. 'I'm so embarrassed. It's really nothing. I thought a constable would come.'

'You've been away I gather,' said Villani.

'I flew to Singapore last Friday,' she said. 'And I got back last night. The duty security man told me there'd been someone murdered in the Prosilio building and I asked when and he said the night before I left and it was a woman.'

She paused. 'Well, I saw something, it's probably nothing but when I heard, it gave me a turn, I thought I should . . .'

'Tell us, Mrs Keller,' said Dove.

'Come over here.'

They went to the window wall, she slid open the glass door, they went onto the balcony into the warming day. It looked onto the west face of the Prosilio building, dark glass unbroken by any projection.

'My husband bought off the plan,' she said. 'We were given the impression we would look over open space to the harbour. A park, I thought, from the brochure. It didn't actually say that.'

'It's not what they say,' said Dove. 'It's what they don't say.'

She gave Dove her full face, her eyes. 'Yes, that's so right. We were in Zurich, Danny wasn't well, we were dreaming of warm weather, the sea. I wanted Byron or Noosa but he was such a city person, he grew up in Gilgandra and he used to say he never wanted to live anywhere with a population under three million.'

'On the Thursday night,' said Villani.

'Yes. Well, I keep late hours, stay up late, stay down late. I was out here having a cigarette, I still can't smoke inside, he's been gone for . . . anyway, it was after midnight and a car went up that ramp.'

She was pointing at the base of the building. A long ramp ended at three roller doors.

Villani said, 'What's behind the doors?'

'Trucks come and go,' said Mrs Keller. 'Deliveries. All day long. A huge garbage truck reverses into the one on the right, where the car parked. It comes every day . . . how amazing.'

A truck was reversing up the ramp. Zooma Waste.

'That's it,' she said. 'The truck. As if I'd arranged it.'

The roller door rose, the truck went in, they could see its snout.

'A car parked there?' said Dove.

'Yes. And a man got out of the front. He was on the phone, and then the door went up. Not all the way. He walked in and the car drove in.'

'And this's around 12.30am?' said Villani.

'Close to that, yes.'

'What happened then?'

'The door went down,' she said. 'And then in a few minutes it went up again, the car reversed out and drove off.'

'You wouldn't have noticed the registration?' said Dove.

'My eyes aren't that good. Anyway, I didn't think a great deal of it. I mean I thought it was an odd way to get into the building but it didn't look, well, illegal. I thought it was just staff.'

Dove was watching the traffic. 'And the make, colour?' he said.

'Black,' she said. 'But that's not all.'

'No?'

'I went to bed but I couldn't sleep and I came out here again and another car arrived.'

Villani looked at her. She ran her palms over her hair.

'The same again,' she said. 'The building door went up, the car went in. But then it was nearly twenty minutes before it came out.'

In the warmth, the feeling on his skin as if a door to an icy place had opened.

'Notice the time?' said Dove, speech too quick.

'Ten to two when I came out.'

Dove turned his gaze on Villani. 'That's precise. You're sure?'

'I went to the kitchen for a glass of milk. There's a big clock. I feel anxious when I can't sleep, so ... well, yes, I'm sure. A quarter to two.'

Dove said, 'So the car left at around two-ten?'

'Yes.'

'That's the same car as before?'

'No,' said Mrs Keller. 'A different car. Also black. The first one was quiet, like a Mercedes or a BMW, something like that. This one made a growling noise, those big exhaust things, I could see them. Like cannon barrels.'

'You didn't see the registration?'

'No. I still didn't think anything of it. The man was wearing a vest.'

'A vest?'

'You know. Undershirt, sleeveless?'

'A singlet,' said Villani. 'What was the earlier man wearing?'

'I don't really know. Fully clothed. Dark clothing.'

'It hadn't happened before, anyone going in there?'

'I haven't seen it. No.'

Dove told her what they would need from her.

Villani considered a question. It was pointless, the city had thousands of black growling throbbing muscle cars driven by muscleheads in muscleshirts. And yet and yet.

He asked Mrs Keller an open question, didn't lead her.

'Three,' she said. 'Two in front and one at the back. In the middle. Little aerials. Is that useful? It caught my eye. I should have mentioned that, shouldn't I?'

'Glad you noticed, Mrs Keller,' said Villani. 'These things can help. And you've been a great help all round. We're in your debt.'

'Well, thank you.'

They went through the sitting room, into the passage, as they walked, she said, 'I heard you mentioned on the radio this morning, inspector. Karen Mellish. She said nice things.'

'I'm grateful for anything nice said about me,' said Villani. 'It doesn't often happen.'

'I'm sure it does. I'm sure.'

In the car, taut, Villani said, 'Get a doorknock there, the first three floors with the view. Might have got the regos, seen under the door. Place's probably full of people don't sleep, see everything. Should have been done straight off.'

Dove said, 'Is that, I should've . . .'

He fell silent.

'Being the boss,' said Villani, 'you get points for all the good work. There's also the reverse. In this case, I came, I took over. So I blame myself.'

'Well, I didn't ask for anyone . . .'

'And then, after I blame myself, I blame you,' said Villani. 'This also might have nothing to do with the girl. Just coke deliveries.'

'Timing's a glove-fit with the phone calls.'

'Mr Bricknell,' said Villani. 'Friend of the high and mighty, patron of the arts, member of the Melbourne Group, raised eight million dollars for the bushfire appeal. You're proposing to interrogate him about his phone calls?'

'A test question is that, boss?'

Villani said nothing, looked ahead. He could sense Dove becoming uneasy, soon he would break the silence. Bob Villani was the master of silence, silence was the way Bob unnerved you, made you prattle, make things worse. Bob reading his school report at the end of year 10, looking at him over the top of it, folding it, putting it in the envelope, looking away as if something on the blank wall had caught his eye. He learned the uses of silence from Bob and he applied them to Mark and Luke.

Last Sunday, Luke with his bit of dumb teenage weathergirl arse, he couldn't bear the look, the silence, he kept amping up his rubbish chatter, eyes darting.

Mark behind his doctor's desk, the pharma reps' trinkets everywhere, the notepads, the Porsche computer mouse with headlights, the tubes of Chinese tennis balls on the shelf, Mark lasted all of fifteen seconds.

Part of the boss manner. And Bob had the nerve to sound as if he disapproved of it, had no part in its creation, didn't like the fact that it intimidated Gordie, the dimwit whose big father, Ken, rolled his swag and buggered off months before Gordie was born. But first he came around and had a fight with Bob, they didn't see it, Bob said stay in the house. The men went behind the corrie-iron shed, they heard Ken's raised voice and felt the violence like pressure on their skin, it lasted a few minutes, then they heard the ute going down the drive at speed and a sound, not quite a bang.

Bob came back flexing his fingers, he went to the tank and held them under the tap. Later they saw the gate lying a good four metres out from the posts, it must have been carried on Ken's bullbars.

Bob said, 'Boy knows what's good for him, he's heading for Broome.'

Mark and Luke were Villani's first children, in a way. And then his proper boy child, Tony. Had he intimidated him with silence? A few times, yes. Not Corin, no, he had never given her the treatment. Well, once or twice when she was briefly a sulky teenager.

And Lizzie? Lizzie wouldn't have paid the slightest attention or she would have looked at him in her direct, sullen way, mouth set, face set. He couldn't intimidate Lizzie.

Laurie? Maybe in the beginning. She was in awe of him for a while, he didn't realise that until later, years later, until she said one day: *You seemed so much older than me, always judging. Much more than my dad.*

But she got over that, didn't give a shit about his silences, his judgments. She just shrugged and walked out, went her own way.

Dove was holding out. He wasn't going to speak.

'Not everything's a test,' Villani said. 'Sometimes you just want an opinion.'

'Can be hard to read you,' Dove said. 'Boss.'

'So Bricknell was at the Orion party,' said Villani. 'You ask him about the calls to the pre-paid. He asks you how you got his phone records. What do you say?'

'For all he knows, we've got the phone,' said Dove. 'We've flashboxed it, got everything.'

'It's been more than a week,' said Villani. 'If he's nervous, he's talked to the people who brought the girl. He knows we don't have the phone because they would have told him. He's not going to panic, he knows we've got fuckall. And even if he's willing to answer questions about his calls, he's going to say someone borrowed his phone, a stranger stole it, they were snorting in the men's. That kind of thing.'

Dove found his dark glasses. 'The blood at Preston.'

'Another mystery,' said Villani. 'This run started with the girl on the Hume. That's looking doubtful. So if the car means nothing, the long-absent Alibani's house has got buggerall to do with Prosilio.'

'Well,' said Dove, 'assuming we know when the girl arrived . . .'

'Assume nothing. To many assumptions already. Get Weber to see how you get to the apartment from the garbage bay.'

In thought, they drove. At the first intersection, Dove said, 'Why'd you ask about the aerials, boss?'

'First it was just a black muscle car. Now it's got three short aerials.'

'I see, boss,' said Dove. 'That's certainly narrowed the field to one or two thousand.'

Villani's mobile rang. Birkerts.

'Tomasic's found stuff at Oakleigh. Want to look?'

'Oakleigh's over. Everyone's dead. What's he doing there?'

'Showbag of Ribaric memorabilia. Could be fun. Well, interesting.'

'Where are you?'

'Base station. Mr Kiely in command mode. Up periscope, number two.'

'Meet me outside in, ah, ten minutes. With air-con that works.'

Birkerts was waiting, leaning against the Commodore, eating something, he wiped fingers on his lips in a lingering way.

'DAY ONE, I thought it's just family shit,' said Tomasic. 'But I had a little sniff at the book again. Wasting your time, I dunno.'

Villani walked around the kitchen table, looking at the items: a brooch, jade earrings, a gold bracelet, half a dozen photographs, one in a pewter filigree frame, a girl in white, white ribbon in her hair, a pale silk scarf, a beaded purse, a page-a-day diary, a slim silver crucifix on a chain of tiny silver beads, worn with touching, with worry.

'So what does this say?' said Villani.

Tomasic scratched his pitbull head. 'The Ribs' nanna's stuff. Valerie Crossley. Died in a nursing home in Geelong about a month ago.'

'That's their mother's mother?'

'Yeah, boss. The mother was Donna Crossley, there's a welfare file like a phone book. Booze, drugs, orders against Matko, kids taken off her three, four times. With Valerie more than their mum. In Geelong.'

'What happened to Donna?'

'Dead in Brissie. 1990. Hooking. Possibly a mug involved.'

Villani picked up a photograph, a bride, a priest and a woman in a cream suit and a small hat. The picture had been sliced vertically, a clean line, cut with scissors. The groom had been excised. The bride had a thin face, pretty in a way that had no legs, heavily made-up eyes, teased hair, lacquered.

On the back was written, shaky hand:

Donna and Father Cusack. Geelong 1973.

'Reckon she got rid of Matko here too, boss,' said Tomasic, he offered another photograph.

Two small boys in a paddling pool, gap-toothed, wet, shiny, happy. The top of the photograph had been cut off, broad hairy male forearms and hands were on the children's shoulders.

Villani passed it to Birkerts.

'Like Russia,' said Birkerts. 'Stalin did that.'

'Cut up photographs?' said Tomasic. 'He did that?'

'All the time. Loved to cut up photographs.'

'Weird,' said Tomasic.

Villani opened a folded sheet of notepaper.

St Anselm's Parish, Geelong
10 July

Dear Mrs Crossley,

Father Cusack has been ill. He says he will try to come and see you tomorrow morning. I hope you are feeling better.

Annette Hogan

'Well, what?' said Villani.

Tomasic picked up the diary.

'Read a bit of this,' he said. 'Old girl was in the nursing home about six months before she carked, she wrote every day or so.'

'Yes?' said Villani.

'About what she eats, people dying, the nurses, lots of religion shit, God and Jesus and Mary and sins and forgiveness . . . sorry, boss.'

'I'm offended,' said Villani. 'What?'

Tomasic didn't look at him.

'Yeah, well, near the end,' he said, 'there's stuff, she wants to see Father Cusack and he doesn't come and she keeps asking the nurses and they just pat her and he doesn't come and she doesn't want to die without confession and then he comes and she's happy. She says she's at peace.'

'That's so nice,' said Birkerts. 'That's such an uplifting story. Might go to confession myself. Confess that I let you fuck around here when you could be doing something useful.'

'There's more?' said Villani.

'The last thing she wrote, she says a Father Donald, he came,' said Tomasic. 'He'd kissed the Holy Father's ring, and he asked her a lot of questions and he said she'd be at God's right hand for telling Father Cusack about the evil. Pretty much a booked seat. Specially blessed. Yeah.'

'What's at the left hand?' said Birkerts. 'What's the scene there?'

'Islamites wipe their bums with the left hand,' said Tomasic. 'Only.'

'It's kissing the ring that's the worry,' said Villani.

He felt uneasy, not just because they were looking at the things an old woman took to the place where she expected to die, the last possessions, the only possessions of worth of all the things acquired in her life, of all the thousands of things, only these had any value, any meaning.

From his own life, not many things he would take to the last stop. There was a meaning here. There was something speaking to them and they did not know the language.

Villani thought about his trees, shimmering in the hot winds, the deciduous leaves browning at the edges, closing their pores, trying to think their way into late autumn, no water evaporating, the chain of water molecules in the limbs ceasing to draw moisture from the roots, the trees telling themselves they could live through this if they remained perfectly still and controlled their breathing.

They deserved some help, his trees.

He should go now, leave this place infused with the badness of the people who had lived here, died close by, deserved to die, leave and drive up the long roads to where he came from, they would let him through the roadblocks, he could put on his uniform, they wouldn't fuck with an inspector, they would let him go on.

His mobile.

'My son,' Colby said, 'I tell you hide under the bed, you go out and treat a minister like street scum. The reward is you are invited to tea with Miss Orong and the AG, Signor DiPalma. How's that? A fucking quinella.'

'Never a quinella man,' said Villani.

'I recall you in enough shit without the exotics,' said Colby. 'And now you have become the force's shit-magnet. They want you now. They await you.'

Colby didn't know the half of it. Or did he? That day in the car, in the carpark behind Lygon Street, Dance reached under his seat and gave him a black and white Myer shopping bag.

'The trick when you hand it over,' said Dance, 'is to avoid photo opportunities.'

Villani put the bag in his boot. He counted it later, it took so long he realised why the big drug players used machines. A few hundreds, fifties, mostly twenties and tens and fives. Thirty thousand dollars in all.

'Well, all very interesting,' said Villani. 'You've got the nose, Tommo. But we don't need any more Ribaric history. Just be grateful they don't have a future. Time to move on.'

AN OLIVE-SKINNED young woman, pinstriped suit, took him up in the lift, down a long corridor hung with paintings, portraits. She opened a door, waved him in.

A woman sat behind a desk, deep lines from her nose. She was a gatekeeper.

'Inspector Villani,' said the escort.

'Thank you,' said the gatekeeper.

The escort left. The gatekeeper picked up a phone and said, 'Inspector Villani.'

A huge panelled door opened and a sandy young man holding files came out. 'Hi,' he said. 'Come in.'

Villani went in, the door closed after him. The attorney-general, Chris DiPalma, behind a desk big enough for three, he was in shirtsleeves, a pink shirt, tie loose, glasses down his thin nose, serious expression, like a magistrate, send you to jail if you didn't cringe.

Martin Orong, the police minister, sat in a club chair. He smiled at Villani, it resembled a smile.

'Sit down, inspector,' DiPalma said. 'You know Martin, I gather.'

Villani sat.

'Call you Steve?'

'Yes, minister.'

'To the point, Steve, You've been giving Stuart Koenig a hard time. He's upset.'

'Routine questioning,' said Villani.

'The Prosilio girl?'

'A murder inquiry.'

'This is between us. Colleagues, strictest confidence. With me?'

'All police work is in strictest confidence, minister,' Villani said.

DiPalma looked at Orong.

'Mr Koenig says he co-operated with you, gave you a full and verifiable account of his whereabouts. Is that right?'

Villani said, 'It's policy not to discuss investigations, minister.'

'And then you apply to get his phone records on the grounds of his involvement in a murder inquiry.'

'That is correct,' said Villani. 'He is involved in a murder inquiry.'

'Jesus Christ,' said DiPalma, 'you don't get it, do you?'

Orong touched his stiff forelock. 'Come on, Steve, this is just a friendly chat, no rank pulled here. All we want to do is the right thing by Stuart, that's not a big ask, is it?'

This was the moment to back off. Villani was going to and then he saw himself encouraging Dove to take Koenig on and he couldn't.

'We want to do the right thing by you too,' said Orong. 'Your career. Future.'

Villani said to DiPalma, 'Minister, we're pursuing a line of inquiry we believe will help us with a murder investigation. That's all I can say.'

DiPalma had an open folder in front of him, he tapped it with his fingernails: manicured, pink. 'I think we're going to have to be plainer with you, Steve. Stuart Koenig's been a naughty boy but that's the limit of it. He's had sex with a prostitute. That's all. Now I want you to back off. You've got a big admirer in Mr Barry, the force is about to have a leadership regeneration, he's considering you for a senior role in the new dispensation.'

DiPalma picked up a fountain pen, black and fat, wrote a sentence in the folder, looked up. 'Is that plain enough for you, inspector? Can I be bloody plainer?'

Villani nodded.

'And there's another little matter you might want to consider,' said DiPalma. 'The renewed interest in the death of Greg Quirk. That involves you and Dance and Detective Senior Sergeant Vickery. We may let this take its course. Or we may not. Is that also bloody plain enough?'

'It is, minister,' said Villani.

'Good,' said DiPalma. 'The election's close, it's not a time for ministers to be touched by murder investigations. However innocent they are. So, we've reached an understanding that you will delete Mr Koenig from your investigation. Nothing will be heard of your visit to him. Absolutely nothing. Fuckall. If this leaks, there will be blood. Yours.'

He stood, they all stood.

Orong coughed, a small-dog bark. 'And this whole Prosilio shit,' he said. 'Let it lie for the moment. There's no upside there for you and it's all bad news for the building. Get on with important work. Career-enhancing stuff.'

DiPalma offered his hand, Villani shook it. Then he shook Orong's treacherous little hand. He left the offices, walked down the cool and self-important corridor. From the walls, the dead watched him pass, they had seen many a coward come and go.

In a short time, he was on the street, orange sun behind the haze, looking for Finucane, unaccountably thinking about the first horse Bob raced, the best horse he ever had, the lovely little grey called Truth who won at her second start, won three from twelve, always game, never gave up. She sickened and died in hours, buckled and lay, her sweet eyes forgave them their stupid inability to save her.

VILLANI sat at the desk, stared at the near-empty inbox. Kiely appeared in the door.

'Checked the active files,' he said. 'Took the liberty. In case decisions were urgently needed.'

'I've been thinking,' said Villani, 'about a bad restaurant where the manager also wants to do the cooking.'

The pink of dawn on Kiely's pale cheekbones. 'A remark made in the heat of the moment,' he said. 'I accept that it was inappropriate. I would also like to say that I had not at that point sent a memo to command. And I did not do so subsequently.'

He'd heard something, he was looking ahead, thinking about the possible price he might pay.

'So, not a dog?' said Villani.

Kiely chewed saliva for a time. 'Not a dog,' he said.

'Welcome to Homicide,' said Villani.

Kiely did not know how to take it.

'That's well meant,' said Villani.

'Right. Thank you.' Relief in his eyes. 'Well, there's progress on some fronts, the drowned woman in Keilor, the husband pumped water into her, he's made a full statement. And the Frankston girl, we've got the two men lived there, so that should sort itself out. The man in the Pope mask, that's proving difficult. Possibly sailor-tossed from the fifth floor.'

'See what's in port,' said Villani. 'Check the *Spirit of Tasmania* crew. They're tossers.'

'Hah. Absolutely.'

He left.

Burgess knocked, files in hand. He was looking remarkably healthy, it was disconcerting. On the very worst of mornings, Burgess had always been someone you could look at and it made you feel better. The Australian Standard for visible hangovers, the benchmark.

'Boss, the girl up there, at the snow? Just about forgotten.'

'What happened?'

'Nothing. It's open.'

'Read those?'

'Not in detail, no. Bit pushed.'

Why at this time was it nagging at him, the icy day, the rutted track, the little body, why did these things arise from nowhere?

'Tell me,' he said. 'I moved on.'

'Me too,' said Burgess. 'Singo wasn't hot on it.'

'Darwin, why do I think Darwin?'

'They kind of ID'd her in Darwin,' said Burgess. 'There was a teenie hooker in Darwin, they said it looked like her. Darwin coppers. Probably fucked her. That was the extent of it. Yeah.'

'Okay, leave those. Why you looking so healthy? Something I should take?'

Burgess winked. 'Love of a good woman,' he said.

'Expensive?'

'Can I tell the next deputy commissioner to fuck off?'

'Where'd you hear that?'

'The birds are singing it. In the trees.'

'Bullshit. On your bike. Trike.'

There's no upside there for you . . . Get on with important stuff. Career-enhancing stuff.

'Get Dove for me, there's a good public servant.'

'Sad boy, the Lovey Dovey,' said Burgess. 'Not a mixer. The Abo chip. Still, the boy took a bullet.'

'Not too late for you to take one. Invite Mr Dove in. And keep taking the good woman.'

Time passed, Dove came, knocked air.

'Close the door. Sit.'

Dove closed the door, sat in the cheap chair, locked his hands, the tendons stood out, thick as spaghetti.

'I'll say to you,' Villani said, 'I'll say I have been told to drop any Koenig stuff, I have been told to put Prosilio on ice. I have been told my career is at risk.'

Dove looked at his hands. 'I see,' he said.

The gear changes, the big motor's sound thinning, thinner, going, going, gone, the silence, Bob gone, he was alone with the boys, the horses, the dogs. No going back to sleep. Things to see to. Sometimes, in the early morning, the burden had felt so heavy, he had pulled the pillow over his head, stopped breathing.

Sometimes Mark would whine about something on a Sunday night and Bob would say, *Steve'll fix it, Steve'll see to it.*

Bob never asked him whether he could do it. Steve would look after things. Talk to teachers, take boys to the doctor, the dentist, cut their hair, buy them clothes, shoes. Never mind that Steve was twelve years old. Perhaps Bob just didn't give a bugger. No, he cared about Mark, came to care about Luke. The horses, he loved them. And then the oaks. They grew from his acorns, they were his beautiful and undemanding children. Water, that was all they asked for. And Steve would see to that too.

'What's that mean?' he said to Dove. A reflex, Singo question, no utterance unexamined.

What did he say exactly? The words. Tell me his words. I'm dying, I can't live without her, I'll kill myself? Did he say stuff like that?

Dove lifted his eyes.

'They're powerful people,' he said. 'They run the world. Why shouldn't they get away with killing a whore?'

They sat without speaking, in the space enclosed from the bigger space, the tin desk, the tin filing cabinets, Singo's trophy protruding from the box, first-round knockout, that was rare in the force's boxing at the upper weights, they were generally mauling affairs.

He thought about the day he told Birkerts he was thinking of looking at some of Singleton's unresolved matters.

Birkerts said, 'They're dead, he's dead, we can only shoot ourselves up the arse.'

'If you don't get it,' said Villani, acid, 'you don't get it.'

Birkerts said, 'I get the principle, I just don't see the utility.'

'The utility?' said Villani. 'Is that what you got your fucking degree in? Working out what the utility is?'

Justice for the dead. Singo's message to new arrivals. 'We're the only ones who can get them justice. That's our work. That's our calling.'

These thoughts had begun to come to Villani in the small moments of his life – at the traffic lights, in the haunted space before sleep, in the wet womb of the shower.

For Koenig and DiPalma and Orong, the Prosilio girl was just a dead creature by the wayside. Roadkill. They didn't get the principle and they didn't see the utility.

He thought of the moment when he saw the dead girl and thought she was Lizzie. Was that some kind of foreshadowing, a premonition? Rubbish.

Singo wasn't hot on it.

The girl on the snow road. No, forget it.

'Well that's it then,' he said. 'See what Inspector Kiely has waiting for you.'

Dove stood up, eyes on him, unreadable.

'Yes?' said Villani. 'Something to say?'

'Nothing,' said Dove. 'Boss.'

'IF THIS is a few,' said Villani, 'it must get a bit crowded when all your friends come.'

Vicky Hendry laughed, expensive teeth. 'This is nothing. Max's great fear is that if we have a party and invite fifty, only ten might show up. So he asks a hundred and they all bloody come. But this is the TGIF gang. Work people. Stable around forty.'

Villani had arrived late, uneasy, regretting the decision long before the taxi stopped. He said his name into the brass grille on the street. The gate was opened by a big smiling man in a suit. Vicky Hendry was waiting at the front door, kissed his cheek, took his hand, led him along a passage and through two huge sitting rooms onto a terrace, he heard the laughter. They went down steps to join a crowd of people beside a pale green salt-water pool, men and women in equal numbers, suits, tieless.

To one side was a bar, a barman, beer and wine bottles in ice in wine barrels, a barbecue the size of a security door. Behind them were two long trestle tables.

Vicky Hendry looked after other guests but he felt that he was her point of departure and return. She made sure he was never alone. She appeared to find him amusing, sought his opinions in a direct way, a slow blinker, she stood close, just a few finger widths from provocative, intimate. His unease went away.

People drifted over, introduced themselves, all connected with Hendry enterprises, many of them to the AirLine project. They knew who he was, a new experience for Villani and it did not displease him.

'Alice, meet Stephen Villani.'

She was north of sixty, overweight, red hair, dyed.

'Alice is called Max's secretary,' said Vicky. 'They have a thirty-year history. I had to be approved by Alice.'

'Calculating bitch was my view,' said Alice. 'But he wouldn't listen.'

'And for not listening he pays every day of his life,' said Villani.

The women laughed and Vicky put a fist against his chest in a mock-punch, pressed, he felt her knuckles, she kept them there the extra half-second and he knew it was flirting, Alice knew it, Vicky knew it.

'Where is he?'

'On his way back from Canberra we hope,' said Vicky. 'He's been talking to the federal government about AirLine.'

Time passed, laughter, Spanish music, he felt easier than he had for, he couldn't remember how long. He drank beer, they moved to a trestle table, platters of kebabs came, bowls of salad, bottles of red and white. Around him the talk was of politics, all sides represented, of the shrunken economy, the endless fires, films, holidays, current events, how bad the media were.

At some signal, Vicky left him and reappeared with Max Hendry, jacketless, tieless, white shirt with sleeves rolled up. He had a big arm around his wife.

Shouts.

About bloody time, mate.

Security, there's a gatecrasher.

Show us the money, Maxie.

Hendry put up his hands.

'You bloody freeloaders,' he said.

Applause.

'So you know where I've been today,' he said. 'Talked to the bastards, six hours. Never met so many dumb people. But we reckon we've finally got it through their thick heads that any alternative that takes traffic off clogged roads is bloody national infrastructure.'

Cheers, clapping.

'Now that is a small step for the dickheads but it's a big, big step for mankind. Which is our cause.'

More cheers, whistles. Max did a boxer clasp, he said, 'Get your snouts back in the trough, you animals.'

Vicky took her seat beside Villani. They watched Max patting shoulders, kissing cheeks, shaking hands, a loved ruler returning from exile.

'They like him,' said Villani.

She was silent. Max got to them, shook Villani's hand.

'Thanks for coming, mate,' he said. 'My dear lady's looked after you?'

A waiter offered food, Max said he'd eaten. The barman came with beaded Coopers, uncapped two.

Max drank from the bottle. He let the world return to pre-Max, told stories about meetings with the prime minister, the treasurer, the federal transport minister.

He asked Villani questions, Villani had the feeling Max knew the answers, knew everything about him.

The dark crept across the space, the guests thinned, everyone saying their thanks, joking with the Hendrys. Villani made to leave. Max put a hand on his shoulder.

'No, no, Steve, stay. Coffee. Quiet Friday nightcap.'

When Vicky had gone to see the last guests off, they moved to the terrace, to big wooden chairs. A smiling silver-haired woman in black brought coffee, chocolates, a bottle of cognac, balloon glasses.

Max poured. Before them lay the dark garden running to the river and then the city and its towers standing in their illuminated self-esteem.

'Cigar?' said Hendry. 'I shouldn't but I might regress. Good word, regress. Sounds like regret, which comes after regressing.'

'I might regress with you,' said Villani.

Hendry left, came back with two cigars and a silver spike, pierced the dark cylinders, handed one over, a box of kitchen matches.

'Thank God for Cuba,' he said. 'Cuba and France.'

They lit up. The smoke hung in the air.

Below them, paw prints of light came on, walking in big strides down to the river.

Villani picked up his glass, he was mellow. The light from portholes in the paving made the cognac a dark honey-gold. Something was coming from Hendry, you knew.

'I want to ask you,' said Hendry. 'Bit of a nerve, really. Ever consider another line of work?'

Villani said, 'Cop is all I know.'

'Not exactly on the beat now,' said Hendry.

'I've got what I hear is called a restricted skill set. I copied my bosses, they copied theirs.'

'That can work,' said Hendry, 'if you don't copy something flawed. Then the copies get worse in every generation.'

'That's what I'm saying,' said Villani. 'I'm several generations flawed. The object will soon be unusable.'

He said it without thinking, drink taken, and he knew it was true. He was a blurred facsimile of Cameron, Colby and Singo. And, to begin with, he was a bad copy of Bob Villani. The looks, the height, the hair, the hands, they were accurate. But all the failings, all the imbalances, they were amplified: the selfishness, the faithlessness, the blindness, the urges, the rutting instinct.

All the worst bits.

But the spine, the guts, the courage, that went the other way. Those things that were large in Bob, they were stunted in his first-born son.

Max laughed, small plosives.

'You just saying that, it confirms my instincts,' he said. 'I like clever people, I can spot them a long way away. That's really all I'm smart at. If my old man had been a garbo, I'd be labouring on a building site.'

They smoked, sipped, the cognac fumes filled the nose.

Vicky came out.

'Rascals at play,' she said. 'Much as I'd love to sit around drinking cognac and smoking a fat cigar,' she said, 'I'm not joining you. Exhausted. I'd say knackered if I wasn't such a lady.'

Villani stood and said his thanks. She squeezed his arms and kissed him half on his lips. He caught the musk of her perfume through the cigar smoke.

'Our pleasure, Steve,' she said. 'You're now a member of the Friday mob. By popular demand, I have to say. Also you must come to the valley for a weekend. I'll send an invite.'

She passed behind Max's chair, stopped, bent to kiss his forehead. 'I know it's difficult, darling, but try to get to bed before dawn.'

'Excellent judge of character, this woman,' said Hendry. 'Only one mistake to date. But back to the point.'

'I've forgotten it.'

Hendry blew a fat rolling smoke ring. 'Learned to do that at school,' he said. 'All I remember from school. Anyway, no point buggering around, I want to offer you a job. Large job.'

'You need a bad copy of some dead cop?' said Villani.

'An operations chief for Stilicho. I gather you know about Stilicho. Bloody monstrous meltdown at the casino but that's teething stuff.'

The publicity people wanted something they could use. Senior police officer. What was needed was a dull prick to organise rosters, check on the bored, underpaid people who checked on other bored underpaid people who checked locks, identity cards, airless 3am rooms, lavatories.

'I don't think I'm cut out for security,' Villani said. 'But thank you.'

Hendry said, 'Don't be so quick, mate. Not some executive-bouncer job I'm talking about.'

A mind-reader.

A hot north-west wind on their faces, another blocking system was idling out in the southern ocean. Two long valleys ran from the north-west towards Selborne, the main road down one of them. The fire would come as it came to Marysville and Kinglake on that February hell day, come with the terrible thunder of a million hooves, come rolling, flowing, as high as a twenty-storey building, throwing red-hot spears and fireballs hundreds of metres ahead, sucking air from trees, houses, people, animals, sucking air out of everything in the landscape, creating its own howling wind, getting hotter and hotter, a huge blacksmith's reducing fire that melted humans and animals, detonated buildings, turned soft metals to silver flowing liquids and buckled steel.

'No?'

'No, no, Stilicho's new territory in security. I don't get some of it myself. Well, a lot of it. Jesus, I was twenty before I understood how electricity worked. This is the future of security technology. They tell me the stuff we've got is two–three years ahead of the curve. That's a huge opportunity.'

What had Dove said?

Stilicho's bought this Israeli technology, puts it all together – secure entry, the ID stuff, iris scanning, fingerprints, facial recognition, suspicious behaviour, body language . . . Stilicho's even trying to get access to the crimes database, the photos and photofits, prints, records, everything . . . Your face's in the base, you show up somewhere . . .

'I thought your son was the boss of Stilicho? Your son and Matt Cameron.'

'Matt's got fifteen per cent. I've got the rest. Hugh's the CEO, no shareholding. Big challenge, operations chief, Steve. There's no job description that fits it. They told me I should bring in the executive-search extortionists.'

'Good idea.'

'I can do my own bloody executive search. Save tens of thousands. They say you don't have problems with technology. They say you're one of the few cops who understand the new technology.'

'I have lots of problems with technology,' said Villani. 'You don't want to offer me a technology job. Any job, really.'

'I do want to.'

'This is not about us nailing those little bastards, is it?' said Villani. 'That's the job. I've been paid for that.'

Hendry said, 'The idea was someone with a broad police background. Someone smart.'

'Rules out about ninety-seven per cent,' said Villani. 'Give or take a per cent.'

Hendry frowned. 'That's pretty harsh. They told me ninety-two. Anyway, before the AirLine thing, Vicky told me the cop who caught David's killers was now head of Homicide. That's how you came up. I asked questions. And people said good things.'

'A cop thing. To say good things about other cops. Your brothers.'

'And the pedigree, I liked that too.'

'Sorry?'

'Your old man. Vietnam. The Team.'

'That's got nothing to do with me.'

Max looked at him for a few seconds, head cocked, said, 'No, sorry, stupid thing to say. Dwelt in the shadow myself, should know better. Yes.'

'I haven't lived in my father's shadow,' Villani said. He didn't want this rich man's job, ordered around by the smooth son.

'No, I'm not saying that. I'm sure you haven't.'

Villani took out his mobile. 'Great evening, Mr Hendry. My day's not over. Unfortunately.'

Max said, 'Stephen, hang fire for a minute, will you? Put that away. Gone off track here.'

Villani waited, poised to leave.

'Hugh's been in my shadow, that's done him no good. I didn't see it until it was too late. Still, he's good at the business stuff, Hugh, good salesman. What I'm looking for is someone who can be the battlefield commander.'

Max sniffed his glass, took a sip.

'Steve, this is going to start as private security, but if we get it right, it'll revolutionise the way we keep public places safe. Protect ordinary citizens against the kind of scum who kicked David to death. We're on the edge of getting the contract for a massive new shopping mall in the west. Also serious interest from a new Brisbane council. Secure a whole retail precinct, civic centre.'

'You don't by any chance think I've got any clout, do you?' said Villani. 'Help get the databases?'

Max put up his hands. 'Steve, we'll get access if we deserve access. If the people who matter see that the benefits outweigh the drawbacks. I want you for the personal qualities you'll bring. That's it.'

Villani's resistance was falling away: the charm of the man, the attention paid to him all evening, the alcohol, the charge to his ego.

'Well,' he said. 'I'm flattered. Need to have a think.'

'Of course you've got to sleep on it. You don't want to know what we're offering?'

'Well . . .'

'More than a deputy commissioner gets. A lot more. Mind you, it's a sixteen-hour day.'

'Get Sunday off?'

'Not as a matter of right.'

Near midnight, Max walked him through the house and the front garden to the street door. The big smiling man was there and he took Villani out to the car, opened the back door.

'I'll sit in front,' said Villani.

He shook hands with Max.

'I know I'm right,' said Max. 'Think hard. I hear Mellish gets in, it's a clean sweep of all senior positions in the force. That's something to factor in.'

'Consider it factored,' said Villani. 'Goodnight, Max.'

He told the driver to take him to St Kilda Road, to his office.

Take him home.

THE BUILDING never slept. Shifts changed, tired people left, less tired people took their places.

In Homicide, in the white light where day and night lost meaning, half-a-dozen heads registered his entrance. He talked to a few of them, to the duty officer, made a mug of tea, sat at his desk, he was sober now, not sure why he was there, sure only that he had no home to go to.

All day he had thought Corin would ring, no question. She had no reason to blame him for anything to do with Lizzie. But she hadn't. Too busy, uni starting, her job, the spunk from the big end of town.

Listen love, I need you to pick up Lizzie. Now.

He should have said that, made her leave her dinner. The oldest, why didn't they always give her the job of seeing to Lizzie? Keeping her up to scratch. Got to school on time. Did her homework.

He could ring Corin.

No, no, no.

She owed him. She owed him many, many things and she could have paid all her debts with just one miserable little phone call. She failed him, his beloved girl. In the end, she didn't care about him.

Leave the job and work for Max Hendry. He came to Homicide to save his marriage, to do clean work. No more gambling, no more women. The clean work he had done. The gambling, he had given it away, he had turned his back on certainties, turned and wept.

He thought about DiPalma and Orong. DiPalma, a lecturer in law at Monash before he felt the calling. Property law. Leases. Conveyancing. Jesus, what did he know of the streets, the scum, the fractured world?

Orong. Orong was nothing. Community Studies degree from the former Footscray Tech. Politics and sociology. Always in politics, a teenage doorknocker, branchstacker.

He logged on, looked up Orong. A photograph from the *Western Citizen* of a younger Orong with Stuart Koenig. Koenig was holding up Orong's right arm as if the prick had just won a fight. The election before last. New MP for Robertsham. He went to a political site called Brumaire18 and searched for Orong. It listed dozens of items, he read an early one.

SNAKES ON A ROLL

On another sad day for democracy, 23-year-old reptile Martin 'Snakelips' Orong this week joins his even viler mentor, Stuart Koenig, in parliament. Koenig, of course, owes his political survival to the product-haired little western suburbs viper. When he was Koenig's office boy, Orong single-handledly stacked Koenig's branch with everything from illiterate Ethiopians to what he famously called the 'Samoan bouncer community'. Koenig and Orong are mates outside of work too. The pair were once trapped by a blizzard in the Koenig ancestral lodge at Mount Buller when they were supposed to be at a party talkfest in Canberra.

DiPalma and Orong assumed that he would do as told. Back off Koenig, Prosilio. They said it as if they had the power to give him orders. And they did have the power if he was scared of what they could do to him.

Was it that way with Singleton? Did people threaten him, make him back off? Singo always talked about *the grip* – people who had it, people who could get things done, undone. Did people have the grip on Singo?

In the job, it wasn't hard to get gripped by someone.

Bent forever, the job. Why not? Terrible pay, the hours, the conditions, the risks. It only took a few days for him to work out who he had signed up with: the dim, the school bullies, body-builders, martial-arts fanatics, control freaks, thrillseekers, loners, kids from cop families, kids brought up by mum.

In uniform, a full understanding of the job slowly dawned. A life spent dealing with the dishonest, the negligent, the deviant, the devious, the desperate, the cruel, the callous, the vicious, the drunk, the drugged, the temporarily deranged and permanently insane, the sick and sad, the sadists, sex maniacs, child molesters, flashers, exhibitionists, women-beaters, wife-beaters, child-beaters, self-mutilators, the homicidal, matricidal, patricidal, fratricidal, suicidal.

Some of them dead.

You could quickly slide into otherness, estrangement from the civilian world, a sense of entitlement. What did it matter if you didn't pay full price for your clothes, your drycleaning, got the free coffee, a sandwich, if people bought you drinks in pubs? You could take lotto tickets, not pay at places. People gave you horse tips, invites to clubs, you could go after your shift with a mate, everything on the house, the best girls.

Just give your name. Expecting you, the bloke.

They gave every sign you were the sexiest thing that year, you had experiences not normally had on a date or with the wife. When you were pissed, someone gave you something. And then one day you got the call.

Shit, mate, bastard pulls me over on the Tulla, goin a bit over, yeah. Not the fine, mate, the fucken points, gonna have to get the fucken push-bike out, have a word, can you? Appreciate it, mate.

You knew someone. You made the call. And you were a fully paid-up mate. A travel agent rang to say you had a free week on Hayman Island, the plane, the hotel, the vouchers. They pointed you to discounts on cars, televisions, washing machines, carpets, gym memberships, booze, plastic surgery, BMX bikes.

Anything.

Every year, there were more bent cops, the number ran in tandem with the number of crims, particularly drug crims, making unthinkable amounts of money from selling ice, GBH, Special K, ecstasy.

The demand was insatiable, a dealer grew rich supplying just one private school, every kid over twelve had tried some of them. No night out was complete without drugs, tradies got stoned after they downed tools for the day.

On any Friday, an army of couriers hand-delivered snort, bazooka, incentive to customers in the CBD, to bankers, brokers, lawyers, accountants, advertising agencies, architects, property developers, real-estate agents, doctors.

The money was visible everywhere and everywhere you heard the resentment from cops.

Mate, the Holden's clapped, the wife's lost her job, now the holiday's at the in-laws. It's like fifty metres of fucking mud before the water. They're all there, the zombie father, the brother, he's a petrolhead bludger, the wife's worse, whinges non-stop, doesn't lift a fucking finger except to paint her nails. Compares with we pick up this piece of shit, he's maybe twenty, he's driving a Porsche, we know him, he's got an apartment in Docklands, it's A-grade whores, fucking Bali, he says you think I'm that stupid boys I'm driving around with shit in my car? Don't waste your time, what do you blokes make? Fifty? Sixty? Fifty on a horse today, mate, fucking thing misses the start. Never mind, tomorrow's another day.

Villani put his hands behind his head, tried to massage his neck.

Dancer had saved him. When the gambling had him by the balls, when Joe Portillo had sent his scum around with a message that there were ways he could pay his debt, Dancer saved him from the grip.

Thirty thousand bucks in the Myer bag.

'Kitty's healthy,' said Dance. 'Had a few big ones. I'm lending. Pay me when you sell your house and make five hundred grand capital gains.'

Save, pay Dancer back five grand at a time, that was the plan. Then Greg Quirk came along and it was on hold. When he offered the first repayment, Dance said, 'Please, mate, no. Long forgotten. Forgiven and forgotten.'

Greg Quirk.

Greg was scum. His brother was scum. And his father. Grandfather too, the dog-killer.

For a long time, lying about Greg didn't bother him. It wasn't a problem. It wasn't until the dreams started. Even then, it wasn't just about seeing Greg die, the way the three of them stood there and watched him bleed out, he foamed, twitched, his legs kicked, little dreaming kicks.

It was about being an honest man. A man of honour.

Honour's not cheap, son. Don't give your word unless you'll do it or die trying.

What the fuck did Bob know about keeping your word? He said he would come back for them in a few weeks and it was years. No car came down Stella's street that Villani did not hold his breath and wait for it to stop. In bed at night, when cars passed, he put his head beneath the pillow, pressed his face into the mattress and with both hands pulled down the pillow.

His child out there, with the street animals, his Lizzie. The sum of his failure as a father and as a man. He simply had not cared enough. When the moment came to go to her, to show her that her father loved her, he turned his back.

Job first, everything else second. And it had always been so.

Bob Villani's boy. The DNA glowed in him.

Did Bob have his Greg Quirk? His Greg Quirks? Small men executed in the dark paddies? A single shot. The trembling knees, the puzzled-dog eyes, the falling.

He could not go back on Quirk. It had entered into his being, his own blood. By his testimony and by his silence, he had given them his word. That was not disputable, he knew that, they knew that.

The dying Lovett. He had sought some redemption for his sins.

I leave you with the thought that we, that's the three of us and by extension the whole fucking squad and the whole fucking force, we have failed the little Prosilio girl.

He switched off his lights and went to the window. Below, the bright ribbons of traffic. Across the road, the dark of the school and its grounds, the botanic gardens. Then, far away, the glow of the highways, and, in the sky, gleaming in the clouds, the full luminescence of the huge city.

BIRKERTS PICKED him up. When they were in the city, at the lights, Villani spoke.

'Western Ring,' he said.

'What?'

'I want to see where Kidd and Larter came unstuck.'

Birkerts rested his forehead on the steering wheel, it was not a sign of respect. 'We'll have to go all the way around to be on that side.'

'Yeah.'

'Jesus,' said Birkerts. 'Feeling okay?'

'I didn't go there, it's been bothering me.'

'Did I not hear you say yesterday that it was time to move on?'

'After this, we move on.'

They drove in the morning rush. Birkerts put the radio on. Villani read the paper, put his head back, drowsed.

'Crash scene coming up,' said Birkerts. 'Blink and you'll miss it.'

Villani sat up, they were in the left lane, closing on the spot where Kidd and Larter came undone.

'Pull over,' he said.

Birkerts indicated, they stopped a good fifty metres beyond the crash scene, just before the exit. Trucks rocked the car.

'Now what?' said Birkerts.

Villani said, 'Just have a look. Sniff.'

'Don't need me, do you?'

Villani got out, choked on the heat. He walked back to where clumps of couch grass had greened, given life by the hosing down of the burning wreck, the seats, the tyres, the oil. On the dirt strip between the highway and a fence, a few stunted native trees clung to life, their limbs ceaselessly moving in the hot road winds. Beyond them was another dirt strip, a fence, then a wasteland, its only feature an abandoned building. A maker of explosives had sprayed its logo on the east wall.

He stood in the scorching day, the trucks howling by, buffeted by their winds, they flew his tie like a narrow battle standard.

There was nothing here. It had been a stupid impulse. Still, he walked across to the trees. As if decorated for some sad impoverished Christmas, they wore shiny chip packets and fast-food wrappings and one held a silver caffeine-drink can caught in its flight from a vehicle window.

Villani went to the fence, followed it for five or six metres, turned back, studying the trivial litter of a million passers-by, shallow-breathing the spent-fuel fumes.

His phone.

'Dove . . . news . . .'

'What?'

' . . . our friend . . . morning . . .'

Looking at the ground, sightless, concentrating on hearing Dove against the booming of the highway, he said, 'Dropping out, call you back.'

Focus came.

Cigarette pack? He moved it with the tip of his shoe, the dusty black brogue toecap of a shiny McCloud's shoe.

Solid object.

Villani stooped, picked it up.

Plastic, gunmetal colour, cracked.

A mobile. Half a mobile, the front was missing.

Thirty, forty metres from the blast? Absolutely no chance whatsoever.

He walked to the Commodore, rocked by two fuel tankers travelling together, a concrete truck, a plastic plumbing pipe-carrier, a tour bus, a jammed Merc looking for a way out, a double-B, all the highway horror.

In the car, he showed Birkerts the object. Birkerts moistened his lower lip. 'Very nice. Resembles a mobile.'

A truck passed half a metre from Birkerts' window.

'Not saying it's Kidd's?' he said.

'No. Roadkill, that's all.'

Birkerts started the Commodore. They waited to enter the bloodstream, classical music, Villani punched the button, familiar voice:

. . . the subject of a smear campaign. In the circumstances, I have suggested to the premier, and he agrees with my suggestion, that it is in the party's and the government's interest that I step down from my position as minister for infrastructure. That's all I have to say at the moment. Thank you.

The woman said:

Well, that's Stuart Koenig a few minutes ago announcing that he's quit his ministerial post. Or been sacked. I lean towards the latter. Political reporter Anna Markham said on the First Light program this morning that Mr Koenig used the, um, services of a young woman of great interest to the police in connection with a murder and has since been interviewed by no less than the head of the Homicide Squad. And Mr Koenig has had his telephone records examined. Small birds say they make fascinating reading . . .

The pulse in his throat.

Anna Markham said . . .

She didn't call him. She didn't think she should tell him she was on the story. What was he to her, then? Nothing of any importance.

Villani rang Dove.

'Hear the Koenig stuff?'

'Yes, boss. That's why I rang you. I heard Ms Markham earlier.'

'Phipps. Bring him in. Now.'

'Just been talking to his mother. He's overseas. Been gone more than a month. Tracy's checking that.'

The flat, barren place, the hard light, the rushing, growling trucks.

Oh Jesus. Conned.

Conned, stiffed. Boned, rolled.

'Prosilio is now to be pursued until there is no rat hole left to go down,' said Villani.

'A change of mind?' said Dove. 'Would you say we've been used and abused?'

'I'd say shut the fuck up.'

He did not know how Prosilio could be pursued, he did not know how to find a rat hole to send anyone down. He had done this so badly.

HCF.

No. Homicide had not come first.

They used a lot of water at Preston.

Four people?

Bomb it to Snake.

He said, for no good reason, 'Let's revisit Preston. Meet me there, Mr Dove.'

THEY STOOD in the passage, chlorine still in the air, the sickly scent.

'Like coming home,' said Dove. 'My mum liked a clean house.'

'Lucky you,' said Villani. 'I cleaned the house.'

'Some say you still do that, boss.'

It took nearly half an hour to give up.

'Too clean,' said Dove. 'Too clean. Should have seen that.'

They went out the front door and walked around to the back.

'Got a smoke?' said Villani.

They lit up. Villani sat on the back step. Dove went to the fence, began a strip walk, up and down.

'Never thought it would be like this,' he said.

Slow steps, eyes down, a man in a trance.

'Be like what?'

'Me and the head of Homicide in some fucked-over back yard in Preston.'

Dove stopped.

He kicked at what looked like a pile of rotting carpet underfelt.

He kicked at it again, in a fastidious way, moved a piece with his right shoe, moved another piece, another, kicked at the earth.

He bent to look at something.

His head came up, lenses sparked.

'Manhole,' he said. 'Up recently.'

Villani crossed the yard.

A square steel cover, rusted, crusted with dirt.

'Don't think they've drained a septic around here since 1956,' Dove said.

The edges were clean.

'What's 1956?'

'Shorthand for a long time ago,' said Dove.

'Tell Trace we want a man,' said Villani. 'With a crowbar. A 1956-type person.'

Three men came. They put on the gear to protect them from a toxic firestorm, one opened the manhole with a crowbar. He stood back.

The smaller man went to a big grey nylon bag and took out a yellow torch, big, a spotlight. He shone it down the hole, had to straddle the hole, he signed to his partner, who looked. They both stood back, the smaller one came over to Villani, offered the torch and a mask.

'Look, boss?' he said.

Villani took the torch, put on the mask, crossed the space, clicking the torch, the foul smell came through the barrier.

He leaned over the manhole, shone the light.

The spotlight lit the pit white, he saw something, couldn't make out what it was.

Then he could.

A rat.

A rat inside a human skull.

Its scaly tail was twitching out of an eye socket.

Villani walked back. To Dove, he said, 'Now we need the full fucking forensic catastrophe.'

In time, the big band arrived, three vehicles pulled in, formation driving, they liked to do that when they could. Villani watched them disembark, the heavy lifters, inured to decay, decomposition, they reached into places other people didn't want to go to.

By late morning, the tapes were up, the street was a parking lot, the media had pitched camp, the helicopters had hung overhead. Sweating scalp, disappointed air, Moxley looked around the small, desperate landscape, the people in overalls, the car bodies, the enlarged hole in the ground

'A female,' said Moxley. 'Youngish, I would hazard. The whole foul thing will have to be excavated.'

'How recent?' said Villani.

'With rats involved, it can be hard to make a judgment. Months, years.'

'No one's ever going to question your rat judgment,' said Villani.

'Not Oakleigh-related this, is it?'

'Who knows?' said Villani. 'We take a holistic view of the world. The whole foul thing.'

'You wouldn't know holistic from a hole in the ground,' said Moxley.

'Holes in the ground, I know. When's this excavating start?'

'As soon as it can be arranged.'

'You'll let me know if, and I say if, you ever learn anything?'

Moxley produced a tissue, blew his nose. 'Which of your handpicked geniuses should we inform?'

Villani pointed. Dove was leaning against the fence, indolent, smoking, talking on his mobile.

'Mr Dove.'

'An indigenous officer who'd now be the only non-bludger on the force,' said Moxley. 'What happened to the wound as a ticket to the Gold Coast on full disability pension?'

'A Homicide officer, professor. We shrug off injuries of all kinds.

Who does your media tip-offs? Do them yourself, do you?'

'I've met Inspector Kiely,' said Moxley. 'A man with a professional manner. He's got some education, I understand.'

'In New Zealand,' said Villani. 'Ranks just ahead of the Congo and Scotland.'

He beckoned to Dove, he came.

'I want you to front up to our media partners,' Villani said. 'Human remains. But until the science is complete, we know nothing. Fuckall.'

'Is that two words, boss?'

Villani saw a pulse in Dove's right eyelid. 'What's wrong with your eye?' he said.

Dove's lips tightened over his teeth. 'Just a tic,' he said.

'What's that, nervous?'

'There would be nerves involved, boss,' said Dove. 'The central nervous system would be involved. In an involuntary way.'

'Not a brilliant look,' said Villani. 'I say that in an involuntary way. Cancel, I'll do it, Detective Dove.'

Villani went out to the cameras and held the Homicide face, grave, concerned, said what had to be said, the natural order of the universe had once more been overturned.

He turned. Dove's hand up. He followed him around the house.

'Found a garbage bag in the pit,' Dove said. 'New bag.'

A man in overalls held a big black plastic bag, knotted.

'Open it,' said Villani, mouth dry. This bag was not months or years old.

The man put the bag on the groundsheet. Clumsy in gloves, he took a while to get the knot undone. He spread the mouth wide.

'Gloves,' said Villani. Someone gave him a pair, he tugged them on.

He lifted out a black dress, put it on the groundsheet. A black bra, tiny black knickers, another bra, more knickers, a cheap Chinese towel, another one, another black dress, one, two, three, four sneakers, cheap ones. A pair of black jeans. A silky shirt, off-white. Nylon zip-up jacket, yellow.

It was in his mind now. The water usage.

Another pair of jeans, blue. Two more blouses. Stockings. More stockings. A white shirt. Nylon jacket, red.

Koenig's words:

An appendix scar, that's all I saw.

Another blouse. A nylon toilet bag, blue.

Another toilet bag, green.

Villani put the bag down, picked up a bra and sniffed it. He put it down, sniffed to clear his nose, bent for the second bra, sniffed that, put it down.

He opened the blue toilet bag. Supermarket cosmetics. Perfume, an atomiser, eau de toilette. *Poison.*

He uncapped it, sprayed the back of his left glove, sniffed. He put the atomiser on the second bra.

Second bag. Same cosmetics. Different atomiser. *Taboo.*

'Give me your hand,' Villani said to Dove.

'Under duress,' said Dove. He held out his left hand, palm down.

Villani sprayed it, lifted it, sniffed.

Dove staring at him.

'Two girls,' Villani said. 'Both at Prosilio.'

AT ST KILDA Road, Villani talked to Kiely.

'Well, we've got a fair bit on our plate,' said Kiely. 'And this doesn't have much of a profile.'

'I want everybody in this establishment not actually engaged in making an arrest,' said Villani. 'That's in the nature of an order.'

'As you wish,' said Kiely.

'Dove and Weber, please.'

They came in, stood in front of the desk.

'In the time frame we have from the Pommy lady across the road from Prosilio,' said Villani, 'on a direct route to Preston, I want every last bit of street vision. Black muscle car, three aerials. Mr Kiely will assign the manpower.'

They both frowned.

'I want this done with astonishing speed,' he said. 'I want a result in hours.'

The men stood. Dove made to speak.

'Go,' said Villani. 'Just go and fucking do it.'

His phone rang.

'Stevo, Geoff.'

Searle.

Deep breath. Be nice to him. He was not dogshit, from a dogshit family. He was a useful member of society, parasite division.

'Yes, mate,' Villani said.

'This Koenig's a fucking landmine, mate.'

'Yes.'

'But I've got another delicate matter here. Free to talk?'

'I can talk, yes.'

'Steve, I hear the *Sunday Age*'s exploding a shit bomb tomorrow.'

'Yes?'

'Tony Ruskin. It's about a senior officer.'

'Yes?'

'Guts is, it's you.'

'Me what?'

'Daughter claims abuse.'

Villani heard himself suck air. A time passed, he had the feeling of being outside himself.

'My daughter?' he said.

'That's right. Youngest daughter. I'm guessing this comes via the welfare. Community Services.'

'Abuse?'

'Of a sexual nature.'

'Come on,' said Villani. 'Bullshit.'

'Haven't been told she's done that?'

'She's on the street with fucking ferals. Steals from her own family. They can't run this kind of shit as if . . .'

'They can,' said Searle. 'They will.'

'Well. Jesus.'

'Sit tight,' said Searle. 'I'm on the case.'

'Appreciate that,' said Villani.

'No worries. Stick together. Your wife, she'll be solid, right? Back you to the hilt.'

What to say? 'Of course. My whole family.'

'Good. United front, that's vital. Drug-crazed kid, yeah . . . Back to you soon, mate.'

Villani sat, holding the phone. Tendons showing in his arm.

How could the little bitch do this? He found his mobile, Laurie's number. She answered in seconds.

'It's me,' he said. 'Where are you?'

'At home.'

'Stay there. I'm on my way.'

HE PARKED in the driveway behind Laurie's VW and knocked on the front door. She opened it.

'What's Lizzie said to you?' he said, closed teeth.

Laurie spoke slowly, as if she had lost her English. 'She called last night, she says she's scared. To come home. She says. She can't live here. Because you made her . . . you abused her.'

'Abused her. How?'

'Made her suck you off.'

The day, the time, the heat, where he was, all went away. He had an obstruction in his throat, he tried to clear it.

'Me?'

'She's told them that, yes.'

'Told who?'

'I don't know.'

'Told them what exactly?'

'You came to her room. Woke her. A number of times.'

'Jesus,' he said, he shivered, inside. 'She's off her face. How can she do this?'

Laurie looked at him and he saw.

'Don't look at me like that, don't look at me like . . . say you don't believe it.'

She said nothing.

'Say it.'

'I don't know what to believe,' she said. 'I'm in shock.'

The violence took him captive, he grabbed her shoulders,

shook her. 'You don't believe her. Fucking say it. Say it.'

She did not resist him, her chin sunk to her chest, and he saw the white skin of her scalp along the parting. All anger left him, he dropped his arms, tried to kiss her head, but she moved away.

'Sorry,' he said. 'I'm sorry. Sorry.'

She backed away, eyes on him. He saw no understanding, saw disbelief. She thought it was possible, thinkable, she could see him doing it. How could that be? How could she not know in her bones that it was impossible?

Laurie turned and walked. He followed her into the kitchen. She went as far as she could go, to the sink.

'Let's be clear,' said Villani, blinking, his eyes were wet. 'I have never touched that girl in my life except to give her a kiss. I have never gone to her room in the night. I have never made her do anything to me, I would blow my fucking brains out if I had.'

Laurie washed a clean plate, shrugged, he could see the shoulder blades shift. 'It's her that's important,' she said. 'Not you.'

He could have punched her in the head, so fiercely did the unfairness burn in him. He gathered himself. 'You know what this is, don't you?' he said. 'It's this scum she's hanging out with. They want money out of her.'

Laurie dried her hands on the dishcloth, dragging it out, rubbing fingers. 'Have to see,' she said.

'Where is she?'

'They say she was in care but she's taken off again.'

'So they lost her?'

'I suppose so.'

'You know where she is, don't you? Don't you?'

'I don't. I don't.'

'Well I'll fucking find her.'

Laurie turned, face set, folded her arms. Deep lines bracketed her mouth. He had never seen them before. 'Stephen, stay out of it. You can only do harm.'

Villani looked at the floor, took two measured breaths. 'Just cop it, will I?' he said. 'She tells the welfare pricks these lies about me, I just shrug it off?'

'Leave it, Stephen.'

He wanted to scream his rage, bang her head against the fridge. He took deep breaths. 'Where's Corin?' he said. 'She'll tell you this is crap. She knows her sister. She knows me. She'll tell you.'

'She's gone away for the weekend. I'm not telling her now.'

'I want Lizzie to say it to my face,' Villani said. 'I want her to look me in the eye in the presence of witnesses and say I made her suck me off.'

Laurie said nothing, tried to walk around him, Villani held out his right arm. She stopped.

'Just say you believe me,' he said. 'Just say that.'

'I don't know what to believe. She's my darling baby. What else can I say?'

'Goodbye, you can say goodbye. You and your fucking slut daughter can both say goodbye to me.'

Laurie pushed back her hair with fingertips, quick, he saw grey at her temples, not seen before either.

'Can I go?' she said.

Villani saw how big and ungainly his hand was, he let his arm fall. 'Say goodbye to me.'

'Goodbye, Stephen,' she said. 'Go away.'

And then he said it.

'She's not my kid anyway. Why don't you send the fucking father out looking for her?'

'Get out,' she said. 'I can believe anything of you.'

DRIVING IN the heat, air-con battling, for a few disoriented moments, he didn't know where to go, what to do, he went through red lights, long hooting.

The rage went suddenly, now he felt sick, dry-mouthed, an ache in the back of his neck.

How did you handle stuff like this? You couldn't carry on in the job if your daughter accused you of sexual abuse. Everyone you knew would look at you in a new way. With contempt. You were a sicko, you were a disgusting pervert, you couldn't be in command, no woman would ever come near you. Anna would draw a shuddering line through his name.

Why would the welfare leak this? If she'd made the allegation, they were obliged to call in the Sexual Crimes Squad. Had they? Called in the SCS and leaked the story to the *Age*?

He was in Rathdowne Street. He turned left at the park, found a space, sat for a time watching mothers watching their small children socialise in the sandpit. One child force-fed another a handful of sand, the victim didn't object but its minder snatched it away, inserted a finger in the gritty, gummy mouth.

Two women, sweaty flesh, big legs, toddlers in all-terrain vehicles, combat pushers. They looked at him, not glances, full-on challenges, women who would ring the police and report a man in a car watching children in a park.

Alleged sex offender watching children in park. Oh, Jesus, this was what Lizzie had done to him, brought him to.

He got out, leant against the car, that was a better look. Not afraid to show his face. What he needed was a smoke.

The newsagent in the next block.

He locked the car without looking, the dull click, walked, turned the corner. He hadn't walked down Rathdowne Street for a long time, since he and Laurie rented in Station Street. Was the pizza place still going? They'd eaten there at least once a week in the old days, just the two of them, then with baby Corin, then with Corin and the baby boy, Cashin often ate with them. By the time of Lizzie, they didn't do that kind of thing anymore.

Plead with Laurie to talk sense into Lizzie. Go on your knees and ask her to save you. How could she take the feral little bitch's word against his?

She could. She had.

He'd lied to her, yes. But she didn't know all of that. Some lies she knew about, he'd told stupid lies, he'd confessed to some lies. You lied because you didn't want people to be hurt. Something that was over, what was the point in admitting it? Soon to be over.

He didn't deserve Laurie, he'd never doubted that. She was a good person, she didn't know how to lie. He had never considered leaving her, not even after the day he opened her mobile phone bill by accident, he was putting it back in the envelope when he saw the amount: $668.45. How did she do that? He turned to the itemised calls. She made long and expensive ones. Most of them to the same numbers.

He wrote down the numbers. At work, he gave them to an analyst. 'Run these for me, will you?'

She came back in minutes with a sheet of paper.

David Joliffe, cinematographer, 22/74 St Crispin's Place, King Street, East Melbourne. Home phone number and mobile.

The pizza place was still there, so was the picture framer who had framed the wedding photograph. Where was that now? He hadn't seen it in years, probably put on top of a cupboard the day Laurie took off the engagement and wedding rings and went bare-fingered.

That was Clem, the interior designer. She appeared to be happy with the odd screw at her place, then when he said stumps, not in an insensitive way, she took to ringing. Christ knew where she got the number, she left messages for him at home.

That was also the end of Mrs Lauren Villani. She took back her family name.

He walked, smoking, rang Searle. The thing was to be icy calm.

'Stevo mate. Item's pulled. For the moment. Had to mortgage the job, sell kids into slavery.'

'I won't say it.'

'No, no, don't. Divided we are rooted.'

'Listen,' said Villani. 'The paper get this from the welfaries or Sex Crimes?'

'Never going to tell me that.'

'But she's made a statement?'

'Not sure. Sit tight, I would say. I'll hear before it goes anywhere, get straight to you.'

'Good on you.'

'The worry for us,' said Searle, 'is if Moorcroft's got the drum. The twat's tight with the welfare lesbo Rotties, he would be their first cab.'

Gary Moorcroft, Anna's little friend, TV crime reporter, who asked whether they were an item.

Unnaturally curious.

'Well, see what happens,' Villani said.

'Not a wait-and-see man, myself,' said Searle. 'Offer a suggestion?'

'Yes.'

'Ms Markham. You've got credit there.'

'Credit?'

'Mate, mate, your car's outside the person's residence at 4am last count, you'd have credit, wouldn't you?'

Searle made a laugh-like sound.

Icy calm.

'I'm surveilled, am I?' said Villani.

'Nothing personal, just the building, the street. The prime minister shows up, he's logged.'

'Who's doing that?'

'Steve, have a word with your friend. She's got clout, she can snuff the little cunt, she's done this stuff before.'

'What stuff?'

'Been helpful. She's a pro. She knows about give and take.'

'She covers politics. How is she helpful?'

Searle made an impatient noise, he was running this. 'Mate, now everything's politics, that's the way it is. Just ask her. Put it on the line. If she takes your word it's bullshit, why wouldn't she do it?'

The years, the things endured, the drudgery, the fear, and now to be patronised, instructed, by this weak dog who knew the job only by the talk of his rotten father and uncles, holders of the slope franchise, said to own much of sea-level Saturn Bay, the working man's paradise. The only justice was that now, at every king tide, the ice-swollen sea enfiladed the ninety-mile dune, soon it would flow beneath the Searle's Hardy Plank palaces, float their boats, their barbecues, the place would be returned to the mosquitoes, the feral cats, dune rats, the gulls, all oblivious to the wind, the ceaseless, sad, sawing wind.

'Get back to you,' said Villani.

Ask Anna to take his word that he had not molested his

daughter? The Anna who implicated him in Koenig's downfall. Searle had no idea what it would cost him to do that. Things like pride and dignity, the man knew nothing of them.

Anyway, what was the point in buying time? Stand down now.

Bugger that. He hadn't done anything except be a mediocre father, since when was that a crime? Standing room only in the jails.

Dad, you only sleep here, you pass over this house like a cloud shadow.

Villani looked at his messages.

Clinton Hulme. Max Hendry's chief of staff.

Stephen. Just to say we'd appreciate an answer today, tomorrow at the latest. Look forward to hearing from you.

Birkerts.

Flashboxed that bit of roadkill you picked up. Unbelievable. It's the aunty's phone. Got some texts. We need to talk.

Yes. Yes. Something going right.

Matt Cameron.

For what it's worth, my advice's make the change, son. Talk to you later. Expand.

Dove.

Boss, can you come in, we've got something.

BLACK-AND-WHITE image, a near-empty city street, car approaching. The digital line said: *0.2.22.*

'La Trobe,' said Weber. 'Looking south-west. Flagstaff Gardens to right.'

'Possibly up Dudley, right into King, left into La Trobe,' said Dove. 'Here it is.'

Second car in view, black, closing on first.

'Honda's going to run lights, changes his mind,' said Weber.

Front vehicle brakes hard, twists.

'Bang,' said Weber. 'Beemer's hit him.'

The driver and passenger of the Honda get out.

'Beemer front-seat passenger,' said Dove.

Big man in black, hair pulled back into ponytail.

'Kenny Hanlon,' said Villani.

'Jesus,' said Dove, looked at Villani.

Hanlon is gesticulating, he is shouting, threatening the driver of the Honda.

'Behind him, boss,' said Weber.

A slight figure is out of the BMW, the back door, chalk face, black hair, black dress, bare shoulders, she does not hesitate, she is running, behind her a bus shelter, she is on the pavement.

'Loses a shoe, kicks the other one off, she's into the gardens,' said Dove.

The camera caught the spike-heeled shoe in the air.

Hanlon cuffs the Honda driver, an open-hand swing of his

right hand, the Honda passenger is trying to grab Hanlon, the BMW driver is out of the car, mouth open, he is shouting.

'Got the vision in the gardens,' said Weber, eyes on the console.

The girl running towards a camera, veering right, no vision.

'That's camera six,' said Weber, 'middle of park.'

Figure coming towards camera, the girl.

'Camera nine,' said Weber. 'Heading for corner of Dudley and William.'

She came into clear focus, wide-eyed, mouth open, breathless.

Lizzie. Oh God.

No, not Lizzie.

'Checked Peel Street?' said Villani. 'Might've gone that way. Must be cameras around the Vic Market. Friday morning, they work early.'

Dove said, 'Three people around there now.'

Villani looked at the men. 'Good work,' he said.

The men looked at him, waited.

'Twins,' said Dove. 'She's the one at Koenig's.'

'The appendix scar,' said Villani. 'Oh Jesus.'

Silence.

'Kenny Hanlon,' Villani said. 'Now.'

'ELECTRONIC gates, cameras, motion detectors, steel shutters downstairs,' said Finucane, the driver. 'They own all of them and the ones behind. Hellhound compound. Gorillas on guard full-time.'

'Beats the old cement factory in Northcote,' said Villani. He chewed the last of the salad sandwich. He crumpled the bag, put it in the cup-holder, pushed it back into the housing.

Four doors down, a big man in a windbreaker appeared, looked hard at them.

'Gorilla at work,' said Finucane. 'Hellhound apprentice.'

Villani and Dove and Weber got out. The man put his head down and spoke to the sheet-steel gate of the second of four townhouses, two storeys, set well back from a three-metre wall. Upstairs, fake windows looked out at useless balconies.

As they approached, Weber said, 'Tell Mr Hanlon the police would like to see him. Homicide.'

The man lifted his upper lip. 'Let's see ID,' he said.

Weber showed the badge. 'That coat. You carrying or just got a dodgy thermostat?'

'Fuck you too,' said the man. He spoke into the grille, an inaudible reply. Bolts clicked. He opened the gate, went in first.

An unshaven man in tracksuit pants and a black T-shirt was in the front door. Big, forties, fleshy, face pocked like a sweet melon, dark greasy hair pulled into a tail.

'What the fuck's this?' said Hanlon, recognised Villani. 'Jeez,

Sergeant Villani, you fucken following me around all my fucken life?'

'Have a talk,' said Villani.

'Yeah. About fucken what?'

'I'll come back with the Soggies,' said Villani. 'Knock your fucking house down and kill you. Accidentally.'

Hanlon said to the guard, 'Okay, buddy, back on station.'

Hanlon turned. They followed him across a tile-floored foyer into a room that was a kitchen and an eating place. He sat at a table of polished granite, two mobiles on it.

'So what?' he said.

'Sure one fuckbrain is enough to look after you?' said Villani.

'Fuckall to do with you, buddy. Area's crawlin with druggies. Did your job, I wouldn't need security. Fucken poodle be enough.'

'Intelligent dog, the poodle,' said Villani. 'It might not want to protect you. Used to live in your batcave, all of you, so shit-scared of the Angels. Still, crapping yourselves kept you warm.'

'Just fuck off,' said Hanlon.

Villani stood at the island bench. 'It's about a woman,' he said.

'Yeah?'

'The one you took to the Prosilio building.'

Hanlon smoothed his hair with both hands, looked at his palms. There was a sheen on them. 'Mate,' he said, 'where do you come by shit like this? What's your problem?'

'Dead girl, that's our problem,' said Villani. 'Account for all your movements on Thursday night a week ago, Kenny?'

Hanlon put a hand into his collar, rubbed himself. 'Every last second. I'm home fast asleep by eleven any night, every night.'

'Someone can confirm that?'

'No. Only about twenty people. And my wife. And my mother-in-law. Good enough? Do you?'

'Live-in mother-in-law, is it?'

'Better lookin than your wife, mate, she cooks like, I dunno, that Pommy poof. Better.'

'So you now transport hookers,' Villani said. 'How can that be profitable?'

Hanlon tapped his forehead with two fingertips. 'I'm in hospitality, buddy. You pricks been over me like slime for years. Want to go again? Go for your fucken life.'

A silence. Dove, face blank, was looking at his clipboard.

'Your car,' he said. 'That's the black Beemer. Involved in a collision in La Trobe Street Friday morning before last, 2.23am.'

'Not me, mate. Had it with fucken German cars, had it with the Krauts. Holden SV now, mate. Aussie car.'

In the doorway appeared a woman in a cream velvet tracksuit. She was snap-frozen at around sixty, blonded, bee-swollen, decorated in a glowing shade of peach, bright pink plump collagen lips.

'Guests, Kenny,' she said. 'So early.'

'Give us ten, Suzie, there's a love,' Hanlon said.

The woman smiled at Villani, it lingered as though facial muscles had gone into spasm. 'So lovely to meet you,' she said. She left, beatific.

Hanlon stood, reached to a counter and picked up cigarettes, Camels. 'Smoke?'

They didn't respond. Villani went to the door and closed it, turned the lock. He looked around the room at the commercial coffee machine, the stainless-steel fridges, the stone-topped counter. 'Our understanding,' he said, 'is that you keep hookers jailed in a house in Preston. Confirm that?'

Hanlon pulled a face. 'Reality check here. Can I go back to planet fucken earth? Rejoin the human race?'

'Rejoining would require prior membership,' said Dove.

'Who's this smartarse boong?' said Hanlon. 'Can't get white people to join you cunts now? Scrapin the fucken barrel?'

Villani looked away, moved closer, balanced himself, hit Hanlon under his ribs, big right hand punch, gave him a left in the ribs, a heavy right into a flabby pectoral.

Hanlon went to his knees and puked, yellow, projectile.

'Respect, Kenny,' said Villani. 'Even if you don't respect the man, you have to respect the badge.'

He found a dishcloth on the benchtop, threw it at Hanlon. 'Clean it up before the Botox witch sees it, Kenny. She might paddle your hairy arse. Or does she do that for you anyway?'

Hanlon wiped his mouth with the cloth, wiped the tiles, stood up. 'Die for that,' he said. 'Fucken die.'

'Detectives, note that Mr Hanlon threatened me with death,' said Villani. 'Kenny, I'm giving you a chance to talk to us. Might save your life.'

Hanlon sighed, Villani heard resignation. 'How stupid you think I am? How stupid are you? Couldn't save my fucken cat's life.'

'Clears that up,' said Villani. He smiled at Dove, turned the smile on Hanlon. 'Enjoyed talking to you. Kenneth.'

'That's it?' said Hanlon. Hands in the air, hairy fingers, two gold rings on each hand, forefinger and pinky.

'Unless you want to say something.'

Hanlon found a cigarette, lit up with a plastic lighter, lifted his head, blew smoke out of his nostrils. 'Goodbye. I want to say that. Goodbye.'

'Those Camels,' said Villani. 'Duty paid?'

'Bloke give me a carton.'

'Bloke in a pub?'

'You know him?'

At the kitchen door, Hanlon said to Villani, 'Occurs to me, you related to Dr Marko?'

'Never heard of him, sunshine,' said Villani. 'Face the wall, close up, hands behind you. You're under arrest.'

'Don't be fucken . . .'

'Draw your weapon, Detective Weber,' said Villani. 'Mr Hanlon is about to resist arrest. Kenny, I'll kick your balls off and then we'll shoot you.'

'Like you done Greg Quirk?'

Villani took back his right hand. Hanlon looked into his eyes and he turned, put his hands behind his back. Weber cuffed him and told him his rights.

Villani pointed to the mobiles on the table. Dove put them in his inside pocket.

'Open the door, Detective Dove,' said Villani. 'You go first, Mr Hanlon. And tell your prick outside to keep his hands out of his clothes or we'll kill him and that will be a pleasure and a public service.'

At the car, Weber in the back with Hanlon, Dove's mobile sang. He plugged it into his ear, talked, put it away, looked at Villani with bright eyes.

'Where you suggested, boss,' he said. 'Tomasic's got a bloke, just come on shift a minute ago.'

Villani rang the number. 'Villani. Got a piece of shit to be taken off my hands. Yeah. Twenty minutes.'

To Dove he said, 'Charge him with accessory to murder, conspiracy to pervert, deprivation of liberty, any old fucking thing crosses your mind. Then he can wait for Monday, have a little time to think.'

IN THE security office, Villani shook hands with the man. He had a big belly and a beard like faded red moss and should have been retired in Venus Bay.

'Tell me, Vic,' said Villani.

'Well, I seen her comin at the Dudley Street corner,' said Vic. 'Light's not bad there, and she run across the street and I seen she's got no shoes on. She sees me, she runs up to me, she can't hardly breathe she's that tired.'

'What's she look like?' said Villani.

'Just a kid. Like sixteen maybe? Thin, white skin, black hair.' He touched his shoulders to show the length. 'She got on like a party dress, black? Those little straps, y'know.'

'Shoelaces?'

'Yeah. Them. Red lipstick.'

'What did she say?'

'Got no English. Very little.'

'So?'

'So I said, come with me and we come around here. She's really scared, she's jabberin on in Romanian and she's lookin back, down Peel and she's kinda tryin to hide in front of me. Y'know? Like gettin in my way?'

'Romanian?' said Villani.

'Yeah. Didn't know what it was. Just wog jabber to me, mate.'

'And?'

'I give the other bloke a call. Made tea, she can't hardly drink it. Anyway, he comes, name's Maggie, he's a wog too. He can't understand her but he says she's a Romanian, he gets that. So he says, get the police and she knows about police, she goes ballistic, no, no, no, she's crying.'

'Common reaction,' said Dove.

Vic laughed. 'So, anyway, Maggie says he knows a Romanian, he'll ring him in the morning. We tell her don't worry, no police, make a bed for her in the back. She just drops off like that, curls up, she's dead to the world.'

Villani said, 'In the morning?'

'Maggie rung the bloke, puts her on, she talks to him. I knocked off but he come around for her. Maggie stayed on.'

'How do we get hold of Maggie?'

'On holiday. With the caravan. By himself. Monday he went.'

'Went where?'

Vic shrugged. 'Dunno, mate. Fishin, mad keen. Mad Collingwood, mad fishin. Go anywhere.'

'Phone number?'

Vic went to a shelf and found a torn folder, put it on the table. It held stapled pages. He ran his finger down one. 'Jeez, the turnover here, mate, you wouldn't believe. Here. Name's Bendiks Vanags. How's that for a name?'

'Means hawk,' said Tomasic. 'Vanags.'

'Yeah,' said Vic. 'He said that. That's why they call him Maggie. Got a pen?'

Dove wrote down the number. 'Mobile?' he said.

'No mobile here.'

'Got a family?'

'No, mate. All alone. The wife give him the arse, that's a while ago. Years.'

'Get the address off you,' said Dove.

They went outside, the scorching day, hard planes of light off the windscreens in the parking lot, Dove on the phone as they walked.

Lizzie. Did it cross her mind that she would destroy him? He took out his phone.

'Mate,' said Vickery, third-pack-of-the-day voice, last drink.

Villani described the man. Dreadlocks, tatts on his face, between his eyes. Dirty did not have to be said.

'I remember,' said Vickery. 'Beat the drums for the cunt now.' Pause. 'Constructive conversations important, not so? So everybody faces the rising sun.'

'Absolutely no question, mate,' said Villani, the taste of copper in his mouth.

BIRKERTS PUT a page on the desk.

'Texts,' he said. 'In a possible time frame, in the LAI. But no date.'

Villani looked.

Received 02.49: WHAT?

Sent 02.50: SOON.

Received 03.01: ?????

Sent 03.04: GOING IN.

Sent 03.22: OTU BANZAI OK.

'Tell me,' Villani said.

Birkerts caressed his shave, found something under his chin. 'New light on the matter,' he said. 'I would say Kidd and Larter do the SAS stroke SOG stuff, kill Vern Hudson, hang the brothers up. Then they hand over to someone.'

'Could be Kidd talking to Larter.'

Birkerts went to the window, prised open two venetian slats, peered.

'I find it hard to believe,' he said, 'that even a cross-trained killer would take on the Ribs and their mate by himself and then send for the other bloke. But that's just me.'

'It's always just you,' said Villani. 'I wish it wasn't always just you. What do we do with this?'

Birkerts turned. 'Have you ever asked a question you didn't have the answer to? Mind made up. Know how much that grates?'

'That's cheeky. Insubordinate. Know how much that grates?'

Birkerts didn't look at him. 'I'm quitting,' he said. 'Monday. Had it.'

'Steady on,' said Villani. 'Don't do this to me.'

'Why not? Anyway, it's not to you, it's to the fucking job. You live in some kind of communion with the dead, you never get a decent night's sleep, it's always on your mind, people treat you like you're an undertaker, mortician, it fucked my marriage, now it's fucked the only decent relationship I've been in since then and another . . .'

Birkerts fell silent. 'Yeah, anyway, I've had it.'

'You'll do what for a living?'

'I don't know. My ex-brother-in-law says he'll give me a job selling real estate.'

'Sell property? Are you mad?'

'What's wrong with real estate? You make money. You don't get called out to some fucking shithole where a mental defective's been burnt to death for fun, you can smell burnt meat a block away.'

Villani got up, went around the desk, no purpose, body humming with tension, kicked Singo's box, full swing of the leg, his toecap dug into it, the boxer shot out, hit the floor with its head, which broke off.

'Oh fuck,' he said, bent and picked up the pieces. 'Typical force shit, can't even give you a bloody metal trophy. I'm supposed to send it to his nephew.'

Birkerts took the pieces from him. 'I know a bloke can recast this. Do it in aluminium. The nephew won't know.'

'I don't actually give a fuck about Singo's nephew,' said Villani. 'I'm quitting too.'

'Come on?'

'Not the only one who's had it, mate.'

Birkerts shook his head. 'Boss of crime, the word's out. You can be the complete bloody sun in all its glory.'

'No,' said Villani. 'Sunset. My little girl says I did things to her. Sex.'

Birkerts frowned. 'Jesus. Well.'

'Smacked-out, on the street, feral scum,' said Villani. 'I'm finished. Fucked.'

Silence. In it, the radio was heard:

. . . the Morpeth–Selborne complex have been told to expect the worst tomorrow when extreme conditions are predicted, temperatures in the mid-to-high forties and winds that could approach . . .

'On Kidd,' said Villani. 'He texts this stuff, changes nothing. Oakleigh is over.'

'My Lord, what is this job?' said Birkerts. 'We drive an hour in the shitawful so you can sniff the fucking roadside and find this, now it means fuckall?'

'Basically,' said Villani.

'I have work to do,' said Birkerts. 'Maybe we can have a drink on Monday when we're both moving on to new careers. New lives.'

At the door, he said to Villani, 'This is why the wife kicked you out?'

'Keep moving,' said Villani. 'Sell inner city, can't go wrong. Is that right?'

He rang Bob's number. It rang out, he tried again, again.

'Yeah, Villani.' Bob.

'What's happening?'

'I'm busy, on a bloody bulldozer.'

'Where'd you get a bulldozer?'

'Borrowed it. Me and Gordie's putting in an airstrip in front of the trees. Talk later.'

End of call. Man in the door.

'Boss, hospital just rang, there's a lady, a Mrs Quirk . . .'

A WOMAN from hospital management met Villani and took him to the fourth floor, along a blank corridor to a room with eight beds, curtains drawn around them.

A young nurse, cheerful farm-girl face, was coming towards them.

'Nurse, please show Inspector Villani to Mrs Quirk's bed.'

Villani said his thanks, followed the nurse to the last bed on the left.

The nurse said loudly, 'Mrs Quirk. Visitor.'

'Who?' said Rose from behind the curtains.

'Me. Stephen.'

'Well, come in the bloody tent,' Rose said.

'Not on her last legs?' Villani said to the nurse.

'Not just yet.' She ran a curtain aside.

Rose on two pillows, head bandaged, face the matching colour. Her right forearm was in plaster to the first knuckles.

'Jeez, ma,' said Villani. 'You've got to stop getting in these fights.'

She drew her mouth down. 'Little shit run me down. What took you so long?'

'Have a heart,' said Villani. 'Only got the message ten minutes ago. You could've said you were okay, not given me a fright.'

Rose made a noise, scorn. 'Probably thought, good riddance, bloody old bag.'

Villani sat on a moulded plastic chair. 'Yeah, that crossed my mind. What happened to your head?'

'Can you believe it?' said Rose. 'The one little bastard knocks me over, the other one's on a skateboard. I'm lyin there dyin, he rides over me head.'

'Who saved you?'

'Across the road come and put a cushie under me head, held me hand.'

'Probably didn't want the street's free veggie supplier to cark it,' said Villani. 'Arm broken?'

'Nah, the wrist.' Rose craned towards him. 'Listen, Stevie, can't stay here, don't want to die here, bloody germatorium. Tell em to let me go home. They'll listen to you. Bloody inspector.'

'Inspector doesn't carry weight with the medical profession,' said Villani. 'Doesn't carry weight with anyone actually.'

'Please, love.'

Rose put her left hand out to him. He took it, chicken bones in a bag of skin, held it in both his big awkward hands.

'They give me all this health shit,' she said. 'Blood pressure's too high. The weight on me heart, surprised it don't shoot out of me ears.'

'I'll lean on them, ma,' Villani said. 'Get you out of here. Those mobile nurses can come around.'

'Don't need em,' said Rose. 'I'm gone. Little arse hit me, saw me spirit float out of me body.'

'Cigarette smoke,' said Villani. 'Out of the lungs. Time to cut down.'

She pointed at the tin cupboard beside the bed, winked. 'Get me bag. We'll have a little ciggy.'

'No, ma. That's the only reason you wanted me here. Got to go, attend to the dead, you're the living.'

Rose sighed. 'Stevie, Stevie,' she said, 'do somethin for me?'

'What?'

'Trust you? Cop scum.'

'Depends. Maybe. No. What?'

'I'm scared about me money.'

'What money?'

She put her head back, closed her eyes, lids of old silk. 'Little treasure chest. Savings. Me float.'

'In the bank?'

She opened her eyes. 'Jesus, mate, wake up to the bloody world. Under the kitchen table, lino comes up. There's a trapdoor, stick a knife in.'

'Yes?'

'Don't bugger me knives either. Little treasure chest.'

'Yes?'

'Keep it safe for me, son? Had a nightmare, house burns down, it's all ashes. Like Black Saturday, I'm walkin around there, pick up a cup. Promise?'

'House locked?'

'Left it locked. Get me bag.'

Villani opened the cupboard, took her bag from the top shelf.

'Giss,' she said. 'Giss.'

'I'm so dumb,' said Villani, 'I should join the police. Treasure chest, bullshit. You want your fags, don't you? Forget it, ma.'

Her eyes closed in slow motion. 'Take the keys, Stevie,' she said, faint. 'Go around and get me chest.'

Villani found the keys, put the bag back in the cupboard.

'Do that, then,' he said. 'Don't worry, Rosie. I'll be back.'

He stood. Her eyes remained closed.

'Giss a kiss, Stevie,' she said. 'Giss a cuddle. Me only good boy. Come too late.'

Villani felt tears coming, he leaned over and took her shoulders in soft hands, pressed his face to her, kissed her riven cheek beneath the bandage and in himself there was a great resentment and a great feeling of the unfairness in his life.

On a winter day, in the big break, backs against the demountable, shelter from the ice wind, clever little monkeyface Kel Bryson said:

They ever find your mum?

In the car, his mobile rang.

Colby.

COLBY LOOKED as if he'd come off the golf course. 'Searle says it's pulled, does he?' he said.

'For tomorrow,' said Villani. 'The question is, did Ruskin get it from welfare or Sex Crimes? Or both?'

Colby opened a file on the desk, flicked to a page, put on thin rimless glasses. 'I can tell you there's no Sexual Crimes statement,' he said. 'Tell me what abused means.'

'Made her suck me off.'

Colby showed nothing. 'You do that?'

Villani stared at him for a while. 'What do you think?'

'Don't know what to think.'

Villani rose, walked down the long room, prints on the walls, he registered every step, chewing the bile in his mouth.

Colby's voice, raised but calm. 'Hey, come back, sunshine.'

Villani turned, hand on the door handle.

Colby beckoned, four fingers tight as a bird wing. 'C'mere, son.'

Villani hesitated. He went back, he could do no other. They sat, chins down, eyes locked, their history hummed. 'Christ, this is hard shit,' said Colby.

'I'll quit,' said Villani. 'Just got some things to finish.'

'How long's she been on the streets?'

'About a week. But she was hanging out with the scum before. Wagging.'

'Drugs?'

'What else?'

'How old?'

'Fifteen.'

'Just a baby, really.'

For weeks and weeks, the baby Lizzie had colic, whatever colic was, her night cries entering his dreams, strange stories developing around the insistent sound. They took turns walking her in the dark, the passage, the kitchen, the sitting room, it was many times in a night, you walked her, she stopped crying, you put her down like landing a soap bubble, went back to bed, she made a sound, it became a cry, a skewer in your head, you got up again.

Sometimes Lizzie slept between feeds. Sometimes he cheated when the cries woke him, nudged Laurie, lied that he'd just had his turn, she rose, no idea of how long she'd been asleep. He said to himself that she'd probably done the same to him, they were both trying to survive. But he knew she wouldn't, she didn't know how to lie.

The difference was that if the phone rang, Laurie didn't have to go to an in-progress. Could be doped drunk fuckwits had a gun and a brilliant 2am idea, could be hardcore, two, three jobs in a night, take a couple of months off, go north, fishing, whoring. Both lots could kill you.

Once it rang as he was changing Lizzie's nappy, gagging on the smell of the yellow purée, first dirty light in the eastern window, everything about him numb, brain, feet, hands, only the nose functioning. Twenty minutes later he had his back against a wall in a lane off Sydney Road, listening to two braindeads come out of the roof, they had lifted a sheet of corrugated iron. Next to him, Xavier Benedict Dance was smiling his dog smile.

'They stop being baby girls earlier now,' Villani said. 'They can go from baby girls to fuckpigs in a very short time.'

'Hasn't escaped me,' said Colby. 'But incest, that's not a barbie-stopper, that's the barbie blows up, kills seven. We have to look at the big picture here . . .'

A silence. Colby's phone rang, a few words, grunts, eyes on the ceiling, goodbye, he stared at Villani.

'So where's she now?'

'No idea.'

'Tell me again it's bullshit.'

'Don't believe me?'

'Tell me.'

'Fuck you.'

'Definite negative. I can probably arrange to squeeze the welfare attack-bitch kennel but we need Ruskin permanently squirrelled. Reckon your missus can talk sense into the girl?'

'Maybe.'

'Okay, we'll find her. Stay nice with Searle. I don't know why he's doing this.'

Villani nodded. If only he could put his head back against the chair and go to sleep, someone else in charge, feel the way he felt when the Kenworth came through the gate on a Friday night, he saw Bob's sharp face, the downturned smile, the raised thumb. It was as if angels had lifted a bag of lead sinkers from his shoulders.

'There's something else,' said Colby. 'Mr Barry tells me the popular belief is that you talked about Stuart Koenig to Ms Anna Markham while fucking her. Do that?'

'I did not.'

'That's the talking, not the fucking?'

'Who's surveilling her building? Or her?'

'How would I know? Who would tell me? Ask your mate Dance.'

'Crucible?'

'I have no fucking idea. What I have an idea about is Greg Quirk. Payback time, son. These babies get back in, new inquest. DiPalma wants to screw you till your earwax melts and you go to jail for twenty years and then the real fun begins. I, of course, remain confident that you and Dancer and fucking Vickery weren't making stuff up the first time around.'

Villani stared at Colby. He seemed less lined around the eyes, forehead smoother. Surely not?

'This Prosilio hooker,' Colby said. 'I understood that was in the vault.'

'It's open, in progress.'

'Yeah. But in the vault.'

'Forgotten about the vault, boss.'

'Stephen, only a brain-dead cunt forgets about the vault. With me?'

'Yes, boss.'

'And you should now personally beseech the blessed virgin several hours nightly for the voters to shaft these arses. And in the day you keep your hands out of your pockets and do nothing to offend the squatters.'

Koenig was there when the girl was killed. Villani knew it in his bone marrow. Never mind him being at home in Portsea. He wasn't there. He was in Kew. How often had Koenig's wife lied for him? Bricknell rang him and he went to Prosilio, parked underground. One girl each.

HE TOOK the fire stairs, millions of them, doors to push, he paced himself and as he went he thought about what the job had meant to him and remembered the moment when he sat back in Singo's chair and thought: Stephen Villani, head of Homicide and he deserves to be.

Bob had no pride in him being boss of Homicide. Cop job, that's all it was. Far beneath foreman, shift boss, night supervisor of anything. But the best his second-best son could do. Second-best until Luke arrived, then third-best. Just a useful body, a cook, guard dog, washer and ironer of clothes, homework checker, reading and spelling tutor, feeder of dogs and horses, mucker-out in chief, track rider, tree planter and waterer.

You're not the doctor, boy, you're the fucking copper.

Mark.

Mark was Bob's achievement in life, the proof that his sperm carried cleverness. He saw no wrong in Mark, he would hear no evil about Mark, he exempted Mark from anything Mark didn't want to do.

He did crossword puzzles with Mark.

Bob never once asked Villani a crossword question. Never.

And then Luke, the bastard by the Darwin whore. The cheeky one, the one who had no fear of his father, demanded affection from him like a puppy, hung onto him, crawled up his legs into his lap, ate off his plate, found sweets in his pockets, fell asleep on him in an instant, safe, safe and home at last. Bob carried him to his bed like some precious newborn, tucked him in, Villani saw that from the door, the tucks, the kiss.

And then, come Monday, it would be his job to see to the whining little shit.

On his desk, a note from Dove about the Preston excavations:

Young female, dead at least three months. Also remains of male, age forty-plus, pictures of rings on little fingers supplied by forensic suggest Hellhound. Armed Crime say strong possibility is Artie Macphillamy, 43, not seen for 18 months since involved in pub fight with Kenny Hanlon and others.

He rang Dance.

'I hear you've left home,' said Dance.

'Where'd you hear that?'

'The most expensive intelligence-gathering operation in police history at my disposal, where do you think I'd hear it? One of my blokes was in a pub.'

'That'd be right. Question for you, I want a straight answer.'

'When did you not? Professional? Personal?'

'Both.'

'I find the phone so impersonal,' said Dance. 'Take a walk down Bromby Street, I'll come along in, ah, ten minutes. I take it you're at work.'

Villani went out, sat on Dove's desk. He was on the phone, finished the call.

'What was his name? Birdy?'

'Maggie,' said Dove. 'No phones in the name. Got his rego, put out a KALOF.'

'Thousands of ancients on the road,' said Villani. 'Sitting in the caravan park looking at other ancients, the wife's inside wiping surfaces, ironing, wearing a housecoat and an apron. That's the reward for a lifetime's work.'

'Koenig,' said Dove. 'I reckon he wasn't at Portsea.'

They were alike, their minds worked in the same strange cop way. 'You reckon, do you? What about Bricknell?'

'Koenig and Bricknell,' said Dove. 'I think we should try to shake Bricknell, boss.'

'Shaking Koenig was so productive,' said Villani. 'Give me something more than phone calls, son.'

He took a smoke off Dove, stole his lighter, went down to the street. The heat pressed on him, it was too hot to smoke. He crossed the avenue and walked down Bromby Street. An Audi pulled up ahead of him, unlawful park. When he reached it, Dance bent his head, looked at him. Villani got in, chilled air, silent engine.

'Nice car,' said Villani. He lit the cigarette.

'So what's this?' said Dance.

'Minter Street, Southbank. A building called Exeter Place. Dogs on it. Yours?'

'Minter Street,' said Dance, thoughtful. 'You have no idea how many people of interest live in Minter Street. They have gathered there, driven by some primitive drug-scum herding instinct.'

'Yes or no?'

'Yes. So if you don't want to be logged entering and leaving Exeter Place, with or without Ms Markham, don't go there. I'm not doctoring logs for you or anyone else.'

'How'd fucking Searle see them?'

'Gillam asked for them. For all I know he passed them around at a Rotary Club lunch, taped them to a hooker's thigh.'

Villani said, 'The story is I leaked the Koenig material to Ms Markham. DiPalma's made it known I'm dead and Quirk's coming back.'

Down his nose, Dance was watching three girls going by, bare, sweaty brown shoulders, midriffs, legs. They were arguing about something, not serious, extravagant gestures, pulling faces, big made-up eyes. He turned his killer-priest's face to Villani as if averting his gaze from sin.

'Well, Stevo,' he said, 'I hear that. There's two possibilities. These tools get back in and try it on. Two, they don't get back and the other lot does it for them. We have to hope the first doesn't happen and plan for the second.'

'Don't know what hoping can do.'

'You hope and also give things a shove.'

Dance was looking at Villani in a way that said: *Don't ask.*

'On election night,' he said, 'if it's necessary, someone will tell the squatter's wife that Quirk is baggage they don't want, that people in the job will make sure they pay a terrible price for revisiting Greg.'

'Price like what?' said Villani. He knew.

'The crypts will be unsealed, the vaults will be unlocked, the dead will walk. For openers, pictures of party icon shagging fifteen-year-old twink.'

Fifteen-year-old. Lizzie's age. Villani said, 'There's something else. My little girl's accused . . .'

Dance raised a hand. 'Heard about that. Vick'll get her found, we'll work something out.'

He took a small player out of his shirt pocket, thumbed it, showed it: grainy picture, two men in evening dress, bow ties. One bent his head to the counter. He lifted his head, put a knuckle to his nose, sniffed. The hidden camera caught an *Aren't-I-a-clever-dog* look.

'When shove comes, Mr Barry will do what's right or he gets the hot shot.'

It came to Villani that Dance was much, much more danger-ous than he had ever thought.

'Bob'd be in that pub up there now, wouldn't he?' said Dance.

'Wait it out in the beer cellar. Too smart for the defend-your-property shit.'

'No,' Villani said 'He's got a firetruck and a bulldozer and he's got Gordie and he's going nowhere.'

Dance looked at him for a while. 'Well, you make a stand somewhere, don't you,' he said. 'Choose your friends, choose your fight.'

He opened the box between the seats and took out a mobile.

'Call you, give you a number.'

Villani took it and went into the day. The wind was in the north now, coming from a burning hot, stone-dry place.

THE PAGE lay on his desk. He looked at it again.

Received 02.49: WHAT?

Sent 02.50: SOON.

Received 03.01: ?????

Sent 03.04: GOING IN.

Sent 03.22: OTU BANZAI OK.

Kidd and Larter near the house in Oakleigh.

Someone waiting for a message from them. Someone also close by. An impatient person, two messages in ten minutes. Who?

What were the two men waiting for? Had the lights gone out in the house? Did they want to be sure the Ribarics and Vern Hudson were asleep?

Four minutes past three: the decision to move. *GOING IN.*

Just shadows moving. At the back door. One kick, take the latch and the screws out of the woodwork. They were professionals.

03.22: Job done. Hudson dead, the Ribarics tied to the steel shed pillars with tape, their mouths would be taped too.

Time to call the impatient person waiting. The man with the knife. This wasn't an ordinary run-through, this wasn't ordinary payback. It was far, far beyond payback. This was a desire to inflict terrible things on the brothers.

OTU BANZAI OK.

Over to you. Banzai. OK.

Why *OK*?

Villani closed his eyes, no energy in him. His last Saturday in the job. You could survive a lot of things but not child sex-charges. Crime commissioner. That prospect hadn't lasted long.

Why *OK*?

Why hadn't he been suspended? Why hadn't Gillam issued the instruction? What were they waiting for? Was it a matter of timing? Did they want him to resign like Koenig?

She says a Father Donald, he came. He'd kissed the Holy Father's ring, and he asked her a lot of questions and he said she'd be at God's right hand for telling Father Cusack about the evil. Pretty much a booked seat. Specially blessed. Yeah.

Villani felt a coldness on his face, as if the room had its own weather, a cool change from the south-west, from Singo's box of junk.

The evil. Telling Father Cusack. Who told Father Donald. What about the confidentiality of confession? Could priests swap confessions with each other? Perhaps in their own confessions they could say things to their confessors, who could in turn . . .

No.

The evil. What story of evil could Valerie Crossley tell Father Cusack? A story she'd waited to tell until she saw her own death.

The thought came to him. He dismissed it. It came back. He got up, the thrumming in his body, he went to find Birkerts. He was half-hidden behind folders.

'A moment of your precious time,' said Villani. 'Where were the Ribarics in 1994?'

'Thought I heard someone say we didn't need any more Ribaric family history?'

'My mood's changed. Experiencing mood swings.'

Birkerts sighed. 'I'll ask the custodian of the Rib family history. Like you, he forgets nothing. I think it's an illness.'

Villani went back to his desk, couldn't resume drowsing, stood up, saw the file Burgess had brought: the girl on the snow road. He went out. Dove was on the phone, put his hand over the mouthpiece.

'Read this,' said Villani. 'My eyes hurt.'

The weekend switch operator's hand up, the phone sign.

'Boss,' said Tomasic, 'in 1994, the Ribs were in Geelong.'

Relief. Not losing it yet.

'How do you know?'

'Six months suspended in the Geelong Magistrates' Court in March 1994. Assault.'

'Dig it out, Tom, the details. Matter of urgency.'

'System's giving lots of shit, boss. Just goes blank.'

'We all just go blank. Talk to the cops there, must be some cunt remembers. And Father Donald. I want Father Donald. If you have to ask the Pope.'

He went to Birkerts. 'Little excursion to Geelong. Pass the time.'

Birkerts didn't look up. 'Rather pass razorblades. In connection with what urgent matter, inspector?'

'Metallic. Oakleigh.'

'Irresistible. Saddle up and ride.'

IT TOOK almost an hour to find anyone connected with St Anselm's Parish and then it was done only by ringing Tomasic.

'There's Annette Hogan,' he said. 'She wrote to Mrs Crossley. See what I can do, boss. Call you back.'

Tomasic rang when they were sitting in the heat, drinking bad coffee at a place on the waterfront. The whole area had been worked on by architects, every place he went back to had been tricked out.

'Spoke to the friend, she'll be home in fifteen,' Tomasic said. 'Newtown. Know where that is, boss?'

'Can you find your dick, son? Address?'

Annette Hogan came to the door, a tall, desiccated woman in her sixties, beaky nose, led them into a sitting room. One of the chairs still had its plastic wrapping.

Birkerts asked the question.

'Father Cusack died about six months ago,' she said. 'He'd had a few heart attacks.'

'He had a parishioner called Valerie Crossley,' said Birkerts.

'Mrs Crossley, yes. She's dead too. A month ago, thereabouts.'

'This is delicate, Mrs Hogan,' said Birkerts, 'but it's very important. Do you know anything about the last confession Mrs Crossley made to Father Cusack?'

Annette Hogan's eyes widened. 'You're not thinking Father Cusack would tell anyone about a confession, are you? Don't you know about the sanctity of the confessional? Not Catholic, are you?'

'No,' said Birkerts. 'Proddy dog. Lapsed.'

'Well, he'd be excommunicated, wouldn't he? In the confessional you're facing the power of God. The priest can never speak of what he hears. He'd be sinning. Good heavens.'

'Sorry,' said Birkerts.

Silence. In the passage, a board creaked. Villani thought that would be the friend.

'There's a Father Donald,' said Villani. 'I don't know if that's the first name or the surname.'

She was still offended at the heathen inquiry. 'Father Donald? Not in this town. Never heard of a Father Donald.'

Villani stood, Birkerts followed.

'Well, thank you, Mrs Hogan. Did you know Mrs Crossley?'

'Not really, no.'

Villani said, 'The place where she died? Where's that.'

Annette Hogan gave them directions. She walked them to her front gate and waited for them to drive away.

'I don't think we're on a winner here,' said Birkerts.

'We may not even be on a horse,' said Villani. 'Look for somewhere to buy smokes.'

They stopped at a fish and chips shop. Villani went in, hunger took him, he had trouble remembering breakfast. He went back to the car with cigarettes and six dollars worth of chips, hacked with a cleaver, six to a big spud. They ate them on the spot, the oily parcel steaming sharp vinegar on the armrest between them.

'This's how the cars get their smell,' said Birkerts, taking the last chip, chewing, thoughtful. 'Egg farts, Whoppers, vinegar, chip fat, cigarette smoke, Old Spice, four-day socks.'

'Put it in an aerosol, subdue the violent with a spray in the face,' said Villani.

'Then shoot them a few times to be on the safe side. Why are we going to this gerry place? I'm not making connections.'

'In time, you may see the utility,' said Villani.

'I'm going to miss you so much,' said Birkerts. 'Just being with you.'

'I'll come around to your house inspections. Shitfaced. Tell everyone I'm the neighbour. Break stuff. Jump in the pool.'

Birkerts turned the key. 'Navigate me,' he said.

IT WAS a T-shape of yellow brick, a tarmac parking area, a dozen splintering *E. nicholi* in a long strip of dead grass.

They went up a concrete ramp with handrails. In a waiting room with brown vinyl tiles, Birkerts pressed a bell five or six times.

A door opened and a sad red-faced balding woman in blue came out.

'Not visiting hours,' she said.

Birkerts showed her the badge, said who they were. She went redder.

'I'll get matron,' she said. 'Have to wake her.'

They went outside, leant against the rails, smoked.

'What happens on a free Saturday night?' Villani said.

'Thought you'd never ask,' said Birkerts. 'Used to take my wife to dinner. Then I took this other person to dinner. Now I get a pizza in. Have to be careful you don't order a Coke with it. Costs a hundred bucks and you don't even get a straw.'

Knocks on the glass door.

They went in, the receptionist showed them to an office. The woman behind the chipboard desk had blood in her eyes, bleached hair, the face of a barmaid turned wardress.

'Shirley Conroy, matron,' she said. 'Police, I gather.'

'Introduce you to Inspector Stephen Villani,' said Birkerts. 'Head of the Victoria Police Homicide Squad.'

'Meetcha,' the matron said, not impressed. 'Sit if you want.'

'Mrs Valerie Crossley,' said Villani.

'What about her?'

'She died recently.'

'Yeah.'

'Someone came to see her a few months before. A priest. Is that right?

'What's it about, this?'

'We're the police, matron,' said Villani. 'We ask the questions. Ever had any benefit from a patient's will?'

Lockdown. Tight mouth, eyes.

'Moving on then,' said Villani. 'Someone other than Father Cusack visit Mrs Crossley not long before she died? Easy question that. I have others. They get harder.'

No hesitation. 'Yeah, a man said he was a relly.'

'Keep a record of visitors?'

'Properly run, this place,' she said. 'Inspected twice a year.'

'I'd be profoundly shocked if it wasn't. See the book?'

Matron pressed a button on her phone, they could hear the shrill sound from the next room. The blue woman opened the door.

'Visitors' register, Judith.'

Judith took seconds. Matron found the page with ease, turned the book to face Villani, pointed at a line.

Name: K. D. Donald.

Relationship: Nephew.

Address: 26/101 Swanston Street, Melbourne.

'Mrs Crossley called him Father Donald,' said Villani.

Matron's thin mouth lengthened. 'Mrs Crossley was not in the full possession of her facilities at the time. Thought her dog was under the bed.'

'What about her faculties?' said Birkerts.

'Heard her confession,' said Judith from behind them.

They turned heads.

The blush upon the flush. 'I heard him say it,' said Judith. 'May the almighty and merciful God grant you pardon, absolution and remission of your sins. He said that.'

A story.

Someone told a story. Where?

In the Robbers, it would have been. In the awed first months, you laughed at any story the hard men told, understood or not. Who told it? What was it? To do with confession? Pardon? Absolution?

It would not come to him, it lay just beyond the breakers, in the deep water, in the dark, slippery moving kelp of the mind.

In the baking car, Birkerts started the engine, the air-con fought the heat. Villani's mobile. Tomasic.

'Getting nowhere on that Rib assault, boss. System's down, no one in Geelong there in '94. Also, the only Father Donald in the whole country died three years ago.'

'Our lucky day.' Villani put the phone away. 'Let's go home,' he said. 'Such as it is.'

HE SHOWERED, put on the gown, went to the kitchen and opened a beer, drained half of it, took it to a chair near an open wall-length window. The television was four metres away, framed in a bookshelf.

He used the remote, waited in mute for the news, unmuted. After the world-in-turmoil graphics, the stiff-faced newsreader said:

Our top story tonight, more shock waves rip through the state government after startling claims by Opposition leader Karen Mellish. Political editor Anna Markham reports.

Anna, the dispassionate professional in all her handsome, calm cleverness. She said:

It's a complicated story Opposition leader Karen Mellish told the media twenty minutes ago. But it boils down to this. The son of Attorney-General Anthony DiPalma, the stepmother of Planning Minister Robbie Cowper, and the ex-wife of Assistant Crime Commissioner John Colby all appear to have made large windfalls from buying apartments in the exclusive Prosilio building in the Docklands precinct.

Footage of the three men: the AG in full flight in the chamber, cow-faced Cowper defending some planning decision in the outer suburbs. Then Colby, in uniform, the hard face, talking about bikie gangs.

Anna: she lifted her dimpled chin, tilted her head.

Karen Mellish says people close to DiPalma, Cowper and Colby *bought apartments off the plan in Prosilio. They put down $80,000 deposits, borrowed from a company called Bernardt Capital Partners. Two years later, the same company sold the apartments to Asian buyers for around $750,000 each. Then Bernardt paid the owners sums ranging from $410,000 to $450,000.*

Karen Mellish, pinstriped suit, a severe, sexy headmistress.

How effortless. These people made $430,000-odd without putting up a cent. Even after paying capital gains tax, a nice little earner, wouldn't you say?

Is this guilt by relationship? Do you know if Mr DiPalma or Mr Cowper or Mr Colby received any benefit?

Mellish laughed.

Anna, watch this space. That's all I'm saying. Watch this space.

Anna:

The Prosilio building is owned by Marscay Corporation, a big donor to both political parties. It's home to Australia's most exclusive casino, the Orion, which is challenging Australia's long-established gambling companies for the patronage of the high-rolling, $250,000 minimum-bet gamblers, almost all of them Chinese.

The quizzical look.

With the state elections just two weeks away, Karen Mellish's charges could be the fatal blow to a government seriously on the nose with voters and which only a few hours ago sacked Infrastructure Minister Stuart Koenig over sex allegations.

Villani terminated the television, finished the beer, the big Geelong chips came back. Colby? Some mistake. Colby was too clever, he would not have taken the risk. His ex-wife? Colby said once the divorce settlement was going to leave him with one ball and a twelve-year-old Holden.

An innocent. He had been used to destroy Koenig. Someone had been watching Koenig's town house, seen the girl arrive with Hanlon, set the whole thing up.

Who would that be? Crucible? Would Dancer do Karen Mellish's dirty work?

Blackwatch Associates? They did surveillance. Cameron's partner, Wayne Poland, had been the force's surveillance expert. Blackwatch would work for anyone.

Perhaps Koenig was bugged. Perhaps they heard him order the girl from Hanlon.

Max Hendry.

His major problem in getting AirLine to fly is Stuart Koenig, the infra-structure minister. Koenig's told the Labor caucus the sky will be dark with pigs before Max Hendry gets government support.

Karen Mellish's words. So Max's major problem went away with Koenig's fall.

So tired. So fucked. A life so completely fucked. What would Bob say when it was out:

TOP COP'S TEEN:

DAD ABUSED ME

Mobile.

It wasn't his mobile, it was the one Dance gave him, squeaking in his jacket where he had thrown the garment.

'Sorry to wake you, mate. Be in the sack, it being all of seven in the p.m.'

The Dancer, cocky, always languid.

'Doing my yoga,' said Villani.

'With your three Filipino personal trainers. Hear the Colby stuff?'

'Just now. Yes.'

'Greed is always so bad. No good comes of greed.'

'Apparently.'

'And I'm bearing other sad news tonight,' said Dance. 'Grace Lovett. Dead. In her pool. Fell in pissed probably.'

A child again, adults telling him things, true things.

'Tragic that,' said Dance. 'Drink and water don't mix. The exception is single malt and ancient spring water, that works. So I think the little cunt's not coming back to haunt us. Grace not being able to testify. Vid's not really admissible now, I'd say, wouldn't you?'

'I'd say. Thanks for the call.' So much more deadly than he'd ever thought.

'Got the saddies, mate? Out of the rip here, boy. No fear of drowning.'

'Just tired.'

'Son. This shit is over. Passed through the system. All crap soon be over. Sit down, have a drink.'

Villani sat for a time, took out his mobile, switched it off. He went to the wall, put out the lights, the room was moonlit. He went to the big leather sofa and lay along its length, closed his eyes, listened to the harsh shrieking, wailing clamour of the city.

The black pipes laid, the water leaking down the hill to the trees, on the summer evenings when he was past sixteen, he would sit, back against the dam wall, and roll a cigarette, acrid chop chop from the Kiewa Valley, from a boy at school who stole it from his uncle. In the yielding day, the valley was so quiet that the thumps of Luke and Mark kicking the football carried to him from a kilometre and more over the hill.

So tired.

In a dream, the phone was ringing, he sat up, stood up, staggered, found the telephone, it was the landline, it was on a shelf.

Birkerts.

'Steve, your mobile's off, they rang me.'

A car came for him. He stood in the hot street, cold to his core. He stood and smoked and they came for him with the siren on.

IN THE van's spotlight, two uniforms, a man and a woman, led him down the mean alley, their long shadows preceded them.

They went by the man with his head back against the wall, they went to the end, to where the small thing lay, a little bundle no bigger than a sleeping dog.

The cop coughed. 'Too late for . . . yeah. Boss.'

Villani took the steps and looked at the deceased, this was what you did in Homicide, if you didn't have the stomach you should go somewhere else.

The small person had been sick, expelled the contents of her stomach, not much, a cup of white liquid, it lay on the cobblestones around her white face.

Lizzie's face was dirty and there was a little sore under her left eye, she'd been scratching at it.

'OD, boss,' said the cop.

Villani knelt and, without thought, touched the child's forehead with his lips, it was cold.

He stood and looked at the man against the wall, head back, knees up, all in black, a black leather cap, dreadlocks hanging from it. He had small triangles, squares and circles tattooed on his cheekbones, a Maltese cross between his eyebrows, barbed wire across his throat, under the Adam's apple.

His eyes were closed.

He had an iPod plugged into his ear.

A rage blocked Villani's ears, his nose, made him feel weightless and enlarged, he took the steps, and he kicked the man in his fork, it was not worth it, it was like kicking a bag of wheat.

'He's dead, boss,' said the woman. 'He's dead.'

Villani turned towards the lane entrance and the spotlight went out and he could see them: Birkerts and Dove and Finucane and Tomasic.

Birkerts came forward, touched his arm. 'Want me to tell Laurie?' he said.

Villani straightened, cleared his throat. 'That's a good idea,' he said. 'Mate.'

He walked to the group, biting his lip, they said nothing, parted for him, patted him, touched him. They had come out in the night because he meant something to them, that was not something he expected. Finucane followed him.

'Where to, boss?' he said.

'I'll just go home.'

'That's home as in . . .'

'As in Fitzroy.'

'Ah, don't know if it's good for you to be alone, boss,' Finucane said. 'Don't think so. No.'

'Let me do the thinking, son. You drive.'

Finucane drove him back to Fitzroy, walked to the door with him.

'I could just come in, sit around,' he said. 'In case you wanted to . . . whatever. Yeah. Just sort of be there.'

'Go home, detective,' said Villani. 'I don't need anyone sitting around just sort of being there. I'm fine.'

In the apartment, he felt compelled to shower, stood in the waterfall for a long time, listened to the landline ringing, let it ring out.

When he was about to pour whisky into a tumbler, the ringing began again. He could not ignore it.

'Villani.'

'It's me.' Laurie. In the two words, he could hear that she had been crying.

'Hi.'

'Stephen, I have to tell you . . .'

She choked, could not speak. He waited.

'What?'

'She rang about two hours ago and left a message. I was out and . . .'

She stopped again. He waited.

'She was crying. She said you never did anything to her. Never touched her. She said they told her to say it.'

Villani felt rage rise in him again. 'Who's they?'

'I don't know. That's what she said.'

Silence, Laurie sniffed, coughed.

'Stephen, do you want . . . would you like, would you like to come home?'

'Not now,' said Villani. 'Corin there?'

'Yes. Tony's coming home, he's getting a . . .'

'Good. I'll call you tomorrow. Got something to take? To sleep?'

'Yes.'

'Okay. Well. Goodnight.'

'I can't . . .'

'Tomorrow. We'll talk tomorrow.'

'Steve, I can't say how . . .'

'You believed her,' he said. 'You thought I was capable of it.'

'You have to . . .'

'Tomorrow. Goodnight.'

He went back to the kitchen, poured half a glass of whisky, took it to the sofa he had slept on earlier. He sipped and a tear ran down his nose. He began to weep. For a while, he wept in

PETER TEMPLE • 375

silence and then he began to sob, softly at first, and then louder and louder.

It came to him that he had never cried out loud in his life. It was as if he were singing for the first time.

After a while, he pulled up his legs, lay on his back. He fell asleep as if clubbed, slept through the remainder of the night, woke with wet cheeks.

IN THE morning, when Villani was walking around aimlessly, trying not to smoke, Birkerts rang.

'Downstairs,' he said.

'Why's that?'

'Thinking breakfast.'

Villani wanted to say no but that would only postpone things. You had to carry on. Bob's saying: *Who speaks of victory? To carry on is all.*

Villani asked him who said that. 'Some German,' said Bob. Now Villani said, 'Just don't talk about it.'

They went to Enzio's. It was too early for the locals, only the clean-living and the unclean-living survivors of the night were out.

'Listen,' said Birkerts. 'I was thinking about Geelong yesterday and I thought about Cameron's son. After that Noske killed himself, what happened then?'

'There wasn't anywhere left to go,' said Villani. 'Noske was it. Never going to trial, mark you. Not unless he sung. Also I suppose when Cameron quit and then Deke Murray quit, there wasn't a driver, other things came along.'

'The idea was Noske by himself?'

'Mad loner, nobody would have helped him.'

Some questions about that cold night in the valley were never answered. The overturned furniture, the broken crockery, the arterial gushes, the cast-off bloodstains from the weapon, the impact splatters, the bloody shoeprints, they all suggested Dave Cameron trying to fight back against one person hacking at him with a big knife or a sword. Then he was shot in the body twice with an unknown weapon and three times in the head with his own service weapon.

But what was Cameron's girlfriend doing while this was happening? Nothing said she had been bound before being shot in the head, three times, with Dave's weapon. But it was possible she had been: she had just come from the cycle track, she was a champion cyclist, she was in full lycra. It would stop her being marked.

'So the Ribs were in Geelong and you thought . . .'

'I have these brain episodes,' said Villani. He was eating mechanically. He needed food, he didn't want it.

'Pardon, absolution and remission of sins,' said Birkerts. 'I like the principle. Now that is clout. That is having the grip.'

The fork was almost at Villani's mouth.

Colby's story that Friday night long ago in the Robbers' offices, the beers out, air grey with smoke. About two Broady boys brought in years before, brothers, Coogan, Cooley, some such. They had done a drive-in bottleshop in Johnson Street, waited until a kid, a student, was pulling down the door, gone in under it like crocodiles, bashed the two workers, homemade knuckledusters, opened their faces, broke noses, cheekbones, kicked the one senseless.

Now, in the spartan Robbers' quarters, the brothers had their turn to know terror. After a while, Colby said, the older one, thinking he was going to die there, expressed a willingness to confess.

He gets them to kneel and say we're so fucking sorry. And then he says, relax boys. May the almighty and merciful God grant you pardon, absolution and remission of your sins. And they look a bit relieved. Then

he says, because almighty God might forgive you. But not me, boys. I'm
going to kill you, you miserable little arseholes.

Villani remembered the laughing, they were mostly proddies,
the Robbers was a proddy stronghold. Kneeler Robbers had to
be special men, they needed hard shells, they had to give it back
in spades.

'Father Donald,' said Colby. 'He made them call him Father
Donald.'

Received 02.49: WHAT?

Sent 02.50: SOON.

Received 03.01: ?????

Sent 03.04: GOING IN.

Sent 03.22: OTU BANZAI OK.

No. It wasn't 'OK'.

Villani chewed, tasting nothing.

'Do me a favour,' he said. 'Ring in and get an address.' He
wrote down the name.

Birkerts did it, blank eyes on Villani. Villani read them: what
kind of father goes back to work six hours after he finds his
daughter dead?

They ate. Birkerts took out his mobile, listened.

'Tell the inspector,' he said, gave Villani the phone.

'Boss, we have Yarraville, that's 12 Enright Lane.'

Pause.

'Looking at it, boss . . . brick, two-storey, industrial, no sign
. . . across the road . . . Speed Glass. Good business, no shortage
of glass breakers. Next door. B & L Shopfitting, less good. From
above . . . a back yard, brick-paved I'd say, pot plants, table chairs,
someone lives there, high walls, not easy getting in that way,
boss.'

Villani said, 'Martin Loneregan, SOG boss. At home, anywhere.
Get him to ring this phone.'

He gave the phone back to Birkerts. 'Take a little trip to Yarraville in a while,' he said.

'Yarraville,' said Birkerts. 'Bought there in the nineties, you're now in Noosa, on the private jetty, toes in the river, you're laughing.'

'So grateful for the real-estate perspective,' said Villani.

They ate, Villani signalled, the coffees came.

'You known here already?' said Birkerts.

'Second visit. They pay attention.'

Birkerts found his mobile. 'Birkerts. He's right here.' To Villani, he said, 'Inspector Loneregan.'

Villani said, 'Mate, need a bit of force in a hurry. Yarraville. Not the full catastrophe.'

'Sometimes not the full catastrophe is the full catastrophe,' said Loneregan.

'One man. Not young.'

'Amazing what shit one man not young can create.'

'Point taken,' said Villani. He told Loneregan who it was.

'My Lord,' said Loneregan. 'Sure you want to do it this way?'

'I'm sure.'

He saw the Ribarics in the big empty shed, just hanging blood-caked meat, sliced and severed and stuck and burnt.

'I'll need an hour,' said Loneregan. 'Got a bit on.'

THEY PARKED beyond Enright Lane and sat in silence for a time, heavy traffic passing, a distant backfire.

'Sure about this?' said Birkerts.

'I reckon,' said Villani. He was regretting the Sons of God. It didn't matter what the man had done, there was respect due.

It was wrong.

'I'm going in,' he said.

Birkerts grabbed his jacket sleeve. 'Steve, Steve, for fuck's sake, don't be, I'm not letting . . .'

'Wait here, detective,' said Villani.

'Well, I'm not . . .'

'You can spell order? The word? Sit. I'll ring.'

Villani got out and walked under the shivering sky, down the ugly little street, the shuttered doors, the windows barred, the industrial waste bins, the litter of takeaway food. The smell was of tar and chemicals.

He stood before the steel entry to number 12. Sweat stuck his shirt to his chest. He pulled at it.

A button. A bell. He pressed and he heard it ring inside the building, far away. The third time he rang, a voice from the speaker beside the door said, 'Inspector Villani.'

'Got a camera, boss?' said Villani.

'State of the art, son.'

'Come in?'

'About what? Not social, I reckon.'

Villani felt the gaze. He turned and saw Birkerts at the head of the lane. A wind had come up, it was moving his hair. Across the distance, their eyes met. Birkerts shook his head like a father.

'Think you know, boss,' said Villani.

'On your own then, Stephen?'

Far away, the roar and keen and whine of the trucks as they rose up the sweeping curve of the great bridge, their sounds as they fell.

'Yes, sir.'

'That's not very clever.'

'Can't say yet, sir.'

Locks clicked.

'Stairs on the right.'

It had been a workshop, a Land Cruiser stood in the middle, doors to the right and back, a steel staircase up the right-hand wall. He climbed them, another steel door.

After all the years. All the years of fighting fear, all the years he could remember, all the years of trying to be a man.

This man would kill him.

Villani opened the door.

A huge room, bare floorboards, bare brick walls, a kitchen at one end, a desk, two chairs, a wall of books, sound equipment, a television.

A dog lay on a rug. Fully extended. A German Shepherd. It did not stir.

'Heard you were coming. Sit.'

Villani crossed the space and sat in a chair in front of the desk. He did not know what to do with his hands. 'How's that, boss?' he said.

'Small world. Come for me?'

The long neck, the crisp curls, the hard sardonic mouth, Villani remembered them.

'Yes, boss.'

'Sure you're by yourself?'

'As you see me.'

'Well, that's pretty contemptuous, isn't it? You could at least have brought the warriors. Even if it wasn't the full catastrophe.'

'They had another job on,' said Villani. 'Might come on afterwards.'

A laugh, genuine laugh, amused, shaking his head. 'Armed, son?' he said. 'At least say you're armed? Give me that.'

'Yes.'

'Not going to be much fucking use sitting down.'

'No, boss.'

'I'm proud of you, then. Stupid prick. What?'

Villani held his eyes. 'Ribarics. The offsider.'

'Guilty.'

Murray's hands came up, a short sawn shotgun came up from under the desktop, it pointed at Villani's chest, at his throat.

Lowered.

'Primitive weapon,' said Murray. 'All show except close up.'

'Kidd and Larter?'

'Psychos,' said Murray. 'Hard to say which one you'd extinguish first. Probably Larter. International killer. Kill his mother, anything.'

Murray looking around the room, looking at Villani.

'Undesirables,' he said. 'But useful. Useful idiots.'

'The car,' said Villani. 'Who did that?'

Murray looked up, waved, a big hand.

'Don't worry about it, son,' he said. 'Let it lie. Saved the taxpayer millions, keeping the pricks in maximum security for life.'

'Why?' said Villani.

'Why?'

'The Ribarics.'

'You know. That's why you're here.'

'I'd like you to tell me, boss.'

'There's a video in the machine, that'll tell you. How'd you get to me?'

'The old lady's confession. Father Donald. I remembered a story from the Robbers, the old days.'

Murray's mouth turned down, he nodded as if agreeing with something. 'And you're not stupid,' he said.

'You do that?' said Villani. 'The torture?'

'No,' said Murray. 'I wanted to. That was the point. But in the end I couldn't. Kidd and Larter. Larter mostly.'

Villani said, 'All this for Matt?'

The winter eyes on him. Was that moisture?

Murray raised the shotgun barrel, pointed, extended his arm until he could pull the trigger and take off Villani's head.

What a stupid way to die.

'No,' said Murray. 'Not for Matt. For myself. Scare you, this shotty?'

'No,' said Villani. 'Go ahead.'

'That's not natural.' Murray sighed. 'You're a good cop, son.'

'Better things to be good at.'

'You never find that out till it's too late,' said Murray. 'Cheers.'

He brought the barrel back, put it under his chin, pulled the trigger.

The blast disintegrated his face, a red mist.

Villani sat, hands in lap, chin on chest, waited.

Inside a minute, the rammer hit the doors downstairs.

The Sons of God.

He went to the door, walked around the dog, which lay at peace. One bullet for the dog, one for himself.

Villani opened the door and shouted. Then he went to the bookshelf, drawn to it, to the four photographs in silver frames.

The Camerons. Mother, father, the small boy was in Matt Cameron's arms.

The Camerons. Lying on a beach, she was in a bikini, lovely, the boy, older now, lying between them.

Donald Keith Murray and Matt Cameron. Walking towards the camera. Tall, lean men, long muscles, flat pectorals, holding the boy Dave's hands. He was off the ground, his little face pure joy.

Three men in uniform posing. Graduation day. The boy, a man now, standing between Deke Murray and Matt Cameron. Even height, three handsome men.

'Jesus,' said Loneregan from the door. 'Jesus, that was fucking silly.'

Birkerts came up beside Villani, studied the photograph.

'Strong family resemblance,' he said.

'Between?'

Birkerts pointed.

'No,' Villani said. 'That's not Matt. That's Deke.'

Dave Cameron wasn't Matt Cameron's son. He was Deke Murray's son, Father Donald's son.

No, Oakleigh was not a run-through, not crims ripping off and killing other crims. It was a terrible revenge for the murder of a son and the woman bearing someone's grandson.

Deke Muray, Matt Cameron's brother in arms. His great friend. Matt Cameron knew who had fathered the boy he called his son.

'Video in this machine,' said Birkerts.

'I know,' said Villani. 'Play it.'

Birkerts pressed buttons. The screen flickered, jumped.

Hand-held camera, all over the place, a room, unmade bed, cans, bottles, plates.

Face close up, unshaven, big teeth.

The young Ivan Ribaric, shirtless, Jim Beam bottle in his left hand, he staggered, slack-jawed, drunk, off his face.

A policeman's cap on his head, the back of his head. He pulled it over his eyes, drank from the bottle.

He raised his right hand, he had a pistol, he pointed it at the cameraman, his mouth made bang noises.

'Service pistol,' said Loneregan.

Dave Cameron's cap.

Dave Cameron's gun.

Ivan Ribaric turned his back to the camera, put the bottle and the pistol on a dressing-table. He picked up something, turned.

He had a short sword in both hands, a cutlass. He made martial-arts movements, slashing movements, hacking movements.

Hacking Dave Cameron.

Ivan Ribaric laughing.

. . . he said she'd be at God's right hand for telling Father Cusack about the evil.

'Off,' said Villani. 'Put it off.'

Outside, Loneregan said, 'Listen, I heard about your girl. What can I say? Strength, mate.'

'Thank you.'

'And thanks about my dad.'

Deke Muray was in his mind, it took a moment for Villani to focus. 'Bob speaks highly of him,' he said. 'Brave man who loved his little boy.'

'Means a lot to me that. Your dad saying that.'

IN THE car, going over the Westgate, how long it seemed since the call to Prosilio.

Villani's phone rang.

'Dove, boss. Boss, sorry, I don't want to . . .'

'Speak.'

'Boss, just leaving a house in Niddrie. With Tomasic. I got this bloke Maggie in Mallacoota. Talked to him, got the name of the bloke who fetched the girl from the market. The Romanian?'

'I'm with you.'

'Tommo's been talking Romanian to them. Took a while to convince them we hadn't come to kill her.'

Nothing for so long and then everything at once.

'She's there?' said Villani.

'No, boss. She's out Heathcote way. She's been staying with the bloke's daughter. But she's going home today. Flight from Tulla in two hours. Austrian Airlines. To Vienna.'

'Who's taking her?'

'The bloke's son-in-law and his brother.'

'Niddrie,' said Villani. 'On your bike. Tulla. Meet you in Depot Drive. That's between Centre and Service. Under the trees, facing west. We want to pick her up without fuss.'

To Birkerts, he said, 'Tullamarine. The Prosilio girl.'

All the way, he thought about Lizzie.

In the seconds when he decided he would not fetch her, he killed her. When he committed her to the cells, he killed her.

THEY DROVE up Departure Drive, Villani and Birkerts in front, parked beyond international departures. Two security men arrived in seconds.

Villani showed them the badge. 'Inspector Villani, Homicide.' The guards left.

'Tell Tommo to check the departure time,' said Villani. 'Get Dove here.'

Birkerts got out, went back and spoke to Dove and Tomasic. Tomasic got out, adjusted his clothing, and walked down the broad pavement.

Dove and Birkerts got in. Dove in the back.

'They'll drive up and drop her or what?' said Villani.

'Don't know,' said Dove. 'I'd say they'll park and come with her. She's got no English, she's scared.'

Villani thought about what to do. It didn't matter much how they arrived.

'What we'll do is,' he said, 'Birk, you and Tommo wait inside the first door. We'll be inside the second one. Warn these security dorks. Tell them to stay out of sight.'

'Boss,' said Birkerts.

'She arrives alone or with the brothers, the door she comes in, we intercept her just inside,' said Villani. 'All badges out, we don't want to scare her, anyone. Say police as caringly as possible. Like a blessing.'

'Jeez, that's a big ask,' said Birkerts.

They got out, immediate sweat, Tomasic was coming out of the building. 'Leaves one-thirty,' he said. 'She's got to check in inside the next forty minutes.'

'Follow me, son,' said Birkerts.

The departure hall was cool, crowded, long lines, two big groups of Japanese men, lean women in sports gear, a hockey team perhaps.

Villani was looking through the glass wall in the direction of the open-air parking lot, they would come from there if she was escorted by the brothers. He had the fear, the tightness in the solar plexus. This was happening too quickly, they should be here in numbers. They shouldn't be here at all. The Sons should be here.

All this in one day.

'Boss,' said Dove, urgent. 'There.'

He was pointing at the multi-storey parking garage across the road.

Two big men, young, T-shirts, cargo pants, dark glasses, one wore thongs. Standing well back from the crossing.

Lizzie.

She was between them, the girl, she barely reached their shoulders, her hair was inside a baseball cap, she was in jeans and a white collarless shirt, a child wearing big dark glasses, carrying a bag, a blue sports bag with the swipe on the side.

The lights changed, they stepped off.

Villani was looking to their left, across the road, through the undercover bus stop. A black car was behind a bus with a luggage trailer, it was nosing out, twenty, thirty metres from the crossing.

A motorbike was beside it, on the far side, the driver's side, two up, full-face helmets, the passenger had his left hand on the car.

In the moment, Villani knew. *Oh, Jesus, no.*

'Car, the bike!' Villani went between two women coming in the door, freeing the weapon as he ran.

The girl was looking at the bike, the car, her mouth was open, the light caught her teeth.

She knew she was going to die.

Villani was halfway across the road, the nose of the black car, an Audi, the tinted windscreen, the biker, he saw the pistol, he did not hear the sounds.

The girl dropped. The man next to her dropped.

Running, he fired, the helmets turned, the bike passenger swung his pistol across the rider's head.

Villani stumbled.

Dove beside him, Dove had his gun in both hands, he fired once, twice, holes in the windscreen, the man on the pillion standing now.

Villani steadied, shot the rider, he knew he had hit him, you knew. He fired again. Dove beside him fired, again, the pillion shooter's helmet jerked, the collar of his leather jacket lifted, he fell sideways.

The black Audi turning left, mounting the median strip, coming slowly.

Screaming, many people screaming, a child screaming.

Villani saw the faces in the car, the head and arm and the pumpgun sticking out of the passenger side.

Run back.

Too late.

'Oh shit,' he said, saw the flame in the shotgun barrel, felt his shirt and his jacket plucked, fired at the shooter, him and Dove, standing side by side, they emptied their weapons.

The Audi stopped a metre away. A hole in the windscreen on the driver's side. Dove had shot the driver. Someone once shot him and now he had shot someone. Not gun-shy, Dove.

Silence.

Birkerts and Tomasic arrived.

They walked to the girl, seeing the slumped men in the Audi, seeing the bikers where they lay, hearing the bike ticking. Villani smelled cordite and hot gunmetal and petrol fumes.

The girl was clenched like a baby with colic. One of her escorts was on his side, losing blood, blood everywhere. His brother was holding the man's head.

She would be dead, dying.

'Police,' Villani said, not loudly.

She raised her head and looked at him, dark eyes.

Not dead.

He knelt by her, Dove knelt too, they turned her gently, she did not resist, she was limp.

Not dying.

Not shot.

'Safe now,' he said. 'Safe now.'

She blinked, she was crying, she smiled a wan little smile.

Not dead. Not Lizzie. Saved.

'Medics,' Villani said. 'Tell them five down. Gunshot.'

THEY SAT in the big interview room, Villani and Dove and two interpreters, a fat sallow man who was also a justice of the peace and a stern young woman who was a court interpreter in four Slavonic languages.

And the girl. Her name was Marica.

The girl did not need to be told her rights. She was not charged with anything. She was giving her testimony willingly. She was a witness to at least one crime.

Dove asked the questions, it was his right.

He was quiet and friendly, smiling, Villani had not seen this side of Dove. He took Marica through her story, from the time in Tandarei when her uncle brought the man to see her and her twin sister and told them they could go to Australia and be trained as hairdressers and beauticians, the Australian girls did not want to do the work, they were also ugly and had big hands and could not do delicate things. His reward would be a small percentage of their earnings when they were qualified, that was only fair.

It took a long time, breaks taken, there was a need to ask for detail. Marica knew some names, just first names, not many.

At length, they came to the night at Prosilio, to the drive from Preston, to the garbage exit, to the stairs and the lift and the rooms in the sky, the bathroom with the glass bath, the champagne and the cocaine.

And the men.

Two men.

The tiny camera. There was a camera.

The things they did. The pain.

Marica cried, tears of shame and humiliation at having to tell strangers, men, these things. The stern female interpreter did not comfort her. She silenced the fat man with a look when he seemed to make an attempt.

And then it was time for the photographs. Dove had assembled them.

It was a delicate matter. Dove told the interpreters how it would be done, what Marica should do if she recognised any of the people in the photographs. But the interpreters could not see the photographs.

The woman explained the procedure to the girl. Dove asked the man if he was happy with the explanation. He said he was.

Dove gave Marica the red pen.

He showed the first print to Villani, A4.

Stuart Koenig.

He slid it face down to the girl. They watched her face.

Marica turned it over, looked, blinked, spoke to the woman.

'She says she was taken to a house,' said the interpreter. 'She had sex with him but did not see him again.'

Dove showed Villani another picture, their eyes met. He put the print on the table, face down.

Mervyn Brody, car dealer, racehorse owner.

She looked, turned it face down.

So it went. Picture shown to Villani, slid to the girl.

Brian Curlew, criminal barrister.

Face down.

Chris Jourdan, restaurants and bars.

Face down.

Daniel Bricknell, art dealer.

Face down.

Dennis Combanis, property developer.

Face down.

Mark Simons, insolvency expert.

Face down.

Hugh Hendry.

Face down.

Martin Orong, minister of the crown.

Softly, Dove said to Villani, face close to him, 'The girl on the snow road.'

He slid the picture to Marica. She looked at it, blinked, blinked.

Face down.

Dove said to the interpreters, 'I want to show her some photographs of groups now. We haven't had time to isolate the people in them. If she recognises anyone, she should ring the face. Okay? We have enlarged the pictures, but she must examine them very carefully.'

The man explained, Marica nodded.

Dove showed Villani the pictures, A5, six of them. Photographs taken at the casino party, the party at Prosilio to launch Orion. Villani looked at them.

Black ties, little black dresses, champagne flutes, facelifts, hair transplants, Botox, collagen, coke smiles, rich people, clever people, talented people, untalented people, freeloaders, charlatans, tax cheats, unjailed criminals, kept women, kept men, toyboys, walkers, a drug dealer, trophy brides.

He gave them back to Dove.

Dove gave the girl the first picture. She studied it. She was tired, she rubbed an eye. She looked like Lizzie, Lizzie when she was alive.

Face down, pushed aside.

Next picture.

Marica was rubbing the other eye, looking at the photograph. She stopped rubbing. She looked at Dove, her eyes were red, her mouth was open.

She took the fat red pen and drew on the picture.

One circle.

Two circles.

She turned the print face down. She pushed the picture back to Dove. He picked it up. Looked. He gave it to Villani.

A smiling man, glass in hand.

A man making a point to a woman, half-serious, his eyebrows were raised.

To the interpreters, Villani said, no moisture in his mouth, 'I'm giving the picture back to her. Ask her if she's absolutely sure. You must impress upon her the seriousness of the matter.'

The woman spoke. The man spoke.

Villani slid the picture.

Marica looked, she nodded fiercely.

Da. Da. Da.

'She is sure,' said the woman.

Guy Ulyatt of Marscay. *We Own The Building.*

Max Hendry.

Villani and Dove went outside. They looked at each other in silence.

'Well, bugger,' said Dove. 'That's a bit of . . . didn't expect that. No. What, ah, what now, boss?'

'Your case,' said Villani. 'You're the boss here.'

'Apply for warrants to search their homes and offices,' said Dove.

'Go for your life.'

'Boss.'

Silence.

'I heard Max Hendry offered you a big job,' said Dove.

'Yes,' said Villani. 'Needed a certain kind of person. But it wasn't me.'

SHE RANG when he was in the lift. She was across the boulevard in her car.

Villani had to wait to cross. He looked at his messages.

Love you, Dad. Always. Corin.

He went to her window, it came down.

'I'm so sorry, Stephen,' said Anna. 'I can't tell you how sorry I am.'

She reached up to him and he stooped. She kissed him, held his head in both hands, fingertips in his hair, pressing on his skull. Then she pulled away.

Villani wiped his mouth. He felt sadness. 'Your lipstick,' he said. 'It's smudged.'

He turned and left but he looked back, he could not help himself. The tinted light made her face pale, her mouth grey. He could not see her eyes.

Home. The telephone unplugged, mobiles off, he showered, closed the blinds, lay down on the big bed. So tired. He carried too much freight. And no pity left in him.

When the pity leaves you, son, it's time to go. You've stopped being fully human.

Singo.

Carrying the knowing all these years. To be with Rose and know they had executed her son. Greg was rubbish but he was hers, the way Tony and Corin were his.

Not Lizzie. She wasn't his. She was Laurie's. He had taken Laurie's child from her as Dance had taken Rose's.

He could not bear the thoughts, went to the bathroom and found Birkerts' sister's tablets, two left. In time, he passed into a sleep of sad meaningless dreams.

He woke just before 7am, lay for a long time, not thinking about anything, overwhelmed by the world, by what was waiting for him. He noticed his hipbones. He had lost weight.

Rose's treasure box. Do that first, he could not face her if something happened to it.

In the kitchen, the radio.

. . . *wind shift that saved the evacuated towns of Puzzle Creek, Hunter Crossing, Selborne and Morpeth and many farm properties late yesterday has only provided a temporary respite. With the fires now largely out of control and extreme conditions again today, emergency services say the best hope is for a change in the weather . . . expected to continue . . .*

In the car, he switched on his mobile. Dozens of messages.

Later. He would attend to them later.

On the freeway, heading for Rose's house, the phone. He plugged in the hands-free.

'Villani.'

'Steve, it's Luke, listen our chopper's been up there and the bloke says Dad's in dead strife, there's no way out, the fucking wind is shifting and . . .'

'He doesn't need a way out,' said Villani. 'He's got no use for a way out.'

'Yeah, well, I'm going in the chopper. The bloke'll put me down, he's a fucking madman too.'

Luke Villani, the snotty, whining little boy, the smartarse teenager who had to be locked in his room, radio confiscated, to do his homework, who sucked up to Bob, who came running for protection every time Mark threatened him, whose highest ambition was to call horse races.

'Talk to the doctor?'

'Waiting for him to call back.'

'Fucking lunatic idea this,' said Villani. He could feel the snare-tight wires in his neck, up into his skull. 'I'm telling you not to.'

It was his duty to say it, his prerogative and his duty.

'Can't tell me what to do anymore,' said Luke. 'It's my dad and my brother. I'm going.'

My brother.

No one had ever said it before. Villani had thought that no one would ever say it. It had not seemed sayable.

'Where's this fucking chopper?' he said.

'Essendon,' said Luke. 'Grenadair Air. Wirraway Road. Off the Tulla.'

'Wait for me.'

'Sarmajor,' Luke said in Bob's voice.

They were waiting on the blistering tarmac beside the shiny bird with its slim silver drooping wings: Mark and Luke and the pilot.

'I reckon I can go to jail for this,' said the pilot. He looked about twenty.

'I know you can go to jail for this,' said Villani.

THEY FLEW across the crawling city and its outskirts and over the low hills, flew over the small settlements and great expanses of trees, flew over dun, empty grazing land. They could see the smoke across the horizon, it stood a great height into the sky and above it the air was the cleanest, purest blue.

After a long while, from a long way, they saw the red edges of the fire, like blood leaking from under a soiled bandage.

The radio traffic was incessant, calm voices through the electronic crackle and spit.

'Got to keep away from the fire choppers,' said the pilot. 'Go the long way around.'

'Took your patient in,' Villani said to Mark. 'Kenny Hanlon.'

'Not my patient,' said Mark. 'Don't have any patients. I'm going to Africa next week. Darfur.'

'Got bikies in Darfur? Got a Hellhound chapter?'

'Fuck you,' Mark said.

In time, they saw Selborne in the distance, they were coming at it from the south-west, and, beyond the hamlet in the direction of Bob's, the world was alight, the road was a snaking avenue of trees burning orange, the air was dark.

'Don't reckon I'm going to jail,' said the pilot, ordinary voice. 'Reckon I'm going to die up here.'

'Steady on, son,' said Luke. 'Just follow the road. Carrying the best cop, best doctor, best race-caller in the country. Don't fuck it up.'

'Dream team,' said the pilot. 'Help me, St Chris.'

Into the dark and frightening hills, they followed the flaming road, the chopper shivering, pushed up and down and sideways by the air currents, everything was adrift in the heat.

Suddenly, they were above the farm, the house, the sheds, the stable, the paddocks.

The forest. Untouched, whipping.

'In the paddock, Black Hawk One,' said Luke.

And then they were on the ground and Luke was patting the pilot, they scrambled out, the heat was frightening, breath-sucking, the terrible noise, the pilot shouted, 'You bloody idiots.'

They ran and the chopper rose, showered them with particles of dirt and stone and dry vegetation.

At the fence, in the fearsome, scorching day, behind them Armageddon coming in fire and smoke with the sound of a million Cossack horsemen charging across a hard, hard plain, stood Bob and Gordie.

Bob spoke. They could barely hear him. 'Don't often get all three,' he said. 'What's this in aid of?'

THROUGH THE dark day and into the late afternoon, in the furnace wind, sometimes unable to breathe or speak or hear one another, they fought to save the house and the buildings.

When they had lost all the battles, when the red-hot embers were coming like massive tracer fire, when the fireballs were exploding in air, Bob took the big chainsaw and, with a murderous screaming of metal against metal, sliced the top off the corrugated-iron rainwater tank.

Gordie propped a ladder against the tank wall and they climbed up it, threw themselves into the warm water, felt the slimy bottom beneath their feet, pushed through the heaviness to the wall furthest from the flames.

Bob came last. First he handed the dog to Gordie, then he climbed the ladder, slipped through between rungs, stayed underwater for a time, came up, hair plastered flat. He looked like a boy again.

They stood in the tank, shoulders touching, water to their chins, nothing left to say. This was the end of vanity and ambition. This was what it had come to, the five of them, all Bob's boys here to die with the man himself, some instinct in them, some humming wire had pulled them back to death's booming and roaring waiting room to die together in a rusty saw-toothed tub.

'What about that Stand in the Day?' said Luke.

'Bloody ripper,' said Bob. 'Need more tips like that.'

They did not look at one another, ashes fell on them, drifted down and stuck to their faces, lay on the water, coated the face of the old yellow dog Bob was holding to his chest.

And, in the last moment, the howling wind stopped, a windless pause as if it were drawing breath. Then it came around as if sucked away to another place, came around and they could feel the change on their faces. The fire stood in its tracks, advanced no further, chewing on itself, there was no sustenance left for it, no oxygen, everything burnt.

They said nothing for a long time. They could not believe that this terrible thing had passed, that they would live. In the silence, they heard the fire chopper coming, it came from nowhere and hung its trunk over them and dropped a small dam of water on the house.

'You never get the air strike when you need it,' said Bob.

They pulled the ladder into the tank. Luke climbed it, they pushed it out and he rode it to the ground. Mark went first, then Gordie.

Villani said to Bob, 'You next.'

Bob looked at him, shook his head. 'Yes, boss,' he said.

Without saying anything, Villani set off. The dog hesitated, followed, looking back for Bob. Bob came, they walked side by side, wet clothes, tank water steaming from them.

They walked across the black smoking paddocks, down to the bottom gate, posts still burning, walked across the road that went nowhere, walked over the rise.

The forest stood there.

Scorched, the outer trees singed. They would lose some. But everywhere, in their circles and clumps and paths, the oaks were in full glorious summer green leaf.

Bob Villani put his right arm around his son's shoulders, pulled him to him, awkward, kissed Villani's temple, his ashy hair.

'Didn't do a bad job with the boys either,' he said. 'Seeing to them. I should've said that before.'

THE LINO peeled back easily. He pushed the table knife into the gap and worked the trapdoor up, got fingers under it, lifted it.

It was a small toolbox such as an electrician might carry, the top held by a hinged clasp.

Villani put it on the table, opened it.

Five or six wads of notes held with rubber bands. Hundreds, fifties, twenties, tens, fives. Perhaps twenty thousand dollars.

Beneath them was a piece of cardboard, cut to fit from a shirt box.

He lifted it with the table knife.

A wire of the old-fashioned kind. A tiny tape-recorder and a button transmitter.

Villani put the money into the toolbox, left the house, put the box in the boot, got into the car. He sat looking at the recorder. It had no speaker. It had to be plugged into one.

Greg Quirk wearing a wire? Whose wire?

He drove to St Kilda Road, took the lift to the techs. The little one who developed games in his spare time took the device. They went to a bench. He gave Villani earphones, pressed buttons.

Mate, I'm not happy. Not happy at all.

Couldn't know they'd pissed it against the wall. How could I know that?

It's your fucking job to know, Greg. Not doing this shit for pocket money, sonny. Risk involved sticking up these dumb pricks, it's got to be worth it.

Yeah, well, fucken risks for me too. Not the only one takin fucken risks.

I need thirty grand quick smart. Help a mate.

Fuck, you're squeezin me now, that's not the fucken way to deal with me, Dancer, that's not the . . .

Villani took off the headphones. He took the recorder. He walked across the buzzing chamber to his office, went to the window and looked at the city.

ON THE day in late autumn, they did the performance for the television cameras, the three of them in uniform, wearing their new insignia of rank.

Premier Karen Mellish made a short speech. She said it gave her great pleasure to announce the new chief commissioner, the new assistant chief commissioner and the new crime commissioner. The force now entered an era of reform, an era of revitalisation, an era that would see the public places of the great city reclaimed for its citizens.

By the time Villani had changed and met Cashin, the cold day was drawing to its end. They walked into the wind, the leaves flowing at them like broken water, yellow and brown and blood, parting at their ankles.

'Saw you on television,' Cashin said. 'Never thought I'd know a crime commissioner.'

'You can live a good life without knowing one,' said Villani. 'A satisfactory life. What's on your mind?'

'You getting back with Laurie?'

'No,' said Villani. 'We screwed that up. I screwed it up. Can't make it good. Can't make anything good.'

'Keep still,' said Cashin. 'The boat will steady itself.'

'Joe, no more Singo. Not ever.'

'It just comes out,' said Cashin. 'I was a sponge.'

'I'm now sponge-like,' said Villani. 'Just water and holes.'

Three runners appeared, two solid men and a lean woman.

The men moved right, the woman ran straight at them, swerving at the last second.

'Cheeky,' said Villani.

Cashin stopped, he was looking up. 'Possum's dead,' he said.

'What?'

Cashin pointed into a tree. Villani saw nothing, then a blob in a fork. 'How do you know?'

'Tail,' said Cashin. 'That's a dead tail.'

'How do you know a tail's dead?' said Villani. 'Could be a sleeping tail.'

'No,' said Cashin. 'Dead.' He walked on, big paces.

Villani caught up. 'Joe,' he said, 'come back to civilisation or join fucking Parks and Wildlife. Take schoolkids on the nature walk.'

'What's it going to be like?' said Cashin. 'Dance as your boss?'

'Nothing Dance can do will surprise me,' said Villani. 'Nothing at all.'

They came to the avenue. Villani looked at the towers, they stood in the sky and the sky was in their glass cheeks. He had walked beneath them, at their hard, dirty feet, a farm boy come to the city.